Shotgun Lullaby

Also by Steve Ulfelder

Purgatory Chasm
The Whole Lie

Shotgun Lullaby

STEVE ULFELDER

Minotaur Books

A Thomas Dunne Book

New York

A THOMAS DUNNE BOOK FOR MINOTAUR BOOKS.
An Imprint of St. Martin's Publishing Group.

SHOTGUN LULLABY. Copyright © 2013 by Steve Ulfelder. All rights reserved. Printed in the United States of America. For information, address St. Martin's Press, 175 Fifth Avenue, New York, N.Y. 10010.

www.thomasdunnebooks.com
www.minotaurbooks.com

ISBN 978-1-250-02808-2 (hardcover)
ISBN 978-1-250-02809-9 (e-book)

Minotaur books may be purchased for educational, business, or promotional use. For information on bulk purchases, please contact Macmillan Corporate and Premium Sales Department at 1-800-221-7945 extension 5442 or write specialmarkets@macmillan.com.

First Edition: May 2013

10 9 8 7 6 5 4 3 2 1

For Steve and Lucy—forever the
heroes of Hot Wheels Land

ACKNOWLEDGMENTS

Sometimes I feel like an exceptionally talented group is conspiring to make me look better than I deserve to look. I do not mind this one bit.

I'd be nowhere without my agent, Janet Reid. My editor, Anne Brewer, improved this book just as she's improved them all. Everybody at Thomas Dunne Books and Minotaur—editors, designers, publicity pros, and others—is in on the conspiracy.

Finally, I thank my partners at Flatout Motorsports and my wife, Martha Ulfelder, for riding out the ups and downs. I couldn't do this without their patience.

Shotgun Lullaby

CHAPTER ONE

If Walmart is too swank for your taste, maybe a little pricey, you shop at Ocean State Job Lot.

Me and Gus Biletnikov were parked outside one, waiting for a thief to get off work.

Marlborough, Massachusetts. Strip mall on Route 20, a busy east-west road that'll take you all the way across the state if you're not in a hurry. The strip mall had grown without any real plan—only locals knew which half-assed access roads led to what. An off-brand super-market, an off-brand clothing store, a rental center, a good barbecue joint, a CVS.

An Ocean State Job Lot.

I spotted the guy leaving the store for the night. Whipping off his blue smock before he was three steps out the door, balling it in a fist. He headed for a black early-nineties Mustang. The Mustang: immaculate, maybe the nicest car in the lot.

I said, "That Andrade?"

Gus nodded. "The one and only. Should I duck?"

"Don't bother."

"You mind if I just wet my pants then?"

I started my truck, dropped it in drive. Turned off the dome light, unlatched my door, held it ajar. Slow-rolled toward Andrade, angling up behind him.

I was on him before he looked. With my dome light off, he couldn't see inside the truck. So the first he knew of me was when I slammed my door into him.

Andrade grabbed his right elbow and went down. I stopped, hopped out, stepped on his chest. "Gus Biletnikov does not owe you any money," I said.

"I sold that little prick a Focus," Andrade said. "I gave him a break, took half up front even though I doubted he was good for the rest. He still owes me six-fifty."

I leaned into the boot on his chest. "You sold Roy a piece of shit."

Confusion flashed in Andrade's eyes. I ignored it.

"You rolled back the odometer," I said. "You cooked up the inspection sticker yourself. The six-fifty *might* make the car roadworthy. He doesn't owe you a goddamn nickel."

Andrade looked at the sodium light above us, waited for his breath to come back. A car slowed to watch. I stared. It rolled on past.

"Fucking junkie owes me six-fifty," Andrade finally said. "I know who you are. I got friends too, tough guy."

Give him credit for guts.

I sighed. Took his right hand, raised it, pistoned his elbow into the busted tarmac.

Twice.

The first time, it made a ball-bat sound. The second time, it made a crunchy sound.

I dropped his arm. "Gus Biletnikov does not owe you any money."

Andrade passed out. It was the first smart thing he'd done.

Then I drove Gus back to Framingham.

He was speechless for a while.

But only for a while.

"I've seen some shit," he finally said, "but that was . . . Conway, you are the *man*!"

I drove.

He said, "My roommate and I had a few encounters with these heavy gangster types. Did I ever tell you about that?"

He said, "You ever hear the term 'noble savage'? You are primitive, man. You are . . . *pure*!"

I drove.

He said, "Who's Roy?"

"My son," I said. "Why?"

"Aha."

"Aha what?" I said. "How do you know Roy?"

"Never mind."

I drove.

And thought.

A few miles later, replaying the parking-lot scene in my head, I figured out how Gus had picked up Roy's name. I felt stupid and simple and easy to read. My face went hot.

When we hit downtown Framingham, Gus said, "I live here, over the sub shop."

It was a halfway house called Almost Home. I know a bunch of guys who've spent time there. A couple are still sober, far as I know.

"I'll pick you up tomorrow at six thirty," I said as he climbed out. "We'll hit a meeting in Milford. You can get up and speak. You're good at that."

"Oh."

I started to pull away, happy for the silence. But stopped, waved Gus to the open passenger window. "I don't know anything about this Andrade," I said. "Watch yourself."

"Will do. Now here's the thing about that meeting tomorrow . . ."

I pulled away.

The kid could run his mouth. I liked him anyway.

Gus Biletnikov had stood out from the second he banister-slid into the church basement for the weekly meeting of the Barnburners, the AA group that saved my life. The Barnburners are semifamous in the tight world of AA. Judges, cops, and counselors send us drunks and addicts who are teetering. Who are set to die or live or go to prison forever, with much depending on how their next few weeks turn out.

The judges, cops, and counselors know we're a hardcore group, so they warn the fresh fish that when they hit the basement of Saint Anne's, they'd best keep their ears open and their mouths shut.

The addicts are usually intimidated enough to take the advice.

Not Gus.

He truly had hopped on the banister and slid sidesaddle to the bottom, hollering "Whee!" like a seven-year-old. Then he'd bopped through the double doors into the big room, causing enough commotion that I stopped fiddling with the microphone and stared.

And opened my mouth.

He looked just like my son.

It was so obvious that a couple of Barnburners I knew well looked from Gus to me and back. They'd seen pictures. They thought the lippy, skinny kid tossing his bangs from his eyes was Roy.

Except in looks, though, he wasn't anything like Roy.

Roy's suspicious of the world. He *hides* behind his bangs, staring out at the world like a stray dog that knows it's going to get hit— but doesn't know who by.

This kid, on the other hand . . . he knew he'd created a commotion. And he loved it. Took three giant strides forward, navigating the aisle between the folding chairs. Put both hands over his heart like a hambone actor and said, "Ah am *here*! Ah am *here*! Ah am *here*, Lord, to be saved by the mighty, mighty Barnburners!"

Then he dropped to a knee like Elvis Presley, made a big show of crossing himself, sidestepped over to a chair, and plopped down next to a fiftyish woman who looked at him like he was from Mars.

Gus never did learn how close he came to getting an old-fashioned bum's rush that night. Skinny Dennis and Pablo, bikers from Medway who would've lassoed a freight train for me, raised their eyebrows in the back of the room. If I nodded, they would take the kid by his armpits and jeans pockets, quickstep him up the stairs, and see how far they could toss him into the parking lot. It wouldn't be the first time.

I damn near nodded.

But the kid had figured out instinctively that in this room, I had some juice.

He was meeting my eyes.

He was not afraid.

And he looked like my son.

I shook my head at Skinny Dennis and Pablo. They went back to their conversation.

We Barnburners set up Saint Anne's our own way. Most of the folding chairs face the podium, of course. But there's a little bump-out in the room's northwest corner, and for as long as I've been around, somebody sets a dozen or so chairs at an angle that lets the leaders and old-timers keep an eye on the entire joint.

To newcomers, they look like seats for a jury. And that's about right.

They're reserved for the Meeting After the Meeting crowd.

I'm part of that crowd, so throughout that night's meeting, I got an eyeful of the kid who turned out to be Gus Biletnikov. He mugged and made exaggerated nods and got a big kick out of himself. Once, while a black woman spoke, he said, "Testify, sister!"

I knew Skinny Dennis and Pablo were itching to toss the kid. Truth be told, I was with them. After the meeting, I figured, I would nod once to the bikers. They would escort the punk to the parking lot and explain that we Barnburners specialized in serious AA for serious people and he'd best find himself another meeting.

But something happened at the end.

As always, we closed by joining hands and saying the Lord's Prayer.

It's hard to explain, but during the prayer, I always feel like I've *done* something. Like I've risen above myself, maybe even done something to be proud of—if sitting on your ass for an hour can fit that description. The prayer is the best part of the meeting. Sometimes it's the best part of my week.

Instinct made me open one eye during that evening's prayer.

I looked at the wiseass kid.

He wasn't being a wiseass.

His hands gripped those of the folks on either side of him. His lips moved as he prayed. His eyes were shut tight.

And he was crying honest tears.

And that meant he wasn't all bad.

So there was no bum's rush. Instead, twenty minutes later, my Meeting After the Meeting pals assigned me to connect with the new kid, to see what he was all about.

I didn't mind.

And that didn't have anything to do with the fact that the kid looked just like Roy.

Hardly anything.

The assignment led me to ask around among counselors and parole officers and rehab operators. Which led me to Almost Home and to Gus Biletnikov. Who, it turned out, had a problem with a shitbox car he'd bought from Andrade.

The morning after I pulped Andrade's elbow, I had an Infiniti on the lift for its 125,000-mile service when a cruiser pulled into my small parking lot. White Crown Vic, FRAMINGHAM in blue filling its flank.

Matt Bogardis climbed from the cruiser. Matt's a good guy, a big guy. The cop gear on his belt jangled and clanked as he came and stood behind the Infiniti. He watched me put on the differential cover with a fourteen-millimeter hand socket.

Matt said, "Wouldn't the job go faster if you used the air gun?"

"The gun's for taking things off. Hand tools are for putting things back together. Ram a bolt in with an air gun, you can strip the threads."

"I've seen a lot of mechanics put things together with air guns."

"Dealerships, Jiffy Lubes, Midas Mufflers," I said. "Those aren't mechanics. They're trained chimpanzees. Only they're not trained."

"Picky bastard, huh?" Matt said it to Floriano Mendes, my partner. Floriano was kicking support arms beneath a Civic at the next lift over.

"Tell me about it," Floriano said.

Matt watched us work.

"Marlborough cops are wondering were you out that way last night," he said after a while. "Route 20? The Ocean State Job Lot?"

"No."

"Reason they're wondering," he said, "some guy got the shit kicked out of him. Kid named Andrade, works at the Job Lot."

"Don't know him."

"Parking lot security cam caught an F-250 like yours. Light in color, like yours. Partial plate that kinda-sorta-maybe starts the way yours does."

I snugged up the last bolt. "Kinda-sorta-maybe, huh?"

He shrugged.

I said, "What's Andrade say?"

"Not a damn word. He was pissed the hospital called us in the first place. Said he'd take care of it himself."

I wiped the differential cover with a shop rag. "Can't help you, Matt."

"Thought so." He paused. "Andrade sells used cars on the side. Shitboxes, nothing over fifteen hundred bucks. He bootlegs the inspection stickers and sells to people who can't afford anything better. Illegals, mostly. They get pulled over and the cop notices the sticker, they're shit outta luck."

"Marlborough cops all bummed out because he got beat up?"

"I didn't get that feeling. But Conway"—he waited until I looked at him—"one of these days, you'll beat up the wrong guy. He'll have a gun, or a bunch of shitfaced buddies. There's only so much I can do. I'm a cop who you know, but I'm not your friend the cop. See the difference?"

I nodded and watched Matt jangle and clank back to his cruiser. Good guy.

A soft spring rain was starting as I pulled over for Gus. He waited under the sub shop's green awning, finishing off a bag of potato chips. Didn't notice me for a few seconds. Under the light brown hair, longish, that fell across his forehead with no real part, he had round brown eyes. Looked even younger than he was, with a peach-fuzz face and a chin that made him look a little like an elf. When you spoke with him, he had a presence, but looking at him there on the sidewalk, I realized he was shorter and skinnier than Roy.

He spotted me. Wiped hands on pants, climbed in. "Anybody else coming?"

"Charlene'll meet us there with a carload of Barnburners."

Gus lip-puffed hair from his eyes. "As I was saying last night, I'm not sure this is the ideal time for me to lose my AA virginity. I'd feel more comfortable doing a little recon, get my drift? Observing and absorbing. I mean, if I speak tonight, doesn't that rob an AA veteran, somebody like yourself, of a chance to lay some wisdom on the flock?"

"You'll speak tonight."

"*Jesus!*" He pounded a fist on his thigh, then folded his arms in a five-year-old's pout. Which is identical to a junkie's pout.

We drove.

"The Barnburners asked me to show you the ropes," I said after a while. "These are the ropes. You want me off your back? Then find a sponsor, get a job, show some progress. Until then, I'm it. Barnburner-appointed."

"The Barnburners this, the Barnburners that. You talk like they're the C-I-fucking-A. As far as I can see, they're a bunch of cliquey old alkies."

Without taking my eyes off the road, I grabbed a handful of his button-down shirt. "The Barnburners saved my life. I do what they ask me to do. Sometimes I throw a scare into shitbirds like Andrade. Sometimes I slap some sense into bigmouth college boys fresh out of rehab." I let go of his shirt all at once, feeling like a jerk. "You'll speak tonight."

He shut up for the rest of the ride. I glanced at him a lot. Wanted to say I was sorry, but couldn't. And couldn't figure out why I couldn't.

I chaired the Milford meeting. Gymnasium, Catholic school next to a Wendy's. Through the gym's open windows, you could hear tires hiss on wet pavement. You could smell french fries.

Usually, the chairman doesn't do much except introduce speakers and pull the raffle ticket. But most of Charlene's promised Barnburners had crapped out, and the ones who did show kept their stories short.

I finally introduced Gus. He rose, dragged himself to the podium, faced the room.

Then he opened his mouth, and he did damn well. Better than any first-timer had a right to. I'd known he would, natural-born bullshitter that he was. He told his drunk log and his drug log, made everybody laugh a few times, pumped out clichés about learning from old-timers like me, and sat to genuine applause.

As I returned to the podium, I shook Gus's hand. Whispered that I was proud of him. Meant it. Hoped he knew I was sorry for roughing him up.

I was fresh out of speakers and had fifteen minutes to fill.

Hell.

I looked at Charlene. She batted her eyes at me, laughing inside, knowing I didn't like to speak but was trapped.

Deep breath. "I'm Conway," I said. "I'm an alcoholic and a drug addict."

Hi, Conway.

I squared up and told my story.

CHAPTER TWO

Back to Framingham in the rain. Gus was quiet all the way up Route 16, most likely replaying his speech in his head. I asked how it felt to stand up in front of so many people. He shrugged, said okay I guess. I told him he did fine.

Downtown Framingham. The GM plant was long since closed. The retail had moved out to malls on Route 9, a busy east-west road. Some sap had bought the old Dennison factory and turned it into yuppie condos, but as far as I could see there weren't a lot of takers.

North of Route 9, Framingham was a nice suburb. Down here, south of 9, it was a beat-up red-brick city scratching its head. Losing its industrial, its retail. Gaining methadone clinics and soup kitchens, puzzling out its next move.

We hit gridlock near the center of town. I figured the gates guarding the railroad tracks had jammed again. Wrong: we cleared the tracks, but not the traffic, and crawled.

A block from Almost Home, the jam was explained: cop cars, fire trucks, ambulances. Parked every which way, the way they park them.

Matt Bogardis was directing traffic with a flashlight, orange poncho over his uniform. I honked, cracked my window. He hustled over, crouching against the rain, strobed blue by his own roof lights.

"Some mess, huh?" he said. "Take a left, try Franklin Street."

I thumbed at Gus. "I'm dropping him off on this block."

Matt looked at Gus for the first time. "Where on the block?"

"Almost Home," Gus said. "The halfway house."

Matt motioned for me to roll my window farther. He flashlighted Gus. "Where you coming from?"

I said, "AA meeting in Milford."

"Let me see some ID."

Gus passed his license over. Matt's visor dripped on it. He passed it back. "Come with me, both of you." He wiped rain from his nose, looked at Gus. "Everybody thinks you're dead."

A half hour later, I stood under the sub-shop awning. Crowded spot: it was the closest shelter to Almost Home. The halfway house itself was out of the rain, obviously—but I got the feeling the cops and EMTs didn't want to spend any more time in there than they had to.

Gus had been pulled aside as soon as Matt Bogardis told the Framingham police chief who the kid was. He was a full forty feet away. I couldn't hear anything Gus said, or the questions they asked him. Had to make do with body language.

Which was pretty plain: this was a clusterfuck. Framingham's big enough to get its share of druggie knifings and the occasional home-invasion murder, but this was way bigger. The fact that the chief, a silver-haired glad-hander who spent as much time in Boca as he did behind his desk, was here in full dress uniform told me that.

The news trucks confirmed it. Channels 4, 5, 7, 56, Fox, Bay State Cable News.

Then the state cops rolled in, silently taking over—the Framingham chief looked relieved about that—and I began to pick up conversation snatches from coffee-drinking ambulance folks and street cops. *Bloodbath. Execution style. Damn near puked. Real Scarface stuff, I shit you not.*

At the far end of the awning, Gus was talking to a guy who had to be a state police detective. He was shorter than most, but otherwise had the look: bowed legs, weightlifter's chest that his Windbreaker couldn't hide, black hair an eighth-inch too long to be called a buzz cut. Gus seemed to be handling himself fine. If the cop was like the others I've run across, he was repeating and tweaking questions to catch Gus in a lie. But Gus had a hole card: he didn't have a lie to tell. Not about something that'd happened while we were in Milford.

I got bored. Watched the TV crews set up, wished for coffee. Every so often, one cop would ask another who the hell I was, then come over and get my story. I told the Framingham cops, then the staties about the Milford meeting. I said fifty people'd seen us there, go ahead and check. Gave phone numbers.

The detective in charge said one last thing to Gus, then came to me. He had a high-mileage face that looked older than the rest of him. Smart brown eyes. And he wore braces—those translucent plastic ones adults get when they want to fix their teeth but are embarrassed about it.

He stood close, looked up, studied me, didn't try to hide it or be polite. Slapped a reporter's notebook against his thigh. Finally said his name was Lima. I told him mine.

"I heard about you," he said.

I said nothing.

"Yeah, I heard a lot about you. Everybody at the Framingham barracks knows you. You're on paper."

"Not for long." It was an understatement. My parole was due to end at midnight. I didn't see any reason to tell Lima that.

"Manslaughter," he said.

"Self-defense. I got hosed by a DA running for office."

" 'Course you did."

"You're new," I said. "In Framingham." Did he blush? I guessed and pressed. "No, it's more than that. You're a new *detective*. Three months ago, I bet you were running speed traps in . . . Fall River?"

He blushed like hell.

"It was just a good guess," I said. "I've never seen a Brazilian detective on the staties." I said the last part in Portuguese. I've learned some out of necessity.

"First in the commonwealth," he said, puffing out his chest. If he was surprised at my Portuguese, he hid it.

When Lima realized he wasn't controlling the conversation, he stepped back and forced his eyes to go flat. Produced a pen, bit off its cap, fired questions at me while writing in his notebook.

Everything he asked I'd already told at least twice. But I played along. Realized I enjoyed having a straight story to tell. It was a new feeling for me. It made things easy.

Lima soon figured out he wasn't going to catch me in a lie. He sighed, made a sharp whistle, motioned at Gus to join us.

"You've lived here three weeks," he said to Gus.

"Yes."

"How long you going to stay?"

"I'm not sure." Gus shuffled his feet. "My counselor suggested six months at least, but I got the feeling that was flexible. Some guys stay longer, but most leave sooner."

"Why?"

"They don't make it. They pick up, you know? They go back out there."

"You mean they take drugs."

"Or drink."

"How does anybody know that?"

"Random testing, for starters," Gus said. "You had to pee in a cup whenever Ellery asked. He's the housefather. Weird dude. But the thing is . . ."

Lima waited.

". . . the thing is," Gus said, "even without the testing, everybody knew. You get a half-dozen junkies all living in a little house together? It was easy to tell when somebody was high."

"What happened when people got caught?"

"They had to split immediately. Ellery would get a phone call with a positive. Then he'd shuffle down the hall—all I ever saw him wear was shower clogs—and knock on a door, and you'd know someone was getting tossed."

"How many guys been tossed since you got here?"

Gus squinted. "There was a black guy who barely lasted a day. I don't even remember his name. Then last week, a guy named Cal split after two weeks."

"Either of 'em pissed off about it? Make any threats? Start a fight?"

"Nah. When guys left, they were mostly ashamed. They couldn't look you in the eye. They just wanted to go back out and use."

Lima closed his notebook. "If this was a movie made in 1954," he said, "I'd tell you both not to leave town. But you"—pointing at me—"got a parole officer I know pretty well. And *you*"—pointing at Gus—"answer to him, far as I can tell. So I don't have to say all that, do I?"

"You know Luther?" I said.

Lima ignored me, turned to leave.

Gus grabbed the sleeve of his Windbreaker. "Who got shot? Why was everybody worried about me?"

The cop faced us. Gus's hand still clutched his sleeve, but Lima spoke to me. "I don't have to tell you this, okay? I'm doing you a favor."

" 'Preciate it."

"Three vics in there. First two look to've been standing in the front hall when the shooter walked in. He could've threatened them, or he could've walked right past. Instead, he blew their innards all over the ugly striped wallpaper." He looked at his notebook. "Only vic upstairs turns out to be Weller, Brian C. Mass license, Winchendon address."

I said, "So?"

Long pause. Lima looked at Gus.

"He was my best friend in the house," Gus said, his face the color of peed-on newspaper. "My *only* friend in the house. We got here the same day. People said we looked and acted like brothers."

"Still," I said, "why the mix-up?"

"Weller was killed in Gus's room," Lima said, "and the housefather gave us a bad ID. Easy mistake. Shotgun, close range. Face was pretty much gone."

CHAPTER THREE

G us was quiet. That was different.

No way was I letting him stay at Almost Home tonight. Or ever again.

Once the bodies were gone, Lima had let him go in and pack his gear. Gus had come out with a duffel and a white face. I wondered how much blood was in there.

We drove.

"Can't take you to my place," I said. "My girlfriend's place, I mean."

"Charlene."

"You knew?"

"Barnburner royalty," he said. "Everybody knows."

I let the *royalty* crack slide. "I'd bring you there, but . . . it's a crowded house right now. Or feels like one. Long story."

I worked a few blocks north and west, parked in front of a four-square colonial. Even on a rainy night, you could see the house was the best one on the street. Fresher paint, a fence that didn't sag, curtains in all the windows. No surprise there: Trey Phigg and his wife, Kieu, loved the place and told me so every chance they got.

Bonus: from the blacked-out third-floor windows, it looked like they were between renters for the in-law apartment.

I had Gus follow me up the flagstone walk.

Five minutes later, he was switching on lights in the apartment. "Not bad at all," he said. "But I have to ask . . . is this a damn safe house or something? Are you Barnburners *that* serious?"

I shook my head. "I once owned this place, and I'm friends with the folks who bought it. Just dumb luck that it's empty."

We were quiet maybe thirty seconds.

I turned and fussed with a blind that didn't need fussing with. "Ask you something?"

"Okay."

"You always cry during the Lord's Prayer."

Gus said nothing.

"At meetings."

"I knew what you meant. When does the question arrive?"

"Why?" Brushing dust from the blind as I said it.

"It . . . it makes me think of my mom," Gus said.

"Gotcha."

"Hang on. There's more. You asked. Now receive."

I turned, leaned on the wall, folded my arms.

"As far as I know, my dad's never spent two seconds thinking about God one way or the other," Gus said. "My mother was raised as what she called a Guitar Catholic in some hippie-dippie church. She fell away from the whole deal. I was never baptized or any of that gobbledygook."

"Only child?"

He nodded. Looked at nothing, recalling something. Then made the nicest smile I'd yet seen on his face. "When I was nine, Mom got a wild hair across her ass for structure and tradition. I think . . . piecing it together, I think she and my dad were having problems, serious marriage problems, for the first time. She was taking stock. She was reconsidering."

I said I could picture that.

"One night as she served dinner," he said, "Mom folded her hands and suggested we say grace. She tried to make it casual, but it came out of *nowhere,* man. She wouldn't have surprised us more if she'd lifted a cheek and farted 'Shave and a Haircut.'"

Gus paused. Took his time. Smiled again, looking at nothing. "If she was hoping my dad would lead the charge and murmur sweet Norman Rockwell-isms, she miscalculated. His cheeks flared bright red—he's Russian, in case you hadn't guessed—and he said, without moving his lips, 'Fine then. Feel free to say your grace.'"

"And?"

"It quickly became clear my mom was stumped. She hadn't thought it through past the initial suggestion, didn't know what to say. She steepled her hands and closed her eyes."

I said nothing.

Gus licked his lips. When he spoke again, his voice was husky, just north of a whisper. "I guess all she could think of, grace-wise, was the Lord's Prayer. So she said it. That was the first time I heard the whole thing, stem to stern. We said it every night at dinner, me and Mom, for the next . . . five years? Six?"

"And your father?"

"Never joined in." Long pause. "Never once, until they split up my freshman year in high school."

"Huh," I said.

"Huh," Gus said. And slapped his thighs. "I should unpack. That might take damn near a minute."

I stepped to the door. Grabbed its knob. Stood still.

"Thank you," I said. "For telling me."

"De nada," Gus hollered from the bedroom.

I left and headed west to Shrewsbury. To Charlene's place.

During the twenty-minute drive, I let my head go where it wanted to. Thought about Gus's story, which led me to think about the danger he was in.

Possibility: some methed-up former Almost Homer with a grudge. Got high, lucked into a shotgun, waded into the place not knowing who or what he was going to kill. Call that the most likely scenario. It was a big part of the reason I'd never liked halfway houses.

Possibility: the kid who got blasted, Brian Weller, was the kid who was *supposed* to get blasted. It'd happened in Gus's room, but so what? They'd been thick as thieves, had shared iPods and sweatshirts and God knew what else. If former-Almost-Homer-with-a-grudge had come looking for Weller, Gus's room would be the second place he looked.

But those possibilities left out Gus.

And my job was to look after Gus.

So seize the initiative, as my buddy Randall Swale always said. Jump to the assumption that could lead to an action plan. Call it possibility three: The killer had come looking for Gus. Maybe he'd been told to hit a certain bedroom. Maybe he'd seen just enough of Weller to confuse him with Gus.

The thought chain had lodged something in my head.

Randall.

My parole officer's son. We met a while back. He helps me out here and there. Former army, knows what he's doing.

Randall was big on seizing the initiative, big on confirmed information, not so big on assumptions.

So get his help confirming some info—or not.

I called his cell. Voice mail. Sketched out what I was after: Brian Weller of Winchendon, shot down at Almost Home. Could Randall sniff around, see what kind of nonsense Weller had been up to? Had to be some—Eagle Scouts don't end up in sketchy Framingham halfway houses.

I clicked off. Drove more, thought more.

What *I* needed was to talk with Gus, figure out who might want him dead. Andrade was the obvious choice. He needed looking at, and he'd be my first stop. But . . . the vibe was wrong. Andrade felt like a bottom-feeder, not a killer. So it was worth asking Gus for more ideas, more jerks with grudges.

I didn't know much about Gus. The Barnburner grapevine said he was a Richie Rich from around here who'd gotten in a jam at college. He'd done the rehab thing, then started showing up at AA and NA meetings. Hard kid to read: he might be serious about staying straight, or he might be smirking his way along to satisfy the court and Daddy.

I'd find out tomorrow.

Checked my watch as I swung into the driveway. Almost midnight. Upstairs, Sophie's light was off.

Jessie's was not.

I sighed, climbed out, let myself in.

Charlene was piddling around with her laptop in the kitchen/great room where we spent all our time.

The laptop's never far away.

Charlene Bollinger made it to the Barnburners a few years after I did. Booze and meth had been her things, and they showed. Back then, she weighed maybe ninety, wore eye makeup that gave her a raccoon look, jitter-jumped at the slightest noise.

The state had taken away her daughters, the ones who were up in their rooms now. For Charlene, that was the bottom you hear people talk about, the thing that finally pushed her to AA.

Over the next few years, she worked harder than anybody else I've seen. Got clean, stayed clean, got the girls back. Found steady work transcribing in Westborough District Court, used that as a springboard to her own transcription-and-translation company.

The business is a big deal now. *Charlene's* a big deal.

"Thanks a million," I said, setting my keys on the counter. "You stranded me up there telling my life story."

"People love hearing your life story." She shut her laptop, leaned back on the red sectional, scratched the head of Dale, one of my cats. "*I* love hearing your life story. That's why I stranded you."

I flopped, sat, yawned. "How is she?"

The way Charlene stiffened was all the answer I needed.

Hell.

You'll never meet anybody works harder than me to stay out of soap operas. But here I was, smack in the middle of one.

My son Roy and Charlene's older daughter, Jessie, are the same age. A while back, when they were high school seniors, they hauled off and fell in love. Trouble was, Jessie'd just gotten out of treatment for anorexia and bulimia. Staying out of serious relationships for a year was part of her aftercare program, right there in black and white.

Like all dumb-ass parents, Charlene and I tried to talk sense into Jessie and Roy.

Like all dumb-ass kids, they told us to pound sand. The two of them moved to Boulder, Colorado, where she waited tables and he worked in a body shop.

Just a few weeks ago, without a phone call or a text message, Jessie had showed up on Charlene's doorstep. She and Roy had broken up. Jessie wouldn't tell Charlene an awful lot, and Charlene in turn didn't tell me everything she heard, but it was easy to see the breakup hadn't been pretty. Neither of the kids could afford an apartment on their own, so Jessie left Colorado and landed at Charlene's place. Roy went back to his mother, my ex. She lives in Lee, Massachusetts, about as far as you can get from me and still be in the state.

I hate to say it, but Jessie didn't add a whole hell of a lot to the Shrewsbury house, where her mother and her sister and I had been doing pretty well. She was as silent and rage-filled as ever. More so, really, because I'd moved in while she was gone. She slept most of the day. Went out every night, never said where or who with. Charlene didn't know what the hell to do. Me neither.

Worst of all, Jessie was skinny. So damn skinny it'd break your heart. Wore a baggy sweatshirt to mask it, but the way she cinched her belt to keep her jeans up was enough to make you cry.

And you know who got the short end, as usual? Sophie, Charlene's thirteen-year-old. She'd been happy as hell when I moved in—I love the kid like nobody's business—had thrived, had let loose her smarts, stunning Charlene and me at the dinner table with these concussive blasts of intelligence.

But Sophie's family role was peacemaker, mood reflector. Since Jessie came home, all that intelligence had gone dark.

What could you do? Family is family.

Charlene had to be thinking along the same lines as me, because she said, "How's Roy?"

I shrugged. "You know as much as I know. Still out in the Berkshires with his mother. I've been trying to get him here to ride the dirt bikes. Been leaving messages."

We were quiet awhile.

Charlene scratched my shoulder. "What happened after the meeting? I got a half-dozen calls from Barnburners. People said the cops were checking up on you and that boy you brought."

I told her the whole thing. It took a while. Halfway through the story she rose, tugged my hand, and led me upstairs to her bedroom. I liked that. Then she stroked my hair while I spoke. I liked that too.

When I was done, Charlene, pillow-propped on the bed now, was quiet a few seconds. "Before noon today," she finally said, "three different Barnburners called to tell me about this Andrade beating. Like all gossips, they had parts of the story wrong. But they had the gist of it right."

"How the hell did word get out?"

She shrugged. "The point is, a lot of people are unhappy about it. There's grumbling about the things you do, Conway. The favors. The muscle stuff."

"Do they think I do it for *fun*? People come to us screwed up in ugly ways. I get them out of jams. And only when I'm asked to."

"I realize that, and I realize that some of the bitchers and moaners are the ones who were once in the ugliest jams." Charlene let a finger play through my hair. "That's half the problem, Conway. People who need help from a man with your talents don't like to be reminded of the fact years later."

I nodded. "Fair enough. Now I know the holier-than-thous are eyeballing me."

Charlene put her head on my shoulder. "Are you worried for Gus?"

"I don't know. I think so. Yes. I *have* to be worried for him."

"What's he like?"

"Cokehead. Rehab kid. College kid. Big bullshitter. Probably doing AA because Daddy made him. I had to guess, I'd say he'll quit the coke and drink like a fish for the next twenty years. Then he'll come back to AA for real."

"Harsh."

"Honest."

"But you care about him a lot."

I waved a hand. "I'm just helping out a Barnburner."

"Nonsense." She smiled.

"Okay. I like the kid. He's got a heart. He's scared. If he works at it, he could be a man."

"What's your next move? As if I didn't know."

"I need to figure out who's got a problem with Gus."

"And look into it." She sighed as she spoke.

"Of course."

"Conway Sax takes in another stray." She said it softly. "He reminds you of your son. You can admit it to me. You might even want to admit it to yourself."

"Everybody's a damn shrink."

"You don't have to be much of one to see it."

"I know," I said. "But there's more to it."

Charlene stroked my hair, said nothing.

"You should have seen the cops and EMTs coming out of this halfway house," I said. "Could barely keep their lunch down, some of 'em, and they were hard-core pros. I didn't want to spook Gus, so I played it light. But it looks like some serious cats want him dead."

"*If* they wanted *him* dead, and not the poor boy they actually shot."

"Yeah. If. But that's the way I see it."

"Of course it is. Because it's an excuse to take in a stray."

Most nights, that would've set me off, started a fight. But the way Charlene was stroking my hair made it hard to get mad.

I said, "Why are you being so nice to me?"

"Something about tonight's meeting. You still make other men in the room seem . . . trivial. It's why I fell in love with you, you know."

"You've told me that."

"A meeting is also the only time you say five words in a row."

"You've told me that, too."

I kissed her.

Soon she broke the kiss. "Davey's yowling."

He's my other cat. Generally speaking, he's a pain in the ass.

"Hell," I said, propping myself on an elbow. "I was getting set to yowl some myself."

"Let him in before he wakes Sophie."

Then Davey kept hopping onto the bed at all the worst times. The more I swatted him off, the more determined he was to stay.

Charlene and I wound up calling it quits and laughing ourselves to sleep while the big dumb cat purred between us.

CHAPTER FOUR

Next morning. Had an '84 Mercedes diesel wagon in for a head gasket and a couple of oil seals. I'd been looking forward to it—we mostly work on Japanese cars now, but it's the Germans I like best. The parts guy was late, though, so my hands were tied.

I'd texted Gus to walk the six blocks to the shop when he woke up. He came at ten thirty with a Dunkin' Donuts coffee for each of us. We stepped to the office, sat, sipped.

"Let's say you were supposed to be killed last night instead of Weller," I said. "Who and why?"

I'd hit him hard partly to scope his reaction. Most guys, you tell them somebody tried to shotgun them last night, they'd flip out.

Gus didn't.

He did raise his eyebrows some, blowing on his coffee. "Whew. Very *Castle*, very *Law and Order*."

"Who and why? For the hell of it."

"The prime suspect would be Andrade, seller of crappy cars."

"I'll check him out," I said. "But why would he go after *you*? I'm the one wrecked his arm."

"You're a tough guy and I'm not. I used Almost Home as my address on the bill of sale, so there's your opportunity, Castle. And as far as he's concerned, I owe him six hundred and fifty bucks. That's motive even if you discount the smashed elbow. As to the means, the shotgun . . ." Gus shrugged.

"You don't owe him a nickel. I erased that debt."

He half-smiled. "You truly see it that way, don't you? Conway Sax declares the debt null and void, therefore the debt is null and void. I doubt Andrade shares your viewpoint."

He was right about that. "I'll look at Andrade first," I said, "even though it feels all wrong. He's a born loser, a creep who rips off poor people and illegals who can't do anything about it. Hard guy with a shotgun? I don't see it. So play along. Who else?"

His eyes dodged. I stared him down, wondered what he was hiding. "There was this guy in Springfield who supplied the dope when I was dealing at college," he finally said. "I was his number-one retailer. I was selling at UMass Amherst and a bunch of the smaller schools out there. This guy loved me because college kids pay twice as much for coke, and you can step on it twice as hard."

"Who was he?"

"Teddy Pundo was his name, aka Fat Teddy, and he was a piece of work. He was a fellow Minuteman, and if he wasn't retarded, he was pretty close to it. He got kicked out, but I heard he went back after a year off. Weird kid. Threw his plentiful weight around, hinted his dad was a Mob guy. I figured he was full of shit. I mean, Mafia guys in Springfield, Massachusetts?" Gus's eyes dodged again.

I shrugged. "Why not?"

"It just seemed *très* dramatic. Especially because Fat Teddy was this freaky loser, shunned and hated by all. And I, ah . . . I finally met the father, Charlie Pundo. Want to know what he does?"

I waited.

"He owns a damn *jazz club*. One that's supposedly a big hairy deal in Springfield. He was mild-mannered, very polite. Seemed more like a dapper retired barber than a gangster."

"What's the club called?"

"The Hi Hat. Fat Teddy said his old man paid top dollar to get big jazz stars into this little club. A regular patron of the arts."

"If you were Teddy's favorite dealer," I said, "why would he be out to get you?" Like I didn't know.

Gus's face confirmed it before his voice did. "I ripped him off for the final nine months of our partnership. Skimming, stepping on the product one final time, taking care of my friends for free."

"Typical college dealer bullshit."

Gus raised his eyebrows. "Painful but true. The *full* truth, since you appear to want nothing less, is that Teddy Pundo's the reason I finally went to rehab. Fat Teddy and some other serious-looking dude came to my apartment one night and beat the crap out of me. Teddy said he knew what was going on. He gave me two days to come up with twenty-five grand. My dad had been bugging me to go to Hazelden anyway. A thirty-one-day trip to Minnesota suddenly looked attractive."

Hazelden: the best rehab in the country, and priced that way. Call it confirmation that Gus's dad was rich.

"I'll hit Andrade first," I said. "Then this Hi Hat, to find Teddy Pundo."

"Seriously?"

"You're a Barnburner."

Gus stared at me maybe twenty seconds.

I said, "Anybody else I should know about?"

He blew on his coffee, looked at me from beneath his bangs. "That's it."

Junkies are liars. That doesn't mean they're good liars.

I sighed. Time for a new tack. "Ever fire a shotgun?" I said. "Hell, ever been *hit* by shotgun fire?"

Gus made a horse noise to let me know it was a dumb question. "Have you?"

"Fired one? Sure. Hit by one? Nah. But a pal of mine was."

"No shit?" He was leaning forward. This was shaping up to be a story a preppy kid from Massachusetts could sink his teeth into. A story he would wish was his own, would likely steal and *make* his own.

"Shot by a watermelon farmer," I said.

"No *shit*?"

I usually stay away from these old stories. It's one thing to outline your drunk log in an AA meeting to show where booze took you. It's another to reminisce. It's tempting, but it's a wrong move—you end up remembering the wacky stories but forgetting the misery that went with them.

An eager audience is tempting too, though. Besides, I had a reason to lay it out for Gus.

So I did.

My buddy's name was Nick. He was five years older than me, and he was mostly deaf and dishonorably discharged from the air force because of what he claimed was a training snafu. Something about high explosives and a plan to scare the shit out of his commanding officer.

Nick had a little-girl giggle you couldn't help but laugh along with and curly brown hair he wore in a mini-Afro. He also had the strangest body I ever saw: wingspan and torso of a basketball player, legs of a near dwarf. Called himself the world's tallest midget when he drank gin, which he freely admitted put him in a self-pitying frame of mind.

During my bad years, Nick and I spent a summer working and stealing and drinking our way down the western shore of the Gulf of Mexico. Once we cleared Corpus Christi, we got sick of the trip. Hailed a pickup full of Mexicans, asked for a lift north, had a little communication problem, wound up fifty miles west of the Gulf coast.

Turned out it wasn't a communication problem after all: the Mexicans had driven us to the middle of nowhere to rob us. They got our last nine dollars, two packs of Winstons, and a brass belt buckle I liked a lot.

The middle of nowhere was Edinburg, Texas.

They grow watermelons in Edinburg.

Hungry as hell, thumbing for a northbound ride that never came, me holding my no-longer-belted jeans up with one hand, we waited for dusk and crawled into a row. Ate watermelon until we got sick, dozed some, talked about our big revenge plans regarding the Mexicans— we both knew the plans were bullshit, but they eased the humiliation— ate some more, got sick some more. Dozed some more.

At least I did.

At false dawn, a racket woke me. Near as I ever figured, Nick had woken up, used his tiny legs to sneak a mile or more to a farmhouse, started an old Chevy truck, and boogied my way.

Which was sporting of him. Back then, I imagine I would have split on my own.

The farmer must've been a light sleeper, because when I woke up, Nick was screaming for me over the clatter of the Chevy's straight-six. Right behind him was a four-wheel ATV, its single angry-insect headlight aimed straight at Nick.

Nick had marked the row where he left me sleeping. As he drew level with it, he braked hard, kicking up dust. He threw open the driver's door and stood on the running board, hollering my name.

I exploded from the row, ran across the Chevy's nose, and dove in the passenger window. Didn't bother opening the door.

I'd been woken from a migraine sleep. I barely knew my own name. My pants were falling down. I'd puked six or eight times in the past five hours. Hadn't had decent food for a week, hadn't drunk water in two days at least.

But my memory of the next few seconds is clear.

Nick began to giggle, the way he did, and swing his long torso back inside the Chevy.

A roar cut through everything.

The giggles stopped.

Nick sagged against the front door.

The ATV's angry-insect light came closer.

"Yeah?" Gus said. "Don't blue-ball me, Conway. For chrissake, what happened next?"

I snapped to. I was breathing hard. The long-buried story had brought more pain and shame than I would've guessed.

I licked my lips. "The point," I finally said. "The point is, it *pulped* him. It *pulped* my buddy Nick."

"*What* pulped him?"

I blinked, realized I'd told it all wrong, had lost track of the reason for the story. "The watermelon farmer's shotgun. Fired from maybe twelve feet back. It took the left side of him, from his ass to his shoulder, everything not blocked by the truck's cab, and it . . . *shredded* him. Turned everything to pulp."

We were quiet awhile.

"What happened next?" Gus finally said.

"The farmer was no killer. He was as surprised as me, went white as a sheet. We just stood there and watched Nick bleed out. It was a double-barreled shotgun, but the farmer never cocked it for a second shot. I never got the feeling I was next."

In a dead voice, I told Gus how the farmer had crossed himself about a hundred times, then fallen to his knees and wept. He told me in Spanglish he knew he'd sinned, he'd done something *awful,* but the wetbacks—his word—had been raiding him all year long. He was going to throw away the shotgun, no, *bury* it, bury it eight feet down.

Then we pidgined our way to an understanding. I made it clear Nick was no relation to me and that I wasn't a guy who would go whistling for the law. Then I helped flop Nick's body into the bed of the Chevy, cover it with a tarp, and haul it back to the barn. In return, the farmer spent the better part of the day driving me to the bus station in Harlingen, where he bought me a ticket to New Orleans.

It was a quiet ride.

"That was that?" Gus said. "No blowback?"

"No blowback."

"You left your buddy in Bumfuck, Texas, to be buried in a row of watermelons."

"It was Edinburg," I said. "And it wasn't a war movie."

We were quiet again.

"Yeah," I finally said. "I left my buddy there. But don't lose sight of the big point."

"Which is?"

"A shotgun is a serious tool. A shotgun is not something you can wise-ass your way past."

Once Gus took off, I told Floriano I had to leave for a while myself. Then I ducked his dirty looks and called Tory Sasaki, who helps out when we're swamped. Or when I go off to do my thing. Which, according to Floriano, is way too often. Which explained the dirty looks.

Tory would be over in fifteen minutes. She always jumps at the work, and she's good. One of these days I'll smarten up and hire her full-time, but for now I can't bear to think of myself as a manager.

Gus's copy of the bill of sale for his shitbox car had Andrade's home address, but I decided to try his shop first.

During the drive, I called Randall. Voice mail again, for crying out loud. Left another message: in addition to checking on Brian Weller, could he do a quick google on the Pundos? Supposedly Mob-connected in Springfield, but that might be BS. I started to click off, then mentioned he ought to see if the Hi Hat jazz club fit in.

I neared Andrade's shop in Marlborough, cut across Route 20 to Mechanic Street. Pulled in behind a low, barn-red building with ten roll-up doors. They belonged to a cast of small garages that came and went. This was a lousy location, hard to find. To succeed here, you had to be a specialist and you had to be good. The minute you could afford to, you moved to a better location. That's what I did a few years ago.

Most of the doors had amateurish, faded signs above. MIDLANDS TRIUMPH USA, EDDIE'S AIR-COOLED VW. I found ANDRADE AUTOMOTIVE, banged on the door. Nothing. So I cupped my hands and peered through smeared Plexiglas.

The one-bay garage surprised the hell out of me. When you know a mechanic, you take a guess at how he'll run his shop. After a while, you get pretty good at it. Same way a realtor can meet a couple and know what their house'll look like inside.

Because of Andrade's dead-end job at Ocean State Job Lot and his penny-ante rip-off schemes, I'd pictured him as sloppy, disorganized, half-assed.

Wrong wrong wrong. Maybe *he* was all those things, but his garage sure wasn't.

The far end was neatly stacked to the ceiling with old tires, new tires, labeled cartons full of parts. Another surprise: the shop floor wasn't stained, beat-up concrete. It looked dead level and was painted in a checkered-flag pattern. A homemade workbench ran arrow-straight down one long wall. Behind it, screwed to the wall, was Peg-Board Sharpied with black outlines of hand tools. And every tool was on its peg.

So admit it: you misjudged Andrade in one way that you know of.

Ten minutes later, I knocked on the door of Andrade's apartment. It was in a maze of two-story red-brick buildings, four apartments to a unit. The development wasn't bad, but it wasn't nice either. It was a place to live.

The woman who answered was very young and short. I'm no expert, but the little boy she held on her cocked hip seemed too old to be working a binky.

The woman looked at me. Pretty blue eyes, round as hell. Her mouth held something halfway between a question and a smirk. Snap judgment: she deserved better than this, and *knew* she deserved better, but hadn't thrown in the towel.

"Andrade here?"

She smiled some, said, "Andrade!" Walked away. Back to the linoleum-tiled kitchen floor, where she was doing something with the kid.

Andrade appeared from the hall that must lead to a pair of bedrooms and a bath, struggling to thread his black leather belt one-handed. A fiberglass cast ran from his right wrist nearly to his shoulder, locking his elbow at a ninety-degree angle.

He stopped dead when he saw me. "You let him *in*?" he said, looking at me but speaking to his wife, or maybe girlfriend. "This is *him*. This is *the guy*."

"*The guy* knocked on the door," she said. "I thought maybe it was Zoller."

Nobody asked me to step in.

I stepped in.

Saw that the woman and the kid were working on a puzzle with fifty pieces, each the shape of a state. The kid's fingers were flying, and he mumbled as he worked. When I heard "Albany, Harrisburg, Boston," I put it together: he was saying capitals as he dropped the pieces in.

People surprise you if you let them.

"Thanks a fucking lot," Andrade said, finally speaking to me. He'd made a quarter turn to thrust the cast in my direction.

"Must make it hard to roll back odometers," I said. "Hard to brew up bullshit inspection stickers."

He ignored that. "Plus the cops came by. Said they know all about me now. Said they're watching me close."

"Good."

"Plus the hospital bill's gonna be like fifteen grand. Plus I got a hydraulic lift on order that costs three grand. No way Jose. So I'm gonna lose my down payment."

"Carson City," the kid said. "Boise, Salem, Sacramento."

I said, "You hear what happened in the halfway house in Framingham?"

"Yeah." Andrade dragged out the word, wondering where I was going.

"What do you know about it?"

"What do you mean?" His eyes: puzzled. Then something clicked. "Fuckin' Biletnikov! He was *staying* there. I *knew* the address seemed familiar."

"What I was thinking, maybe you dropped by. Maybe you got all beered up and brave."

"You gotta be shitting me."

"Were you over in Framingham last night?"

"Piss up a rope. You bust me all up, then you drop by my home and . . ." His face went red. "Piss up a rope. Or smash my other arm."

My reaction must've given away the way I was starting to feel, because Andrade pressed. He took a step toward me, making a show of presenting his good arm. "Yeah, Mister Hard Guy, Mister Drunk's Best Friend. Bust up my other elbow in front of my kid and my girl. Why not, tough man?"

"Whyn't you just tell him?" his girlfriend said, not even looking up, tapping on Alaska because the kid had lost it beneath his own ankle. "Your brothers came over and you all got drunk hooting about your million-dollar lawsuit. The cops pounded on the door at eleven, then ran your brothers off at midnight. Just *tell* him."

Hell.

Andrade was alibied to the gills. He didn't have anything to do with any killings.

As I drove off, I felt like a real man for destroying his elbow. Kid at home, hydraulic lift on order. And I'd crippled him to show off for Gus. Why? Because Gus reminded me of Roy.

Hell of a reason to blow up a guy's elbow.

I felt like a million bucks.

CHAPTER FIVE

With Andrade ruled out, my next stop had to be Springfield. I called Randall again, hoping to grab an address.

"Great Caesar's ghost," he said after picking up on half a ring. "Talk about an interesting google. Why are you curious about Charlie Pundo?"

"It's the son Teddy I really wanted to know about."

"Forget Teddy. Teddy is nothing. It's Charlie that makes for a spine-tingling read."

"You got an address? Or was your spine too tingly to notice?"

The line went so quiet I wondered if the call had crapped out.

Randall finally said, "You're not going to *visit* Charlie Pundo, are you?"

"Sure."

"That's a bad idea, Conway."

"You got an address or not? I can find it on my own if I have to."

He sighed. "Swing by."

"You're coming?"

"As if you didn't know I would when you dialed. Bastard."

Randall clicked off.

I may have smiled.

Ten minutes later, I watched him rattle down an outdoor stairway from the second-floor apartment he rented in Framingham's Saxonville neighborhood. Watching him zip down the shaky iron stairs, tablet computer tucked under one arm, you could just about forget one of his feet was made of titanium and high-tensile-strength plastic.

Randall Swale was the son of my parole officer, Luther. We met a while back. Randall wasn't overseas for three weeks before an IED under a trash-can lid in a godforsaken village blew his right foot and half his shin over a wall. He came home, learned to use his prosthesis, showed zero self-pity, said he was never looking back. Had standing offers for full-boat academic scholarships from most of the best colleges in the country—but had spent over a year bumming around, helping me out sometimes, getting himself into relationships with women that started out serious but dried up.

A few weeks back, Luther'd asked me to talk with Randall. If he was going to start college in September, he needed to make a commitment soon.

I'd tried. Randall had muled up right from the start, the way I'd known he would.

The kid was going through something. And whip-smart though he was, I got the feeling he didn't know himself what was holding him back. He had to get through whatever he had to get through, and he had to do it mostly on his own.

I knew a little something about that.

When I was in an honest mood, I admitted all this worked to my benefit. A dude who'd been first in his class at officer candidate school was good to have around. And if that dude was black to boot . . . well, Randall could go a lot of places I couldn't.

I aimed us west on the Mass Turnpike.

"Helping you out," he said, "ensures me a lengthy stay in hell. Standing on my head in a bucket of shit, as the old joke goes."

"What are you talking about?"

"This morning, I spent fifteen minutes on the phone with the late Brian Weller's guidance counselor."

"How'd you manage that?"

"She may have had the impression I was writing a feature for the *Worcester Telegram and Gazette*."

"Nice."

"I'll treasure that compliment when I'm in hell."

"Well?"

Randall pushed up a pair of imaginary glasses on his nose. It's his tic when he gets set to tell me something juicy. "Poor wrong-place, wrong-time Brian Weller was a great kid. A great kid who drank exactly once, according to the counselor. The first time he sampled old John Barleycorn at a neighborhood party, he backed over the knee of the high school track star, a girl who was a lock for the Olympic team in both the two hundred and four hundred meters."

"It's not easy to back over a knee."

"It's somewhat easier when the girl is passed out under your mom's car."

"Oh. So Weller got a choice between Almost Home and jail, one of those deals?"

"It's actually a bit more complex. The poor dumb kid wanted to do hard time. He *begged* the judge to send him to MCI Cedar Junction. A fit of conscience, that sort of thing."

"Which proves he wasn't much of a hard case," I said.

"Agreed."

"So I'm going to assume he was shot by accident. By somebody who was after Gus."

"Who is Gus?"

I gave him a three-minute fill-in.

Then Randall spent twenty minutes zipping around his iPad, reading me Charlie Pundo horror stories.

"This is one bad hombre," he said. "Took over Springfield in the late eighties, and had to step on a lot of New York Mob toes to do it. Apparently another family, the New York–approved Santosuossos, were getting big at the time, too. So it was 'This town ain't big enough for the both of us.' High noon in Springfield, et cetera, et cetera. A full-on gang war broke out."

"Charlie Pundo won the war."

"Clearly. And ran Springfield for a quarter century or so, and didn't make a lot of friends doing it. But starting a few years ago, he backed off. Ceded turf back to NYC, which from what I gather is simply not done. Now he plows money into the Hi Hat and jets around to jazz festivals, but otherwise keeps a low profile."

"What about the son?"

Randall shrugged. "Theodore's a nonentity. Well, I shouldn't say that. I found news stories about an aggravated rape charge a few years back. But the case was dropped for no reason I could find."

We exited the pike onto Route 291, nearing Springfield. I tried to resist. Couldn't. Pulled my cell. "Since we're this far west anyway."

Randall said nothing, and bless him for that.

I called my ex-wife. Got voice mail. Said I was in Springfield on business, be a shame to come so far and not see Roy. Said I'd call back later, maybe I could take him to dinner.

Randall said nothing.

I nearly missed the Hi Hat on my first pass, assuming the bombed-out ghetto we were rolling through couldn't be home to a big-time gangster's place. Springfield's a sad little city and a familiar story: a manufacturing hotbed until fifty years ago, in decline ever since as the jobs went first down south, then overseas. Old-timers will tell you the Feds drove a stake through Springfield's heart when, using typical Fed wisdom, they built I-91 on the bank of the Connecticut River, which used to be and ought to still be the city's best feature.

Springfield's a city that just gave up. It must have fifty neighborhoods like the one we were passing through: good homes gone to seed, good people who just couldn't make it.

But ghetto or no, Randall whacked my arm and pointed right—at a short block that looked like 1965.

"What the hell?" I said, cutting the wheel.

The club was wedged between a barber shop and a men's clothing store. A haberdasher, I guess, or so said the old-fashioned sign. Directly across the street: a deli and general store, complete with a rack of fresh fruit out front. Overhead: another fancy sign.

I craned my neck. Anchoring the other end of the block was a church in red-brown brick. Catholic, I was guessing, though I had only a glimpse.

Although the streets leading here were pure inner city—Hondas on cinder blocks, pit bulls with rib cages showing, dead-eyed kids staring at us—this block was pristine. I half-expected to see a white-uniformed man working a push broom.

In the window of the club itself: a neon sign, HI and HAT alternating, a drum cymbal opening and closing every other pulse. You put a sign like that most places in Springfield, it's busted out an hour later. It's that kind of city.

"Charlie Pundo," Randall said, "appears to have built himself a gangster Disneyland."

"See that fruit, just sitting out front of the deli? He must be respected as hell."

"Or feared."

"Same thing."

"No it's not."

"Around here it is."

Randall thought that over. Didn't argue it.

We parked.

Inside, the Hi Hat was long and narrow and more contemporary than I would've guessed. Jazz came from speakers I couldn't see.

Exposed brick, polished floors, restored bar and woodwork. Low but decent-sized stage filling the far end. Two old-timers at the bar watching ESPN with no volume. Young bartender in a white shirt, his head shaved, his soul patch perfectly symmetrical, his cuffs folded precisely.

I forget how sad bars make me until I'm inside one.

We stood at the bar. I asked for a Diet Coke. Randall asked for ice water. We waved off the lunch menus the bartender extended. I asked for a pen. When he brought the drinks, I slid him a note on a cocktail napkin: *We are not cops. We need to talk with Charlie Pundo about Gus Biletnikov.*

The bartender was good: his expression changed not at all as he read. We took our drinks to a table and listened to jazz.

Soon another man appeared. He was dressed like the bartender, but built more solidly. Had the shaved-head look but wore no soul patch. His ears, nose, and scalp belonged to a man who'd boxed. But not well.

He looked at me, nodded, jerked a thumb over his shoulder. Randall and I rose, but the man shook his head once and gestured for Randall to stay there.

I shrugged.

Randall shrugged, sat, sipped.

The man led me to a short hallway with doors for the restrooms, the kitchen, and something else.

The office.

The man knew what he was doing. He waited until I was hemmed in, with doors on all sides and limited movement available, then turned and held his arms out, shrugging some at the same time—pantomiming *Sorry, but I'm gonna search you and there's not a goddamn thing you can do about it.*

I extended my own arms. He searched me.

Then he nodded me in and closed the door behind me. Never did say a word.

Staring at me from a cheapo rolling chair was the man who had to be Charlie Pundo.

I nodded to him and looked around.

It was the working office of a man who didn't give a rat's ass what anybody thought of him. Office-grade carpet, old schoolteacher's desk with a laptop, mix-and-match lamps, hospital-colored walls.

It was cold, too.

I turned to take in the wall behind me. It was floor-to-ceiling custom shelves, sized perfectly for records. Actual vinyl LPs.

"Best move I ever made," Charlie Pundo said, waving an arm at the LPs. He rose, shook my hand, passed me a business card, sat again. "Forty years ago, all the experts and know-it-alls wanted me to put the music on reel-to-reel and throw out the records. Then it was cassettes. Then they wanted me, they *begged* me, to digitize everything and save the space, the hassle. I stuck to my guns. Now those records are worth I can't even tell you how much. I've had three Hollywood guys and the chairman of Blue Note Records write me a blank check. They told me fill in a number. Uh-uh. I guess they'll end up in a museum when I'm gone."

I slipped his card in my wallet. "The records why it's cold in here?"

"Also why I keep the lights low." He sighed so long and loud that I turned and really looked at him for the first time.

Give Gus credit: he'd said Charlie Pundo reminded him of a retired barber, and I saw what he meant. Nearly as tall as me, thirty pounds lighter, call it twenty years older. Mostly bald, salt-and-pepper ring of hair that could use a trim. Droopy mustache, also salt-and-pepper. Heavy brown eyes. He wore a perfectly tailored gray suit, pinstripes, white shirt, purple necktie. Looked about as menacing as the grandpa from a cookie commercial.

He gestured at me to sit. When I did, he sighed again. "You shouldn't have come here."

"I didn't know what else to do."

"You say you're not a cop, and as far as I can tell, that's true. Are you a private cop?"

"I'm a mechanic."

He smiled, shook his head. "A mechanic. Go figure. Now why'd you come here asking about one"—he looked at the cocktail-napkin note—"Gus Biletnikov?"

I told him about the shooting at the halfway house, about Gus's claim that he got in trouble dealing for Pundo. When I finished, Charlie leaned back in his chair and looked at me over his reading glasses.

"You put me in an untenable position," he said, unbuttoning his suit coat and clasping his hands behind his head. "You force me to make the I'm-a-legitimate-businessman speech, the can't-an-Italian-American-get-a-break speech. But I *am,* and I *can't.* I run the most important jazz club in New England. That's not according to me, that's according to *Downbeat* magazine. I showcase the American art form to folks who'd be line dancing in hillbilly bars otherwise."

"So if Gus Biletnikov says he dealt drugs for you, he's lying."

"Or delusional."

"Then I guess I'm glad he didn't say that."

Pundo frowned, looked a question at me.

"He said he dealt for your *son.* For Teddy."

Charlie Pundo's jaw dropped half an inch. His teeth weren't so great for a rich man. He must be too old to care.

"Yeah, for old Fat Teddy he called him, no offense, just repeating what I heard. Guess they would've been at UMass around the same time, huh?"

He was so quiet, so moveless for so long that I decided to rise.

Pundo just sat there, staring at his wall of LPs, hands locked behind his head. Ignoring me, maybe making connections in his head.

"You put this whole block together," I said. "The deli, the tailor. Even the church, I'm guessing."

He didn't look at me. "Is there a question in there?"

"Why?"

"You've got to spend it on *some*thing."

I stepped to the door, opened it, hesitated, turned. "I've got a son myself," I said, not sure why I was telling this to Charlie Pundo. Not sure why I liked him. Why I felt for him. "They're not always easy."

He said nothing.

"Sons, I mean."

He said nothing.

I closed the door quietly.

CHAPTER SIX

"What now?" Randall said three minutes later. We sat in my truck kitty-corner across from the club, close enough but not too.

"We wait," I said.

"What for?"

"For Teddy, the son. Charlie just about dropped dead when I mentioned him. Put that together with things you told me and you get a picture."

"The father truly *has* backed out of *La Vida* Gangster," Randall said. "Or is trying to."

"But the son's trading on Daddy's rep, trying to be a hotshot drug dealer."

"It's conjecture."

"But it's good conjecture."

"That it is." Pause. " 'Just when I thought I was out . . .' "

An SUV slammed to a stop in front of the club. "That's got to be him," I said, pointing. "He must've been nearby."

"Agreed," Randall said as the driver's door of the SUV opened. "No critique of my splendid Pacino?"

"Be glad. And hush."

The guy we assumed was Teddy Pundo climbed from the SUV, a Mercedes Geländewagen you couldn't touch for less than a hundred and ten grand. It was black, of course, with twenty-four-inch chrome rims, of course. Then he steamed into the Hi Hat, looking neither left nor right.

He was gone so soon we didn't get much of a look at him. Impressions: long brown hair, greasy. Expensive high-top sneakers topped by jeans topped by a black leather car coat. Fat Teddy? You could see where he got the nickname. But he moved well beneath the weight. He wasn't sloppy fat; he was powerful fat.

"That it?" Randall said, keying the SUV's license number into his tablet. "Are we done here?"

"I guess we are," I said, finger-drumming the steering wheel. "But we got a lot. We know the club, including the layout of the office. We're pretty sure Charlie Pundo really is trying to go legit, and that his numbnuts son is gumming up the plan."

"But what did we learn about the likelihood of Clan Pundo shooting up the halfway house?"

I thought that through. "Charlie's a definite no. He's got his club, his records, his little make-believe block. An old-school shotgun party feels like the opposite of what he's into now."

"I'll buy that. And Teddy?"

"I dunno. For a hard-case killer, he sure hustled over when Daddy called. Maybe he . . . hell, look at that."

As I'd pulled from my parking space, the white-shirted guy who looked like an ex-boxer had stepped from the club. He was now wearing, but hadn't zipped, a black Windbreaker.

He stared at my truck.

He made eye contact with me and mouthed my license number twice.

He stepped to the driver's-side rear corner of Teddy's Geländewagen. There was nothing but thirty yards of empty street between us and him.

He set hands on hips, pushing the Windbreaker back a few inches. He had a goddamn cannon tucked in his waistband.

"Jesus Christ," Randall said. "Desert Eagle, maybe the .50-caliber model. I'm surprised his pants stay up."

I drove away, right past the man.

He tracked us with his eyes. When we eased by, he wasn't more than ten feet from Randall's window.

" 'They pull me back in,' " Randall said a few seconds later.

"Shut up."

We were quiet after that.

When he answered the door of the apartment I'd set him up in, Gus was surprised. He looked at his watch. Then I thought he looked over my shoulder. "Done for the day?"

"I've been to Marlborough and Springfield," I said. "Need to talk with you." I stepped in, told Gus to swap his pajama pants for jeans.

Then I told him about the day.

When I finished, he shook his head. "So you walked into a wise-guy bar and wrote a note asking to see the man in charge of cocaine sales?"

I shrugged.

He rubbed his temples. The move annoyed me—it was like *he* was a teacher and *I* was a student being a giant pain in his ass.

"You're fantastic to let me stay here," he said. "And all the world knows you'll give any Barnburner the shirt off your back. Subtlety, however, is not your strong suit."

"We're assuming somebody tried to kill you," I said. "I am, anyway. If you're looking for *subtle* help, you're out of luck."

"Damn straight."

I wanted to shake the little bastard. Why the hell *was* I helping him? What the hell wasn't he telling me?

You know the answer to the first question.

I took my time. Breathed myself calm. "You named two possibilities," I finally said. "Andrade and Teddy Pundo. I checked them both out. Andrade didn't do it, and I'm pretty sure Pundo didn't either."

"Conway, he's a *drug dealer*. He's a *gangster*. His father was *bull*shitting you."

"Nope. Charlie Pundo didn't know Teddy was dealing until I told him so, and he didn't know anything about Almost Home. And if Teddy was badass enough to be blowing people down with a shotgun, you can bet his dad'd know. So we're back where we were before: who else has something against you?"

"I'll say again that maybe whoever killed Brian Weller was trying to kill Brian Weller."

"Nope. We read up on him. He was a damn choirboy, and you know it."

Gus folded his arms. "Be that as it may, why is this your mission in life all of a sudden? Why am I your big fucking project?"

"The Barnburners asked me to keep an eye on you. I'm doing that."

"Is that all? Really? How old did you say your son is?"

I said nothing.

"His name's Roy, I believe you said."

Charlene says I'm transparent. I hate being transparent.

I wanted to tell Gus about Roy. I wanted to ask Gus about his father, to see what their relationship looked like from his vantage point.

I wanted to ask him if Roy would come back to me.

"You ever ride a dirt bike?" I said. "I know a great spot."

He could ride, all right. I watched him clear a hill twenty-five yards ahead of me. He tabletopped his jump, laying the little 125cc Yamaha sideways in midair, then snapping it wheels down just in time to land.

We'd been riding the power lines near Route 495 for a good forty minutes. I was beat. I hadn't ridden for a couple of years, had forgotten how punishing it was.

I goosed the throttle, squirted alongside Gus, made a drinking gesture. He nodded, pulled over at the next power-line tower.

We killed the bikes and took off our helmets. First impression when you shut down: quiet, quiet, quiet.

I stepped off, stretched, pulled water bottles from a fender carrier, tossed one to Gus. On his face: big smile, goggle marks. "Killer idea," he said. "These little one-twenty-fives are a hoot."

"You ever race?"

"I wanted to, but my old man wouldn't let me. I did most of my riding in the backyard."

"Must have been some yard. Over in Sherborn, you said? Nice town."

Gus shrugged. "I used to whip around in the woods. I even hacked out my own little course. *Man,* did I want to race. But when I hacked too close to the neighbors' yards, they bitched to my dad. He gets scared shitless when anybody disapproves of anything, so he rolled over and made me quit riding. He used to say, 'Do you want to read about it in the police log on Friday?' That was his worst fear, a police log write-up in the *Sherborn Sentinel.*"

From the north, the deep-noted engines of bigger bikes pounded our way. "High school years are tough for the son and the father both," I said. "Things any better now?"

Gus said nothing.

Three guys on big green Kawasakis busted past. Friendly waves all around.

I said, "I used to ride here with my son Roy."

"How old is he?"

"About your age. Tried college, but it didn't take. He's a good body man." To our left, the Kawasakis jumped a hill and disappeared. "It's been a while. He doesn't ride with me anymore."

"He's nuts. This place rocks." Gus whipped his empty water bottle at me, grinned, straddled his bike. "Looks like you got the wrong kid and I got the wrong dad." Lit up his Yamaha, tire-fired dirt at me as he took off.

I followed as fast as I could. Smiling big.

CHAPTER SEVEN

H ello?"
I walked down a short flight of steps, stutter-stepping in the dark. Felt half-ridiculous, half-mad at Charlene.

"Anybody home?" As I said it, I pushed through the church basement door. It was unlocked, which was good. But I couldn't see three feet in front of me, which was bad.

Goddamn disorganized drunks.

Here's what'd happened: while Gus and I had trailered the dirt bikes back to the shop, I'd found a rambling voice mail from Charlene. Breathless, almost panicky, not like her at all. The gist of the ramble was that a couple of good eggs we both knew, longtime Barnburners, were trying to launch a new AA meeting. Greek Orthodox church out in Hopedale. The meeting wasn't getting off the ground. To change that, a big crew was planning to swarm the joint tonight and lay down some Barnburner mojo. Upshot: could I come by? It'd mean a lot, blah blah blah.

"That's a hell of a sigh," Gus had said as I glared at my phone. He looked like a reverse raccoon: white skin where his goggles had sat, dirty everywhere else. I guessed I looked the same.

I'd been looking forward to a hot shower, an hour with Quick-Books, then dinner and TV. I told Gus all this. The little bastard hadn't seemed sympathetic. If anything, he'd smirked as I dropped him off.

Anyway, here I was in Hopedale, which makes Framingham look like Chicago. Showered but still hungry, I'd made it three minutes early for the eight o'clock meeting.

And the parking lot was empty, and the building was dark, and Charlene wasn't picking up.

"Hello?" I let the door shut behind me.

Nothing.

Something beneath my feet crinkled. I barely noticed.

"Well fuck me sideways," I said to the darkness.

"For that," a man's voice said from a far corner, "you want the Congregational place down the street."

And a hundred people cracked up.

And the lights snapped on.

And there they were.

The banner behind them said FREE AT LAST.

And I'm so thick it took me another second to remember: my parole had ended at 12:01 that morning.

They were hooting and clapping and smiling, but in my head everything went silent as I took them in.

All of them.

There were Charlene and Sophie, front and center. I even spotted Jessie, arms folded, along the back row. All the key Barnburners were there: Butch Feeley, Mary Giarusso, Carlos Q (the world's meanest Colombian, and that's saying something), a bunch more. Floriano and his wife Maria stood off to one side, not knowing most of the others. Eudora Spoon and Moe Coover, my two favorite old-school AAers, smiled and clapped. Randall stood with his father, Luther. Luther was beckoning me for some reason.

Hell, even Gus Biletnikov was there. He must have been in on the setup—it explained the smirk that afternoon when I'd dropped him off.

Roy wasn't there.

No reason he would be, really.

Luther Swale's beckoning was nearly out of control. I took a step forward, and the hooting and hollering doubled. Luther cupped his hands to be heard. "How does it feel to be off paper?"

I looked down. They'd taped newspaper just inside the door. It explained the crinkling when I stepped in.

It was a long way to go for an inside gag. See, parole is called being on paper. The best day of an ex-con's life comes when he gets off paper. No more weekly PO visits, no more travel restrictions, no more peeing in a cup.

Charlene strode across the basement and planted a big honkin' kiss on my lips, putting extra Hollywood on it for the benefit of the crowd. Then the rest of them flooded over and ringed us. Somebody cranked music on a boom box.

It was a good night. Who says drunks don't know how to throw a party?

The good vibe ended when my eyes snapped open the next morning. My first thought wasn't of dirt bikes or parties: what popped into my head was the dude outside the Hi Hat. A dude who walked around with a giant handgun stuffed in his pants and didn't mind showing it to you.

The dude was Charlie Pundo's muscle man. But was he also *Teddy* Pundo's muscle? Or was he more like Teddy's babysitter?

Hell, that was just one thing I needed to look at. First, I'd decided to drop in on Gus Biletnikov's family. Unannounced.

Whether Gus acknowledged it, it sure felt to me like whoever'd done Almost Home was trying to kill him.

Which meant I had to bail out of work today.

Which maybe happened more often than it should, thanks to Barnburner chores.

Which didn't go over so great with Charlene or Floriano.

I slipped from bed, took the world's quietest shower, and escaped the house without waking Charlene. Which meant I didn't have to explain to her that I wasn't going to work.

Phew.

Called Randall while driving east, told him where to meet me.

Dropped by the shop and told Floriano I had errands to run. His raised eyebrow and the Silent Sam routine as he looked over the day's appointments were his version of a hissy fit. I told him I'd call Tory again to ease his workload, but he said she was out of action for the rest of the week—getting trained up on the new direct-injection fuel systems.

Hell.

Well, Floriano would just have to stay pissed. I needed to keep tugging threads.

On the ride home last night, I'd worked through it in my head. I'd given Gus two chances to level with me about anybody who might have it in for him. Each time, he'd fed me Andrade and Teddy Pundo. Each time, he'd acted sketchy when I pressed. He wasn't telling everything there was to tell.

Far as I was concerned, that gave me license to end-run Gus. And the place to start was with his dad.

Or I hoped it was. Couldn't think of anybody else.

Randall had agreed with my thinking. Our plan was to meet at the Biletnikov place and see what made the family tick.

Sherborn is ten minutes southeast of my shop. It's also a different world.

The last address I passed in Framingham was a squat cluster of Section 8 housing. Once I crossed the town line, the first address in Sherborn was a horse farm. It's up there with Wayland and Weston as the ritziest towns in the state.

A few horse farms later I climbed a hill, angling northeast now, and turned where the GPS said to. Cleared a stone wall, drove up a steep gravel driveway.

The house: a McMansion. New, designed to look old. Vast, designed to look modest. Flowing, designed to look rambling.

I parked, rang the bell.

A young woman in jeans answered. Chinese looks. Shoulder-length black hair thick as a horse tail. Perfect skin, sweat-sheen on her forehead. "Yes?"

"Mr. Biletnikov in?"

"I'm afraid not." Her accent was vaguely familiar and not what I'd expected.

"There a Mrs. Biletnikov?"

"I'm afraid I can't help you." She began to close the door, but a phone clipped to her jeans buzzed. She raised a finger and took the call.

Then everything changed.

She hung up, smiling and half-bowing, and opened the door wide.

"Come this way. Mrs. Biletnikov has been down in the cottage lately." In addition to the cell clipped to one belt loop, she had a pink and white walkie-talkie clipped to another. She saw me looking at it. "I'm Haley. Nanny for little Emma."

"Emma is . . . Mrs. Biletnikov's?" I knew Gus's parents had split up. Looked like his dad had remarried and had a kid.

"In a manner of speaking." Haley said it with a locked jaw. While I puzzled that through, she led the way.

The house was clean and tidy, but with baby stuff scattered here and there: a dozen bottles on the kitchen counter, nipples to match, a stuffed giraffe with a bow around its neck. I checked out the place as we walked. Wide pine floorboards, probably scavenged from an old farmhouse. Overstuffed chairs with preworn arms. New paintings that looked like folk art. The most authentic country money could buy. Snap judgment: this was a poser house, the home of people who didn't know who they were. If a decorator walked in tomorrow and told them to change over to midcentury modern, they'd write a check to make it happen.

We walked a long hall, then down a flight of stairs. I tried not to stare at Haley's rear end. I failed.

We moved through a walk-out basement to the backyard. Wildflowers, oaks, a patio with thousand-dollar steel chairs prerusted. Patina, they call it. It costs extra. I kid you not.

The lot was three acres, easy. And though the spring leaves were still puny, I couldn't see even a hint of any neighbor's house. No wonder Gus'd had room to hack out a motocross track.

Haley led me down a short path to a green-trimmed cottage screened by trees. To my left, Randall's Hyundai crunched gravel. He climbed out and joined our wagon train, introducing himself to Haley on the fly.

She gestured toward the door of a cottage half-hidden in the woods, smiled without really smiling, and walked back the way we'd come.

I knocked. Heard "Yes." Entered a room with walls the color of peach ice cream.

"I'm Rinn Biletnikov," she said, stepping into the room from a hallway.

I took a fast breath. Heard Randall do the same.

Everything about her was just right. Genuinely blond hair, chopped at chin length. Smart blue eyes that said *If you play your cards right* and *You wish* all at once. Nose freckles, tiny gap between her front teeth. Cross a 1950s Hollywood starlet with a frog-catching tomboy, you had Rinn.

Age? Call it late twenties.

"I'm going to take a wild guess," Randall said. "You're not Gus's mom."

She laughed. "We're only a few years apart, which makes for an odd relationship and then some. It's one of the perils of being a trophy wife. Drink?"

She fixed a Diet Pepsi for me, bubbly water for herself and Randall. She looked us over, not trying to hide it, while we sat in a white sofa and matching armchairs. "Haley seemed nervous about you," she said to me. "I see why."

"I'm not Sherborn material."

"And thank God for that. It's a dull little slice of paradise."

"Rinn," Randall said, crossing his legs. "What an interesting name."

"Better than Brittania Whitney," she said, staring at his plastic ankle.

"Brittania?" he said. "Not Brittney or Brittany?"

"Brittania Whitney," she said. "Of the Wellesley Whitneys."

He made an exaggerated wince. "Rinn it is, then."

She laughed.

They made merry eyes at each other.

I rolled mine.

I should say Randall is considered handsome. I've personally seen three strangers tell him he's a dead ringer for that guy (they say, snapping their fingers), you know, the guy from *The Wire,* the one who's a bad guy but you like him anyway. When Randall points out that half the cast fits that description and asks which one they mean, they get flustered—they don't know how to distinguish one black guy from the next.

Point being, he's handsome.

Rinn Biletnikov sure thought so.

Yeesh.

We sipped.

"Out of curiosity," I said, "why'd you want to meet with us? With me? You had no idea who I was."

"You looked interesting. It gets lonely down here, Mr. . . . ."

I said my name and Randall's. "Why *are* you down here?" *While your baby's up at the main house?* I thought. *And your nanny seems pissed about it?*

She said nothing.

"We came to talk about Gus," I said. "Came looking for his father. Your husband, I guess."

"About?"

"We're worried."

"How so?"

"You hear about the shooting at Almost Home, his halfway house?"

"Yes."

"We think they were trying to kill Gus, not the other kid."

She put a hand over her mouth. "What makes you say that?"

Randall jumped in, telling her what hadn't been reported on the news. That Gus and Weller looked alike. That Weller had been in Gus's room when he was shot. He told her about Andrade, about Teddy Pundo and his pedigree.

Randall told her so much I nearly kicked him. He was enjoying her attention, her focus. It was hard to blame him. Hell, I'd balance my Diet Pepsi can on my nose if it'd buy *me* a minute of that. Something about the way she looked at you. Like you were the most interesting man she would talk to all day.

Randall's story finally petered out. "So that's about it," he said. "We're wondering if you or Gus's father know about other problems Gus is having. Things he might be hiding from us."

"Before he went to rehab," Rinn said, taking her time, editing as she spoke, "Gus was on terrible terms with his father. Peter is the *last* person he would have confided in."

"How about you?"

She hesitated. Did her face flare red? She made a flitting gesture with her hand, but too late. "We were pals," she said, shooting for breezy. "We were probably closer than most stepmoms and stepkids in this situation. Which is a tricky one, and that's an understatement. But he never *confided* in me. We never talked about anything serious."

It was quiet awhile.

"So you met Gus a few months ago in AA?" Rinn finally said to me. "And that's the . . . extent of your relationship? You're certainly going above and beyond to help him."

"It's a tight group. I told them I'd keep an eye on Gus, be an informal sponsor until he gets a real one."

"And then," she said, "you proceeded to beat the living daylights out of one man, then beard a gangster in his lair." She sipped bubbly water and looked at Randall. "Your friend keeps one hell of an eye."

"He's known far and wide for the eye he keeps."

"And the company," she said.

"Who am I to argue?" he said.

"Oh for chrissake," I said.

Rinn blushed some.

We sipped.

I said, "What does his father do?"

"Investment banker. He is"—Rinn tucked her chin to her chest and used a newscaster voice—"the driving force behind Thunder Junction Partners, the red-hot Cambridge firm that's the envy of Wall Street and Silicon Valley." In her own voice: "Thunder Junction made a splash when it refocused on green tech at just the right time. Peter was hailed as a genius. The company's done well these past few years, while everybody else has been flailing."

I started to ask something, but she snapped her fingers and interrupted. "You know, if you want a *truly* interesting take on Peter, here's the man you should talk to."

"Interesting how?"

She ignored the question, peered at her phone, wrote a number on a notepad, handed it across the table. It read *Donald Crump* and a number that started with 713, an area code I didn't recognize.

I pocketed the paper. "I'll call. How long have you two been married?"

"A year and a half. We met the summer between my junior and senior years, when I interned at Thunder Junction."

"What college?" Randall said.

"Harvard."

"Where else?" he said. "How silly of me."

She smiled. "My application for the internship caught Peter's eye. It was a memo. Six pages, single-spaced."

"What did it say?"

"It said Thunder Junction should dump high tech and biotech and jump into green tech." She used two fingers to pull a lime wedge from her water glass and pop it in her mouth. "With both feet."

Rinn Biletnikov chomped the lime, sucked its juice. If it struck her as bitter, she hid it well.

"My my my," Randall said when the two of us left the guesthouse.

"Married," I said. "Six-month-old baby."

"Killjoy." Long pause. "She is something, though. That you must concede."

I conceded it. We stood on the gravel drive, our backs to the cottage, each with car keys in hand, looking up the rise at the main house.

"She's down here," Randall finally said, "and the husband's up there."

"No sign of any baby in the cottage, either. That's the part gets me. Ever seen the mother of a six-month-old move out like that?"

"And she lied about her relationship with Gus," he said. "Or, at the very least, omitted much."

"You picked up on that even with those stars in your eyes, huh?"

"Shut up."

"Even with those little cupid arrows."

"Shut up." He smiled, though. "What's next?"

I held up the slip of paper Rinn had passed me. "Guess I'll call this guy."

"Geese to be chased," he said. "Herrings to be . . . reddened, I guess."

"The hell is *that* supposed to mean?"

"You're going to a lot of trouble, my friend. Heck, I'll just say it: *we're* going to a lot of trouble. Over a shooting that *may* have something to do with young Gus."

I said nothing.

"Or may not," Randall said.

"I got that." Long pause. "You saw the dude with the Desert Eagle."

He shrugged. "Beard a gangster in his lair, as lovely Rinn said. He puts on a show of bravado. This is a surprise?"

I said nothing.

"You go off on tangents," Randall said in a different voice, the voice of a man talking to a nervous horse. "You charge after causes. You misspend energy. You often do this when your actual life, life its own damn self, grows stressful. This is not news, Conway. This is not something of which you're unaware."

We were quiet maybe twenty seconds.

I searched my head.

Then shook it.

"I feel it," I said. "They're trying to kill him."

"Who?"

"That's what I need to find out. With you or without you." Held up the slip again. "Next stop, this guy."

Randall Swale and I stared at each other, perfectly still.

Then he sighed. "What do you want me to do?"

"See what you can learn about Rinn's husband. And about her."

"Brittania Whitney of the Wellesley Whitneys."

"Yeah."

"It's a dirty job," Randall said.

CHAPTER EIGHT

The voice at the other end of the phone belonged to a black guy who talked a hundred miles an hour. Donald Crump said he felt like a late lunch, asked was there any decent barbecue around here. I thought of the place in the Marlborough strip mall where I'd crippled Andrade a couple nights ago, told him how to get there. Once I clicked off, I realized I didn't know how to spot him.

It wasn't hard. When I rolled up, a man who had to be Crump was pacing out front, talking on a cell. I took him in.

Tiny man. He wore ostrich-skin cowboy boots with heels that jacked him up at least two inches. His cowboy hat, whose band matched the boots, added another six inches up top. But he would still barely come up to my chin. His suit and shirt were the color of lime sherbet. He wore a bolo tie. Its silver clasp was shaped like a cow's skull. The cow's eyes: two tiny emeralds.

When I neared him, he mouthed my name and his, but stayed on his cell. He pumped my hand like a hummingbird and pulled open the door. Stayed on his cell while ordering, waiting for the food, finding a booth.

When I was about set to take his phone and stomp it, he snapped it shut. "I could see soon's I pulled up this food'll be horrible," he said. "Don't know why you don't get better barbecue around here, man who opens a decent barbecue joint up north is an instant millionaire. Gonna put my hat on the table here, you don't mind. Cost more'n most folks make in a month, I leave it on a hook it'll walk right out the door. That all you eatin', little pulled-pork sandwich? Help yourself you want any of my sides."

He waved at his tray. It bowed under a full rack of Memphis-style ribs, cucumber salad, dirty mashed potatoes, red beans, and three squares of corn bread.

I said, "How much food do you order in a decent place?"

His laugh: high-pitched. "Good one, good one." His skin was very dark, very smooth. His head was shaved, his goatee precise, his eyes quick. He took a long strip of the brown paper towel they use for napkins, tucked it in his collar, smoothed it. "You looking at my paper towel? Got to protect the suit, suit costs more'n most people make in six months. Now why'd sweet young Rinn Biletnikov put you in touch with me?"

I shrugged. "You tell me. Where you from?"

"Everywhere. Anywhere. Now? Houston. Lot of opportunity there. Texas where a hungry man wants to be."

I ate a bite of my sandwich. It'd be easy to let Donald Crump, whoever the hell he was, steamroll you with the patter. He probably counted on it. So I focused, took a deep breath.

"Rinn told me you'd have something to say about her husband. Peter. Something I ought to hear."

"Why you want to hear about him in the first place?"

"Why do you want to know?"

"You're the one called *me* for a download, fool."

"Yeah, but *you're* the one with a thing for Rinn," I said. "You'd step off a building for her."

It was a guess.

It was a good one.

"She is something," Donald said. "Ain't she?"

We ate.

"Here's why I want to know about Peter Biletnikov," I said, and laid out a two-minute version of Gus's story, ending with the Almost Home shootings.

Crump eye-locked me. "You want to know did the father put a hit on the son."

I said nothing.

"Truth is I never seen him do anything that heavy," Crump said, wiping the corners of his mouth. "Nor heard tell of it."

I read his eyes. "But."

Half smile. "But. Hell yes, but. Wouldn't put it past him. Ain't much I'd put past Peter Biletnikov."

"Why? What's he to you?"

"Question is, what am *I* to *him*. And what I am is Willie McCoy." He smiled, waited.

I didn't get it. And I guess that showed on my face, because he shook his head, dropped the smile, waggled a finger at me. "You're weak on pop culture. Remember Jim Croce? Willie McCoy's the dude tugs on Superman's cape." He started singing, banging his rib on the table edge to keep time. "You don't tug on Superman's cape." People turned. Crump banged his rib harder. "You don't spit into the wind. You don't pull the mask off that ol' Lone Ranger, and you don't mess around with Jim."

Quiet laughs from nearby tables. A kid two booths over clapped. I looked at him. He stopped clapping.

"Peter Biletnikov took all my money," Donald Crump said. "And it may sound funny, but I come to get my money back."

CHAPTER NINE

I'm listening," I said.

"Think of me as a serial entrepreneur."

"How many times you been arrested for entrepreneuring?"

Hummingbird laugh. "Good one, good one." Then his eyes sharpened up fast. "Tell you what, Sax. Don't ask about my arrests, I won't ask about yours. You ain't no virgin. Fair?"

"Fair," I said, smiling, admitting to myself I got a kick out of this cat.

The tiny man had demolished his food. Now he fished a silver toothpick from his jacket pocket and began to use it while he told his story.

He was born in Holyoke, Massachusetts. Had headed south twenty years ago and loved it right away. He'd hoped to die without ever again traveling north of Washington, D.C. But business was business. And business eventually pulled him to Westborough, a couple towns over from Framingham.

Without saying exactly how, Crump said he was named CEO of a tiny company called SoPo Industries LLC. SoPo made lightweight glass and plastic products, mostly for solar-powered cars.

"You, a CEO? No offense, but it's hard to picture."

"You got to understand what a mess the company was," he said. "It was like being CEO of a lemonade stand. At first, anyway."

When Crump rolled into Westborough, SoPo hadn't met payroll for two months. Judging from the state of the building, he figured most of the employees had simply stood and walked out one day. Some left their computers turned on.

He poked around and found a frazzled but loyal receptionist running the switchboard through her cell, a pile of dunning letters and liens, and two Chinese engineers who didn't know a dozen words of English between them, playing NERF soccer in the conference room.

Crump taught the engineers enough English to fire them, then persuaded the receptionist to stick around. Together they sifted through records and assets, looking for any way to turn a dollar before Crump folded up SoPo and headed south.

There were not a lot of assets to pore through.

Crump was about to throw in the towel, stuff a bunch of laptops in his car, and split when the receptionist came across a query letter from a division of DuPont, the giant chemical company. The letter expressed interest in a process developed by SoPo for applying anti-reflective coatings to extremely thin plastics molded in complex curves.

"Ka-ching," I said.

Crump called DuPont. Then he called Thunder Junction Partners. Said have Peter Biletnikov buzz me: SoPo is reorganizing and needs capital.

I said, "Why him?"

"Hell, he'd been on the cover of *Forbes* the month before. He was hot and heavy on green tech."

"So Biletnikov and Thunder Junction dropped a truckload of money on you?" I said.

"And it was a good-sized truck."

"How come, though? I know investing is what he *does*. I get that.

But come on. It sounds like you won this SoPo outfit in a poker game. Why should a hotshot take a risk on you?"

"Walk on the wild side. He liked slumming. He liked getting down and dirty with a genuine negro." He said it *JEN-yoo-wine NEE-gro,* smiling.

"Seriously?"

"Hell yes. Not the first time I seen it." Crump shrugged. "Didn't matter to me, baby. His check cleared."

Peter Biletnikov, who was uptight about his kid riding dirt bikes around the yard of his three-million-dollar Sherborn home, rubbing elbows with a guy like Donald Crump?

The man might be more interesting than I'd given him credit for.

Crump said the big check, and some smaller ones from local businessmen Biletnikov strong-armed, had resuscitated SoPo. DuPont and other defense contractors licensed the company's technology. Head count grew to twenty-five, then fifty, then a hundred and ten.

Biletnikov helped out—or so it seemed at the time—by stacking the board of directors with gold-plated Boston business names. "Instant pedigree," Donald said.

"Bet that's how you got screwed in the end, though."

"Bingo. Like I said, you ain't no virgin."

Soon SoPo, in a rotten business climate, was one of a handful of start-ups that could realistically think about going public. Analysts predicted it. Business magazines speculated about it.

When the time was right, Biletnikov screwed Crump.

He dropped the hammer via leaks to the business press. Stories began to circulate about SoPo's CEO. Turned out he had quite a few names, and convictions or injunctions to go with most of them. This was poison to a company setting up an IPO. The drumbeat built until SoPo's board of directors—all those fancy Boston and Cambridge types who'd once seemed like a godsend—demanded Crump's resignation.

"What'd you do?" I said.

"I resigned. I'd been played. I'd been got. Know when to hold 'em, know when to fold 'em."

"Then what?"

"Biletnikov came in as a white knight. Handpicked a new CEO, made sure the board pulled my stock options and threw me out on my ass. For his trouble, he helped Thunder Junction to eighty percent of the company."

"You seem like a man who knows how to fight dirty," I said. "Think about any tricks? Maybe the media play? The race card?"

"Peter ain't stupid. He made a preemptive strike there. Went to a *Globe* business columnist he knows, put his own spin on things. Said he'd invested in *me*. In my dreams. Sure, he should've checked my background better, but I'd told him a moving story."

"So he was the hero who invested in the black community. You were the con man who let him down."

I tore open a Wet-Nap. Donald picked his teeth.

I said, "I hope you at least squeezed some severance out of them."

"Chump change, bus fare, an insult. Pissed me off. Professionally, I admired Biletnikov's moves." He did a perfect English accent: "Well played, old chap."

I smiled.

"But throw me a few bucks," Donald said in his own voice. "Send me back home with a smile on my face."

He leaned toward me. As he spoke, he tapped the table hard enough to make ribs jump. "Biletnikov tried to *crush* me, *destroy* me, *humiliate* me. He made a mistake there, boy."

"Okay, so you want to take down Biletnikov, hurt him, get back a piece of what's yours. But why now? And what's the Rinn connection?"

"Recent events done painted a bull's-eye on Peter Biletnikov's back," Donald said. "I'm here to squeeze him the way he squeezed me. It's professional, but if I get a little pleasure from a job well done, we'll call that a bonus."

"Recent events," I said. "Tell me more."

He smiled and said nothing.

"This got anything to do with Gus Biletnikov, addict?" I got fired up as I said it, felt like I was headed in the right direction, pressed harder. "Were you leaning on uptight Peter Biletnikov over the fact his kid was a dealer who landed in a halfway house?"

"That all you know about the Biletnikovs? That your big secret stash of dirt? Man, you don't know shit."

I sighed. "Then frigging educate me, Donald."

With a con man's timing, he made me wait while he tucked the toothpick back in his pocket, folded his arms, looked both ways. "Emma," he finally said. "Rinn's baby girl."

"Yeah?"

"Who's her daddy?"

"Aha."

"Bet your sweet ass aha."

We split up not long after that. Donald Crump, having eaten everything on his plate and half of what was on mine, somehow climbed into his pearl-white Escalade without a stepladder. He fired it up, lowered his window. "It may sound funny," he said, "but I come to get my money back."

"I believe you will."

He looked at me maybe ten seconds. "You a serious man, Sax."

I said nothing.

" 'The enemy of my enemy is my friend.' Ever heard that one?"

"No."

"Think on it," Crump said, and backed out and drove away.

I got myself pointed at the shop and listened to messages as I drove. One of those messages—from Floriano—turned out to be lucky. He'd found an auto-parts place down in Medfield that had in stock an oddball part we usually have to order: a fender liner for a Mazda3. Could I swing down there and pick it up?

I guessed I could. Slammed a quick right into a menswear store lot to turn around.

That was the lucky part.

Because that was when I spotted the Impala tailing me.

CHAPTER TEN

It was silver. The driver called attention to himself by squalling into the lot so sharply that his bumper cover graunched as it bottomed out.

I didn't put it together just then, though. Dumb drivers aren't a rarity in Massachusetts. Just took a quick look in my mirror, shook my head at the dimwit, spun around, and headed for Medfield.

But a few miles later, a glance in the mirror told me the Impala was still there.

Huh.

I slowed, used the mirror some more. There were at least two people in the car. Guys.

I tried saying "I've picked up a tail" out loud. Felt paranoid, ridiculous.

But just for the hell of it, I pulled into a Mobil and gassed up, even though I had a half tank left.

The Impala did not drive past.

When I got back on the road, the silver car floated out of a strip-mall lot. Confirmed: two guys inside. Big guys.

Click.

Teddy Pundo.

Holy shit.

First thought: I'd been right about Almost Home. Gus was the target all along. It was impossible now to see it any other way. By steaming into the Hi Hat, Randall and I had stirred up something serious.

Second thought: thanks to the stirring, Gus was in deeper trouble than ever. And I was in pretty deep myself.

I mirror-drove, ID'd the passenger as Charlie Pundo's muscle, the ex-boxer-looking dude who walked around with a Desert Eagle shoved in his pants.

I didn't like it one bit, especially now that we were moving south on Route 27 through high-end exurb. There was mucho dead space along this road. All Teddy Pundo needed was a little luck with traffic.

I thought. I planned.

I made my move.

First, I hightailed it to a busier road, looping clockwise back toward Framingham. Toward my shop.

Five minutes later, pointed more or less north, I called Floriano. "You know that F-350 out back?" I said when he picked up.

"The junker?"

"Yeah. Think you can get that truck started? In a hurry?"

"It's a Ford diesel, Connie. It start fine when you and me both dead."

I told Floriano what I wanted him to do. When I said I'd picked up a tail, he laughed out loud.

But he never hesitated.

"I see you there in fifteen minutes, Magnum P.I."

Good old Floriano.

I grabbed another right onto Route 126. Now I was headed straight for the shop.

The Impala had grown more aggressive. Fat Teddy knew I'd made him—my guess was the ex-boxer had told him so—and Teddy didn't give a shit. Teddy was coming.

That was good.

He slipped over the double-yellow line and passed a minivan. Now he was riding my bumper. The ex-boxer was looking at Teddy, maybe giving him an earful. But Fat Teddy was stupid or stubborn or both.

That was good, too.

I slowed, giving Floriano time.

Now we were two miles south of downtown Framingham. Two- and three-family houses to my right. To my left: scrub forest running down to a lake.

We cleared a gentle curve.

Up ahead was the small parking lot of an out-of-business dry cleaner. In the lot sat the rust-brown Ford F-350, its neglected diesel engine pumping exhaust smoke like a crop duster. I knew why: Floriano was doing a brake stand. Had his left foot hard on the brake, his right foot deep in the throttle. It was the only way to build enough revs to make the diesel accelerate.

When Floriano saw me, he snapped his foot from the brake. The truck took off harder than I thought it could. It bounced from the parking lot and shot past my door, two and a half tons of iron moving arrow-straight. Floriano never second-guessed, never lifted. Was probably going thirty, and still pulling hard, when he hit the front corner of the Impala—which was going thirty-five.

The sound was like a plane crash.

I braked, looked in the mirror. The Impala's nose was swayed. Its hood had buckled. Its radiator spewed steam.

Teddy and his passenger were on queer street. They sat motionless with unfocused eyes, bloody noses, white air-bag powder covering their faces. The pair of them looked like the final shot in a Laurel and Hardy scene.

I may have smiled.

The F-350 idled, half-buried in the corner of the Impala. Floriano hopped out, trotted over, climbed in my truck. We were rolling before the first looky-loo dialed 911.

I said, "You okay?"

He rubbed his neck. "*Mi pescoço*. Killing me. Get us the hell out of here, Magnum P.I."

"We need a name for this dude," Randall said, tearing off a chunk of bagel, when I wrapped my story. "We need to call him something."

"Who?" I said. "The ex-boxer-looking guy?"

"Bingo. I christen him Boxer."

"Suit yourself." I sipped.

We were in a Dunkin' Donuts that sat next to a Red Roof Inn and fifty yards from a Mass Pike on-ramp. Randall had chosen the meeting site. I wanted his help puzzling everything through. Truth be told, though, I wasn't getting his best effort. From the way he kept looking at his watch, he seemed all fired up to hop on the pike and go somewhere.

"So our sniffing around Springfield has smoked out Teddy Pundo," Randall said. "Is that a good thing or a bad thing?"

"Both. Good because it gives us a solid target. Bad because Fat Teddy doesn't seem too bright, and he might make a panicky move on Gus."

"Whom you've warned, I assume?"

I nodded. "Told him to lay low. He ought to be safe in that apartment."

We sipped.

"What I'm wondering about Teddy," I said, "is what he had in mind before Floriano totaled him. Why follow me?"

"Maybe he thought you'd lead him to Gus."

"And I might have, if he hadn't been the world's worst tail artist."

"He probably thought he could scare you off with a burst of desedem-dose talk," Randall said. "Remember, Fat Teddy is gangster born and gangster bred. Those guys get most of what they want just by scaring the whiz out of people."

"No argument," I said. "But the shooter . . . Boxer, I guess we're calling him now . . . that's a serious dude. You don't need that dude along just to scare somebody."

"So you think Fat Teddy had something heavier in mind?"

"Yeah, but that's not the interesting part."

He looked the question at me.

"Here's the interesting part," I said. "In Springfield, Boxer vibed as *Charlie* Pundo's man all the way. Top lieutenant, personal security, that kind of thing."

"And?"

"And we know Charlie's ripshit at Teddy for dealing. That was obvious from the way he called him on the carpet yesterday."

Randall nodded, getting it. "Boxer's loyalty is to Charlie. Consigliere, faithful servant, and advisor."

"And if he's like most guys in that position, he thinks the boss's kid is a complete pud."

"Especially if the kid *is* a complete pud."

"Especially then, yeah."

"I'll buy it. But where does it take us?"

"Boxer could be end-running the boss by serving as Teddy's muscle," I said. "More likely, though, Charlie put him on babysitting duty. 'Keep an eye on Teddy, make sure he doesn't get hurt.'"

"And if that's the case, Boxer the hard-core pro is holding his nose while following orders."

"And not happy about it. At all."

He finger-drummed the table. "So if you want to learn more about Pundos *père et fils*, Boxer may be your pry bar."

"Pry bar," I said, "or shooter."

"You're thinking a man as comfortable with a Desert Eagle as Boxer is a man who could walk into a halfway house with a shotgun."

"Couldn't he?"

"At whose behest, though? Charlie's, to protect Teddy? Or Teddy's, to establish a tough-as-nails reputation?"

"Good question."

"So tell the state cop, what's his name. Lima. You said he's meeting you here, right?"

"He is. Any minute now. And maybe I will."

"Or maybe you won't. Maybe you'll keep after the Pundos on your
own."

I said nothing.

Randall sighed and stood.

I sipped coffee and looked him in the eye. "Behest," I said.

He smiled some and left.

CHAPTER ELEVEN

L ima parked his unmarked Crown Vic, gray, three minutes later. Entered Dunkin' Donuts, nodded at me, flirted in Portuguese with the gal at the counter, came over with a small black and a muffin.

We sipped coffee. Lima peeled the wrapper from his muffin. His thumbnail was longer than I would've guessed. Shiny, too. A state cop with plastic braces and a manicure. Go figure.

He said, "Thanks for meeting."

"I was here anyway."

"With Luther Swale's kid. What's his name again?"

"Randall." Man, this Lima didn't miss much. Must've passed Randall in the parking lot.

"Randall. That's right. War hero." He blew on his coffee. "That's a nice place you found for Gus Biletnikov. Shitty neighborhood, but a nice place. I had a hard time communicating with the Vietnamese lady downstairs, but I guess she's a friend of yours?"

I said nothing.

"What's Biletnikov to you, Sax?"

"Sponsee."

"Is that even a word?"

I shrugged. "In AA it is."

"Spare me the AA. What's Biletnikov to you?"

"He needed a place."

"Why *that* place, though? It's almost like you stashed him away."

But you found him, I thought. *That's impressive.* I said, "Whoever lit up Almost Home likely went there to kill Gus."

"Says who?"

"I checked. Nobody'd want to kill Weller."

"Maybe so, Eliot Goddamn Ness. Then the question is, why would anybody want to kill Gus Biletnikov, lightweight druggie?"

I shrugged. "You got me. I'm just watching out for him."

"Why?"

I wiped a clump of sugar from my Styrofoam rim. Lima was trying to push me in a direction, and I was damned if I could figure out what it was. *So keep tap-dancing.* "Because the Barnburners asked me to."

"The hell is a Barnburner?"

"My AA group."

"Jesus, AA again. Was Biletnikov a member of this group? Couldn't've been for long."

"Two months. Maybe three."

"So you knew Gus Biletnikov a couple months. Your AA buddies asked you to keep an eye on him. A kid got shot in his halfway house, maybe had nothing to do with Biletnikov. But all of a sudden you're stashing him in a safe house? A safe house you used to own?"

Lima: smart and thorough both. He'd checked real-estate transactions to learn the history of that house.

I said nothing.

"It all strikes me as horse shit." He finished his muffin, began to neatly fold the wax paper. "Were you involved with Biletnikov?"

"Involved?"

"Romantically?"

"No."

"You queer?"

"No. Why?"

"It's an angle. It's something you look at." Lima tapped the muffin wrapper. "These things are loaded with sugar, you know. That's how they make them taste good and call them reduced-fat at the same time."

"Trade-off."

"Yeah. Trade-off." He sipped.

I took a guess. "You've spent the past couple days looking at the Weller kid," I said. "Same way I did, only slower. And you haven't found anything that'd make anybody want to kill him."

Long pause. "Not a damn thing. That's why we're looking at Biletnikov."

The way he said it made me sit up straight. "Looking at him how? As the guy who was supposed to get shot? Or as a suspect?"

"You tell me."

"Gus was with me at a meeting that night. I know you checked that out."

He shrugged. "There're a lot of ways to have a guy killed. Plus, I was surprised when I tracked him down yesterday and knocked on the door of that little apartment."

"Surprised how?"

"What with you being Mr. AA and all."

I didn't like the way Lima's eyes danced while he said it. He was savoring something.

"Surprised how?" I said.

"Surprised at the way it smelled in there." He paused, sipped. "Did you know he was smoking weed in your little safe house? Man, it reeked."

Ten minutes later I pulled up to the house, feeling only a red-mist pulse in my head. The pulse had been quiet for months now—I feel it just before doing something stupid—but I knew better than to think I'd beaten it for good.

I eyeballed the house, the ancient outdoor staircase to the upstairs apartment. Me and Randall had busted ass in hot weather fixing, scraping, and painting those stairs.

As Lima and I had chucked our trash and left Dunkin' Donuts, I'd said, "You knew that would burn me up."

He'd shrugged. "Thought you'd want to know. You're doing a lot for Biletnikov. What's he doing for you?"

Lima was using me the same way I wanted to use Boxer: stir up some shit and watch what happened.

Stairs, apartment door—spare key behind a shutter a few inches to the left—enter, cross the kitchen. I stopped, opened the cupboard beneath the sink, pulled a white trash bag. Stepped into the biggest bedroom, which stank of cigarettes and young dude and reefer and an overmatched air freshener.

Gus lay on the bed in a pile of comforter and sheets.

I slapped open the curtains.

"The fuck, man?" Gus blinked as he said it, shielding his eyes from the light.

"Get out. You got five minutes."

He sat and rubbed his face. "That frigging cop. Lima. He dimed me out, am I right?"

"Hell yes. Five minutes."

I went to the main room and looked around. Saw an eighteen-inch-tall bong, orange, on an end table. *Dark Side of the Moon* graphics ringed it. I felt the red-mist pulse, but with something else mixed in. Tears. Tight throat. Helplessness.

Off in the bedroom, Gus stuffed his things in the trash bag. "Wish everything looked black and white to me," he said. Loudly, for my ears.

But it wasn't black and white. It was red mist. I felt it. Didn't trust myself to speak.

"Wish everything was binary for me," Gus hollered. "You're drunk or you're sober. You're fer us or agin us. Join the Barnburners or we'll burn down your barn." He laughed.

He came out with the bag slung over his shoulder. Jeans, gray T-shirt, camouflage backpack. Smoking a cigarette. He started to wise off again but took a good look at me and decided to be quiet.

I was staring at the bong. At the joint where the aluminum bowl met the plastic tube, a toy action figure wearing a blue helmet was perched. A typical stoner joke.

I recognized the action figure.

I stepped to the table, held up the toy. "Where'd you find this?"

"Oh. I had a buddy over yesterday. We got a little high, as your cop friend clearly told you. My buddy found that little guy under the dresser. I told him to leave it be, but he didn't listen. We goofed with it. Sorry, man."

I hit Gus with a looping right. He took two crossover steps, dropped his bag, and fell sideways. His head hit the hardwood floor.

After that, I only half-knew what I was doing. Dragging Gus across the floor, beating him, kicking him, screaming in a voice I barely remembered. I opened the door, pulled him from the apartment by his backpack, got a work boot on his hip, shoved him down metal stairs in an ugly tumble. Threw the trash bag after. Stormed the apartment, grabbed the bong, came outside, whipped it down at him, didn't miss by much.

Screaming the entire time, tunnel-visioned from the red mist. After a while, I recognized what I was hollering: "It was all there for you! You should've been one who made it!"

Over and over, Gus looking up at me from the bottom of the stairs.

I only stopped screaming because my voice gave out.

Then there was a weird near silence. A man working under the hood of a Civic across the street had stopped turning his wrench. Two boys on the corner who ought to be in school looked at me over orange sodas.

Gus said, "I need help."

I closed the door.

I picked up the action figure. Sat on the sofa, looked it over. It's a cheap GI Joe knockoff, a three-inch-tall soldier. Oversized biceps, gold bandolier on each shoulder. Vaguely Asian features, visible rivets. His arms, legs, and torso move. When you stretch him, you can see the elastic cords that hold him together. His right foot is missing, snapped off at the ankle.

I bought him at a flea market in Grafton when my son was four.

I was freshly sober. After maybe a dozen phone calls, my ex had agreed to bring Roy for a visit. By then, the two of them had moved to the Berkshires.

It was a good weekend. Sunday morning, I took Roy to a big flea market on Route 140. There was a lot to see, must have been five acres of junk for sale. Roy sat on my shoulders, pulling my hair like a horse's reins when he wanted to change direction. I'll never forget that.

I told Roy I would buy him one thing. *Anything*, but just *one* thing. He wanted to examine all his options. He's still that way. He steered me to every table. I carried him on my shoulders for two hours. He finally chose the action figure. I paid a buck. It was a big deal.

To both of us.

Then we went down the hill to Dunkin' Donuts. In line, he dropped the cheapo toy. Its foot broke off, just like that. We didn't have time to go back for another.

With Roy staring at the action figure in one hand and the broken-off foot in the other, tears welling, I had to think fast. I named the toy Brokenman, said now he was special. Then I launched into the first in a series of stories: "The Adventures of Brokenman."

Brokenman got the bad guy every time, see. But it always cost him a foot.

I wouldn't meet one-footed Randall Swale for more than a decade. Funny how life works out, huh?

Roy loved Brokenman stories until he was seven. Then he didn't. One weekend, he left the toy on his bedside table at my apartment. I called and promised to put Brokenman in the mail the next day.

"That's okay, Dad. You keep him."

I remember the way my heart dropped in my chest when Roy said that.

I did keep the toy, though, kept it a long time—right up until I'd moved from this apartment. The time had seemed right to pass Brokenman along. I guess I'd pictured a little kid starting his own series of adventures.

I hadn't pictured a stoner goof.

I locked the apartment and walked down the stairs. Took Brokenman with me. I would offer him to Roy again.

You never know.

CHAPTER TWELVE

I said, "Balboa the explorer dude was beheaded?"

"Yes!" Leaning across the table, Sophie whacked her plate with a breadstick. "Pedrarias *claimed* Balboa was setting up a rogue government, but really he was just jealous—"

"The hell is a Pedrarias?"

"I *told* you on the ride over, he was the new governor of the colony! A total political hack."

"What colony?"

She dropped her breadstick, grabbed her head with both hands.

Jessie said, "He's screwing with you, Sophie."

"I know." She grabbed her breadstick. "Anyway, Balboa got back from . . ."

Charlene and I smiled at each other across the table and let Sophie build a head of steam. Charlene looked at her watch. We were at an Olive Garden in Marlborough, across the road from a mall. A kid with spiked hair and two different-colored eyes had taken our order, brought us salad and rolls, and disappeared. Charlene gets testy if the main course doesn't hit the table in fifteen minutes.

Dinner out was a way to fold Jessie back in, according to one of the experts Charlene was paying to figure out the anorexia deal.

When I'd picked up the ladies, Charlene had palmed me a note: *Per shrink, don't mention J's eating.*

All I could think about was Gus, out on the street with his gear in a trash bag. I would have skipped the dinner to look for him, but it was one hell of a big deal—the first time we'd been able to talk Jessie into going anywhere with us.

Sophie wore a blue, gold, and white Windbreaker that said COLO-NIALS on its left breast. Against all odds, and for no reason Charlene and I could figure, she'd joined Pop Warner cheerleading in her final year of eligibility. Most of her teammates had been doing it since they were six, and Sophie's lack of experience showed at every practice. But she was gung ho, and the other girls were less snotty than I would've predicted, so it was fine by me—something new for a kid who maybe spent too much time by herself.

What we hadn't known when Sophie signed on was that these days, cheerleading is a sport unto its own damn self. Hell, it's a whole *lifestyle* if you let it be. When Pop Warner football ended, the cheerleading competitions kept rolling along. And wouldn't you know it: the Colonials were damn good this year, which meant at least one road trip a month to Boston, Hartford, Kittery, Albany. I didn't mind, but the cheer fests, with the makeup and the primping and the stomping and the hugging and the crying (win or lose), were quietly driving Charlene nuts. She wasn't wired for that kind of thing.

We made small talk, everybody keeping a sneaky eye on Jessie. She hid behind her hair and mostly looked at her plate. But she gave us reason to hope, too. She'd agreed with Sophie that the waiter was cute, with his blue eye and his brown eye. And while the rest of us pretended not to look, she scooped a few spinach leaves and olives onto her salad plate and even tore off a quarter of a roll. Whenever she took a bite I held my breath, felt Charlene doing likewise.

More than anything else recently, that hitch in my breath when Jessie lifted a roll made me understand parenthood.

Jessie. The older one, the one Charlene had always butted heads with. Her face as I remembered it was frank, strong, dominated by powerful eyebrows and nose. It was more handsome than pretty, maybe a tough face for a girl to grow up with, but a damn fine face for a woman once she knew what she was about. But you had to wonder if Jessie would get that far: now the face was slack and pale and formless, collapsing into itself behind a wall of dyed black hair. She'd been a jock until sophomore year in high school, when the usual combo—the addict's gene, the things she'd been through—had shunted her to self-puking, pills, and parties she was too young for. She'd put Charlene through hell.

Which Charlene said she deserved, and then some.

When the Department of Social Services took the girls away, Jessie was eight and virtual mom to Sophie, who was a toddler.

Eight years old. Imagine the weight.

"Phew," Charlene said to the waiter when our food finally came. "We thought you'd fled the country."

Sophie rolled her eyes. She tried to make a joke of it with her sister, but Jessie hid behind her hair.

I ate chicken parmigiana. Sophie talked about Balboa. Charlene talked about the great gal managing her new office in Augusta, Maine.

"How were things at the shop?" she finally said, looking down at her veal something or other, trying for casual and almost making it. But I knew her too well to buy it: Charlene and Floriano had been chattering. They did every day. I wished they didn't, but there wasn't much I could say about it: she holds the paper on the garage.

I looked at Sophie while I answered. "You know the junker F-350 we use to plow the lot?"

She nodded.

I felt Charlene's stare but kept my eyes on Sophie's. "Things were great," I said, "until Floriano totaled it."

"What?" Sophie's eyes went big.

"On purpose."

"What?"

"To take out a pair of gangsters who were tailing me."

"Holy shit," Sophie said.

"No shit," I said.

Charlene threw her napkin on the table, rose, walked out. Never looked back.

"Crap," I said.

Behind her hair, Jessie smiled for the first time since she'd come home.

The four of us headed back to Charlene's place. It was a quiet ride, though I tried.

"We talked this through," I said.

Charlene said nothing. Left her arms folded.

"Me, I've got my Barnburner thing," I said. "You, you're no Martha Stewart. And you don't want to be. Remember?"

Charlene said nothing.

Which was too bad. I would've liked to talk with her—with *someone*—about Gus. About tough love. About zero-tolerance policies. About how rotten they feel.

They sound good in meetings, in counselors' offices.

But try to *live* tough love. Try to throw a kid out on his ass for smoking a little weed.

It's harder on the thrower than it is on the thrown.

And the thrown know it. They leverage it. They leverage anything, *everything*. Drunks and Junkies 101.

Which is why tough love is the way to go.

Full fucking circle.

I parked Charlene's Volvo SUV in her driveway. We all climbed out. I handed Charlene her keys, unpocketed my own, unlocked my truck.

She didn't ask where I was going.

———

I spent an hour prowling Framingham. Gus wasn't answering his phone. I wondered if it was the GPS kind that could tell you its location. Probably. But how did you go about that? Cops? Court order? I thought about calling Lima. Decided against. Asked myself why, decided it was con's instinct. You don't tip your hand to the law. Period. Not even if he seems okay, as Lima did.

So you're on your own. Think like a junkie who's got a few hundred bucks in his pocket and is on foot. And favors cocaine.

The map in my head told me after being chucked down the stairs, Gus would've headed a few blocks south to Route 135, gravitating toward noise and traffic and shops. From there, east would mean Natick and nicer towns. West, on the other hand, meant Framingham's downtown—train station, Salvation Army, alleys, and all. It's not a big city, not hardly, but Gus could find what he needed there.

West it was.

I crawled the little downtown. Hit every street, every loading dock, every doorway. Framingham's mostly made up of workers. Blue-collar: too tired on a weeknight to raise much hell. But there are some places you don't want to be after dark.

I looked in those places.

Tough love.

No Gus.

I asked a dozen creeps in a dozen spots. White kid, probably looking to score? All his stuff in a backpack or a trash bag slung over his shoulder?

Nobody'd seen him, or would cop to it. A Bahamian outside the train station wearing three hoodies mumbled and pointed enough so that I stuck a pair of fives in his hand, which was missing its ring finger. "Well?" I said.

"Thatum," he said, pointing west. "Or thatum." East. "You got a light, mon? You got a smoke?"

I took back my fives.

"Aw, *mon*," the Bahamian said to my back.

I kicked my truck's tire out of frustration. Climbed in, heel-rubbed my eyes, checked my watch. Midnight. Thought about calling the Framingham cops, but Matt Bogardis was the only one I trusted, and what were the odds?

"Hell," I said out loud to nobody.

And called Luther Swale.

"Sorry," I said when he picked up on four and a half rings. "It's late, I know. But I'm looking for a kid."

I listened to Luther breathe for maybe fifteen seconds. "How old?" he finally said.

"Twentyish."

"And yet you called him a kid. When I was twenty, I was a supply sergeant down at Otis."

I rolled my eyes. "Yeah yeah yeah. And these days they're boys until they're thirty, and even then half of 'em want to take the easy way out and be stay-at-home daddies. Hell in a handcart. We've covered all that, amigo. But I'm helping this one."

"Helping. The way you help. Your Barnstormer pals."

"Barn*burners*."

He sighed. "What do you need?"

"He might have hopped on the commuter rail, looking to get out of Framingham and score. If you take Boston, I'll take Worcester."

"You don't even know what *direction* he went in?"

I said nothing.

"What would he be after?" Luther finally said. "Ups or downs?"

"He's a cocaine boy. Limited funds, so I'm guessing crack."

"Mattapan by moonlight, looking for a white boy who's looking for a rock. That ought to make for a nice evening."

I gave a twenty-second description of Gus. "Luther," I said, "I owe you."

"You made it off paper," he said. "You don't owe anybody any-thing." Click.

Parole officer's view of the world. You're on paper or you're off.

I headed for Worcester.

"I need help." The last thing he said to me. Junkie leverage, like when the dog gives up the fight and shows his belly.

And the hell of it is, it's true. He does need help, and he knows it. But he's also showing his belly to play you, to con you. Truth and bullshit both.

I pounded the steering wheel. Shook my head, felt stupid.

Felt stupider at daybreak, having burned half a tank of gas, dodged two stickups, and found not a whiff of Gus.

Luther hadn't made out any better. We'd called back and forth every hour on the hour. At five, I'd told him to go home. He'd said why bother, he was headed for a diner.

Both Swales, father and son, must curse the day I clown-shoed into their lives. I brought them nothing but hard work and misery.

I gassed up, tried to think.

Downtown Framingham, such as it is: ruled out. Cocaine safari to Worcester or Boston: hard to say definitively, but rule that out too.

Home? Sherborn?

Could be. Family was family.

But Rinn Biletnikov had told me Gus and his father weren't ex-actly seeing eye to eye. No, it'd been more powerful than that. *Gus was on terrible terms with his father,* she'd said. *Peter is the* last *per-son Gus would have confided in.*

I'd overlaid that on my own situation with Roy, had found it easy to believe.

Which is why you didn't check Sherborn first, I admitted. *Which you should have done out of common sense. It's home and it's close.*

It was time to visit Peter Biletnikov.

I felt bad over what I'd put Luther through.

I would feel worse soon.

Because about the time I flipped down my sun visor at an off-brand Worcester gas station and aimed my truck at Sherborn, somebody blew a hole in Gus Biletnikov.

CHAPTER THIRTEEN

Haley, the nanny, answered the door. She wore running gear—had an iPod clipped to her upper arm and everything—but held a baby on her hip in that way that looks so natural for women. In her other hand she held a plastic baby bottle and wadded-up earbuds. How she'd managed to open the door I couldn't figure.

It took her half a beat to remember me. Then she said, "Oh," and looked at her runner's watch.

"Early, I know," I said. "But I figured this for an early house. Looks like I was right."

"You were," Haley said, nodding me in and kicking shut the door. "Usually I can squeeze in five K on the treadmill before she wakes up. But you were a restless, hungry girl this morning, wasn't you, sweetie? Wasn't you? Is she not the bee's knees?"

"I guess." Never have gotten the hang of baby talk. It makes me grind my teeth. "Uh, how old? Is she, I mean."

"Just over six months. And perfect. Seventy-fifth percentile for length, weight, and head size."

I guessed that was good.

We stood in the warm front hall. Slate floor opening onto a massive, cathedral-ceilinged kitchen and great room.

Haley nuzzled noses with the baby. Who seemed okay with it. Maybe she was cute. I'm the wrong guy to ask.

"Well," I finally said. "Is Peter here? Awake?"

"Peter," she said. "Interesting."

I looked a question at her.

"Because *Rinn* can't stop talking about you and your compadre, Randall."

I said nothing.

"You fascinate her. She finds you very *genuine,* very *real.*"

"What the hell do you have against me?"

"Why, nothing. Sir. Mr. Sax. What makes you say?"

"Knock it off," I said. "The eye rolls, the sneer every time you open your trap. What's it about?"

She started to mouth off. But she was a good kid deep down, as I'd thought, and so she deflated instead. "I'm sorry. I'm transferring frustration to you. Uncool. Not fair."

"Transferring from where?"

She swept an arm. "From here. From this. From *them.*"

I waited. She was dying to tell more, to spill. My best move was to say nothing.

I'm good at that.

Haley looked at the baby, then her watch. Cocked her head, hearing a household noise that meant something to her but not to me. She sighed, tossed earbuds onto the black granite countertop, and turned to present me her arm. I figured out she wanted me to de-iPod her. I ripped Velcro, set the rig next to the earbuds, waited for Haley to spill.

She didn't get a chance. Peter Biletnikov pounded in.

He was almost tall. He was almost handsome. I would have guessed Russian even if I hadn't known already, from the weak mouth, the apple-red cheeks, and the way his hairline was moving up his forehead, leaving a widow's peak that was his second-best feature. His best: quick blue eyes. They took me in, resented me, and filed me away as a nuisance in the time it took to cross to the stainless fridge and pull out a bottled smoothie.

"Haley," he said, reading the smoothie's label instead of looking at either of us, "who is this gentleman and why is he here so early?"

"Peter Biletnikov, Conway Sax. The man who's been helping Gus."

"Gus was staying with some friends of mine," I said. "Since the shooting at the halfway house."

"I see. And why are you here?"

Haley'd had enough. She popped the bottle in the baby's mouth and began to make a casual break for a long hallway.

"I'm here," I said, "because Gus is missing. And I'm afraid he's using."

Haley stopped dead. Peter read his smoothie label. "Missing?" he said.

Time to come clean. I sighed. "I ran him out of my friend's place for smoking weed. Haven't seen him since. I, ah . . . I feel responsible."

"Correction. You *are* responsible."

I hadn't known Peter Biletnikov two minutes, and I wanted to slap the smoothie out of his hand.

But he was right. Damned if he wasn't.

"What I was wondering," I said, gritting my teeth, balling my fists, "I was wondering if he'd shown here. Come around looking for money, maybe. Or a bed."

"No," Peter said.

"Yes," Haley said.

"Huh," I said.

"He came by last night," Haley said. "He wanted me to take him to the ATM and withdraw the maximum on your card, Peter."

"And?" he said.

"He made me nervous. He was either high or desperate to get that way. I gave him a hundred dollars to get rid of him. Then he went down the hill toward the guesthouse."

"Of course," Peter said.

"Did you see him after that?" I said.

"No," Haley said. "You can get back to the road from the guest-house. There's a path."

The baby began to cry.

"Take her," Peter said.

"I know, I know," Haley said, and this time she did disappear down the hall.

I said, "Did you ever visit Gus at Almost Home?"

"No," Peter said.

"Mind if I ask why?"

"It sounds like you've been part of this world, this AA-rehab-counseling-drug thing"—he made a circular motion with his drink—"for a while now. So you must know how hard it is on the family."

"It's kind of hard on the person doing the AA-rehab-counseling-drug thing, too."

His eyes flashed. "I've helped Gus every way I could, make no mistake. I've nodded like a good boy and done whatever the guidance counselors, drug counselors, policemen, shrinks, and rehab sales reps told me to do. And do you know what I never heard from any of those people?"

I waited.

He slammed his smoothie on the countertop hard enough to fountain purple berries. "What they never said, not one of them, was, 'Your son is a spoiled brat, Mr. Biletnikov. He's sucking up trust-fund income and laughing at you while he does so. He's happily riding his monthly check until the big score, the inheritance, comes in. *That*, Mr. Biletnikov, is what Gustav Biletnikov the Second looks forward to most. Your son gets a little thrill of anticipation every time you board an airplane, every time you cross a busy street.' "

He panted, nostrils flaring, cheeks redder than ever. These Russians have a way of coming across as royalty and white trash at the same time. Not sure how they pull it off, but they do.

He pinched his nose, breathed deep a few times. Finally looked at me again. "I wish nothing but the best for Gustav. I bid you go find him. Talk to Rinn, talk more with Haley, do as you wish. As for me, though"—he dry-washed his hands—"I am done with it. With him. With you."

Peter Biletnikov clapped once, fished car keys from a wicker basket, and walked out without looking back.

The word that hung in my head: "inheritance." It meant a lot more than Peter seemed to know. It meant a lot even if you didn't have two nickels to rub together.

Like my dad.

I thought about him. Fast Freddy Sax: stock-car racer, welder, drunk.

I had experience on the receiving end of an inheritance, all right.

Now I was on the giving end, which turned out to be a lot harder. By the time you understood how important it was, you'd already screwed things up a dozen ways.

Maybe your kid was waiting for you to die.

Maybe your kid wasn't taking your phone calls.

Fathers and sons.

"Hell," I said out loud in the empty kitchen. Heard a V8, looked out the window, watched a black BMW SUV tear down the gravel drive faster than it needed to.

"Welcome to my world."

I spun. It was Haley, without baby and with sweatpants now. She'd catfooted up the hall.

I said, "What's his story?"

"He's got a hundred million dollars or more," she said, "and he feels like a failure."

"Why?"

"His father was Gustav Biletnikov the First, the man Gus was named for. Does this ring a bell?"

"No."

"He may be the reason we're not speaking German. He worked as a nuclear physicist for the Nazis during World War II. They worked on their bomb while we worked on ours. A lot of smart people say they were on track to beat us to fission, thanks primarily to Gustav Biletnikov's brain."

"What happened?"

"He defected in early '44, with help from Richard Feynman. There are books about it. By then it was nearly impossible for anybody, let alone a key scientist, to get out of Berlin."

"Who's Feynman?"

"Not important. Gustav Biletnikov became one of *our* Russians. After the war, Cornell wrote him a blank check to start a physics department."

"What's all this got to do with Peter?"

"Peter grew up in a house of titans. Feynman, Oppenheimer, Bethe, and Lawrence dropped by whenever they could. Albert Einstein gave Peter a Batman comic book for his eighth birthday."

"Son of a great man," I said, thinking of a few I'd known. "Not an easy thing to be."

"Precisely."

"But Peter's done okay for himself. And then some."

"That's how I see it, too," Haley said. "That's how most *anybody* would see it. But he grades himself on a different curve, and he sure didn't save the world from Hitler."

I started to answer.

But was interrupted by the longest, loudest scream I'd ever heard.

It made my neck hairs stand up, and that hadn't happened for a long time.

We stared at one another, frozen for half a beat.

Then we pounded down the back stairs, me in the lead. Exited the walk-out basement to the wildflower-lined yard that separated the main house from the guesthouse.

I paused. I thought the scream had come from farther back in the yard, to my right as I stood now, but it was hard to be sure.

Haley pulled up behind me, put a hand on my back.

Another scream. It had less shock this time around, but maybe more pain. It was definitely coming from my right.

We ran.

"Path," Haley said. "Angle left just a little."

I did, found it, led her over pine needles at a dead sprint. A corner of my head wondered if this was the motocross track Gus had cleared when he was a kid, the one that'd pissed off his father.

We popped into a ragged clearing piled high with compost—mown grass, storm-wrecked branches: the place the landscapers brought yard junk—and there she was.

Rinn Biletnikov.

Squatting, her back to us. Tiny sneakers, off-white slacks, a thin kelly-green sweater riding up.

She turned, looking in our direction but not seeing much—had the thousand-yard stare.

The smell in this clearing: rot under sweet, like a dead rat in a candy shop. It was the mown grass, I knew: dumped here for years, composting, collapsing in on itself.

We stepped toward Rinn. Whatever she was screaming about was mostly hidden by her body, by tall grass, by scrub oak.

It became clear as we drew closer.

Basketball shoes.

Blue-jeaned legs.

Sweatshirt.

"Oh God," Haley said, and stopped walking.

I didn't.

Couldn't.

It was Gus.

On his back. Eyes open wide. One lazy fly walking his cheek.

His black sweatshirt said FLATOUT.

His middle, from the bottom of the word to the button of his jeans, was just a red-black mess.

"Shotgun," I said to nobody.

CHAPTER FOURTEEN

I *need help."*
   The last thing he said to me.
   I helped by throwing him down a flight of stairs.
   Because some sixteen-thousand-dollar-a-year counselor once told me tough love was the way to go.

"For God's sake, Conway, what should we *do?*"

I snapped to.

It was Rinn. She'd risen from her crouch, was hugging her arms.

"She's doing it," I said, nodding in Haley's direction. She had dialed 911 and was saying the address.

"What happened?" Rinn said, looking down at the body.

"You tell me." She'd made a pretty quick transition from helpless screaming to analyzing the situation, hadn't she?

I stepped toward Gus's body. I made myself a camera. Needed to suck up info now, while I had a chance. The cops would hustle us out of here in a hurry.

I looked. It's a sucker bet to play *CSI*, but common sense can tell you a lot.

Common sense told me right off the bat that Gus hadn't been

killed where he lay. His back arched across a slab of protruding stone the size of a card table, and there wasn't enough blood for him to have been blown open there. But that didn't mean he hadn't been killed nearby, on his father's grounds.

I turned to Rinn. "Did you hear it? The gun?"

She shook her head.

"Maybe overnight?" I said.

She shook it again.

"You?" I said to Haley, who'd finished her phone call. "Middle of the night, maybe? Anything?"

"No," she said, biting her lip. Then, firmer: "No. We're only a hundred feet from Emma's bedroom window, and she's easy to unsettle. A gunshot would have woken her."

I nodded, turned back to the body, made myself look hard at the belly. *Camera. Capture info. Anything else comes later.*

The blood was three or four different shades, running from crusty near-black through rose. So try common sense again: Gus had been killed, then moved—to a car, maybe—then moved a final time, to the spot I was staring at. With each movement, crusted blood would crack and fresh blood would flow.

Maybe it was a *CSI* sucker bet, but I didn't think so. It felt like a starting point.

Sirens. From the road. All three flavors: cruiser, ambulance, fire.

"They won't know how to find us," Haley said. "I'll show them." She backtracked up the path.

"Gus," Rinn said. "Sweet Gus."

My head swiveled, sharper than I meant it to. She'd only said three words, but they carried backstory.

She caught me staring, hugged her arms again, shivered.

It was a fake shiver. A good one, but a fake.

The sirens died, which meant we had a minute or two, no more.

Camera. I took a step to my right, changing my angle to make myself see things differently. Gus's big eyes, wide open. That brown hair, not really parted. That goddamn fly, still cheek-walking. Gus's back arched across the flat gray stone he'd been dumped on. Deep-green moss creeping up the stone's edges where it protruded . . .

There.

In the moss.

A heel print, clear as day.

And another next to it.

Deep prints. Prints you'd make if you were dragging a body by its armpits, walking backward—awkward, stooped over. You had dragged the body quite a way already. You were tired. Maybe you had sweat in your eyes. You wanted to get this the hell over with. By now, you were just digging in your heels and hauling.

"Huh," I said out loud.

"What?" Rinn said.

"Nothing," I said. Behind me: trotting footsteps on the path, cop radios, the rattle of a gurney on uneven ground.

What were those heel prints from? I knew, but I didn't know. Who looks at shoes?

They were small, but not spiky like high heels. No, call them the shoes of a small-footed man.

Click.

Not shoes. *Boots.*

Tiny cowboy boots.

I was thinking about stomping the prints to get rid of them—I wanted to handle this *my* way, not the official way—when a dozen cops piled into the clearing.

And that was that.

"Tiny cowboy boots," Lima said to me ninety minutes later.

I leaned back in my thousand-dollar patina'd chair, stared at him, said nothing.

It wasn't the first time cops had given me the hot-box, hurry-up-and-wait business. Not by a long shot. But it was the first time they'd done it in a place this pretty.

The way it had played out: the crew that had first crashed the clearing was led by a sergeant with smart eyes and a voice like a cement mixer. The moment she saw the body, she hollered, "Stop right where you are," and believe me, everybody did—that voice. Then she snapped cell phone pics of me and Rinn where we stood, I guessed to show the techs when they rolled in, and she had us step back to the clearing's mouth. No cuffs—not for the lady of the house, not in this town—but each of us got our elbow held by a patrolman.

They'd set up the backyard as their command post, had even made a cozy arrangement of Adirondack chairs and a picnic table. Somebody brought a pitcher of lemonade down from the kitchen.

Sherborn.

The politeness didn't mean they were dimwits. Lima had rolled in not thirty minutes after the local cops. He led a full-court press of staties, and before you knew it the place was a bona fide crime-scene nuthouse.

Just like Almost Home had been.

I passed the time looking at Google Earth on my phone, trying to figure how Gus had ended up where he did. The bird's-eye view didn't help much. Sherborn was woodsy, but it wasn't Green Acres: Biletnikov's house was close enough to schools, ball fields, and a cemetery that whoever'd dragged Gus here could have come from a half-dozen spots without drawing attention.

After letting me simmer a good long time, Lima had stepped from the path, walked straight to the picnic table, poured himself a lemonade, and sat next to me.

And said: "Tiny cowboy boots."

There was no sense playing dumb. "In the moss," I said.

"He tried to be careful. But he had to be beat by then. You ever drag a body a long way, Sax?"

I said nothing.

Lima laughed. "I had to try. Seriously, though. We're talking a couple hundred yards. From the school parking lot, probably."

"Maybe," I said. "But check the cemetery first." Held up my phone, showed him Google Earth.

"Dammit, you're right. That little spur road's the shortest route. As the crow flies, anyway." He sipped lemonade. "You're not stupid, are you?"

I said nothing.

"Most of the crooks I run across are dumb as a post."

I said nothing.

"Tiny cowboy boots," he said. "Just right for the tiny black guy you ate lunch with yesterday."

"You're not so stupid yourself," I said.

He smiled.

"Most of the cops I run across are."

Lima's eyes went stormy, then cleared. He put his free hand behind his back, pantomiming like his arm was being twisted. "Uncle," he said, and maybe he even tried to smile. But he didn't try hard. "Now tell me about Donald Crump."

"Who?"

"Cut the shit. From yesterday."

"Businessman from Houston."

"There's a little more to him than that, according to the Georgia Department of Corrections, the Louisiana Registry of Motor Vehicles, and the IAFIS."

"What's that last one, fingerprints?"

He nodded. "FBI database."

I said nothing.

"We picked him up forty minutes ago, you know. They're sweating him at the Framingham barracks right now."

I said nothing. Noticed that Peter Biletnikov had shown up. He stood near the driveway's edge, gray and deflated.

An ambulance backed to the very end of the gravel drive, making that obnoxious *beep-beep-beep* while it was in reverse, then onto the lawn.

I saw that not only had Rinn slipped away from my area, which felt like the suspect holding pen—she'd had Haley bring her the baby to boot. Peter, Haley, Emma: brave family in tragic circumstances.

"We'll talk to her, too," Lima said, following my gaze. Goddamn cop knew what I was thinking. "Bet on it. In a town like this, it's tricky. Takes finesse. But we'll get to her."

Two uniformed staties trundled the gurney, now topped by a sturdy-looking navy zipper bag, up the path and into the yard. The Sherborn sergeant with the cement-mixer voice tried to gentle Peter away from the ambulance.

But he wouldn't be gentled. He rushed the gurney and sort of half-collapsed onto it. He moaned. He stroked the body bag.

All the while, though, I had the feeling he was cutting his eyes our way. Putting on a show. Doing his damnedest to act the way he thought he was supposed to act.

Rinn stepped to her husband, who by now was crying loudly into a forearm that rested on the gurney. When she shifted the baby to her right arm so she could rub Peter's back with her left, she damn near dropped the kid, and wound up holding Emma like a schoolbook. In my head I contrasted this with the natural, million-year-old way Haley had held the baby on her hip.

"Huh."

Didn't realize I'd spoken out loud until Lima said, "Don't read it too close."

I looked at him.

"One thing I learned in a hurry when I got this gig," he said, tapping his detective's shield. "Everybody does it his own way."

"Does what?"

"Grieves."

CHAPTER FIFTEEN

I drove.

Everybody grieves his own way.

I should've gone back to the shop.

Instead, I drove. A long loop. Millis, Medway, Milford, Mendon. Angle northwest: Hopedale, Upton. Cut east again: Bryar, Hopkinton, Ashland, rolling toward the place I was supposed to be.

And didn't want to be.

You know who'd be nice to talk to right about now? Sophie. Sophie would get it.

She wouldn't be out of school for another hour and a half.

Hell.

I pulled into a parking lot that used to be a Cadillac dealership. Killed my truck. Shifted my head left, then right.

My neck made a sound like a stepped-on twig.

My head weighed half a ton. It pulled itself down and forward until my forehead rested on the steering wheel.

Gus Biletnikov.

I need help.

Of course he had. He needed help and a fix both. He wanted the fix more.

But he wanted the help, too.

I need help.

Truth and bullshit both. Junkie 101.

They break you, these motherfuckers. Try to help them and they break you.

I cried onto my air bag.

Not for long: my cell snapped me out of it. I sleeve-wiped my eyes and looked at a number I didn't recognize.

Three rings. Four.

What the hell. I picked up, said nothing.

"Sax."

My breathing hitched. It was goddamn Crump.

He said, "I didn't kill your boy."

"Sure you did. And he had a name."

" 'Course he did, 'course he did, sorry. Gus. I didn't kill him. Pay no mind to what these cops telling you."

"They didn't have to tell me. I saw 'em myself."

Pause. "Saw what?"

"Boot prints."

Longer pause. "Shit." He said it *sheee-it*. "So that's what they got? That's *all* they got? You should see 'em, walkin' in and out of this room like they got me dead to rights. They got shit."

"The Rhinestone Cowboy getup did you in, asswipe. Where are they holding you? Still at the Framingham statie barracks?"

"Yeah."

"Live it up, Crump. Next stop's a lot worse. Trust me. What phone are you on, anyway?"

"Listen while I tell you one thing," he said, ignoring the question. "You don't like what you hear, you bring a tub of popcorn to my trial every day and have a ball. Fair?"

I said nothing.

"For a tight-ass commie state," he said, "y'all surely have a lot of shotguns floating around all of a sudden."

I said nothing.

"Shotgun here, shotgun there. Whole lot of people got shotguns. Know what? I ain't one of 'em."

I said nothing, heard a background voice behind Donald. He'd conned somebody out of their phone, and they wanted it back.

"Take a look at that," he said. "I know you will. If you want to find out who killed your boy. Sorry, sorry. Who killed Gus."

Click.

Crump's question was fair.

Who's got a shotgun?

How about a man who walks around with a Desert Eagle in his pants? A man who serves as the right hand of a gangster?

I needed to talk with Lima.

You need to go to the shop. To your shop.

I needed to talk with Lima.

I thought during the five-minute drive to the police barracks.

Maybe Crump was bullshitting me for some reason I hadn't figured out. But he had a point. Truth is, cops take the path of least resistance. Why shouldn't they? Experience tells them the obvious answer's the right one almost every damn time. Boot print? In a size that matches a funky black guy who's connected to the Biletnikovs? Bingo.

So unless the staties had found a shotgun in Donald's Escalade—or in the Sherborn woods with his prints all over it—the idea was worth checking out. Massachusetts ain't exactly lousy with shotguns.

Not legal ones, anyway. In Massachusetts, it's easier to get a pet zebra than a shotgun.

As to extralegal ones . . . well, now we were back to gangsters and guys who wore Desert Eagles the way janitors wear key rings.

The question, I thought as I trotted across the parking lot toward

the red-brick building, was how eager Lima would be to look at anybody other than Crump.

"Go fuck yourself," he said three minutes later, speed walking from
the reception desk into an old brick-walled room retrofitted with drop
ceilings and cubicles. He hurled himself into his rolling chair hard
enough to make two other detectives look up from their sandwiches.
He glared at me. He didn't tell me to sit.

I sat. "I was in your shoes, I'd like Crump for it too. But listen—"

He tapped a folder on his desk. "Crump, Donald. From his Social,
it looks like he was born here in Mass. Aliases include David Cringle, Danny Cringle, Dwayne Chapparal. I love that one. Also John
Anthony Randle. Know who that is?"

"Football player."

He nodded. "It's not my game, but I guess Randle was good. Hall
of Famer. Two years ago, Crump was arrested at a boat show down in
Cary, North Carolina. But not before he signed autographs for two
hours. You know how they send third-string celebrities to those things?
Crump walked in and said he was *the* John Randle, former Minnesota
Viking, who I guess was on the bill. Crump made himself at home,
signed football cards, posed for pictures, the works. Funny part is he
would've walked out with a couple grand in his pocket and nobody
the wiser, but he grabbed a girl's ass and she hollered for show security." He shrugged.

I eeled into my chair and said nothing.

"Got to give Crump credit for balls," Lima said. "The cat's maybe
five-three, one-twenty-five, and he convinced everybody he was a
Hall of Fame defensive lineman. So whatever he conned you into
believing, Sax . . . don't take it hard."

I needed to slow Lima down before he gave me the bum's rush.
"What do you know," I said, "about Charlie Pundo out in Springfield? And his kid Teddy?"

The room went still.

The other two detectives, who'd been doing a pretty good job pretending they weren't listening, flat froze.

The only personal item in Lima's cubicle was a snap of him and a man who had to be his father on the back of a fishing boat.

The old building's HVAC system kicked on. Near the ceiling, two red streamers tied to a vent cover went from limp to horizontal.

Lima had straightened. He tapped a pencil eraser against his front tooth—or, I guess, his braces. "What do *you* know about the Pundos?" He said it slowly, carefully, aware of his audience.

I told him. Leaned forward and kept my voice down so the other detectives couldn't hear—ex-con instinct told me not to tell any cop anything if I didn't have to. The pair of them must have wanted the story pretty badly, because they looked hate rays at me while I spoke.

And I spoke for quite a while.

Told Lima about Gus's run-ins with the Pundos. About the trip Randall and I made to Springfield—Charlie Pundo's frustration at his son, the way Teddy'd been summoned to the Hi Hat on the double. About Boxer. About the way we'd taken Teddy and Boxer out yesterday when they tailed me.

Lima slapped his thigh then. "I *knew* something stank about that wreck."

To show a little balance and let him know I didn't have tunnel vision for the Pundos, I told him about Andrade, too. Even though it went against my ex-con's grain to spill so much to a cop.

Lima must have known this, because he looked at me a long time, chin on fist, when I finished. He finally said, "Feel any better?"

"No."

"Good. 'Cause Biletnikov's just as dead now as he was ten minutes ago when you started."

I said nothing. I took it.

"And if you'd come to me with all this—*any* of this—a day or two ago, he might be alive."

I looked him in the eye. I deserved it. I took it.

"But no. You bring me this cock-up *now*, when I've got a viable suspect in hand, complete with forensic evidence." He waved a disgusted hand. "Andrade with the car. Teddy Pundo 'cause he *might* own a shotgun. Colonel Mustard in the goddamn drawing room."

I rose.

"Sit," Lima said. "Hang on."

I sat. He logged on to his desktop computer, keyed around a while. Rose, walked to a printer on the far side of the room. That was good because it gave the other two detectives, who hadn't moved an inch, fresh opportunities to look hate rays at me.

Lima returned, sat. He squared the printout he carried, stapled its top left corner, scribbled something on the last page. He rolled the papers into a tube and rolled his chair toward mine until our knees about touched.

"If you want to run around like Castle looking for the guy who killed your buddy, Sax, that's your choice. But back in the cells"—he jerked a thumb over his shoulder—"I got a three-state felon who had a beef with Biletnikov's daddy and left boot prints all over my crime scene. I like what I got."

He paused. Started to speak, but didn't. Tapped the paper tube on his thigh. If I hadn't known better, I would've thought he started to choke up.

"But," I said.

"Yeah, *but*. You mention Teddy Pundo around me and the boys here—anytime, any context—you'll find we're all ears."

Then he thrust the rolled-up papers at my chest.

"What's that?"

"Take it and scram."

CHAPTER SIXTEEN

I sat in my truck in the parking lot and read.

It was a police report. Filled out by a detective in Chicopee, a fading mill town next to Springfield. It was written in constipated cop-report language, but rage trembled through.

Just over a year ago, early April. A man later ID'd as Theodore Joseph Pundo pulled up next to a twelve-year-old girl walking home from a Chicopee middle school just east of the Connecticut River. The girl's parents were Guatemalan. The family had come north thirteen months ago. The girl had already picked up a lot of English. She read at a twelfth-grade level, had single-handedly revived the school debate team, and was considered a rare gem in the city's shitty school system. As she did every day after school, she was walking straight home to tend her seven- and four-year-old brothers so her mother could pick up a few hours at a dry-cleaning shop.

Along came Teddy Pundo in a teal-colored Mustang GT convertible, later found to be stolen from a nail-salon parking lot. It was a warm day, and Teddy was rolling with the top down.

He asked the girl if she wanted a ride to Dairy Queen in his slick new car.

No dice.

He asked her to help look for his puppy, which had jumped out of the car somewhere around here.

No dice.

Those must have been the only come-ons Fat Teddy knew, because he looked around, apparently didn't see anybody, climbed out, hit the girl in the head with a little souvenir baseball bat, and stuffed her unconscious in the Mustang's backseat. It was a small seat, but the girl fit just fine. Hell, she only weighed seventy-six pounds.

Then Teddy Pundo put the top up, drove to a shut-down distribution center for a convenience-store chain, and raped the little girl until nightfall.

Me: gut-punched. I set down the report, breathed deep a few times.

Red mist. It starts in the temples.

I made myself pick up the report.

Fat Teddy Pundo had tied the little girl up and done awful things to her for three-plus hours. The cop who'd written the report laid it all out. I could barely stand to read it.

At dusk, Fat Teddy set the girl's clothes on fire, left her there naked, and drove off in the Mustang, top down again now that he had nothing to hide in the backseat.

Bottom of the last page, block printing, Lima's message to me: *Girl, parents, & sibs all gone. No forwarding addr, probably back to Guatemala or dead. Owner of Mustang recanted, claimed she loaned car to suspect. All charges dropped.*

I felt like throwing up. Tossed the report on the passenger seat. Had a hundred questions for Lima. Why had the staties gotten involved in a local crime? Had they been trying like hell to make something stick to Teddy Pundo? If so, it looked like they'd failed. Was that because Charlie Pundo, for all his I'm-just-a-jazz-bigwig bleating, still had juice?

It sure looked that way.

And what message was Lima sending? Was he telling me not to bother, the Pundos were above my weight class? No, that felt wrong—especially when I recalled how the other detectives' ears had pricked up when I mentioned the Pundos. There was a vendetta here, something personal. Maybe Lima was green-lighting a run at Teddy Pundo, letting me know the state cops wouldn't mind one little bit.

Yeah. That felt right.

I fired up the truck and checked my watch. "Springfield bound," I said out loud.

"What the hell for?" Randall said into his phone three minutes later.

"To rattle the Pundos," I said. "Especially Charlie. You know that pry bar we talked about?"

"Boxer."

"Right. Supposed to be Charlie's guy, but now he's sporting around with Teddy."

"Yeah." He drew the word out, made it half a question.

"I'm going to work that pry bar into the crack. Work it in deep. Let Charlie know his world's being rocked."

"Your voice is shaking, my friend. That police report put you in a bad place. It's making you stupid. Here's what you—"

"No!" Maybe I barked it harder than I meant to. I took a breath, softened my voice. "Well . . . put me in a bad place? Okay. If you'd read it, you'd be there too. But I think Lima's doing two things. First, he's letting me know what Fat Teddy's all about. What he is at his core, what he's capable of doing."

"Possible. And the second thing?"

"I think he's letting me know it's okay to take a run at Teddy. He pretty much said so in the cop shop. Imagine the things Fat Teddy's done that *don't* show up in any reports. I think Lima was letting me know *he* knows Teddy did Almost Home and Gus. And he was telling me to do whatever I need to do."

"Listen to yourself," Randall said. "You've just talked yourself into believing you're a state-sanctioned killer, or something frighteningly close to it. Is this you, Conway? Is this what you envisioned when you swore you'd never turn away a Barnburner in trouble?"

My face went hot. I said nothing.

We were quiet for what seemed like a long time.

"Here's what I was going to advise before I was interrupted," Randall finally said. "Head over to the shop. Do a brake job. Tidy up the books. Engage in commerce. Remember commerce? Productive exchanges of goods and services for currency?"

"Fuck you."

I could picture Randall closing his eyes, counting to five. "I'm sorry," he finally said. "Condescending, I know. Bad habit. I realize you were close to Gus."

"You're not exactly tearing life up your own damn self. Your old man's after me to lean on you about picking a college. And he's not the only one."

Randall went quiet.

"Come with me," I said.

"To Springfield? I can't."

"Why? What's so important?"

"I . . . can't. Won't."

"Tough love," I said. "That it?"

He said nothing.

"You been talking with Charlene, or maybe Floriano? The three of you been jabbering about how Conway's screwing up again?"

"Don't be an asshole."

"Give me a yes or a no. You and Charlene been talking about me?"

Randall started to speak.

But I clicked off. Felt red-cheeked shame, knowing I'd been a jerk. Tried to breathe it away as I pulled up at my quick stop before the Springfield run: Andrade's apartment complex.

His short girlfriend with pretty round eyes let me in. Andrade sat in a ratty wing chair watching a game show I'd never seen.

I said, "How's your elbow?"

"Still busted. What do you want?"

"Wondering if you want to come work for me. I'm busy as hell with other stuff right now."

"He'd love to," the woman said. "You want a soda?"

"I got one good arm," Andrade said, raising his cast an inch. The cast had sparkles glued to it now, and a drawing that might be a dragon. "Not sure how much help I'd be."

I didn't say what I wanted to say: that I'd thought that through. That Andrade was likely as not to rip me off. That everybody would say I was nuts to even think about hiring him—which was why I hadn't asked anybody's opinion.

Something tugged at the key chain clipped to my belt loop. I looked down, saw Andrade's kid. Ignored him. "Don't make this harder on me than it needs to be," I said to Andrade. "You can handle the phone and the computer. Just do whatever you can until you're healthy."

"He'd *love* to," the woman said.

"There is only one state capital that contains three words," the kid said, still tugging my key chain.

"I know your guy Floriano," Andrade said. "He's a good tech."

"He says the same about you." A lie, but a good one.

"He does?" Pause. "I'm sorry about the Biletnikov dude. Even if he did owe me six-fifty."

I gritted my teeth and let that slide. "I'm sorry I busted up your elbow. Why don't you head over now and get a feel for the shop? I'll call Floriano, tell him to expect you."

The woman pressed a cold can of Coke into my hand as she let me out the door. "Thank you," she said.

"Least I can do," I said.

"Salt Lake City," the kid said.

Ninety minutes later, I sat in my truck eating a pair of roach-coach hot dogs and eyeballing the Hi Hat. I'd looped the block before parking, hadn't seen any sign of Fat Teddy's Mercedes SUV. Also hadn't seen anything that looked like heavy security. There was a camera bolted above the Hi Hat's alley door, but that was par for the course at a city nightclub.

All this suited the plan I'd come up with during the drive: to grab a few minutes alone with Boxer.

Given some one-on-one time, I could feel him out, see which way he leaned. Charlie or Teddy? Was Boxer babysitting the boss's kid and hating every minute of it? Or was he working with the kid to overthrow a weak boss who had one foot out the door? Hell, was he the actual trigger man who took out Gus?

My next move would depend on the answers.

I finished the dogs, hopped from my truck, wiped hands on jeans as I angled toward the front door. Didn't go in, though—veered away instead, looking as sketchy as possible. Which wasn't exactly a stretch. I was betting the front door had a security cam, too, and I wanted to look wrong in a way that would catch Boxer's eye.

Rounded the corner, walked the twenty yards to the Hi Hat's delivery alley. Stood at the corner, looked both ways a few times—piling on the sketchiness for whoever might be watching—and headed down the alley. Passed a Dumpster, a stack of milk crates, a tangle of old rolled-up chain link . . .

. . . and smiled inside as a steel door opened and Boxer stepped out.

It's nice when a plan works.

Over his white shirt/black slacks uniform he wore—I'm not kidding—a sky-blue cardigan sweater. Unbuttoned. As I neared he made the move I'd seen before, putting casual hands on casual hips to show me the Desert Eagle that wasn't one bit casual.

"Help you, friend?" He said it *frind* in an accent that was almost familiar, but not quite.

"Hell yes you can help." Without looking at the camera behind and above his right shoulder, I said, "That thing got audio?"

He paused half a beat. "Negative."

"Good." All the while I walked toward him, keeping my voice and my moves casual. We were just two guys talking.

The dude was good. As I neared he didn't back away, didn't flinch or overreact, didn't touch his gun for reassurance. He just stood, hands on hips, until I was close enough to slip a stick of gum in his shirt pocket. Then he said it again, with an edge this time: "*Help you, friend?*"

"You can help me figure something out."

He waited. He had shark eyes. They gave me nothing.

"You can help me figure out why a pro like you, who looks to've spent time in some serious places, is babysitting Charlie Pundo's nothingburger baby-raping turd of a son."

The right corner of his mouth gained enough altitude to show a hole where a tooth belonged. I was pretty sure that was a smile. *So he is Charlie's guy, and he does hate Fat Teddy's guts. Your instincts were right. Now press it.*

"Yeah, that Teddy's all man," I said. "At least when it comes to twelve-year-old Guatemalan girls. Which made for quite a mess, the way I figure it. Whole family had to get disappeared. Were you in on that?"

Boxer squinted and tugged at his right earlobe. I took it as a sign I was getting to him.

Which was dumb.

"You think you're in a certain line of work," I said, "until one night the boss tells you to crash some immigrant janitor's apartment. To snatch him and his wife and his kids. Not exactly what you—"

I didn't get to finish.

Because Boxer, who'd been cocking his fist when I thought he was tugging his ear, knocked me cold with the quickest, heaviest right hand I'd ever felt in my life.

Or ever hope to.

CHAPTER SEVENTEEN

I came to in a place that smelled like sweat and sawdust. High windows, dirty light. I fuzzed out, fuzzed in. My head hurt like hell. I felt a blurt of puke, kept it in.

Heard a voice, soft but urgent. *All due respect. Nowhere near this place. Not today.*

That voice. I remembered. Boxer. He'd tugged his earlobe.

When I pushed to a sitting position, my left cheek screamed pain. I touched it. Big swelling, like I'd tucked a golf ball in there.

I'd been wrong about a lot of things but right about one: that dude had surely spent time in the ring.

I finished sitting up—it took a while—blinked, took things in. Warehouse, a big one, ten thousand square feet easy. Curving plywood ramps, most of them badly patched and graffitied. Over there: a Coke machine lying on its side. Far corner: the weight of an HVAC unit had pulled down a chunk of ceiling. The stench clarified itself: bums, rats, junkies, beer piss, slow-rotting plywood, human shit, rubbers, bird carcasses.

Soundtrack: *Thunk. Thunk. Thunk.* Unhurried. A patient sound, soft on soft.

I shook my head once more and turned and figured out a couple of things.

I was in an indoor skateboard park. In fact, I was sitting at the bottom of a giant ramp, a half-pipe I think they call them. Damn thing had a diameter of thirty-plus feet. This one was the pick of the litter—it still looked usable, which was more than you could say for most of the ramps there.

My eye was drawn upward, where the half-pipe's rim was painted to look like swimming-pool tile, and I saw the source of the patient noise: Charlie Pundo, sitting sixteen feet high, long legs dangling, running shoes *thunk-thunk*ing plywood. Even with those shoes, he wore a sharp suit and tie. He stared straight ahead at nothing. He sure didn't look at me.

He's sixteen feet away, and he doesn't have wings. Get up and run away now.

"Ahem."

I cranked my neck, heard it rattle, spotted Boxer behind me. He stood easy, one foot on the half-pipe, the Desert Eagle in his right hand.

So he punched like a steam engine and he could read my mind.

Great.

"Sax," Pundo said.

I looked. He beckoned with a white tube that looked like a baton. "Come on up."

I made a *how the hell?* shrug.

"I did it," he said. "You can, too."

"Sir?" Boxer said to Pundo, not liking the idea.

Pundo waved him off with the baton. "Don't worry about it. Go see how the guys are making out."

The guys? As Boxer walked off—after hesitating, like he *really* didn't dig the idea—I noticed footsteps here and there. Wondered how many guys there were.

Pundo whistled through his teeth, made a pendulum motion with his free hand.

"What the hell," I said out loud. And started to run back and forth.

It's probably easy for fourteen-year-old boys who weigh a hundred and ten, but it sure wasn't easy for me in Red Wing boots. I trotted up one side of the half-pipe as far as I could, spun a clumsy one-eighty, and trotted back the way I'd come, using momentum to gain a little altitude on the other side.

Once.

Twice.

Three times. Sweating now, the one-eighties tricky because my body was nearly parallel to the floor, the way a skateboarder would be.

I decided I had as much momentum as I was going to get. Put together a burst, ran up Pundo's side, flung my arms, grabbed the edge. I pulled, boot-scrabbled, heaved a leg, pulled some more.

And made it. I sat to Pundo's left, hot as hell, panting but trying to hide it.

He was back to his thousand-yard stare now. He said nothing. In his right hand, close to his chest, he held an old-school Colt Detective Special, blued. With his left hand he tapped the baton on the ramp. Now I saw it wasn't a baton, but rolled-up papers.

I patted the inside pocket of my jacket.

The police report on Teddy's rape was missing.

Pundo held it, rolled up, in his hand.

Which probably explained why we were here.

Pundo said nothing. Held his revolver as easily as most people hold a breadstick.

While he brooded, I used the time to scope the warehouse from this vantage point, figuring angles.

Off near the hole in the ceiling a guy came into view. He walked backward, splashing a trail from a red plastic jug.

"You're torching this dump," I said as gas joined the other smells. Pundo said nothing.

I craned my neck, still checking angles, escape routes, possibilities. This half-pipe had once been reachable by a ladder made of two-by-fours, but the ladder lay on filthy concrete now, torn up like everything else.

I spotted another guy, this one with an orange beard, also dumping gas. So call it Boxer plus two, and assume they were all armed.

Good news: they were preoccupied. Lugging around a gas can and a lighter does focus the mind.

Bad news: they were Boxer's men. He knew his shit. They would, too.

When I looked at Pundo again, he was looking at me. He'd unrolled the police report, had set it neatly in the space between us. The Colt, pointed at my belly, shook not one bit.

He said, "I bought this place for him."

"For Teddy."

"Eight years ago? No, nine. He was a big boy even then, and he wasn't exactly setting the world on fire, you'll pardon the pun, when it came to school. Or friends. Or anything else." He turned his head to look straight out over the skate park—*his* skate park—and he half-smiled. "He expressed interest in skateboarding, rode around our driveway for a few weeks. I bought him this place so fast, and at such a price, my accountant quit."

Then we were quiet some more. Below, men moved around while Boxer gave instructions.

Wait. Was that something else in my peripheral vision? Off to the left, where my view was blocked by the downed HVAC unit, it seemed the light changed for a second or two.

Could be anything. Could be a cat running past a window.

But it could be something else. And something else, *anything* else, had to be better than the box I was in.

So stall. Keep the clock running and try to get lucky.

I said, "Did he like it here? Did he skateboard a lot?"

"He loved it. He made friends, cut down on the video games, even dropped a few pounds." Pause. "For four months. Then a twelve-year-old called him a fat whale, and Teddy bashed all the kid's teeth out on the cast-iron railing they were doing tricks on, and the kid's dad had some juice here in town, and before I knew it Teddy was enjoined from coming within two hundred feet of the motherfucking skate park I bought him."

Pundo never raised his voice while he told it.

While we said nothing again, Boxer approached the bottom of the half-pipe with a plastic bag from Home Depot. He pulled items from it one by one, arranging them at the edge of the ramp.

A stout eighteen-inch screwdriver.

Duct tape.

Zip ties, huge ones.

Finally, an eyebolt with a shaft two inches long. The type of thing you'd screw into a tree branch to make a tire swing.

With the gear laid out, Boxer looked up at me and made that smile that revealed the missing tooth. He raised his eyebrows once, then again, like a silent-movie bad guy.

Then he picked up the eyebolt and the screwdriver. He used the screwdriver's handle like a hammerhead, pounding the eyebolt into a half-pipe support to get it started. Then he screwed in the eyebolt. When it was too deep to turn by hand, he shoved the screwdriver blade through the hole and used it for leverage.

"The place went to hell after that," Pundo said, ignoring Boxer below. "Lay fallow a long while. Last year I thought about rehabbing and reopening, but I'll be damned if my people could find three skate parks outside California that turn a profit. So up in smoke it goes, a nice write-down. I shouldn't be here, of course. Christ, I should be in another state, with a half-dozen witnesses to boot. But when I heard about this"—he tapped the police report—"I needed to speak with you."

"Before you set me on fire."

"Yeah. Before that."

Below, Boxer was finishing up. He'd run the eyebolt in deep enough to work up a sweat—wanted to make sure once they zip-tied me to it and torched the warehouse, I stayed put.

"You've got a son," Pundo said. "You told me so when we met."

"Haven't seen him for a while now," I said.

"They disappoint you."

"Or you disappoint them."

"Is that the way it played out for you?"

"Yes."

He nodded, tapping the report. "For the most part, though, *they* disappoint *you*. You stand by them. You'd do anything for them. And they let you down."

Boxer and his two guys came together near the bottom of the ramp, and I recognized the third guy as the bartender from the Hi Hat. Shaved head, crisp white shirt. The three of them must be finished setting up, because nobody held a gas can. Boxer looked at Pundo and tapped an imaginary wristwatch.

"Well," Pundo said, rolling the report and tucking it away.

"One question," I said. It was a stall: off in that corner, light had shifted again. Something was going on. I hoped.

Pundo raised eyebrows.

"Why kill me?" I said, thinking fast and talking slow. "I don't count for shit. Your kid's no worse off than he was. I got my hands on a year-old police report. So what? But if you take me out, you take a big risk and a step backward. So why?"

It seemed to surprise him. "For family. Of course."

Then Charlie Pundo pushed off and slid down the half-pipe on the ass of his fine suit. He rose and walked out of sight dusting the seat of his pants. He never looked back.

The three guys formed an arc in the bottom of the half-pipe. Holding a fistful of zip ties, Boxer finger-crooked. "Drop in, friend."

Again, *frind*. What the hell was that accent? Australian? No, but almost.

Boxer was trying for easy confidence, like I had no alternative but to slide down, get myself zip-tied to an eyebolt, and then burn to death.

But I was looking at shoes.

And the shoes damn near made me smile.

I put weight on my hands like I was getting set to slide.

I wasn't.

All three of them wore dress shoes. No way were they climbing the half-pipe with leather soles. That must have occurred to Boxer—he'd been trying to bluff me down.

I leaned forward even more until I felt him relax just a hair.

Then I threw myself backward and flattened out on the deck.

A handgun fired three fast rounds.

Boxer said, "Knock it off! Knock it off! You've got no angle!" Then, quietly: "Fuck *me*."

As long as I stayed flat, they couldn't see me from where they stood. And they couldn't shoot what they couldn't see.

So I could stay right here, prone atop a half-pipe in a rat-turd warehouse, for the rest of my life.

It didn't sound so great. Until you compared it to burning alive.

I looked around, spotted a length of two-by-four hanging where there used to be a railing, wrenched it loose. Two big-ass deck screws protruded from one end.

Something new. I sniffed. Smoke?

Sound: dress-shoe footsteps. I watched the edge of the half-pipe, cocked my two-by-four. Heard a slip, a heavy thump, a howl. "Take your shoes off and try again," Boxer said. Then: "Socks too, for Christ's bloody sake."

No question about it now: I smelled smoke. It was gathering near the ceiling. Maybe Boxer's boys had lit their matches early.

The now-barefoot guy tried again. I couldn't see him, but I heard his back-and-forth footsteps build height, as I had a few minutes earlier. The footsteps neared. I regripped my club and eye-scanned the top of the ramp.

I saw a hand. Then another.

I uncoiled with my club.

I rammed an honest inch of galvanized deck screw into a knuckle.

The hand released. The man screamed, fell, hit like a sack of doorknobs.

When the guys below spotted my arm and club, they cut loose with what had to be semiautomatics. They were good, but they weren't lucky: bullets chewed the lip of the half-pipe in front of my face, but all that hit me were splinters.

Then a bunch of things happened. They happened fast, but my brain processed them slow. That was a good sign—it used to work the same way in a race car.

The smoke grew heavy enough to sting my eyes. Since I was near the ceiling, it was harder on me than it was on Boxer and his boys. I'd have to jump soon, like it or not.

I flipped onto my belly to pick a landing spot. Stayed as flat as I could, but Boxer saw movement and snapped off a couple rounds. They whistled past the ass of my jeans.

Boxer knew what I was getting set to do. He said, "Go around back!" I heard the second guy move. The third was rolling around in the half-pipe, moaning and useless.

I looked down. Shit. Sixteen feet straight to polished concrete, a guaranteed busted ankle. But I had no choice: the smoke now had me coughing, squinting. I got ready to drop.

Motion. There, that damn far corner again. What the hell was going on?

I blinked against smoke, then blinked again as I tried to understand what I was looking at.

A couch. A raggedy-ass cushionless sofa the color of blood.

The couch was sliding my way.

I got it: someone was pushing the couch, doubled over, using it for cover. He was coming *fast*.

Boxer's guy—it was Redbeard, which meant Barkeep was the one whose hand I'd wrecked—cleared the corner of the half-pipe and caught me exposed. He had an angle on me, a shot.

But the motion caught his eye the way it'd caught mine. He stared. His jaw dropped. I guess he'd never seen a raggedy red couch move so fast. "Hey," he said, frozen, as the couch came at him.

The couch rammed Redbeard, rammed him *hard*, knocked him on his ass.

Then Randall Swale straightened.

I may be mistaken—like I said, things were moving along at a good clip—but I'm pretty sure I smiled.

Randall came around the couch, took one step, and kicked Redbeard in the head. He kicked with his good foot, like an old-fashioned straight-on football kicker. He kicked with power and form.

Redbeard did not move.

Boxer, who'd stayed put in case I backtracked into the half-pipe, couldn't see any of this. But he sensed things were going badly. "You got him?" he said, hollering it, his voice losing its cool for the first time. "What in fuck-all's going on over there?"

Randall grabbed Redbeard's semiautomatic and tucked it in his pants. Then he shoved the couch in my direction. It was still one hell of a drop, but at least it wasn't to concrete. Without letting myself think, I rolled off the edge, held my breath, and crash-landed on my feet. Felt it in my spine and hips, lost balance, splayed out, rose.

Randall pointed at the corner he'd come from.

We took off.

We ran hard.

Boxer must have figured out it was time to ditch his post, because he came around the corner of the half-pipe and tossed shots at our backs.

We ran harder.

Randall crash-barred a set of double doors like they weren't even there.

I followed.

Right about then I would've followed Randall Swale any-damn-where.

CHAPTER EIGHTEEN

T hat was an intriguing way to answer a question," Randall said two hours later, pushing away his plate.

"What do you mean?" I said. "What question?"

I smiled at Sophie as she cleared the table. When Randall and I had stiff-legged our way into Charlene's place a half hour ago, Sophie'd taken one look at us and announced she would make omelets. I had no idea how hungry I was until she said it.

Damn, she was a good kid. Bustling around, cleaning up in a yellow apron, acting like she was thirty-five. All she asked in return was that we ignore her, pretend she wasn't listening to every word as we talked things through.

From Sophie's point of view, the invisibility act had another benefit: by the time I realized we shouldn't be discussing things in front of her, we'd said so much already that I could only shrug.

She was the only female in the house taking an interest, that was for sure: neither Charlene nor Jessie had bothered to come downstairs.

"The question was," Randall said, "whether Boxer was Charlie's guy. Or whether he and Teddy were planning a mutiny."

"Looks like he's Charlie's guy all the way."

" 'Twould certainly appear."

I thought. "That might do us some good," I said after a while, "if we could turn Boxer against Fat Teddy."

"I don't see it, though. Boxer looks like a loyal soldier. Keeps his opinions to himself, including his opinion of Teddy."

"*Especially* his opinion of Teddy."

Randall nodded. "And does as the boss man says."

From the corner of my eye, I saw Sophie frown. And could tell she *wanted* me to see that.

"What is it?" I said, gesturing. "Spill."

"Did you come any closer to figuring out who killed Gus?"

The kitchen went quiet.

"If Teddy did it," Randall said after a while, "Charlie's warehouse move was to protect his dipshit son. Which would make sense."

"Or," I said, thinking it through as I spoke, "*Charlie* shot Gus—or had Boxer do it, same thing—to clean up after the mess Teddy made when he was dealing drugs without his father's okay."

"This would also make sense," Randall said.

"Meaning my banzai run to Springfield netted us jack shit," I said.

Randall and Sophie agreed by saying nothing.

We sat.

"Either way," I said, "we did learn *something*. Charlie Pundo was willing to take one hell of a risk."

"Killing you, or trying to."

"And torching a dump he owned, and being there while it all happened."

"A man with his history," Randall said, nodding, "might as well tattoo PRIME SUSPECT on his forearm when pulling a move like that."

"Well," Sophie said. Standing at the sink, she didn't bother to turn as she spoke. "He must have had one hell of a strong reason."

"You kiss your mother with that mouth?" Randall said.

"Oh please," Sophie said.

"You're right, kid," I said. "But there's a disconnect. He said he was doing it for family, but he could barely mention Fat Teddy without spitting."

"Huh," Randall said.

"Huh," Sophie said.

Charlene came in. Evening wear: fluffy slippers, cotton pajama pants, an old POWERED BY YATES T-shirt of mine that nearly reached her knees.

"Hey baby," Randall said.

"Hey," she said without looking at either of us. She started to microwave a cup of tea, then circled the room pulling shades—it was dark now.

"Care to hear a tale of derring-do and manly skill?" Randall said.

"No."

Randall, Sophie, and I froze until Charlene pulled her tea from the microwave and headed upstairs.

"What's that about?" he said, mouthing it, barely audible.

"I hired a tech," I said.

"Oh?"

"With a busted elbow."

"Oh."

"Conway busted it," Sophie said.

"Thanks, punk," I said.

"*That* guy?" Randall said.

"Render a man useless, then hire him out of guilt," Sophie said. "It's the Conway Sax way."

"A one-armed grease monkey," Randall said. "If only your shop worked on unicycles."

The two of them cracked up.

"Who needs enemies," I said.

Once their laughter petered out, we were quiet.

"What comes next?" Randall said.

"The day before Gus was killed . . . the day before I tossed him out . . . he was hanging around with some dude in his apartment. Partying, getting high. He said so himself."

"So?"

"So I need to know who the dude was."

"Because?"

"Because it's a blank space," I said. "A space that might tell us something. Think about the timeline. This dude was one of the last people to see Gus alive."

"Maybe *the* last. Other than the killer."

"Unless the dude *was* the killer."

"Pardon me," Randall said, "but aren't we pretty damn sure at this point that some combination of the House of Pundo killed Gus? Or, failing that, this Houston con man?"

"Pretty sure's not sure enough."

He finger-drummed the table. "The cops must be looking at this mystery friend."

"I don't think they know about him. Lima told me he stopped by the place and it reeked of weed, but he didn't mention anybody other than Gus. So maybe the dude was gone by then. Or in another room."

"Naturally, you haven't mentioned this critical bit of intelligence to Lima."

"I may have forgotten to."

Randall sighed and pushed his chair away from the table. "So you're not going back to work tomorrow, to train the one-armed mechanic who hates your guts. Instead, you'll chase after Gus's mysterious pot-smoking comrade."

"I might."

Randall squeezed and kissed Sophie. "Great omelet, Muffy." He'd been calling her that since he first saw her cheerleading getup. "See if you can talk some sense into Charlie Chan here, 'kay?"

"Fat chance," she said.

"Fat chance," he said, and started toward the front door.

"Randall," I said.

He stopped. Turned.

"Thank you," I said.

"*De nada,*" he said, and left.

"Did he really save your life?" Sophie said, turning on the dishwasher.

"Pretty much." I explained what he'd told me once we cleared out of the skate park and he was driving me back to the Hi Hat to fetch my truck. He'd felt bad about stiffing me, so he'd headed for Springfield. He found my empty truck, failed to raise me by phone, spotted a Town Car easing from the club's alley. He followed, watched Pundo's men lug me into the skate park, reconnoitered, and decided the best move in an unarmed one-on-four attack was to set fire to the dump before Boxer and his men were truly ready for it.

"Not bad for a gimp," Sophie said. She undid and hung her apron, then patted me on the shoulder as she walked past. "Turn out the lights when you come upstairs to face the music."

How was I supposed to not smile?

The smile faded, though, as I was left alone on the first floor with household noises.

I sat at the kitchen table a good long time. Thinking about fathers and sons and how disappointment runs in both directions.

When I finally padded up the stairs, ready to take whatever Charlene dished out, Jessie stepped from her room and we nearly banged into each other.

She said, "Howdy, stranger."

I could have let it slide. Should have.

But it'd been one hell of a long day.

"What's that supposed to mean?"

"Haven't been around much lately, have we? Since the problem daughter returned. We're brave when it comes to bad guys, but in the domestic realm we're all flight, no fight."

The "we" bugged me. "Bullshit." I hissed it, trying to keep quiet.

Jessie kept her voice low, too. "Is it? You've sure been dreaming up excuses to be elsewhere. Between work and the Barnburners, I never see you."

I stammered.

Stopped.

She was right.

Hell.

"The disappearing act is fine by me," Jessie said, "but your two *devoted* Bollinger gals, the paycheck and the fangirl, miss you around the house. They miss you *a lot*. And what hurts them hurts me."

"What about when *you* hurt them?"

She stared at me, hands on bony hips.

I stared back. "You break her frigging heart," I said. "How could you not? Look at you."

"You think I don't know it?" A tear rolled—even in the mostly dark hallway I could see it. "You think it's something to be *fixed,* like . . . like a leaky head gasket?"

Why not? I thought.

I was smart enough to not say it out loud.

Barely.

Jessie let her single tear fall to the carpet. Then she stepped into the bathroom and pulled shut the door.

When I let myself in the master bedroom, Charlene had the lights out and lay with her back to me. Asleep.

Or faking it.

Either way was fine by me.

CHAPTER NINETEEN

At six thirty the next morning, I stood in the apartment I'd chucked Gus from.

There wasn't much to see. He'd grown accustomed, junkie-style, to living out of a backpack. All his gear had fit in it and a plastic trash bag. The apartment was bare.

So look around anyway.

For what?

Hell, I'd know when I found it.

If.

I started with all the trash cans, glad my friend Trey hadn't yet emptied them, and plucked every nasty item individually. Kleenex, fast-food Styrofoam, a couple of bags from the Osco Drug down the street.

Nothing interesting, nothing that pointed me anywhere, nothing written down. Which was no surprise, really. In the age of smart-phones, what twentyish kid jotted notes anymore?

Living room: nothing.

Eat-in kitchen, with its yard-sale table and its Target plates and glasses: nothing.

Bathroom: less than nothing.

Bedroom: nothing.

Just to be thorough, I checked every teenager's favorite stash space: pulled the twin-sized bed on its black metal frame away from the wall, leaned over, looked down . . .

. . . at nothing. Not even dust bunnies.

Hell. I sighed and worked the bed back where it belonged . . .

. . . and saw something.

Knelt on the bed, looked close.

"I'll be damned," I said out loud.

Scratched into the wall near the head of the bed, barely higher than the mattress itself:

4315 AGR

It was etched lightly into the off-white drywall, so I'd nearly missed it. Maybe it'd been scratched by a pen that had run out of ink. Or by a pushpin, or a tack.

In any case, it was fresh: I spotted fallen drywall powder on the baseboard beneath.

I straightened, keyed it into my phone's notepad: 4315 AGR.

What is that?

I knew.

Almost.

It meant something to me.

Almost.

It would come to me if I didn't focus on it.

So I forced my head elsewhere by policing trash into a single bag. Felt my mind humming, sifting possibilities all the while.

License plate? Not in Massachusetts, where the plates were still six characters max.

Initials? Maybe.

Address? That felt right.

I let it work its way through my head.

Left the apartment toting a full trash bag, was halfway down the steps when it hit me. I stopped and said out loud: "Arms at Granite Ridge."

Then I smiled.

Chucked the trash in a barrel, hopped in my truck.

The Arms at Granite Ridge was the latest name of a big-ass apartment complex on Route 9, Framingham's main drag. It was built into a hillside—the granite, I guessed—overlooking the road and, beyond it, a reservoir. Four buildings, maybe two hundred units apiece.

Driving past the tennis courts and health club nobody ever used, I thought for the hundredth time this was the type of place people lived when they were starting out or starting over. I'd known a dozen Barnburners who spent time here after a divorce. The apartments were okay, but turnover was fierce because whoever built the joint in the 1980s took the easy way out and installed electric heaters in each unit. They were cheap for the builder, but brutal for renters. New tenants would get their December electric bill, faint dead away, put on an extra sweater, and vow to move out before the next winter hit.

I parked at the 4000 building, the one farthest from Route 9. Stood at the doorway pretending to search my pockets for keys until a young woman came out. Slipped in before the glass door latched, made sure the woman wasn't eyeballing me, walked across a green-carpeted lobby to look at mailboxes. Found it:

4315 B. BLOOMQUIST

Back in Minnesota, you couldn't throw a rock without hitting a Bloomquist. But I'd never met one around here, so the name seemed worth searching.

I used my phone to do a Google and a Switchboard.com. Didn't find anything helpful—no address for a B. Bloomquist, which might mean something or might not.

I thought for a minute, then googled bloomquist and "university of massachusetts."

Boom. There he was in an article from an Amherst newspaper: Bradford Bloomquist. Hometown: Brewster, Massachusetts. Graduated a year before Gus Biletnikov.

This was starting to make sense.

Two minutes later, I stood with my ear to the door of 4315.

Pink Floyd.

Really?

I knocked. Volume dropped, somebody spoke.

"It's Conway," I said. "Friend of Gus."

As the dead bolt turned, I kicked out hard. My left foot went through the cheap door, but the door didn't open—I'd timed it wrong, and the dead bolt hadn't yet released. My ankle stuck and I fell backward, sitting down hard in the hallway with my foot higher than my head. Not to mention stuck in the door.

All the detective cred I'd built by finding the address and googling Bloomquist pretty much disappeared right then.

A guy in a bathrobe and a shaggy beard was looking down at me. "Dude," he said.

I pulled my boot from the hole, rose, bulled him into the apartment, slammed the door. We walked—me forward and pushing into his personal space, him backward—until he had nowhere to go and half-fell onto a futon.

I stood, breathing hard. Feeling like a jackass.

Bloomquist: long brown hair, that hippie beard. The bathrobe was terry cloth the color of red wine. Plaid flannel pajama pants, bare feet. I couldn't help but do a double take at the feet: they looked like kayaks.

I eye-locked him, saw he was stoned to the gills. "Gus Biletnikov."

"He was a friend of mine. He's dead."

Had he stutter-stepped at *friend*? Maybe just a little? "Tell me when you saw him last," I said. "Tell me what you did with him. Tell me everything."

"Are you a police officer?"

"No. My name is Conway Sax. I was Gus's friend."

"He never mentioned you."

"He never mentioned you to *me*."

Bloomquist nodded, scratching his beard. "Fair point. May I, ah, ask why you kicked in the door of my castle keep?"

"Sorry. Had to make sure I got in. Didn't realize you'd be mellow. I don't run across much mellow. What happened to Gus wasn't mellow at all."

"What *did* happen? He was shot, this much I know. You seem to know more." As Bloomquist spoke, he rose and recinched his bathrobe. Gestured me to a sofa covered by a Mexican blanket. Turned down the stereo, sat facing me on one of those giant exercise balls.

Behind him was a folding table covered with hobby gear. Atop the table: a torso-only half-mannequin draped in a brown leather vest. The vest's back faced me. It looked like an art project: a portrait of Bloomquist and, arced above the portrait, words:

THE DUDE ABIDES

I sniffed, realized that under the scent of weed and cigarettes and incense and bachelor pad hung the clean smell of leather. Looked harder at the table, was impressed at the array of tools. Adzes, awls, hole-punches, a dozen small knives, a whetstone and oil to keep their blades sharp.

Bloomquist saw me looking. "My passion," he said. "My calling. The vest is just inked for now. I'm getting ready to do the hard part. You like?"

"I guess."

"My friends call me the Dude, see. After the movie."

"What movie?"

His shoulders dropped. "Never mind. So . . . are you a *family* friend or something? I ask because I was pretty close to Gus, and like I say, he never mentioned you."

"I met him when he got out of rehab and started AA."

He nodded. "That would explain it. I didn't see much of him once he went to Hazelden."

"I was showing Gus around AA, helping him when I could. I put him in the apartment where you two got high the other day."

He didn't bother to deny it. He said nothing.

"I know a little about homicide cops," I said. "Two things make their jobs easy. First, if there's a husband or a wife or a boyfriend or a girlfriend, that's who dunnit. Bet your last dollar."

Bloomquist's eyes sharpened up for just a second.

"With Gus," I said, "there was no girlfriend. Brings us to the second thing cops look at. Who saw the vic last? So far, the cops don't know that was you. If they find out, they'll flood this place. They'll find whatever you're selling"—I paused to let that sink in. It'd been a guess, and not a tough one—"to pad all that money you're making off your leather goods."

He leaned forward, struggling. He was a small-time dealer with no use for the likes of me. On the other hand, I could see Gus had meant something to him. He needed a push.

So push.

"Brad," I said, "they cut him in *half.*"

"Bullshit. What?"

I'd phrased it that way on purpose. Bloomquist's reaction had been the right one. "With a shotgun, I mean. They didn't *actually* cut him in half. Blew a big-ass hole in him, though."

His lower lip quivered. The beard added ten years visually, but this was a kid I was bullying around, a kid Gus's age. "What do you . . . what do you want from *me*?"

"Tell me things," I said.

"Tell you what?"

I made a big circle with my arms. "Everything. You, Gus, UMass. Tell me anything that'll help me find out who killed him."

He closed his eyes for a long time.

When he opened them, they looked different. Straight, or the closest to it he'd been in five years.

CHAPTER TWENTY

They met in Melville Hall, a dormitory at the Amherst campus of the University of Massachusetts. Bloomquist was a sophomore, Gus a freshman. Early in the year, Bloomquist's roommate dropped out. "Boy, was he a hillbilly," Bloomquist said. "From Gill, a hick town way out Route Two. Amherst was like Manhattan to him, and he couldn't hack it in the big city."

Meanwhile, Gus's roommate was a New Jersey kid. All night every night: Bon Jovi air-guitar fest. The room became a magnet for Jersey kids. Somebody put a sign on the door: NEWARK NORTH. The roommate was too dumb to know it was an insult. Gus phased himself out of the room. He wandered the halls a lot, crashing on couches and floors.

Eventually, the floor he crashed on belonged to Bloomquist. They hit it off. They liked the same music. They hated Bon Jovi. They liked smoking weed.

And how.

With Bloomquist's roommate gone, it was simple for Gus to swap in.

They became pothead best friends. Lived together in various

dorms and apartments for the rest of their UMass careers, sold high-end reefer to finance their own stash, dabbled in whatever other drugs fell into their laps.

"Dabbled," I said.

"At first," Bloomquist said. "I'm getting to that."

Like every other stoner who ever dealt on the side, they couldn't keep their hands off the for-sale merchandise. I nodded as Bloomquist said so, remembering Gus had told me the same thing without mentioning any friend.

They dug themselves into a hole smoking weed fronted them by higher-ranking campus dealers. They added meth, cocaine, and pharmaceuticals to their inventory to pay off the reefer debts.

By the time Bloomquist was a senior and Gus a junior, they were both into cocaine in a big way. Debt deepened. They robbed Peter to pay Paul. Campus dealers stopped fronting them drugs. They got skinny. Bloomquist sold his five-thousand-dollar car to a townie for seven hundred bucks in fifties. "Technically," he said, "it was still my dad's car. But the buyer was willing to overlook the discrepancy."

With an index finger I gestured to speed it up. "I hear this story three times a week. Get to Teddy Pundo."

The name jarred him, as I'd hoped. "Man, why didn't you say you knew that twisted, pants-shitting whale? Not a figure of speech, sad to say. Gus was in the same freshman dorm as Teddy. Teddy's roommate got the hell out because Fat Teddy shat himself on a semi-regular basis. Word got around the dorm, you know? A psych major told me when it comes to predicting who's going to be a total psycho murderer, pants shitting is right up there with torturing small animals and setting fires."

"Go ahead."

"Fat Teddy lasted two semesters. Then he got busted stalking a senior. He broke into her room, went through her panties, videotaped himself jacking off in her bed, delightful stuff like that. The girl's parents didn't want the publicity that would've come from pressing charges, so Teddy was quietly invited to absent himself from campus."

"Tell me about the drugs."

"Before Fat Teddy got tossed, he used to drop hints that his dad was the Tony Soprano of Springfield. We all assumed he was full of shit, ha ha, pardon the pun. But when Gus and I looked into buying weed in quantity, we heard Teddy Pundo was indeed the man to see, due to the fact that his daddy was indeed a top hoodlum. This was a drag. We wanted nothing to do with Fat Teddy. He was no longer matriculating by then, but he hung around town a lot in typical loser fashion."

"You had no choice," I said. "By then, the drugs were choosing your friends for you."

He tugged his beard. "I'm not going to argue that now. Anyway, Fat Teddy was like a puppy dog when we knocked on his door. He couldn't wait to be our main man. He made sure we got fronted our weed. Later, he lent us the dough for the other stuff, the pills and coke."

"Did you ever deal with the dad? Charlie Pundo?"

He shook his head. "We knew *of* him, of course, but we never once saw him. I didn't, at least. Although . . . come to think of it, Gus might have. Ninety-nine percent of the time, he took on the lovely task of meeting with Fat Teddy. Say, do you mind if I do a bong hit? Just to clear my head?"

"Yes. Why was it Gus who dealt with Teddy?"

"His money, ergo his problem. Or his daddy's money, to be precise."

What?

Bloomquist had finally told me something new.

I straightened. "Slow down. What the hell are you saying? Was Gus draining a trust fund or something?"

He shook his head. "Dude, once we got seriously into the hard stuff, Mr. Biletnikov was *buying* the shit. He had a hot little trophy wife to take care of. She used to visit every weekend, and she had"—he touched his thumb to the side of his nose—"*needs,* if you get my drift."

"You're talking about *Rinn* here?"

"You know her? Devil woman, huh? She was sweet at first, but . . . anyway, we were the Three Musketeers for a while. But Lord, she could suck up the coke." Bloomquist tugged his beard again. "No offense, but this is my *casa* and I'm going to break out the bong. I need to get motivated to patch that hole in the door."

I told Bloomquist to fire up his bong. I patched the hole myself with a pizza box and duct tape.

While I worked, I wondered what the hell was going on with the Sherborn Biletnikovs.

"Come with me," I said a half hour later, shoulder-jamming phone to ear while I rummaged through a cardboard box in Charlene's basement.

"It's not that I need a lot of convincing to drop in on Mrs. Biletnikov," Randall said. "But why, exactly? What's my role?"

"She likes you, for starters. You know . . . *likes* you."

"Hoo boy. Maybe I'll take her to the malt shop after the big game with State."

"Knock it off," I said, flipping past my Milford High School diploma and a rubber-banded brick of snapshots. I hesitated, lowered my voice, feeling ridiculous even as I said the next bit: "The nanny said Gus went down to see her at the cottage, remember?"

"When he came by to cadge money. So?"

"So as far as we've been able to find, that makes Rinn the last one who saw him before he turned up dead."

"You're joking."

"In her yard."

"Please tell me you're joking."

"And she found the body."

It was quiet so long I wondered if the call had dropped out.

It hadn't.

"Really?" Randall finally said. "Think it through. We've been looking at a pair of hard-core gangsters, one with a well-established drug connection to Gus. Said gangsters are sufficiently worried to have attempted to turn you into an Ohio Blue Tip match. Moreover, the state police have enough evidence to be holding your buddy Donald Crump while they build a case against *him*. And yet you're saying Rinn Biletnikov, movie-star-gorgeous socialite, worth eighty million via her older hubby, had a beef with her stepson? Whereupon she Rambo'd into a halfway house with a shotgun? Whereupon she killed three people, including the wrong kid? Whereupon she rectified her error by shotgunning said stepson for real in her own backyard? No, it's even better. She shotgunned Gus somewhere else, then *dragged* him to her backyard. *Really,* Conway?"

"I know. I know." I pinched the bridge of my nose. "But all that money opens up new possibilities. If you've got eighty million, you can kill a man without pulling the trigger yourself. Besides, what else am I supposed to do?"

"Um, fix cars? Earn a paycheck?"

I ignored that. "She's starting to look like a real piece of work, you've got to admit that much."

He said nothing.

"The nanny said Rinn was fascinated by you. Did I mention that?"

His sigh told me I'd hooked him. I was smiling even before he said, "Give me half an hour."

As we clicked off, I found what I'd been looking for in the box, wrapped in my first checkered flag from Busch Grand National.

I unwrapped. A thin book, its dust jacket mostly green.

Goodnight Moon.

Thanks to the checkered flag, it was pristine despite spending a decade-plus in the box. I opened it to the first blank page. Black pen, my handwriting:

Roy—This was my first favorite book, can't wait to read it to you. Love, Daddy

I was on the road when Roy was born. Heard the news on my way out of Darlington. Bought the book in Saint George, South Carolina.

I never brought it home. I stayed drunk a long time instead. By the time I got serious about my amends and came to know Roy, he was too old for it. I would have been ashamed to give it to him anyhow.

Maybe this was the time to pass it on.

I pictured myself handing Rinn the book. We'd chat. It would turn out we'd both loved *Goodnight Moon* as kids. We'd recite lines to each other. I'd tell Rinn my first memory was warmth in my stomach when my mother read the opening lines: *In the great green room / There was a telephone.*

Shook my head, snapped out of it.

Knock it off with the kid stuff. Why Rinn? Why now?

I made myself look at the questions. Why now? Because, I figured, I felt like I was hip-deep in parenthood, whether I liked it or not. Roy, Gus, and even Jessie had made damn sure of that. I chuffed a half laugh as I realized Sophie was, in her own way, the most mature of them all.

So why Rinn? She barely looks at her own baby. What's she done to earn a book that means a lot to you?

Huh. That was the tougher question.

What had Charlene said the night I brought Gus to that Milford AA meeting? *Conway Sax takes in another stray.*

Was I taking in Rinn? Trying to make her something she wasn't? Something closer to what I wanted her to be?

"Hell," I said out loud. "Too much thinking."

I fetched a razor blade and ruler, sliced out the page I'd written on.

Was in my truck in the driveway, set to hit Sherborn via Randall's place, when my phone rang.

I squinted at the incoming number.

No goddamn way.

I picked up.

"Meet me at that barbecue joint," Donald Crump said. "The awful one."

"You're out?"

"I'm out and I'm hungry. *Told* you I didn't do nothing." He clicked off.

I sighed, texted Randall that I'd be a while. He could have Rinn all to himself.

He texted back a smiley face.

CHAPTER TWENTY-ONE

When I rolled up, Donald was rattling the barbecue joint's doors, trying to explain to a Latino dude that he was fresh out of a holding cell at the Framingham barracks and he was *hungry*, dammit.

"They open at eleven," I said.

"I call it close enough," he said, putting tiny fists on the hips of his sky-blue slacks and explaining the whole thing again—in Spanglish this time.

The poor Latino dude finally let us in, then went back to warming up the fry-o-lator and slicing cucumbers.

"Why'd they kick you loose?" I said a minute later in a booth. We each had a cold root beer in front of us, and Donald was working on a bag of chips. They seemed to've calmed him some.

"They didn't tell me exactly," he said. "Don't have to tell you shit, so they don't. Hold a man twenty-two hours, serve him nothin' but nasty McDonald's, don't even have the decency to admit they know he didn't do what they been swearing he done for twenty-two motherfucking hours."

He sipped root beer. I kept my mouth shut, betting Donald Crump wasn't finished talking.

I won my bet.

"So they didn't tell me shit," he said. "But I been to my motel, and I believe I figured out a few things."

I said nothing some more.

"They tossed the room, of course," he said. "When I straightened 'er up, something come up missing." He smiled a challenge at me.

"A pair of boots," I said.

He slapped the table. "Good one, good one! You ain't so dumb. Way I got it figured, they thought they nailed me when they found boot prints my size. But when they went looking for the boots"—he made a big shrug—"no boots! Oh, they found two, three pairs in the same size, same brand—I favor Dan Post—but they must've been looking to match an exact print. And they couldn't. And I'm guessing when Lima took that to the DA, she made him cut me loose. Told him without those boots, he didn't have shit."

"So where are the boots?"

"Don't know."

I slapped the table. "Come on, Crump. We can help each other here. But not if you jerk me around."

He raised his hands. "Dead serious, Sax. My mouth to God's ear. My charcoal twelve-inch Dan Posts gone missing. Stolen, you ask me."

"You mean . . . come on, you're getting paranoid here."

Donald set finger to lips as the Latino dude lugged over a tray loaded with beef ribs, baby back ribs, dry Memphis-style ribs, wet Memphis-style ribs, sweet-potato fries, a half-pint of cucumber salad, and six Wet-Naps. Donald reached in his powder-blue Western-style jacket, pulled a wad, peeled off a fifty, and thanked the dude for his trouble, saying he truly did appreciate the extra effort.

"Paranoid?" he said after tucking in his brown-paper-towel bib. "Nah. I was set up. Who the cops gonna look at closer than an out-of-town negro with a chrome-yellow cowboy suit and a grudge?"

"Just for kicks, let's work that angle," I said. "Who'd want to set you up? You had twenty-two hours to think on it."

"Who had a beef with Gus Biletnikov?"

"Andrade," I said.

Donald's face told me he'd forgotten about him, or his name anyway.

"The guy who sold Gus the shitbox?" I said.

"You're cold."

"He's alibied up anyway. Cops were at his house twice that night."

"*Ice* cold, then. Who else?"

"The Pundos, Charlie and Teddy both. I bumped up against them while you were inside. I'll have to tell you about it."

"Some other time. For now, you're still cold. Who else?"

I finger-drummed the table.

"Give you a hint," Donald said, tossing another rib in his bone bucket. "I am an, uh, altitudinally challenged American."

"It's possible I noticed that."

"With hands and feet sized proportionally."

"Where the hell are you going with this?"

"Who had a beef with poor old Gus and could walk around in my boots?"

"*Nobody,*" I said. "Hell, a *girl* maybe."

"Ding ding ding," he said, popping a square of corn bread in his mouth.

Then it was quiet a long time.

"Come on," I finally said.

"Tear me off another yard of paper towel," Donald Crump said, "and listen up while I tell you about Rinn and Peter Biletnikov. And it ain't no accident I said her name first."

We left a half hour later. Donald cradled his belly like a newborn child, yammering about how rotten the food had been.

I wasn't really listening. Was putting pieces together instead. Or trying to.

It had been quite a download.

I didn't hear the voice at first. Then Donald tapped my arm and pointed.

"Conway?"

Huge guy, three hundred pounds easy. Blond mullet. His T-shirt said JEFF GORDON, with a faded cartoon of Gordon's race car stretched across the belly. Over the T-shirt, despite the day's warmth, he wore a faded blue flannel shirt, unbuttoned. In each hand he held a brown shopping bag full of takeout.

"Conway Sax," the big man said. "Now don't you dare say you don't remember me."

"Mensa Mulligan. You crewed for Ricky Craven when he was running Busch North." I introduced Donald, but he and Mensa ignored each other.

"Knew it was you," Mensa said. "Been ten years, easy. Where you been at?"

"Around. Got my own shop now. Mostly Japanese stuff. How about you?"

"Workin' on them ricer cars, huh? I get it. Pays the bills. I'm a tech up at Florio Jeep-Chrysler. When Craven got his Cup ride, the weasel dropped me like a bad habit." He squinted. "Tryin' to remember when's the last time I seen you race. Didn't you have a Busch ride?"

"I had a cup of coffee, yeah." I shifted on my feet. I looked at my watch.

Mensa snapped his fingers. "Hell yes! You had a primo ride. Won some races, am I right? Yeah you fuckin'-A did, pardon my French. Your ass had Cup wrote all over it. Then you disappeared."

"Your takeout's getting cold, Mensa, and I need to split. You see any of the old boys, you say hi for me, okay?"

He looked half-pissed, half-puzzled as he made for a Jeep Commander with a COURTESY VEHICLE sticker on its rear window.

"Hot diggity damn," Donald said. "You used to drive race cars, you cracker? You got to translate that conversation for me. What's bush? What's cup?"

"You kidding me? Where you're from, it's hard to *not* know at least a little about racing."

"I take all necessary steps to avoid that cracker shit."

" 'Cup' used to be Winston Cup. Now it's Sprint Cup, the NASCAR you see on TV. Busch Grand National, *B-U-S-C-H,* like the beer, has a new name too. It's one rung down the ladder. Think of triple-A baseball."

"Were you on TV?"

"Sure."

"How fast did you go?"

"We ran one-eighty-five at Daytona."

"Were you scared?"

"Not in the car."

"Crash much?"

"I crashed about the right amount."

I saw the question in his eyes.

"You can drive around in circles and cash paychecks," I said. "Or you can push hard and wreck once in a while."

"And you weren't about drivin' in circles."

I shrugged.

"Did you make it to the big leagues, the Whatchamacallit Cup?"

"I drank myself out of a ride."

"This is *interesting,* Sax. Side of you I didn't see coming. But I do believe you'd rather be talking about anything else."

"It was a long time ago. And I need to get to Sherborn."

"Your redneck buddy there, Mensa, made it sound like you dropped out hard and fast."

"I walked away from a good ride in the middle of the season."

"Why was that?"

"Team owner heard I was drinking before I climbed in the car. I walked before he made me run."

Long pause. "You were driving drunk. At a buck-eighty-five."

"I need to *go*, Donald."

"One last question. Your buddy didn't look like no Einstein. He called Mensa because he's some kinda weird genius, what they call a savant?"

"No. He was the stupidest guy anybody knew. Too stupid to know his nickname was an insult."

"Who made up the nickname?"

"I did."

"You proud of that?"

I climbed in my truck and drove east.

CHAPTER TWENTY-TWO

Read a text from Randall while I traffic-thumped toward the Biletnikov house:

> *Holmes: Have arrived solo at scene of crime in selfless bid to comfort mourning stepmom. No sacrifice too great. Yr hmbl & obt & etc Watson*

I shook my head. In spite of everything Donald had told me, which had my head spinning, I guess I smiled.

I parked behind Randall's Hyundai. The main door of the guesthouse was open, and I heard their voices. So I opened the screen door . . .

. . . and barged in on a three-alarm flirting session.

Giggles. Arm touching. Big-eye making.

Spare me.

"Fix yourself a drink," Rinn said without looking my way.

I waved off the drink and sat across the room from the pair of them. She was sunk deep in an armchair. He was as close as he could get to her in a sofa that ninetied up to the chair. His left knee kept bumping her right.

I said, "When's the funeral?"

It hushed them up.

"Tomorrow at ten," Rinn said, shooting eye lasers at me for killing the vibe. "Pilgrim Church, right up the road. Randall says your AA friends . . . Barnburners, was it? . . . will make their presence felt. They're welcome, of course."

"Peter okay with that?"

"*I'm* okay with it," she said. I'd gotten to her—her eyes flashed. But only for half a tenth of a second. She was good.

"Yeah," I said, "and what's okay by you is okay by Peter. Or else. So I hear, anyway."

"For crying out loud," Randall said.

"What exactly do you hear?" Rinn said.

"I hear you lead him around like a baby goat on a very short strap," I said.

And stared at her feet, picturing them in Donald Crump's boots.

"Conway, old chum," Randall said. "A moment outside?"

I ignored him, locked eyes with Rinn. "I hear you won a bet. Tell me I'm wrong. Or tell Randall about the bet."

She said nothing. But her eyes went angry again, and this time they stayed there.

Push. Don't let her off the hook.

"Show Randall the matching Harleys," I said. "The matching BMWs."

"What's he talking about?" Randall said.

Rinn said nothing for a long while.

Then she set elbows on knees, buried her face in her palms, and began to cry.

Soon enough, the tears turned real.

Rinn sobbed something into her hands.

"What?" Randall said, popping up and grabbing a Kleenex box from the kitchen table.

"Everybody hates the trophy wife," Rinn said.

No *mercy. Push push push.*

"Tell him," I said.

"'I am your spaniel,'" she said, addressing Randall. "'And the more you beat me, I will fawn on you. Use me but as your spaniel. Spurn me, strike me, neglect me, lose me.'"

I said, *"What?"*

Randall said, "'What worser place can I beg in your love, and yet a place of high respect with me, than to be used as you use your dog?'"

I said, "What the *hell?"*

"A Midsummer Night's Dream," Rinn said.

"Jesus Christ," I said.

"No," Randall said, "Helena. To Demetrius."

They made big eyes at each other.

"I'm guessing you're not Helena," Randall said to Rinn.

"Of course not. Peter was Helena. Is." She put her chin on her fist and leaned toward Randall. I might as well have been in the neighbor's yard. "He was supposed to be a big visionary, but the first thing he ever did that I knew of was rip off a bullet list from my job application." She explained what she'd told me already—that Thunder Junction's perfectly timed shift to green tech was her idea.

"So you knew he was a poser from the get-go," he said. "That's a bad place to start as far as respect is concerned."

Rinn nodded. "When we became a couple, I turned cruel."

"I find that difficult to believe," Randall said.

I found it difficult not to barf. But kept my mouth shut.

"I began putting Peter through torture tests," she said. "Spurnings and strikings."

"Like what?"

"Okay, here's one. I'd drag him to these dive bars, then flirt like mad with the biggest jock I could find. If Peter ignored the flirting, I'd berate him for letting his girlfriend get hit on in the Chicken Bone Saloon. But if he stood up for me, I'd call him a jealous prick and sic the jock on him."

"Oh."

The story had cooled Randall some, I saw.

Rinn saw it, too. "That wasn't *me,* I swear to you." She took his hand in both of hers. "It was a strange, confusing time. I was seeing a man twice my age. Things were getting serious. And there were . . . other factors."

I put a thumb to the side of my nose and made a huge, exaggerated sniff.

"You're such a jerk," Rinn said.

"I see," Randall said.

"And Peter was buying," I said. "For the three of them. Open bar, an all-you-can-snort buffet."

"You're *such* a jerk," Rinn said.

"The bet," I said.

"I *would* like to hear about that," Randall said.

It was quiet maybe twenty seconds.

"Around this time," Rinn finally said, "I was getting to know Gus."

"And Donald Crump," I said. Saw Randall's puzzled look. "He came on the scene around the time Peter and Rinn started dating. Made himself very chummy. Always looking for an angle, like any self-respecting con man." I glanced at Rinn. "I got that right?"

She waved an impatient hand. "That little . . . yes, you've got it right, but Donald's not important to the story. To *this* story. Which you've succeeded in prizing from me, so I'd appreciate it if you'd shut up while I tell it."

Fair enough.

"Peter introduced me to Gus, of course. He was a sweetheart, and so was his best friend, Brad. We became quite a trio. I spent nearly every weekend at UMass. Sometimes with Peter, but usually without."

"Did those trips have anything to do with this?" Randall said, and touched his nostril the way I had mine.

"Of course," she said. "It was a wild year, a whirlwind. But it wasn't all about the drugs. We had a Three Musketeers scene going. It was genuinely fun. It was sweet."

Then she stared past him long enough so that Randall said, "But."

"Yes, but. Or *until*, actually. Gus didn't have a lot of affection or respect for his father. The three of us used to amuse ourselves, in callow fashion, I concede, by talking about what a fool Peter was. We had a ball congratulating ourselves on how we were using the squaresville sugar daddy. It sounds awful when I say it out loud, I know. Anyway, we used to dream up spurnings and strikings. The idea was to see how far I could push Peter before he pushed back."

"What was the bet?"

"For a hoot, Brad, Gus, and I went on an honest-to-God hayride one weekend. I think a sorority put it together. The hayride ended up at a square dance in a barn, and all the local couples were dressed in matching clothes. It was the funniest damn thing we ever saw."

Rinn forced a laugh, looked around to see if it caught.

It didn't.

"You know, the way those chubby Midwestern cruise-ship couples wear identical Hawaiian shirts. It was so . . . Walmart!" She tried again with the laugh.

"I know what you're talking about," I said. "Not my style, but I think it's kind of nice."

"Of course you do."

"It's almost like the couples care more about each other than about what some douche-bag college kid thinks."

She skated past that, but her face went red. "Gus and Brad made me a bet right there. My assignment was to go all-in on the matching shtick with Peter. We knew it would horrify him and his BSO/MFA crowd. But would he put up with it? For li'l ole me?"

Randall read the question in my eyes. "Boston Symphony Orchestra. Museum of Fine Arts."

"The finish line," Rinn said, "or the money shot, as charming

Brad called it, was a square dance in the same barn two months later. To win the bet, I had to bring Peter and do-si-do all night in matching duds."

Whatever else came out of this meeting, one thing was for sure: Randall was taking a hell of a fresh look at Rinn Biletnikov. "And you . . . *did* this?" he said. "You put thought and energy into this endeavor?" He probably didn't realize it, but as he spoke he reached down and rubbed his prosthesis.

"Damn you," Rinn said to me.

CHAPTER TWENTY-THREE

They started with identical running outfits in a five K," I said, speaking to Randall but locking eyes with Rinn. "Then she walked him up the ladder. His-and-hers cowboy hats, matching Harleys, identical cars. Like that."

"Who told you all this?" Rinn said. "Donald or Brad?"

I said nothing.

"For what it's worth," she said to Randall and only Randall, freezing me out again, "I'm not proud of that period. I'm ashamed, in fact. A lot of history led up to it."

"I'm listening," he said.

Rinn looked at her lap, pulling her story together.

"There are many nice things about dating older guys, as I always have," she said. "Money is the obvious one. In high school, my girlfriends were lucky if their boyfriends paid for their Burger King. I was eating at L'Espalier and finding diamond earrings on the dessert cart. An older man fortunate enough to get in a young girl's pants will do anything to stay there. *Anything.*"

"Spurnings," Randall said. "Strikings."

She nodded. "But there are downsides, too. Think about the older men a girl meets. Coaches, teachers, family friends. Taboos, taboos, everywhere you look. I lost my virginity when I was fifteen, to my across-the-street neighbor. My parents had known the family forever. My first home wrecked, my first shrink sessions."

I said, "He in jail now? I hope?"

"You're missing the point, as they all did. I'd had a massive crush on Mr. Freed forever. *I* seduced *him,* and believe me, he played hard to get. But my parents and the police couldn't accept that. Even the shrink kept trying to turn things around. Eventually, I gave up explaining."

Randall said, "Can we skip from Mr. Freed to Peter?"

"It's a long way to Tipperary," she said. "I want you to have the whole picture. There are also certain . . . physical disadvantages to seeing older men. They are not, generally speaking, stallions. Sorry about the icky background. I'm trying to establish that where tending to older gentlemen is involved, I'm something of an authority."

"So?" Randall said.

But something had clicked for me. "Peter Biletnikov couldn't get it up. Can't." I said it as much to myself as to them.

They looked at me.

Randall said, "You serious?"

At the exact same time, Rinn said, "How did you know?"

I shrugged. "Everything about him points that way. He's all front, all shell."

Rinn said, "That's an impressive intuitive leap."

"For you," Randall said.

I tried not to smile, looked at Rinn. "Keep going."

"Peter was, shall we say, unable."

"Even in this age of chemical miracles?" Randall said.

Rinn snorted, waved a hand. "Viagra, Cialis, Levitra. Hypnotists, fortune tellers, oysters, powdered stag antler, eye of newt, something flown up from Mexico that gave him hives. You name it, we tried it. Colossal failures all. This turned out to be a lifelong issue for Peter. The problem was up here"—tap tap—"not down there."

"Bummer for you." Randall said it with soft eyes.

Rinn smiled and shrugged. "I was encouraging and helpful and understanding. At first, anyway. Peter grew angrier and angrier, frustrated, mean as a snake. He lashed out, tried to blame me." Her eyes hardened. "I set him straight on that."

"Dumb-guy question," I said. "If this was a long-term deal, where'd Gus come from?"

"Not to mention Emma?" Randall said.

"Even a stopped cock is right twice a day," Rinn said, then looked around for laughter that wasn't there.

I said, "You met Peter when you interned at Thunder Junction, right? I'm surprised he was interested. Given what you've said."

"Peter had a long tradition of using interns as beards." Rinn half-laughed. "Heterosexual beards, to make the other dudes think he was a hound dog just like them."

"Dudes still think that way?" Randall said.

"Empty ones," I said. "Ones who're all shell."

"For us it was different," Rinn said. "With the others, the arm candy, Peter hadn't dared broach the impotency topic. I don't know if he fell for me or what—"

"He fell for you," Randall said. "Trust me."

I rolled my eyes.

Rinn ignored Randall and plowed ahead. "From the start, he said I was the one, that he wanted to have kids with me. I think he believed I could . . . cure him. The promise of a family was part of his sales pitch. He assumed I wanted kids, just as he assumed I wanted a big white-dress wedding."

"Was he right?" Randall said. "Did you want either of those things?"

Rinn started to speak.

Then stopped. Stared at nothing.

Randall let the silence grow. I followed his lead.

Rinn finally said, "Am I allowed to pass on the question? To say I'm not sure *what* I want? May I plead youthful indecision?"

"I do believe I'm younger than you," Randall said.

"You don't seem it. And that's a compliment."

Randall smiled. "I'll rephrase. Was it reasonable for Peter to *believe* you wanted the big wedding? The big family? The big house in Sherborn, the slightly smaller one in Chatham?"

"It was indeed reasonable. I let him believe I was just dying to have two or three wailing, puking, shitting joy-bundles."

"Why?"

"He wasn't the only one doing a sell job. Peter is an empty suit who stumbled into a pot of money. He's a copycat in an industry that's about vision. When he dumped his first wife and married me, he was imitating a thousand other fiftysomething business swamis. Pumping out a baby or two with the trophy wife is part of the pose."

"Wailing, puking, shitting," I said. "That's how you think of your daughter?" Tried to keep the disgust out of my voice. But failed.

"I love her!" Rinn said.

Randall and I said nothing.

"I *love* her," Rinn said.

Randall and I said nothing.

"I . . . oh God, I can't believe I'm going to say this out loud. Conceptually, I love her. But in detail, in the day-to-day . . ."

"The wailing, puking, shitting day-to-day," Randall said.

Rinn nodded. She looked at nothing. She especially did not look at me.

"Let's get back on point," Randall finally said. "The more I hear about Peter, the more I want to hate him. But if you look at it from his point of view, it took a twisted brand of courage to make his move on you. To open up."

"I'm not unaware of it," Rinn said. "He wanted something badly enough to risk a lot."

"He risked ridicule," Randall said. "Which I gather is something he greatly fears."

"More than anything."

"And you proceeded to heap ridicule on him. Spurnings and strikings and matching cowboy duds."

"I said I'm not proud of it."

Randall said nothing. He rose.

So did I. And then looked at what I held in my hand. Had forgotten about it.

My gaze drew Rinn's, and hers drew Randall's, and then it was too late for me to stash it behind my back. So I held it out.

"*Goodnight Moon,*" Rinn read.

"I, ah," I said. "It's a good book. For babies. For little kids. For Emma."

She took it. Set it on an end table without really looking at it. "How sweet."

Randall and I left.

"She wouldn't have looked much different if I'd handed her a steaming dog turd," I said in the driveway, not looking at Randall as I spoke because we both assumed she was watching.

"She's probably not going to make Mother of the Year," he said. But seemed reluctant to admit even that much.

"I told you she was a piece of work."

"Which doesn't make her a murderer. Especially up close and personal with a shotgun. Can you picture it?"

I took my time answering. "I've seen a lot of things I couldn't picture before I saw them."

"Fair enough."

"So have you."

"That's different," he said. "War . . . it's different."

There wasn't much I could say to that. He'd been there. I hadn't.

So we stood quiet awhile.

"What's your take on Rinn?" I finally said. "Anything jump out?"

"Her lack of connection to the baby, her disdain for Peter, they're . . . *palpable*."

"Spurnings and strikings."

He nodded. "And the running around with Gus and Brad. I hate to admit it, but now you've got *me* wondering if she had anything to do with the murder. There's something worth teasing out here."

"So tease it out."

"What do you mean?"

"Make yourself Rinn's best new pal. Charm her. Tell her about the time you jumped on that grenade. In that foxhole."

"To save those nuns," he said.

"And orphans. Meanwhile, I'll talk to Brad again, see if I can learn more about Gus's relationship with his dad. And I need to figure out where Lima's headed with this thing. I should talk to Peter, too. I need a better handle on him."

"That all you've got planned? Easy peasy," Randall said, and I heard his smile, though I still wasn't looking at him. "What about your good friend Charlie Pundo? Aren't you worried he'll take another run at you?"

"Worried? No. Dead sure? Yes." I shrugged. "We'll cross that bridge."

"Anything I can do, amigo? Besides the arduous duty of making myself available to Rinn?"

"Yeah," I said, heel-rubbing my eyes. "Make sure Charlene doesn't kill me while I'm screwing around with this."

CHAPTER TWENTY-FOUR

Guilt drove me to the shop to see how things were going.

They weren't going well. I found Andrade parked in the office, one-handing the computer. He said he was learning our software, but his fast mouse click when he saw me looked like a telltale for solitaire. Or porn surfing.

Floriano was working on two cars at once and trying to handle late drop-offs at the same time.

I really wanted to visit Brad Bloomquist again.

"Hell," I said.

If Floriano heard, he didn't respond.

I sighed, grabbed my coveralls, stepped into the flow.

Spent the rest of the day doing boring maintenance on boring cars. Thought about Rinn Biletnikov, Donald Crump, Brad Bloomquist. Especially Brad. Something about his story didn't click. I waited for it to come to me.

It didn't.

What did come to me: flashes of Gus. The banister slide into his very first Barnburners meeting. His hero worship when I beat up Andrade. His hidden nervousness about speaking in AA, followed by the smooth talk itself.

The way he tabletopped his dirt-bike jumps, like he was born to do it.

The way he looked like Roy: slender, big brown eyes, uncombed hair, that unfinished look to his features.

The way he looked gut-shot in a sweatshirt, his back arched, one hand clutched delicately like he was holding an imaginary piece of chalk.

The way I'd walked out on Roy. The way I'd tossed Gus down a flight of cast-iron stairs.

These flashes would come, and I would feel so . . . heavy. Like I needed to sit right away. But if I sat, I'd want to lie down. And if I did that, I'd want to sink through the floor.

I worked slow that day.

At five thirty, we all drove to Marlborough for Andrade's tools. Three wide on my F-250's bench seat. Nobody said a word. When Floriano saw Andrade's immaculate shop, he made a tight little nod, and I knew he understood why I'd hired a new guy with one good arm.

You can't lift a loaded rolling tool chest. We had to empty every drawer by hand, and even then Floriano and I could barely wrestle the piano-sized chest into the back of my truck. By the time we got everything to my shop, unloaded, and squared away, it seemed like I should take the guys to dinner. And then we had to wait twenty-five minutes for a table at T.G.I. Friday's. And still none of us said much of anything.

Long day.

"No man should have to do this," I said to Peter Biletnikov the next morning, extending my hand. I had made my way up front, to the pews reserved for family.

He stared at the hand until I pulled it back. Then he turned and put his arm around Rinn, who stiffened but let him leave it there.

I walked to the back, wanting to serve as an informal usher when the Barnburners rolled in.

It was a small church, but pristine. The paint was fresh, the blue carpeting was new, all the Bibles matched—it was what you'd expect in a town like Sherborn.

Those reserved pews weren't anywhere near full. It was just Peter, Rinn, Haley holding the baby, and a pair of great-aunts who looked just off the Trans-Siberian Express. Everybody wore black. Nobody spoke.

Even at two minutes of ten, the joint was nearly empty. Maybe the Barnburners had stiffed Gus—hell, they barely knew him.

The preacher, a woman who didn't look much older than Gus, spoke quietly in a corner with a man who must have worked there. Brad Bloomquist sat in a back pew, as far from the Biletnikovs as he could manage. He was the only one who'd arrived before me. His suit was neat enough, and he'd trimmed his beard.

And he was crying. Silently, steadily. Bolt upright, hands between his legs, making no effort to wipe the tears that rolled into his beard and eventually dripped from it.

The organist started up.

I checked my watch. One minute past.

Gus Biletnikov would go out in an empty church, with a eulogy from a preacher who likely never met him.

Hell.

Then I heard a twenty-one-gun salute of car doors.

It could only be the Barnburners. Drunks always meet at a Dunkin' Donuts, and they always pile in five to a car. It's where the best conversations take place. The best therapy, the best confessions. The best AA.

I opened the church doors.

Mary Giarusso was first, decked out in 1961 clothes all the way up to a velvet pillbox hat. She touched my arm. "We got lost," she whispered. "Chester said he knew where it was, and everybody followed."

"Chester can't find his ass in a telephone booth," I said.

"That's what *I* said."

The organist noticed the open doors and played filler to kill time.

The musical vibe changed somehow—the organist seemed as relieved as I was that some warm bodies had showed.

In poured the Barnburners: nearly two dozen of them, ones I knew and ones I ought to. Chester Bagley, his wig a full inch off to one side, explaining to some kid how he hadn't *really* been lost. Carlos Q, a man who refused to speak to anybody without a year of sobriety—but would empty his wallet and his pantry for anybody with one. Charlene slipped in, and Sophie, too, looking grown-up in a midnight-blue dress. Then came Butch Feeley, a retired cop, the closest thing there was to a leader of the Barnburners.

The Brazilian gal who almost never talked but spoke better English than me when she did; the biker with a cobweb tattoo who'd slipped me a free raffle ticket at my first meeting; a bunch of old ones, a few young ones. Bringing up the rear, helped up the church steps by a heavy gal in a muumuu, was my pal Eudora Spoon. We go back.

I kissed her cheek. It was like kissing a moth's wing. She was eighty, or close to it. Her buzz-cut hair was whiter and stiffer than ever.

"Thanks for coming," I said.

"Never met the young man," Eudora said. "Those who did meet him didn't much like him. They said he was oleaginous. I came for you, Conway. We all did."

"I know."

She was scanning the front of the church, and I knew why. "Don't worry," I said, "no casket in here. Burial's out in the cemetery after. Family only."

"Thank God." Eudora patted my arm, and she and her helper found seats. She'd had some kind of scare when she was a little kid—an open-casket funeral where the mortician did a hack job. It'd left a scar eight decades long.

The service was lousy. It wasn't the preacher's fault: you could tell that not only had she not known Gus, she probably hadn't met Peter and Rinn more than a couple of times. So the talk was all generic, about a life too short and making amends and bearing up after loss.

Near the end, when she'd said her own say and led the prayers and most of the hymns, the preacher invited people to stand and share memories of Gus.

She blew it there, misreading the crowd.

The church went quiet.

Nobody spoke. Nobody raised a hand.

The silence grew long, then embarrassing.

From the corner of my eye, I could see Brad Bloomquist. I hoped he would rise and speak. In my head I begged him to, *willed* him to.

He didn't.

Neither did Rinn.

Neither did anybody else.

The silence became awful.

I sighed.

I stood.

I cleared my throat.

"He was a hell of a dirt-bike rider," I said.

They all turned and looked.

"What I mean," I said. "What I mean, he could *do* things. That thing, anyway. A kid his age, from a town like this, that's easy to skim over. Nobody *does* anything anymore. Kids especially."

Peter Biletnikov was trying to burn a hole in me with his eyes. Most everybody else was staring like I had a snake in my sport-coat pocket.

But a few—Carlos Q, the cobweb-tat dude, a few others—were nodding. The nods fueled me to push ahead.

"I got him out on a Yamaha one day," I said. "He hadn't ridden for years, but he could tabletop a jump like nothing. When he was a kid, he wanted to be a motocross pro. Hacked out a little track in his backyard and everything. I believe he could've made the big time." I locked eyes with Peter, watched his cheeks go extra red. Screw him. "With a little encouragement."

There was more in my head. More about kids in nice towns who never *did* anything. There were no paper routes anymore. Kids didn't shovel snow from driveways or fix bicycles or comb the dump for treasure or build tree houses. They never got a chance to show they *could* do anything except work a cell phone and a credit card.

But the words wouldn't form up, wouldn't organize themselves. Which was typical for me.

I sat.

The preacher had learned her lesson: she didn't ask for more volunteers. Went straight to the final prayer instead.

When the organ started up and most people rose, flipping through hymnals, Peter Biletnikov began to moan. It came from nowhere. He doubled over. He cried loudly. He raked his face with his hands. Rinn took one shot at comforting him, but it wasn't much of a shot. She looked at Haley next to her, and I was pretty sure she rolled her eyes.

The hymn chugged along, with the preacher and not many others singing. Peter built a head of steam, putting on a show for all the Barnburners who'd never seen him before and never would again. "No, no, *no!*" Screeching it, raking the cheeks, shaking like somebody'd wired him to a battery.

As the hymn ended, the preacher closed her hymnal, glided down to Peter, and dropped to a knee. She tried to comfort him with words nobody else could hear. The organist stutter-stepped, then rolled into a tune that apparently excused us. Only the preacher and the family stayed: Peter blubbering and howling, Rinn cold-shouldering him, Haley bouncing the baby, Trans-Siberian aunts crossing themselves over and over.

I held the door again, wanting to be last one out.

"Quite a show," Eudora said. Deadpan.

Carlos Q squeezed my arm. "I liked what you said."

"There was more, but . . ." I shrugged.

"Was good. What you said. Was enough."

"And the Oscar goes to," Charlene said, tossing her head in Peter's direction.

I said nothing. Wasn't ready to make fun of a man who'd lost a son. There're plenty of ways to grieve. What had Lima said in Bilet-nikov's backyard? *Everybody does it his own way.*

As he slipped past, the last Barnburner to leave, Butch Feeley caught my eye. "Parking lot. Meeting After the Meeting."

I raised eyebrows in surprise, but nodded I'd be there. Was about to let the door close when I scanned the church one last time.

Brad Bloomquist still sat.

As I approached, I saw his tears had slowed not one bit. They rolled: eyes to beard, beard tip to lap. The lower third of his necktie, his shirt, and the front of his pants were all soaked.

I sat next to him.

I didn't know what to do.

I took his hand in both of mine.

He left it there.

We sat.

We watched the preacher and the church worker herd the Bilet-nikovs through a door.

Brad watched them leave like a puppy watching his new owner close the basement door for the night. "They wouldn't let me go to the burial," he said. "I asked Rinn. She asked Peter. Peter deliberated long and hard before opining that I should go fuck myself."

"Family only is what I heard."

He looked at me. "Did anybody ever tell you you're not too quick on the uptake?"

Every goddamn day, pal.

I didn't say it. Hell, between the beard and the tears and the sad smile in his voice, I didn't even get mad.

"Gus wasn't just my roomie," Brad Bloomquist said, "and he wasn't just my partner in crime. He was my love."

I said nothing.

"My first love."

CHAPTER TWENTY-FIVE

I'm easy to fool. I don't notice things.

Charlene, Randall, and Sophie make fun of me. "Gaydar," Sophie calls it. I don't have it. Randall says I'm one thick SOB, but Sophie and Charlene say I'm sweet. "Everything *you* have, everything *you* offer the world, is right there, front and center," Charlene had said one night while we watched a TV show about singing teenagers. "You're subtle as a motorcycle chain. And that's nice. But you expect everybody else to be the same way. You get snookered over and over. And will forever."

I said nothing. Watched teenagers tap-dance and sing their way up a subway escalator.

"Jazz hands!" Sophie said.

"Shut up," I'd said that night.

Now the church worker opened the door he'd just led Gus's family through, spotted Brad and me, frowned like he wished we'd leave, and closed the door.

"Tell me," I said.

"I'm surprised Rinn didn't bend your ear already. The little twat never could keep her mouth shut, not to mention her legs."

"You and Gus, that's your business. What I want is anything that'll help me find out who killed him. That's my job."

"Your *job*? Your *job* is grease monkey. You knew Gus what, a few months? I knew him five *years*." Brad spoke in a harsh whisper, knowing he sat in a church, not liking his own direction but unable to turn back. "Were you fucking him?"

"No."

"What's your interest then?"

"I told you before. I was showing him the ropes in AA." Explaining it again pulled me back to Brad's apartment, and that lit off a recollection: when I'd told him cops always suspected the boyfriend or girlfriend, it'd thrown him for a loop because he *was* the boyfriend. I'd been too thick to make the connection.

He took his hand from mine, made a tell-me-more gesture. "And?" Stretching the word.

"And he got killed."

"Simple as that."

"Simple as that."

"Bullshit. There's more."

Long pause.

"I threw him out," I said.

Brad said nothing.

"He reminded me of my son. I never did right by my son. Ditched him when he was a baby."

We sat. To our left, the sun was working its way around the building. Stained-glass windows hummed with the light. They were something to see.

Brad pulled tissue from the back of the pew in front of us. He winced. His fingertips were peeling. He saw me looking at them. "Heat gun," he said. "A leather crafter's best friend. And mortal enemy." He blew his nose, wiped his eyes. "I'm sorry about what I said."

"Cops know about you and Gus?"

"Of course. Detective Lima saw right through me."

"So he probably asked where you were the night Gus got killed."

He nodded. "And the night of the Almost Home shootings."

"What did you tell him?"

"Without even consulting my ultra-busy social calendar, I could tell him precisely where I was both evenings. Sitting in front of the TV, high as a kite, waiting for customers to call or knock. It sounds so depressing, doesn't it? And it is. Of course, he didn't take my word for it. I had to dish up a few client names, and I signed a release allowing Lima to look at my phone records without a search warrant."

Behind us, the front door opened. I didn't bother to turn—figured it was the church worker again, trying to nudge us out so he could police up the joint. Well, he could wait: I was shuffling thoughts and memories, and I was getting somewhere.

Even with Brad and Gus factored in as a couple, something wasn't right. I felt like I was just starting to tighten a small bolt that was cross-threaded. With enough experience, you learn to feel it before wrecking the bolt.

I shuffled through things Brad had told me, things I knew about him.

Click.

"You're from somewhere on the Cape," I said.

"Yes?"

"Got family down there?"

"Four generations of Bloomquists have called Brewster home. Not one of them amounted to anything, but that's another story."

"To me," I said, thinking it through as I spoke, "the Cape seems like a sweet place to live if you work with leather and deal weed . . ."

"And are queer as a two-headed quarter."

"I didn't say that."

"You didn't have to. What *are* you saying?"

"If I was queer as a two-headed quarter, worked with leather, and dealt weed on the side, I wouldn't be in a hurry to leave the Cape for a dumpy apartment in Framingham. Boston, maybe. But *Framingham*? In a complex full of secretaries and divorced dads?"

Brad's eyes had gone hard. I looked at him. He looked straight ahead.

I said, "How long did you say you've been here?"

He said nothing.

"The phone company doesn't have a number listed for your landline yet. You must be pretty new."

He said nothing.

"Did you move up here around the time Gus got out of rehab?"

Nothing.

"You did, didn't you? You moved to the next town over from Sherborn."

I felt, rather than heard, someone behind us. I ignored the presence.

"You say Gus was your first love," I said. "Hell, you probably believe it. But is there any chance Gus thought of *you* as a reminder of a bad time? As a stalker?"

Then Brad Bloomquist got very, very lucky.

A hand fell on my shoulder.

I whirled, ready to make the pushy church worker regret touching me.

But it wasn't the church worker.

It was Butch Feeley.

"Everybody's waiting," he said.

Brad scuttled out the door.

Most of the Barnburners had left. The remaining half dozen gathered around a pair of picnic tables just behind the parking lot.

This was the Meeting After the Meeting crowd. The ones who saved my life.

A long time ago, after more tries than you could count, I finally put together some sobriety. A couple of months, my longest dry stretch since I was fourteen.

It was awful. I didn't know what I was doing. My knuckles were white, my teeth were ground to nubs, my nightmares lasted all day.

It was slipping away, and I knew it. I was feeling shame already over the next backslide. Had a feeling it would be the last one, the one that carried me all the way down.

And then I stumbled into a Barnburners meeting.

They were different. You saw it the minute you stepped into the basement at Saint Anne's. The old-timers arranged fifteen or so chairs jury-style, so they could watch the speaker at the podium and keep an eye on the crowd, too. Anybody who spoke or laughed or sneaked out for a smoke earned a dirty look or a little talking-to. I learned that night the Barnburners' watchword was "serious AA for serious people."

Soon enough, I would learn more. The Barnburners were born after World War II of a bizarre wreck between AA, which was new at the time, and a vigilante biker group—combat veterans who trusted nobody but fellow dogfaces and took a blood oath to watch each other's backs.

Barnburners take care of Barnburners. And the small Meeting After the Meeting crowd runs the show.

Working your way into the Meeting After the Meeting takes patience. You need to show up at Saint Anne's for every single meeting, keep your mouth shut, and do as you're told.

You also have to have skills that'll be useful to the group.

When I found the Barnburners, I'd spent the better part of a decade as a full-tilt bum. Hobo jungles, county lockups, bars, barges, underpasses, a grate in the Bowery.

Like that.

You want to survive that way, you learn skills.

Ugly skills.

Skills that come in handy.

The night Butch Feeley told me to stick around for the Meeting After the Meeting was and is the best night of my life. My silent vow: I would do anything this crowd asked me to.

And I do.

And I take the weight that comes with it.

Mary Giarusso—Switchboard Mary, gossip queen, organizer of events, keeper of the telephone tree—patted the bench next to her.

I sat, listened to my friends wrap up some new business. A Barn-burner needed babysitting help or she'd have to quit her job to get her kids off the school bus. The job was keeping her sane. If she quit, she'd spiral downhill, would be using again before you knew it.

A ninety-two-year-old Barnburner who got confused easily had been ripped off by gypsy roofers. They'd squeezed him for eight thousand that he knew of, maybe more.

"Keeps it in a focking cigar box," Carlos Q said. "I'll take that one. Kick the shit out of these gypsies, then talk that fool into get-ting a savings account."

"Isn't that one more up my alley?" I said.

Most everybody looked at their hands or the picnic tables before them while Butch Feeley slipped Carlos Q a picture of the roofers' license plate.

"What?" I said, picking up the vibe. They'd talked about me before I joined them. It was obvious.

Butch cleared his throat. "Whyn't you sit this one out, Conway? Looks like your plate's pretty full as it stands."

I felt redness crawl up my neck. "I can handle both."

"Don't look to me like you can handle neither," Carlos Q said, eye-locking me. "They putting one of yours in the ground right now."

Full-bore red face now. I felt the heat of it.

"I," I said.

And looked around. A few of the newer ones, maybe ones who

were scared of me, were interested as hell in the picnic table. But most of them were staring at me.

A jury of my peers.

"I," I said again.

But couldn't think of anything else to say.

The Barnburners. The Meeting After the Meeting. Serious AA for serious people. Talk meant shit. Results meant everything.

I stood.

I walked to my truck.

Climbed in.

Drove away.

Felt Barnburner eyes on my back the whole time.

"Uniform and cruiser?" I said, crouching to set my face at passenger-window level. "Don't tell me you got busted back to trooper."

"Get in," Lima said.

I did, but passed him a coffee first. It seemed to surprise him. He set the coffee on the dashboard, leaned over the huge center console they cram in those police Crown Vics, and moved junk to make room for me.

"Busy times like these, they let detectives earn time and a half on details," he said. "But you got to wear the uniform. Public don't like guys in ties sitting in cruisers."

I knew what Lima meant by busy times even before he gestured with his coffee: the Boston Marathon had been run less than two weeks before. On the phone he'd told me to find him in Ashland Center, where he silently strobed his blue lights while a work crew broke down the course. They were picking up orange and white barrels, power-washing mile and kilometer markers from the road, hauling out Porta-Johns. Like that.

"I always get out of Dodge the weekend of the marathon," I said.

"For me, it's a good weekend to earn four weeks' pay."

"Amen." I toasted with my own coffee.

We sat awhile watching a man in a Boston Athletic Association Windbreaker argue with a lady in an Ashland Public Works Windbreaker.

"You're wondering where we're at," Lima finally said. "With the Biletnikov thing."

"Yes."

"Why should I tell you?"

"Because I remembered you take a large black."

"Do better."

"How about this? You think Crump killed Gus Biletnikov. It looks obvious to you. The boots, the grudge against Peter Biletnikov, all that. But the DA won't buy in. He prosecutes lead-pipe cinches only. It makes for pretty stats. When you couldn't get an exact match between Crump's boot and the print in the moss, the DA said cut him loose."

"Which is fucking re*tard*ed, because how definitive a match can you expect from something as springy as moss? Keep going." He sipped. "By the way, the DA's a she."

"I don't think Crump did it."

"Because you like him. Because he's charming. Smarten up, Sax. He's a con man. Charming and likable, that's his *job*."

"Nah, it's more than that. You must've looked hard at Crump's record. He ever do anything even a little bit violent?"

From Lima's silence, I knew the answer was no.

"The funeral was this morning," I said. "I talked with Brad Bloomquist. Turns out he and Gus were an item."

"No shit, Sherlock."

"Yeah, he told me you figured it out pretty quick. How'd you find Bloomquist, anyway?"

"We did cop work. You didn't know they were an item?"

Jazz hands.

I didn't say it out loud. Instead, I said, "You must've taken a hard look at him. He said he gave you phone records. Is he alibied up?"

"Hard to make a definitive call with phone records. But on the Almost Home night and the Gus night, *somebody* answered a bunch of calls in Bloomquist's apartment. The callers say it was Bloomquist."

"Stoners making thirty-second phone calls," I said. "Probably using dumb-ass weed-dealer code, like 'I need half a cruller.' I was you, I'd want something better than that."

"Pound sand, Sax. Put the calls together with the boots. You see the size of Bloomquist's *feet,* for crying out loud? It doesn't work."

But he sounded like he was trying to sell himself.

So maybe I could sell him another idea if I kept working at it.

Good to know.

Across the street, a forklift tried to lift a pair of Porta-Johns on pallets. One of the green plastic toilets was off-center. It rose three feet and fell from its pallet. The man in the BAA Windbreaker threw his hands up.

"Your tax dollars at work," Lima said.

"Where's the shotgun?" I said.

He sighed. "Damned if I know."

"No *CSI* crap on that?"

He half-smiled. "Like, 'Oh, it was a left-handed Eskimo with high blood pressure'? Come on, you been around. That shit never helped any working cop. Specially when a shotgun's involved. The barrel's not rifled, you know? Everything just blows up." He sipped. "Though there was one thing."

Lima looked through his windshield.

My best bet was to say nothing, but *man* did I want him to go on.

He would or he wouldn't.

He did. "The shot used on Biletnikov wasn't the same stuff used at Almost Home." He looked to see if I got it.

I did. He meant the size of the pellets in the cartridge. "What was the difference?" I said.

"They used one-aught at Almost Home," Lima said. "Serious stuff, big stuff. About what you'd expect from a killer."

"What'd they use on Gus?"

"Bird shot. *Mid*-sized bird shot, but still."

"Hunting shot," I said.

"Yeah. Nasty way to die. Little holes everywhere. Bigger spread."

I thought of the black-red gash in Gus's middle when we'd found him.

The memory hurt my chest.

I said, "What do you make of it?"

"Nothing, most likely. They probably ran out of one, so they used the other."

"Bullshit, Lima."

He said nothing. His eyes went stony.

We watched the workers.

After a while I said, "Have you guys tossed Peter Biletnikov's place?"

Lima stared at me. "Tossed? Sax, you *toss* a junkie's apartment when he runs in the door with some lady's pocketbook. You don't *toss* the mansion of a swell who's got a picture of himself deep-sea fishing with John Kerry."

"Not even if you think he killed his kid?"

"You want the truth? No. Not even then. What are you, a child?"

My face was good and red, but there was an angle here. *So press it.*

"You're trying hard," I said, "but you're not pulling it off."

"Trying what? The hell are you talking about?"

"Trying to fit in."

"With who?"

"With these burnout detectives who wake up every two weeks at paycheck time," I said. "The cops who only make cases when one dealer dimes out another, or a husband wanders into the barracks with a bloody hatchet in his right hand and his wife's head in his left."

"Get out."

I ignored it. *Press press press.* "You're ambitious. You want to go somewhere. The braces give it away." I touched my front teeth with my thumb.

Now it was Lima's turn to go red in the face. He put his free hand across his mouth, went redder, dropped the hand.

I kept pressing. "I think you're good-ambitious, not asshole-ambitious. I think you want to get something done. So if the burn-out detectives got to you already and taught you how to coast . . . that's a damn shame. But what do I know? I'm a child."

He stared through the windshield at the Keystone Kops across the way trying to right the Porta-John. Stared for a good long while. Like he was counting to a hundred in his head.

"What's your pitch?" he finally said without opening his mouth, and I felt bad about mentioning the braces.

"I get that you can't toss Peter Biletnikov's house. But *I* can."

"How's that?"

"I've got an in with the nanny."

He sipped. His coffee had to be cold. Mine was.

"Let's say you toss it," he said. "What happens then?"

"If there's no gun, there's no gun."

"Which doesn't prove much of anything."

"Prove? Maybe not. But it's good info to have, huh? Points you in other directions, maybe. And if I *do* find anything . . ." I shrugged.

"That," Lima said, "would be *really* good info to have."

CHAPTER TWENTY-SIX

My cell rang while I drove to Sherborn. It was Crump. "I was just with Lima, the cop," I said. "He still thinks you killed Gus."

"Fuck Lima. Need to tell you something."

"Okay."

"Not now, not on a cell. Let's meet."

"That restaurant again?"

"*Hell* no. Dark and private. Tonight. This here's your town. You say where."

"Everything all right?"

"Say where." Donald's voice: tight in a way I hadn't heard before.

"Hopkinton State Park. There's a gate they lock at sundown, but in a truck you can just drive around it. What you do, you take Nine west to Eighty-Five south—"

"I'll google it. Got to go." Donald Crump, near-midget cowboy con man, was rattled as hell.

"Hang on, Crump. From the minute Rinn gave me your number, you've fed me info in bits and pieces to suit your needs. Now you're in a jam, and I'm supposed to drop everything for a *Mission: Impossible* meeting?"

"Says who I'm in a jam?"

"Says everything about this call, for chrissake. You want help? Fill me in. Tell me about you and Rinn and the Biletnikovs."

"Tonight."

"*Now*. Or there *is* no tonight."

Donald Crump went quiet.

He was out of options. And didn't much like it.

I knew the feeling.

Finally, he let out one hell of a long sigh. "She was at Thunder Junction, working for nothing, *interning* they call it, nice racket, when I called Biletnikov to invest in SoPo."

"You and Rinn had something in common," I said. "You both wanted to squeeze money out of Peter."

I meant it as a pump-priming joke, but Crump was quiet a few seconds, considering.

"You're only half right," he finally said. "I was shopping for dough, sure. But Rinn? I believe she truly fell for the man. Or thought she did. *Convinced* herself she did. She's . . ."

I waited.

"She's half traditional and Godly and sweet. Old-fashioned, even."

"What's the other half?"

"Like all kids her age, specially rich ones. Rinn and her little boyfriends used to tell me they was *a*moral, not *im*moral. Difference seemed real important to 'em. Tried to act all cynical, like they was bored 'cause they seen it all." He snorted. "They ain't seen shit."

"Amen to that."

"Thing about Rinn, thing you got to understand, these two ways always pulling at her, see? Pulling her apart."

It made sense to me. It even made sense for a girl who liked older men. I couldn't tell you why it fit, but it did.

I told Crump to go on.

He'd met Rinn at Thunder Junction's offices on a day Gus happened to be hanging around. Crump, not knowing about any connection between Rinn and Peter, had taken a smooth run at her. Rinn, who had plenty of practice stiff-arming such moves, had turned Donald away without breaking a sweat. But Gus witnessed the whole thing, and that night, when he, Rinn, and Brad Bloomquist went out partying, he told the story of the little black guy with the brick-red suit and the matching cowboy hat so well that Brad insisted on meeting Crump.

"And for two, three months," Crump said, "they kept me around for kicks. Making like we was all buddies, then laughin' at me behind my back. You know."

"And you went with it," I said, "but only while Peter Biletnikov looked like a hot prospect." I remembered Donald telling me the first time we met that Peter got his kicks slumming around with a black guy who struck him as streetwise. That was making a lot of sense now—Peter would've known Crump via Rinn, would've known the Houston con man was all front.

"Yup," he said. "I put on a show for the rich white kids, never paid for a drink, learned all sorts a info for future reference."

"Such as Rinn's baby's real father."

"I told too much already," Crump said. "Ten tonight at this Hopkington place."

He said it *Hopkington.*

A lot of people do that.

It's an easy mistake to make.

In Sherborn, I knocked on the front door of the main house. If somebody answered, I'd ask for Rinn. If nobody did, I'd break in and search the joint.

That was all the plan I had.

"Overthinking a situation," Randall once told me, "is not a malady from which you suffer."

Here's the thing, though: I've helped a lot of people out of rough spots. Before they got to those spots, every damn one of them had a clever plan.

So maybe clever plans were overrated.

Haley answered the door.

I said, "Somebody weld that baby to your hip?"

The way she looked at the kid told me a lot. It was a mother's gaze, pure and simple. "I would do anything for this child."

"Glad somebody would."

She looked me in the eye. "Yes."

"How do you work for her? For Rinn?"

She ignored the question and bounce-walked to the kitchen, cooing to the baby. Didn't tell me to scram, so I followed.

Haley plucked a bottle she must have just warmed from the island's granite countertop, popped it in the kid's mouth.

It didn't look like I'd get my chance to toss the house, so I might as well dig for info. Which meant loosening Haley up. I thought of the accent I'd noticed, how it and her looks didn't sync up. "I'm going to take a guess," I said. "You from the Dakotas?"

She blinked. "North. Horace. Outside Fargo."

"I know where it is. I grew up in Minnesota. Mankato."

"I didn't pick it up. In your voice, I mean."

"Been in Massachusetts a long time. How'd you wind up here?" I made a circling gesture. "In the middle of all this?"

"I interned at Peter Biletnikov's firm."

"Another Harvard kid?"

She smiled. "Undergrad, yes. I applied to the business school. People said interning at Thunder Junction guaranteed I'd be accepted."

"Because Rinn did the same thing."

"She wasn't the first. How much did she tell you about her internship?"

"I know about the arm-candy bit, if that's what you mean. She said there were others before her but that Peter was serious about her."

"Fair enough. That jibes with what I heard." She set the bottle down, put Emma over her shoulder, patted the baby's back. "Before Rinn, and incidentally before Peter's divorce, there was a regular stream of Harvard girls who spent a summer at Thunder Junction, then sashayed into the B school."

I knew that, of course. But made a snap decision: play along, learn how much Haley knew. She seemed innocent, at least for this crowd.

"Oho," I said, popping eyebrows. "Tell me more."

She half-smiled and shook her head. "Slow down. I did my due diligence. The casting couch wasn't part of the contract. A couple of my predecessors said Peter simply enjoyed having female company at parties and receptions."

"There a lot of parties and receptions in his world? I thought banking was pretty dry stuff."

She looked at me like I was a second-grader. "*Investment* banking. Peter's job, his business, his expertise lies in connecting people who need funding to people who have it."

"Middleman."

"A middleman steering very big money around."

"How big?"

"If you're after less than fifty million, Thunder Junction doesn't want to hear from you or about you. They don't even know your name."

I whistled.

Haley nodded. "Men bowing and scraping for that kind of capital will do just about anything to lubricate the deal. And I select the word 'lubricate' carefully."

Emma belched. From Haley's reaction, you would've thought the kid had written the Declaration of Independence.

"Vegas stuff?" I said. "Shows and booze and hookers?"

"It all depended on the deal and the players. Pebble Beach, a private day on the Formula One track at Dubai, pheasant hunting at a ten-thousand-acre retreat in Georgia. And yes, Vegas debauchery was a standard gambit."

"That how you pictured your career going when you were at Harvard?"

Pursed lips, a hard headshake. "You didn't let me get to it. What I learned from the girls who came before me—all brilliant, by the way, eminently qualified, now successful financiers themselves, thanks in part to Peter's recommendations—it was as if Peter wanted a pretty young thang on his arm almost as a defensive measure, a way to ward *off* the excesses. He was big on excusing himself early from the bacchanal, throwing a big wink at the others, and escorting me out."

"And?"

"And as soon as we were out of earshot of Team Viagra, he would thank me for my usual top-notch work and go to his room."

"Alone."

"Alone."

If Haley knew more about the *real* reason Peter never made a pass at her, she hid it well. And she didn't strike me as the type who would or could.

Down a hall, a buzzer buzzed and a clothes dryer stopped humming. Haley said something about clean onesies. For a split second, it seemed, she considered asking me to hold Emma.

Then she took the kid with her down the hall.

Not knowing exactly where she was or how long she'd be gone, I couldn't do a lot of searching. I doubted Peter Biletnikov kept his shotgun—if he had one—with the corkscrews and vegetable peelers. I did flip lightly through stacks of paper, wicker baskets, a junk drawer.

Nada.

While I rifled I thought about Peter Biletnikov, trying to put him together. His daddy saved the world. He himself had made a pile of dough but didn't give a rat's ass about it. He'd named his first son after the daddy, but had a hell of a rough time with the son. He lived in a four-million-dollar house with all the personality of a furnished apartment. He hired pretty interns and made everybody think he was fooling around, but he never laid a glove on them. Even when his son died, he hadn't known how to behave. It was like he'd picked out tired movie scenes—*Collapse when you see the body! Tear your hair out at the funeral!*—and imitated them as best he could.

And then there was Rinn, who called herself a trophy wife. She bore Peter Biletnikov's midlife-crisis baby but wouldn't have anything to do with either of them. Half-wanted to be a picture-book mommy, according to Donald, whose observations I trusted, but couldn't handle the real-world details of the gig.

And I kept nibbling around the edges of Gus's murder, but I still hadn't nailed down where Peter or Rinn fit in.

It all made my head hurt.

When Haley came around the corner without Emma, I was standing with both hands on the granite, looking innocent. I hoped.

"Asleep," she said to a question I hadn't asked. "A warm onesie and a warm blankie, and she goes down like *that*."

"Why are you still here?" I said. "You working through business school as Peter's nanny? Is that part of the deal?"

"The well-trod path from Harvard College to the B school via Peter's arm didn't work out for me. Guess why."

I thought it through. "Rinn pulled something."

"Right you are. She has this power over older men. I swear, she bewitches them."

"She does okay with younger ones, too," I said. Thinking of Randall. And maybe myself.

Haley smiled. "So stipulated. Anyway, Rinn may have thought I had designs on Peter. I didn't. Or maybe he had designs on *me* that I didn't pick up on. Whatever the case, my B school application was rejected."

"You sure that was Rinn's fault? It's got to be a tough place to get into."

She laughed. "My mother's father was an Inuk. Talk about a prize pedigree. For a woman with Inuk blood and a four-point-oh at Harvard College who interned at Thunder Junction, getting into the B school is anything but hard. Trust me. It had to be Rinn's doing. She whispered in Peter's ear, and he then whispered in a few ears himself."

I pointed. "The baby urped on your shoulder."

"Thanks." But she didn't wipe it off—left it like a merit badge. "The minute I got the bad news about grad school, *this* job miraculously opened up. Housekeeping for Mister Thunder Junction himself. The two of them invited me for dinner, then presented the offer as if I were Orphan Annie and they were Daddy Warbucks. You should have seen Rinn's eyes."

"What do you mean?"

"They'd done their research. My dad's on disability, and my mom drives a school bus. And I had four years' worth of student loans."

"Come on, Harvard. You must've had other options."

Haley looked at the floor, said nothing.

"They had something on you," I said. "Dirt."

Haley looked at the floor. I liked her even more for not lying to me and for feeling, as far as I could tell, shame. Between Rinn, Gus, Brad, and all the partying, I could imagine a dozen levers they might have on this kid. I decided not to press.

Instead, I said, "Is the pay okay?"

"Obscene. It was part of the reason I took the gig and it's part of what keeps me here. And Rinn knows it."

"It doesn't make sense," I said. "Why would Rinn screw you on the school application, then guarantee you stay this close to Peter? Hell, you live under his *roof,* which is more than she can say."

Haley started to answer, but the doorbell rang. She answered it and came back with a woman who looked like a thirty-year prison guard but turned out to be a babysitter. "Even Fargo girls get an afternoon off," Haley said to me.

I took the hint and split.

Outside, I finally did get something semi-useful out of the trip. All three of the garage doors had been opened by a kid who was detailing a black BMW X5. Next to it sat an identical SUV. License plates: HIZZUN and HERRUN.

I shook my head. SPURN and STRIKE must have been taken.

I looked in the third bay. Parked in tandem, kickstands and forks at identical angles, were a pair of black Harley-Davidsons. They were tricked out yuppie-style, with whitewalls and GPS units and better stereos than most homes and all the other crap that makes true Harley guys' skin crawl.

The cars and bikes backstopped Rinn's story about the jackass bet where she'd whipped Peter into playing twinsies. Poor sap.

"Is nice, uh?" It was the detailer, a boy working on a pencil mustache. He'd seen me staring.

I nodded. "Nice."

"Big money." He rubbed thumb across fingers.

"The biggest." We nodded good-bye and I climbed in my F-250.

CHAPTER TWENTY-SEVEN

I'd left my cell charging in the truck. It buzzed as I climbed in. I picked up.

"Conway?"

I said, "Sophie?"

"Hi, stranger!" She spoke too loud, trying for casual but forcing it.

"You okay?"

"We had a half day at school. When I got home, Jessie was here with her friend Kaydee and two men. I don't like diming anybody out, but I think they were . . . partying."

I sighed and smiled at the same time. *Diming anybody out*. Gangster Sophie.

Kaydee: Jessie's best friend, or what passed for it. I never had liked her. She wore this look on her mug like your fly was down and she'd rather Facebook it than tell you.

Charlene felt pretty much the same way I did about Kaydee. But a friend's a friend, especially when your kid doesn't have many. And she sure as hell wasn't anorexic. That struck us as a good thing.

I said, "Where was your mother in all this?"

"Office." Long pause. "I think she forgot I had a half day."

"Oh."

"Yeah, oh." Long pause. "It's just . . . they were *men,* you know? Not old high school boyfriends or anything. They had tattoos, and one had a beard, and when I came in they looked like they hated me. Everybody was smoking, and the men were drinking wine, and I'm pretty sure Jessie was too except she hid it when I walked in, and I was *scared.*"

"Don't blame you." I looked at my watch. "Your mom'll be home soon. Did the men leave yet?"

"They all did. Jessie couldn't even look me in the eye, Conway. She told me to watch TV til Mom got home, and I swear she was almost crying, like she was making a mistake and she knew it but it was too late, and then she *left.*" Sophie talked fast, staying just ahead of tears.

My heart hurt. "I'll be there in twenty-five minutes."

"No! Please don't. I want you . . ."

"What?"

"Can you find Jessie?"

"I doubt it."

"They left in the men's truck. It had a bumper sticker that said QuinsInk." She spelled it.

"Sounds like a tattoo joint."

"It is. I googled. It's in Worcester, right on Lake Quinsigamond. Hence the name."

"Good stuff, Sophie. But not much help. Anybody can get a bumper sticker."

"I eavesdropped, and the men were talking all about tattoos. To impress Jessie and Kaydee, I think."

"Well."

"It was a green Dodge pickup truck. The huge kind, with four doors and extra tires on the back."

"A duallie."

"Yes! A duallie."

"I'll get going. Text me the address."

"Already got it. Ready?"

Sheesh. A force of nature. It was a side of Sophie I hadn't seen before.

"I'll do what I can," I said. "But kid, keep in mind Jessie's an adult, and—"

"Chronologically, maybe. Please find her."

Click.

I got to QuinsInk as fat raindrops began to fall.

A green Dodge duallie sat out front. On its front doors: magnetic signs for a house-painting outfit.

What do you know.

I parked across the street. Sighed.

If Gus'd had a heads-up sister like Sophie . . . well, who knew?

It was a poisonous thought, but I couldn't help but chase it.

What the hell was I doing, looking to bail out Jessie when I ought to be running down Gus's killer? I had no connection with Jessie. She'd resented me from the get-go, had done everything in her power to turn Charlene and Sophie against me. Then she'd hauled off and moved two thousand miles away. With my son. Giving us all the finger every way she could dream up.

I caught myself, felt embarrassed at the direction of my thoughts, took a deep breath.

Roy is not here. Gus is not here. Jessie is here.

I heel-rubbed my eyes, looked up and down the block. Lake Quinsigamond, which is built more like a wide river, slices down the eastern edge of Worcester, separating it from Shrewsbury. Leave it to Worcester to waste what ought to be primo lakefront real estate on a tattoo parlor flanked by dive bars. Charlene says Worcester could screw up a ham sandwich.

It hit me that I'd pulled a few Barnburners out of this place before, when it bore a different name. I don't understand why drunks always want to stumble off for a tat, but they do.

QuinsInk's windows were blacked out, and I didn't see anybody enter or leave. Maybe people were still too sober for tattoos. But the apartment above seemed occupied. Its window was cracked open, and what looked to be a beach towel served as a curtain. I thought I heard music, but couldn't be sure.

There'd be a staircase around back.

Why couldn't I haul myself out of the truck? I felt so . . . tired. Didn't want to see what I was pretty sure I was going to see.

"Goddamn Jessie," I said out loud.

Hell. If I was going to do this, I ought to do it fast. I took three deep breaths and climbed out.

Two minutes later, having eased up an outdoor stairway and gentled the knob of an unlocked door, I piled in.

The smell of pot was dense, ugly-sweet. The music was hard, loud, angry, fast. The beach towel/curtain featured Buzz Lightyear upside-down.

I strode into the living room. Between the weed and the music, it took them a few seconds to notice me. I used the seconds to scope.

On the couch sat a doughy kid, maybe twenty. Round face, gray sweatshirt, painter's pants. Next to him was a guy ten years older, with a prison-seamed face and a cropped beard. Same sweatshirt, same pants as the doughy kid. An intricate, all-black tattoo crept from the sweatshirt's neck.

Kaydee knelt on the floor, lighting a Marlboro over a yard-sale coffee table. Next to her, Jessie was bubbling a hit from a green bong. She popped her thumb from the airhole, sucked smoke, held it in.

Then she looked at me for the first time. She was so high it didn't register right away that I shouldn't be here. She smiled and waggled her fingers.

When the beard finally noticed me, he didn't hesitate at all. He sized me up and reached for a Carhartt work jacket next to him. He was the one to worry about. He'd obviously done state time, and now he was going for a weapon he kept close by out of habit.

Taking the shortest distance between me and the beard, I giant-stepped onto the table, flattening it. Ashtrays, wineglasses, and the bong all tumbled. The beard scrambled in his jacket pocket. The doughy kid came out of a stoner dream and said, "Hey."

I stepped again, onto the couch this time. Needed to crowd the beard, get between him and whatever he was scrambling for.

I knee-slammed his ear. His head bounced off the sofa's arm just as he pulled a three-inch lock-blade knife from his jacket.

Then time slowed in a good way—my brain clicked into some kind of animal mode I don't understand, all senses maxed out. I took in everything. *Everything.* I knew what had just happened. I knew what was happening right now, every movement of every player in the room, including the ones I couldn't see.

Best of all, I knew what was *going* to happen in the next few seconds.

Past, present, future: I saw it all.

I can't explain it any better than that.

I stood on couch cushions looking down at the beard, who was on queer street.

Under the music, the girls bitched about the mess, the spilled bong. Kaydee was whining at the doughy kid to *do* something, don't be a pussy. I felt bad for him. Kaydee and every movie he'd ever watched were nagging him to back up his pal, but his belly was telling him to run like hell.

His belly was the smart one.

As all this worked through my head, the beard shook his to clear it. He made a blind move for his lock-blade.

I'd been waiting for that. Hell, I'd been looking forward to it.

I pulled back until it seemed my elbow would brush the ceiling. Then I freight-trained a right into his temple. My allies were gravity, adrenaline, fury at the wicked knife, heartbreak over Jessie. To me, the punch felt like dropping a cinder block. From an airplane.

Don't know what it felt like to the beard, but something in his head cracked and his eyes rolled back.

I grabbed the knife and turned to the doughy kid.

Kaydee had convinced him, for a few seconds anyway, to stop being a pussy. He stood in what he probably thought was an Ultimate Fighting stance: bouncing on the balls of his feet, holding up loose fists in a southpaw stance.

I stared at him maybe ten seconds.

He stopped bouncing.

I flicked open the knife and used it to point at the door twelve feet behind him.

He looked at Jessie, Kaydee, the out-cold beard, the knife.

He looked at me.

Then he turned and walked out fast without looking back.

He'd listened to his belly. Smart kid.

With all threats gone, I thrummed and panted. I was adrenaline-jacked, with nobody left to hit.

I took it out on the music. Two fast steps brought me to a black component stereo. I kicked it, stomped it, killed the awful noise.

The quiet almost hurt.

Kaydee said, "You *prick*!"

Jessie, arms folded, stood by the sofa looking down at the beard. "I think you killed him." She wore a ratty-ass bathrobe a foot too long for her.

Bathrobe?

My heart fell another inch in my chest.

Kaydee said, "You fucking *prick*!"

I looked at her for the first time. Her hair was in pigtails. She wore a white blouse with a black bra showing through. The blouse was tied off, showing soft pale midriff. She wore a plaid miniskirt, kneesocks.

My heart sank into my belly as I stepped down a short hall, knowing from the girls' getups what I'd find.

Sure enough, the apartment's only bedroom was rigged as a studio. Tripod, expensive still and video cameras, banks of lights. The queen-sized bed was covered by a little-girl spread. A dozen stuffed animals were parked against the headboard. Some of the animals still had price tags. Target.

I wondered if they took them back for a refund when the shoot was over.

Somehow, that was the thought that lit me off.

I'm not proud of it.

I wrecked everything. Destroyed the room, screaming while I did it. Cameras, tripods, reflectors, all other gear: out the window. I used the lock-blade to slash a giant X in the mattress. That wasn't enough, so I did the box spring, too. Stomped the bed frame, made it matchsticks. Picked up an old six-drawer chest, held it head-high, dropped it.

Again.

And again. Screaming, stomping, keening, losing myself in it, not knowing who I was or what I was doing.

Then I stood, panting and looking the room over.

"I call it good," I said in a voice that didn't sound like mine.

On my way out, I grabbed another bathrobe from a chair I hadn't noticed before, one partially hidden by the door.

Then I chucked the chair out the window.

Then I snapped the door off its hinges and chucked it after the chair.

When I got back to the living room, both girls were staring at me with huge eyes.

Jessie pointed at the beard. "He's not dead."

I went to Kaydee, shoved the robe at her. She folded her arms and let it drop. I picked it up, grabbed her, spun her, began to force the robe on.

She said, "Hey!"

I pushed her arm through a sleeve.

She fought me. "Copping a feel, pre-vert?"

I pushed her other arm, spun her again, cinched the robe. Kaydee stared at me and curled her lip in her version of a smile.

"Oh my God," she said. "Are you *crying*, pre-vert? Jessie, the pre-vert is *crying*."

Jessie said, "Shut up, Kaydee."

It was the nicest thing I'd heard her say since she came home.

CHAPTER TWENTY-EIGHT

I managed to not punch Kaydee in the face during the ride to her folks' house. They weren't home, which spared me a tough decision—tell them or don't?—for now. On the one hand, she was twenty. On the other, she lived in her parents' basement when she wasn't clerking at a toy store. Or making porn vids.

Without Kaydee calling me a faggot and mocking me with *boo-hoo-hoo* noises, my truck was quiet.

"Remember the other night," Jessie finally said, arms folded like she wanted to cut herself in half at the waist, "when you said I was breaking her heart?"

I knew who she meant. "I remember."

"If you mention this, it really will."

"Yes."

"Bad memories. The acorn falling close to the tree."

"Yes."

We stopped at a light. The rain had settled in. Mental note: get new wiper blades.

"So," Jessie finally said. "Are you?"

I said nothing.

"Going to tell her?"

"I knew what you meant."

The light turned. I waited to make my left. I licked my lips. "How's Roy doing?" I said.

"Aha. Quid pro quo."

"I don't know what that means. How is he?"

She said nothing.

"He doesn't return my calls," I said. "My texts."

"His silence speaks volumes."

Traffic opened up. With my front tires cocked left, I hit the throttle harder than I needed to. On the slick road, the truck's back end jumped wide and stayed wide, and I spent a few busy seconds working the wheel and the gas to catch up.

"If you're trying to scare me to death," Jessie said as I got us pointed more or less straight, "try harder."

"For chrissake, Jessie," I said in a voice that made her head swivel my way, "just tell me one thing. *The* one thing."

She knew what it was.

She said nothing.

She was going to make me beg, make me ask out loud.

So I did. It came out raspy. "Is he using?"

We were in Charlene's neighborhood now, and the rain made for an early dusk. Between that and the wet roads and the excitement back at the traffic light, I was driving like an old lady.

But there was another factor. We were in a bubble. I had Jessie on my turf, or as near to it as I could hope. The second we pulled up and her door opened, the bubble would pop. She would hustle to her bedroom fortress and her phone and her laptop and her TV, and that would be that.

I drove slow and kept my mouth shut. And hoped.

Prayed.

Prayed she would tell me that one thing. Prayed that the goodness inside Jessie Bollinger—a smart, watchful, deadpan girl who'd served at age eight as a two-year-old's mommy—would trump the hate and darkness that'd steamrolled her these past few years.

I could feel her, truly *feel* her, waffling. Waves rolled from her. I sat dead still, like a man who just found a finch on his shoulder.

My prayers almost worked.

She almost turned to face me, human to human.

She almost talked.

About Roy.

I could tell.

But then we pulled into the driveway. Jessie opened her door before I even got the truck in park. She pounded up concrete steps, hunched against rain, thumb-typing a text message without looking back.

I stayed in my truck so long Sophie came to fetch me.

Charlene closed the bedroom door, waited two beats, and whipped it open.

I said, "Looking to bust Sophie spying?"

"You bet I am. And not without reason."

She shut the door for real. And locked it. "What was that all about, Conway Sax?"

"What was what about?"

"What was *tonight* about? Don't play dumb. You know I hate that."

I did know it, but I was in a jam. The whole evening had been an unspoken agreement between me, Sophie, and Jessie to keep Charlene in the dark. Jessie had it easy—she'd spent an hour in the bathtub before locking herself in her room. I'd been scared that if I said much of anything, Charlene would know something was wrong and pry it out of me. Sophie must've felt the same way, because she was so quiet Charlene asked if she felt okay.

"Guess everybody was just tired," I said, closing the blinds. I had a plan to sidestep Charlene's curiosity, and it was one the neighbors didn't need to see.

"Tired my ass," she said. "There was another grand conspiracy going on. I'm *sick* of those."

I needed to show her a little leg, throw her off the scent. "Sophie had a half day today."

It worked. Charlene grimaced, then pinched the bridge of her nose. "*Dammit!* Dammit dammit dammit."

"Not a big deal. She's old enough."

"I know, but she needs new cheer shoes, and I'd promised today was the day. The two-month-old white sneakers she's worn a half-dozen times apparently aren't white enough for the big competition. Can you explain that to me?"

I was too busy feeling relieved to say much.

So I crossed the room and kissed her.

She kissed me back like a Freightliner. Damn near knocked me backward to the bed. Which maybe she'd wanted to.

To show her who was boss I crouched some, got my hands under her rear end, and lifted. She didn't have much choice but to wrap her legs around my waist. I got us turned around, so now it was *me* dumping *her* onto the bed, falling atop her. Both of us giggling and kissing the whole time.

I forget which of us switched off the lamp.

After, she slept and I dozed. Couldn't afford to do more—had to meet Donald.

At twenty past nine, I slipped out of bed and dressed.

There's a certain look to a woman's shoulder blades in half-light. So pretty. So lonely.

The rain had pushed through by the time I eased to the locked main gate at Hopkinton State Park. Deep mud ruts told me Donald had driven around it, the way I'd explained. But he had four-wheel drive, and I didn't.

I rolled into the ruts. Bogged. Fought three seconds of worry that I'd get stuck and have to tap-dance with a local cop. But my rear tires found enough grip to shove me through.

It's a decent-sized park, but most of the roads are gated off at night, so there's really only one place you can drive. I killed my headlights. With clouds still blocking the moon and stars, I had to move slowly.

Bear right, up and over a hill, bend left to a string of parking lots serving a reservoir I could feel but not see. I'd chucked a few guns in there—it was one way I knew this place.

The other: most summer Sundays, Floriano and his kin, along with half the Brazilians in the state, mob the place for all-day grill fests and beach parties. I'd joined the Mendes clan here a few times, eating my weight in Brazilian sausage and beef.

Damn, but it was dark. Even the dashboard light would screw up my night vision, I knew, so I dimmed it all the way down.

I drove, listened, looked.

I heard only halfhearted waves tickling the reservoir's angled sides.

Rolled forward twenty yards at a walking pace, stopped, looked, and listened again.

Nothing.

Did all this again. Again. Again.

After five minutes that felt much longer, I was cursing myself for being vague about the location of the meet, wondering if Donald had managed to find another lot somewhere. I pulled my cell. He was probably close enough to hit with an apple core, but in this dark I'd best call.

That's when the gun went off.

I wish I didn't know that sound so well, but I do. And it wasn't anything other than a handgun. I fumbled my cell, ducking instinctively in my seat even as I registered the sound and a white flash to my left.

I came out of the panicky duck and looked that way in time to see another flash, hear another pop. Sure enough, the flash told me it was Donald's big-ass Cadillac SUV. As I'd guessed, it was no more than fifty yards away.

I jumped out. I ran toward the truck's outline. It lit up a third time and I flinched, stumbling—but this time there was no pop to match the flash. A dull thunk told me a door had closed, and I began to fear what I was going to find.

Hit the Escalade's left side running hard, both hands out to stop me. I half-registered slop on the driver's window, grabbed the handle, pulled hard . . .

. . . his lime-sherbet-green cowboy hat fluttered past my shoulder.

And Donald Crump, all five foot two of him, a man who could eat barbecue all day long and never admit he liked it, a man who could impersonate an NFL lineman one week and run a solar company the next, fell into my arms with a little hole in his right temple and a big hole in his left.

I saw it all by the Escalade's dome light. I saw more than I wanted to see. I saw too much.

The keys were still in the Cadillac's ignition. A chime went *ding-ding-ding*.

Donald's dead weight took me down slowly. I ended up splayed on the tarmac with his body between my legs.

I spoke. I babbled. I said something. I didn't know what.

Later on, the Hopkinton cop who made the scene first said I kept saying, "Aw, hell." Only that. Over and over.

Until they pried me away from Donald and cuffed me and shoved me in a cruiser.

They didn't haul me out of holding to speak with Lima until eight the next morning.

Don't know whether I ought to tell this—it's an embarrassing thing to know—but when it comes to jail, most everything you see on TV and movies is horseshit, pure and simple. Unless you're a prize jerk, most cops treat you okay.

The night before, cuffed in the back of the cop car, I'd told the Hopkinton PD they ought to call the staties before deciding what to do with me. They had. I spent the night in a decent one-bunk holding cell in a back corner of the staties' Framingham barracks. Sure, I wore prison orange—but only because they offered to have my clothes washed overnight. Dinner and breakfast were from Burger King. I'm a McDonald's man, but I hadn't complained.

So don't picture that squirrelly guy who begs the detectives for mercy because he spent all night on a bench fending off rapists. At 8:00 A.M., when they nodded me into the interrogation cube, I had a good night's rest, a full belly, and lemon-scented clothes.

I also had cuffs on my wrists. That part's not horseshit.

Neither is the worry. If I'd had my phone, the staties would have let me call Charlene—the one-phone-call bit is more TV nonsense—but I'd dropped it in my truck when the shots were fired. And, the guard told me after checking, my truck was part of the crime scene. It was getting the full forensics treatment.

"The hell for?" I'd said to the guard. "All I did was drive into a parking lot and watch my friend get shot."

"Don't tell me," he'd said, squinting at his clipboard, "tell Detective Lima."

And here he sat, lips pressed together, both hands flat on the beat-up table, manila folder open before him.

"Why am I here?" I said. "I drove into a parking lot and watched Donald Crump take two in the head."

"Sit."

I sat.

"Pure as a mountain spring," Lima said. "That's you. Billy Bob Bystander. So why'd you bust into a state park with a locked gate and clearly posted hours? And why'd you black out your truck while you drove around?"

"Donald called. He wanted—"

"Fuck Donald Crump!" Lima screamed it, blowing his top for the first time I'd seen. "Everybody loves Crump! Everybody wants to hug him and take him home for dinner! He wasn't a pint-sized black leprechaun committing pranks, Sax. He was a fucking-A thief/con man/douche bag who'd steal your gold fillings if you gave him half a chance."

Boy, was he pissed.

I counted to five. Maybe Lima did, too.

"Donald Crump called me yesterday," I said. "He was shook up. He wanted to meet in a quiet place. I told him the place."

Lima stared at the report in his folder. He looked like a man trying to will the ink on the pages to shift until it said what he wanted it to say.

Huh.

I thought.

Then I thought out loud. "You've got his cell and mine. So you know it's true he called yesterday afternoon."

"Right. So you remembered the call and fed me BS that would fit. Big deal."

But Lima was trying to sell himself. And failing.

Then there was a nice click, and I half-smiled in spite of everything.

"You knew I was rolling with my lights turned off," I said. "You've got a goddamn witness."

CHAPTER TWENTY-NINE

It was quiet for a long time.

"Two." It killed him to say it.

I said nothing.

"Plus cell-phone video."

"*What?*"

Lima sighed, leaned back. "You get many handjobs when you were thirteen, Sax?"

"That's a hell of a question."

"Young Mica . . . hell, you don't need last names. Young Mica met young Alexa in the state park last night. Facebook friends. Thirteen years old. Both of 'em Hopkinton kids, but they go to different schools. Sneaked out for a handjob that had apparently been promised young Mica by young Alexa."

"They met at the reservoir," I said, nodding, seeing now where he was headed. "It's a big makeout spot. Or was. Floriano said that's why they started locking the gates at night."

"Who's Floriano?"

"Never mind. Was I right about the kids?"

"'Course."

"What about the video?"

"In this day and age, what red-blooded boy wouldn't secretly record his first handjob?"

"It was dark as hell."

Lima shrugged. "Night-vision app. No problem."

"Can I see the video?"

"No."

"It tell you anything new?"

"Yes." He looked at me awhile. "It told me somebody was trying to set you up."

I said nothing.

"Want to tell me who might do that, Sax?"

I said nothing.

"Want to talk about the Pundo family, Sax?"

"How'd the video tell you this?"

He leaned back, stared at the ceiling awhile. Sighed, dropped his shoulders. "Young Mica's video was pretty crappy, especially when things got exciting."

"I'll bet."

He worked hard to hide the smile. "Once the gunfire started, I mean. We miss the first gunshot flash altogether, though we do hear it. We see the second gunshot flash. Then we see your truck's dome light when you climb out. Then we see Crump's dome light, presumably when the shooter climbed out, and then again when you open the door and find the body."

Donald's body. The cowboy hat, the burst left temple. I'd managed to bury all that overnight.

"Guess what we see next," Lima said.

I thought of the sequence. "Hopkinton PD pulls up. And now that you mention it, they must've been tipped off to get there so quick. I doubt they even have keys to the main gate."

"You're right about all that, but guess what we *see*."

I waited.

"We see your truck's dome light again."

"Huh?"

He opened a drawer, pulled from it a big Ziploc bag, laid the bag on his desk. It held a slip of paper, some sort of evidence ticket.

And a pair of thin, purplish rubber gloves.

I recognized them right away—we buy them by the boxload at the shop. They keep grease off your fingers while leaving most of your touch for threading small nuts.

"Surgical gloves," Lima said.

"I know." I explained how.

"Found 'em in your truck's center console."

"Are you going to say what I think you're going to say?"

He nodded. "Powder residue. Near-microscopic grit. Good stuff."

"Didn't you say that *CSI* stuff never helped anybody make a case?"

"You work with what you got. If it wasn't for young Mica, these gloves would have me looking at you a whole nother way. Walk in my moccasins, Sax. Can you see it?"

I thought. Nodded. "While you were rushing the gloves through the lab, you must've checked the inside for DNA."

"Sure. No go. Instead, they found traces of the powder that keeps the gloves from sticking together in the box." He looked a challenge at me.

I said nothing for a full thirty seconds. Then: "Two gloves, one worn on top of the other. The outer glove held the gun that shot Crump. The inner one trapped the actual shooter's DNA."

"That's how I see it. The inner glove's long gone, the outer one ends up in your truck."

"Would the setup have worked? Without the video, I mean?"

"For a conviction? Who knows? Doubt it. It sure as hell would've kept you inside these walls awhile, though."

"Huh."

"There's more."

"How much more can there be?"

"I don't know if I'll ever change your mind on your pal Crump," Lima said—sitting straight, savoring something—"but we found a shotgun in his spare-tire well."

I sat. I stared at nothing. My ears hummed. I focused on the humming, tried to make it stop.

It didn't.

"Bullshit," I finally said.

"No bullshit. Wicked little thing, on the short side but not a sawed-off. No branding whatsoever, looks like a full-on custom job. I got three civilian experts trying to figure out who made it. Turns out if you got a checkbook big enough, there're six or eight guys in various parts of the world who'll build a gun exactly to your specs. It's just like getting a hot rod built, or a custom motorcycle."

"You found *a* shotgun. Is it *the* shotgun?"

Lima shifted in his chair. "Well. Hell, why am I telling you all this? You know, you're sneaky in your own way. Sit there saying nothing, or close to it, but somehow egging me on to share the family secrets. How do you do that?"

I said nothing.

"I deserve that," he said, half-smiling. "Like I said yesterday, shotgun ballistics are a pain in the ass. The nature of the weapon, you know?"

I put my hands together, made an explosion sound with my lips, let my fingers fly apart.

He nodded. "Right. So here's the way we're looking at it. The gun from Crump's SUV has *not* been ruled out as the murder weapon from both Almost Home and the Biletnikov killing."

I said nothing.

"That's not lazy, Sax, and it's not a clock puncher's cop-out. That's good police work."

"Can I go?"

He set elbows on the table, rubbed his eyes with fingertips. "You know," he said, "the media's turning up the heat on this one. The

Almost Home triple homicide was rough enough. Framingham's Framingham, and it *was* in a halfway house. But still."

Finished rubbing his eyes, then opened them to stare at me. "Then a rich kid got it, in Sherborn no less. And now Crump, in a state park in another nice town. Guess who called our press gal at six this morning?"

I said nothing.

"Only *The New York Times,* that's who. They're going to dump me, Sax."

"*The New York Times* is going to dump you?"

He shook his head. "The bosses. They love a shiny minority, but only until the shiny minority screws up."

I felt bad for him.

I said, "Can I go?"

"Talk to me about Charlie Pundo. Talk to me about Fat Teddy."

"I guess I can go."

I rose. I walked out. I felt Lima fume behind me.

At the front desk, they handed over my phone, wallet, and keys. And told me to have a nice day.

Lima was right about the Pundos—they'd done a solid job taking out Donald, and if it weren't for a horny thirteen-year-old, I'd be waiting trial right now instead of heading for Sherborn on a sunny spring morning.

It had to be the Pundos who'd done it. Fat Teddy and Boxer, most likely. But maybe Charlie himself had been in on the act, sending a Mob-style message: *You got lucky and didn't burn in my skate park. But I can burn you anytime I want.*

There was one question: how'd the Pundos learn about Donald in the first place?

Easy. I could think of a couple possibilities. Donald had partied with Rinn, Gus, and Brad Bloomquist, and Fat Teddy had been their connection. Bingo.

And if that wasn't it . . . hell, I'd met with Donald in public around the time Teddy and Boxer were tailing me. The Pundos would have cop connections—they could've run his plate and known everything there was to know in ten minutes.

After texting Charlene and Sophie to say I was okay and would explain everything, my gut had told me to round up Randall and make a hard run at Springfield. Bull-rush the Hi Hat, kick the snot out of anybody we found inside, take out Boxer if need be.

I ignored my gut.

I wish I hadn't.

That one time I should've let the red mist, the blind fury, take over. Instead, I played it civilized. Told myself I'd get to the Pundos when I got to them. I figured they had to be holed up and alibied up after what they'd done last night.

I actually congratulated myself on my thinking. It seemed like the smart move. It seemed grown-up.

For a while.

So instead of running dead west at a hundred and five, I rolled southeast at city pace, easing into Sherborn.

Every few minutes, a flash of Donald busted through. A green cowboy hat. A head that didn't look much like a head anymore. Dead weight that carried me to the parking-lot tarmac.

Interspersed: Gus memories. A black sweatshirt that said FLAT-OUT. A bloody middle in three different shades of gore. That wrist, twisted so delicately, the wrist of a boy.

I fought the memories. I tamped them. I knew from experience they'd fade as time passed.

But they'd never go away altogether. I knew that, too.

It was pushing ten when I knocked on the Biletnikovs' front door. Nothing.

Gave it five minutes of knocking, ringing, calling out. Then went through the same routine at the guesthouse.

Nothing.

Peered in a garage window. One of the black BMWs was gone.

Well, now.

Looked like this was my chance to search the house, the way I'd wanted to yesterday. But did that still make sense? The idea had been to look around for a shotgun, or anything else that might clear or point a finger at Rinn or Peter. Now Lima had his shotgun. As far as he was concerned, he had his shooter, too: Donald Crump.

Me, I still needed one hell of a lot of convincing on that.

So convince yourself. Or not. Look around. Now.

It was a big risk with low odds on a payout.

But hell, I was going to do it.

I may have smiled when Randall's favorite army saying came to me: *Half a plan and your dick in your hand.*

I'm no cat burglar, and thin tape strips on the house's front windows told me there was some kind of security in place. But people are always the weak link, and in a big joint like this, with a nanny and a kid and cleaners and deliveries all the time, I expected no trouble.

And had none. Two-thirds of the way around the north side of the house, hidden from the road, a small window was open an inch. There was a screen, and because the yard fell away here I was working at shoulder level and above, but those factors didn't slow me much.

I used my multitool to pry out one of the pushers that held the screen in place. Set down the screen, shoved the window higher, untied my boots, put hands on the sill, jumped-pulled-scrabbled until my shoulders were inside.

My face was six inches above a toilet bowl.

CHAPTER THIRTY

The toilet smelled like flowers.

Sherborn.

I wriggled until my waist set on the sill, then kicked off my boots. It was worth a few seconds of my time: they kept the house clean as a marine's sock drawer, and there'd be no quicker giveaway than to tramp dirt all over the place.

Then I was all the way in. I stepped from the powder room and got my bearings. I was in the hallway Haley'd disappeared down during my visit. To my left: laundry room, a few other doors. To my right: the bulk of the first floor.

I stood and listened. Even today, with electronics everywhere beeping and buzzing, you can feel when a house is empty. Especially if you've been breaking and entering since you were thirteen years old.

Which is another story.

I felt the B&E tingle, the ugly little thrill you get when you have the run of somebody else's home, for five seconds. Then I reminded myself what I was here for, set the bezel on my ancient Seiko diver's watch, and ran upstairs. It's where you start. That way, you're always flowing back toward your escape point.

That was one thing a certain woman had taught me long ago.

Another: you never want to be inside more than eight minutes. Six is better.

It took me eleven to do the second and first floors. I was out of practice, and it was a big house, with lots of storage in lots of rooms.

I stood by the basement door. Two more minutes for a search down there?

Hesitated, grabbed the knob, bombed down.

It paid off the instant I opened another door, one that looked like it led to the unfinished part of the basement.

I whistled long and slow in the room lit only by a pair of slot windows in the foundation.

Knives. Swords. And tools for working them. A four-foot-by-three-foot butcher-block table, a stool, a pair of magnifying safety glasses. A variety of oils and whetstones like I'd never seen. Most of the stones looked a hundred years old—God knew how many sharpenings had worn in them soft, deep valleys.

On the room's walls, there had to be a hundred knives and swords. Some were three inches long, some were thirty. Three were Confederate swords from the Civil War, and many looked even older.

You've been in the house thirteen minutes. Get the hell out.

Two walls were lined with cabinets. I rifled them *fast.*

I found nothing. They were junk cabinets, had been crammed full long before Peter Biletnikov began using this as his hobby room. Which it had to be.

Yeah, I made the connection: not-quite-a-man Peter liked playing with swords, blades, knives.

Duh.

But that armchair shrink talk always struck me as BS, the kind of palaver stupid people throw around to sound smart. So as I zipped up the stairs, I made a note to wait and see where Peter Biletnikov's hobby led. If anywhere.

Twenty seconds later, when I pushed away from the powder-room windowsill, I had jack shit to show for all those minutes.

Don't get me wrong: in the old days, the Biletnikov place would've counted as a gold mine, maybe my best score ever. I'd found eighteen hundred in cash, a half-dozen men's watches worth more than my truck, a tiny pistol in a tiny velvet-lined box, cameras, laptops, and all sorts of other crap. Had left it all in place, of course.

As for *real* guns, though? Shotguns, handguns, cleaning supplies, trigger-lock keys, any indication this was a weapon-savvy household?

Jack shit.

As I pulled my boots on and replaced the screen, I thought about something else I hadn't seen in the Biletnikovs' master bedroom. The dog that did not bark, as Randall sometimes said.

No woman's stuff. None whatsoever. It was a man's space, flat out.

Rinn Biletnikov's move to the guesthouse was long-standing and permanent.

Huh.

Which means you haven't searched the joint, not really, until you've searched the guesthouse.

I looked it over. A white bungalow, trellis covered on the side facing me. There was no second story, and a concrete slab told me there was no basement. It was what, fifteen hundred square feet tops?

You pressed your luck already when you took too long in the main house. Am-scray.

"Hell," I said out loud. My voice, *any* voice, sounded funny to me—hadn't heard one since leaving Lima.

Half a plan and your dick in your hand.

What swayed me: Donald Crump's tiny boots. Boots only a girl's feet could fit inside, as I'd said myself. Crump's suspicions hadn't convinced me, not really. But didn't I owe him a three-minute search of the guesthouse?

The way his sherbet-green cowboy hat fluttered from his SUV. The way his left eye bulged under the side of his head that'd been blown out.

Yeah, I owed Donald three minutes.

I crossed the yard to the bungalow's door. The key wasn't under the mat. Which meant it was parked atop the casing, I knew.

It was. It always is.

I pushed key into lock, set my watch bezel again, stepped inside.

Bedroom first was the smart way to go. As I crossed the living room, green caught my eye on a big square end table.

Goodnight Moon. Under a stack of junk mail and women's magazines.

My face reddened as I walked the short hallway to a pair of bedrooms and a bath. I felt like a sap for handing the book over to Rinn Biletnikov.

Each bedroom was twelve by twelve. A glance told me one was for sleeping, the other for dressing and primping—it'd been turned into a giant closet with a makeup table and mirror.

I tossed the true bedroom first. Didn't find a shotgun with I KILLED GUS etched on the barrel. Didn't find much of anything.

Checked my watch. Nearly two minutes left.

In the second room: nothing nothing nothing. Clothes, tossed here and there, some still with tags from high-end stores.

Hell. Now what?

I gave each of Rinn's clothing drawers a five-second look-through. And there were a lot of them—she'd brought in a second full-sized dresser. I guess she liked clothes.

Nothing.

Finally, with less than a minute before I ought to get out, I rifled each of the dressing table's smaller drawers.

Looking for the world's smallest shotgun, numbnuts?

But once you start, you've got to finish.

Top to bottom on the left: makeup makeup makeup, blow-dryer, Q-tips and cotton balls.

Nada.

Top to bottom on the right: makeup makeup makeup, a half-dozen varieties of tampon-type stuff, and . . . my head knew I was a few seconds over my three-minute limit now, whip that drawer open . . .

"Well," I said.

A stack of gift boxes. Each one the size of a deck of cards, all identically gift wrapped in primo-looking silver paper. I finger-shuffled. There were a half dozen of them. They gave off a sad vibe, though I wasn't sure why. The topmost one was dusty.

I plucked the box second from the top, leaving the top one and its dust undisturbed. Professional gift wrapping had covered the box and lid separately, so I could open the box without tearing paper.

I did.

And blinked at a silver iPod.

That was it.

What the hell?

I thumbed the power switch on. The little screen told me only that the battery needed juice.

I opened another box.

Same deal, right down to the iPod's silver color.

Then a third, just to be dead sure.

Looked at my watch. I'd been inside nearly five minutes.

Get out.

I did.

But I took two boxes with me. Two was the right number—if Rinn opened the drawer, which I doubted she did often, the stack wouldn't look different.

There was something going on with these damn iPods.

You don't feel the I-got-away-with-it-again rush until you're away from the home, counting the cash and planning where to fence the rest. That's the way I recall it, anyway. But my memory's not always so hot where those days are concerned.

I was sitting in a Dunkin' Donuts parking lot on Concord Street in Framingham. Had backed my truck into a slot so I could watch the street and check for cruisers. My cell's charger didn't fit the iPods, so I was staring at them, wondering why they'd felt worth taking.

When in doubt, call Randall.

He picked up on three.

"I tossed Peter Biletnikov's home," I said. "Including Rinn's quarters. Found something you should see."

"Slow down there, my good man," Randall said. His voice wasn't quite normal.

I said, "Everything all right?"

"As rain. I'm squiring the party in question even as we speak."

I said nothing for a while. My ears began to whine. Finally: "You're with her? With Rinn? *Now?*"

"Rinn, Peter, Haley, and little Emma. We're on a window-shopping expedition in Wellesley. Rinn's a native, you may recall."

"Why'd she haul you along? Where do you fit?"

"Personal security was mentioned."

"Horseshit." I thought for maybe three seconds. "She likes you the way you like her. She brought you along as a power play, something to shove in Peter's face. He's gritting his teeth and taking it. Am I right?"

"Astutely guessed as usual. Hang on, she's telling me something."

Back-and-forth chatter while he covered the phone with the heel of his hand.

When Randall came back on he said, "Would you care to join us? An invitation has been proffered."

"You don't sound too thrilled about that."

"I'll take that as a no?"

"No. Yes. I mean, yes, I'm coming. You on the main drag there, where everything costs an arm and a leg?"

"The very one."

"Fifteen minutes." I clicked off.

Randall was hanging out with Rinn? If you looked at it one way, it was no surprise. He was doing as I'd asked, and doing it with extra thoroughness.

But her *husband* was along for the ride?

Yikes.

Poor bastard.

No way was I going to miss it.

CHAPTER THIRTY-ONE

Lord, she is a perfect little thing. Aren't you, Emma? Aren't you a perfect little thing?"

The woman leaning over the navy-blue stroller was a friend of Rinn's parents. Twenty years older than me, she looked five years younger. Straight blond hair, blue eyes, toned arm muscles in a green silk T-shirt.

That's how they grow 'em in Wellesley. Rinn must feel right at home in Sherborn. She'd moved from one of the state's ritziest towns to another.

I'd found them—most of them, anyway—on Washington Street, the main drag.

"Where's Peter?" I'd asked Randall when I climbed from my truck, which was the only non-Prius or -BMW in sight.

He jerked his thumb at a restaurant across the street, Blue something.

"He got hungry?" I said. It was barely noon.

"Thirsty," Randall said.

"Oh," I said.

"Yes," Haley said. "Oh."

I had a dozen questions for Randall, but they had to wait—we glided down the sidewalk in a pack that felt, I could tell, as awkward to Haley and Randall as it did to me.

Not to Rinn, though. She was the queen bee. She moved and smiled like there was an invisible documentary team trailing her. She'd greeted me with a better kiss than I deserved. Then she'd tried to get me to ooh and ah over a new baby blanket. It was no bigger than a bath mat, and it cost a hundred and forty bucks. I had a hard time oohing.

When Rinn spotted her parents' friends, she snapped the stroller from Haley's grasp and trundled ahead, leaving the rest of us to grouse amongst ourselves. That's when I figured out the real point of the trip: for Rinn Biletnikov, formerly Brittania Whitney of Wellesley, to show the hometown gang what a model mommy she was.

At the same time, though, she'd brought Randall, disguised as security. I didn't know where the two of them stood—they hadn't had a chance to do much more than flirt—but her decision to parade him through her hometown clicked with things I already knew about her. The split in her soul that Crump had mentioned, half of her wanting to be Little Miss Picket Fence while the other half whiffed cocaine with rough trade. *Look at me, I'm with my hubby and my baby . . . and this studly black dude.*

A man holding two Starbucks cups crossed the street and handed one to the blond woman. The man kissed Rinn's cheek, then leaned over the stroller and said most of the things his wife had said already. They made a good couple: the man had snow-white hair, but all of it. Pro haircut, Polo T-shirt, Rolex Daytona, no belly.

He glanced at me, Haley, and Randall, then asked Rinn when her folks were coming up from Longboat Key. I guessed it wasn't unusual for a young mom in Wellesley to go shopping with a nanny and two guys who looked like security.

Rinn: chatting, poised, easy, looking like she belonged here and nowhere else. She was something to see. Had me half-convinced she was ready to join the Garden Club. It was tough to picture her sniffing cocaine in a crappy UMass apartment.

Emma stepped on Rinn's buzz, though, by crying out.

Then again, louder.

The couple said "Awwww" and laughed understandingly. Next to me, Haley took a half step forward, then froze. She clenched and unclenched her hands.

I said, "You going to help her out?"

Haley's eyes never left the stroller. "Rinn said to let her handle things. She wants all of Wellesley to think she's a real mommy."

I looked at Randall. He shrugged.

We watched.

Rinn's shoulder blades tightened, but she kept conversing.

That was fine for a minute or two, but Rinn kept it up even as Emma's crying grew throaty, insistent.

The man and woman seemed puzzled now. They looked into the stroller, then back at Rinn, waiting for her to do what moms do.

Still, Rinn ignored Emma. She kept talking about problems at the marina on Longboat Key.

Emma's squalling gained momentum, volume.

Finally, the blond woman said, "Is the little sweetie hungry?"

Rinn acted as if she'd just noticed. She reached into the stroller like she was baiting a bear trap. She lifted Emma, but not like any mother I'd ever seen—she plucked her from the stroller by the waist and held her at arm's length, elbows locked. She half-glanced back at Haley.

I said, "Now?"

"I don't know," Haley said, damn near crying. "Rinn told me three times to back off while we're here. Things get ugly when I disobey her."

But while she spoke, the three of us crept closer like a bunch of kids playing red light–green light. I guess we won, because we didn't stop until we'd made ourselves part of the group.

A look passed between the couple. The woman, anyway, had seen through Rinn. She said she remembered those days well and that

Rinn should kiss her folks for them. She tried to smile while she said it, but didn't have much luck. The couple walked away whispering. The man looked back once.

Emma's squalls were now making people across the street stare. The baby was twisting, torquing, red-faced. Even I knew her head shouldn't be whipping around like that.

Haley couldn't stand it anymore. She took Emma from Rinn, held the baby against her own chest, supported her head. She rocked. She cooed. She reached in a shoulder bag and came out with a bottle.

Rinn looked at me, then at Randall. She breathed through flared nostrils, tears at the corners of her eyes.

"Fine," she said. "Fucking fine." And she crossed to Starbucks.

Right in the middle of the street, stopping traffic in both directions—but cars don't honk in Wellesley—she spun and said, "Haley!"

"Shit," Haley said. I'd never seen her flustered this way. She looked at me. Looked at Randall.

"*Haley!*" Rinn again.

Looking miserable, the nanny shoved Emma into my arms and trotted after Rinn.

"That went well," Randall said.

I ignored him.

I'd been hit by lightning.

It's the only way to describe the feeling. Holding a baby. *That* baby, anyhow.

She was ignoring the bottle, which I handed to Randall. She was holding tiny fists to her chest, gazing at me with blue eyes.

I gazed back.

I couldn't do anything else. The lightning strike had taken me places, put me places, racked me with recollections and visions and half dreams and I don't know what else.

I was Emma. I was me now. I was six-month-old me. I was my mother in Mankato, *holding* six-month-old me. I was everything, everybody, everywhere. I was all of it, all of *them*.

If I could describe it better, I would.

Mostly, though, I was . . . warm. Not warm now, in Wellesley springtime sunshine. Warm in Mankato. Six-months-old warm, mother's-arms warm.

I was loved completely.

I was forgiven completely.

I was pure.

"Are you all right?"

Randall's eyes told me he knew something was up.

I wanted to explain.

How could I?

I wanted to stay wherever that feeling took me.

But it ebbed.

It took everything I had to shift gears.

"You got an iPhone charger in your car?" I said.

"Of course. Why?"

"Tell you later. Take the two little boxes from my pocket." I shoved my hip at him.

He shrugged, reached, pulled. "Soon as you can," I said, "juice those up enough to tell me what's on them."

"Juice what?"

"You'll see."

"Do I get to ask what the hell's going on?"

"Do I get to ask why you're sporting around with Rinn Biletnikov? And her husband, for crying out loud?"

"I was *supposed* to cozy up, was I not? I have. And I've learned things. Things I'll tell you later."

"But the *husband*. Seems to me enough people have made him a doormat."

Randall's face went shiny, which meant he was mad. And maybe feeling guilty. "Rinn's invitations carry a certain insistence, a certain urgency."

"She's a spoiled brat who's never been told no."

"There's a whole boatload you don't know about her. Come to think of it, though, that's seldom a barrier for you."

"She's also married."

"Not in any meaningful sense."

"*Aha*!" I tried to laugh, but it came out more like a horse noise. "I get it. You two been having deep chats? *Meaningful* chats?"

"Don't be an asshole, amigo. And smile. Here comes Haley."

I handed her the baby and stomped across the street to find Peter. The lightning jolt I'd felt when I held Emma faded so quickly I wondered if it was real.

Other than a pair of old-timers eating grilled cheese sandwiches at the far end of the bar, he was the only customer. He stood with one foot propped on the brass rail. The white-shirt, black-slacks bartender, a gal with a brown ponytail sticking out directly above her left ear, was slicing lemons and filling bowls with maraschino cherries.

When Peter spotted me in the mirror, he slapped the bar hard. "There he is! Come join me, friend."

Experience told me he was on his third stiff one—deep into I Love You Man, ready to cross the border to Fuck 'Em All and Fuck You Too.

He hoisted his highball. "Join me."

I said, "Nah."

"Too early for you?"

"Too late."

He spent five seconds figuring it out, then barked a laugh. "I forgot! A teetotaler. A dedicated alcoholic, and don't you forget it."

I said nothing. It was starting, and I had to let it run its course. I wanted to see, for the first time, Peter Biletnikov act the way he felt— not the way he thought he should act.

Booze'll do that for you.

"This temperance," he said. "It does not suit your persona."

"What do you mean?"

He set down the drink, balled his fists, and flexed his arms like a weightlifter. Or a gorilla. "Conway Sax, man's man. He-man. *All* man. You really ought to be a two-fisted drinker to complete the pose, don't you think?"

Man. Man. Man. Pose. If I hadn't known already about Peter Biletnikov's problem, I would have figured it out then and there.

I thought while he babbled about Hemingway and real men and the good old days. Everything about him—job, house, wife, the string of pretty young women he liked to be seen with—looked right from the outside. But it was all a series of shells. Where it counted, he didn't consider himself a man.

Next thought in the chain: Emma. Rinn had said Peter was her father. But she'd said it on the fly, had tried to breeze her way past it.

And Crump, whose payback plans got him killed, had sure smelled a rat. What had he said? *Rinn's baby girl . . . Who's her daddy?*

And Randall agreed with me that Peter showed no connection whatsoever to Emma, who was supposed to be his midlife-crisis baby.

Huh.

It needed looking at. Not because I cared about the Biletnikov richfolks soap opera—nothing would make me happier than to walk away from the whole twisted group—but because some subplot in that soap opera might help me figure out who gut-shot Gus. And while I was too late for a lot of things and a lot of people, I wasn't too late to do right by him.

Right now, though, I had to change the subject. Wanted to learn how well-lubricated Peter truly felt about his son.

"Gus was a good kid," I said. "On his way to being a good man."

"The things you said at the funeral. It should have been me who said them."

"You were too choked up."

"Was I?" Peter thumped his glass to the bar. "Or was I chicken? Was I incapable?"

I said nothing.

"It should have been me," he said.

I could barely hear him.

He stared at nothing, shoulders down.

We were quiet awhile.

The bartender looked at Peter's glass, then at me. I shook my head. She moved down to the grilled-cheese guys and let them flirt with her.

"I helped with the track," Peter finally said.

"What track?"

"The motocross track in the yard. I helped Gus build it. Did he mention that?"

" 'Fraid he didn't."

"Of course he didn't. This is the story of our relationship." He sipped. "He was twelve at the time. He needed help, and lots of it. We cut down saplings. We dug out banked turns until our palms bled. For God's sake, he convinced me to buy a truckload of soil to make jumps and whoop-de-dos. Do you know what whoop-de-dos are?"

"Sure."

"You are one of the few. Gus explained them to me." Peter rattled the almost-gone ice cubes in his glass. "The awful thing. Or is it a funny thing? In either case, the thing is, I truly don't think Gus remembers my help, the father-son aspect of the project. He became such an angry teenager. And he's a storyteller by nature—"

"A natural-born bullshitter," I said, hoping Peter would take it the right way.

His smile told me he did. "I believe he can twist even his clearest memories. He can make them fit his narrative, make them suit his purposes."

"Gus said you tore the track apart when the neighbors griped. Did he have that part right?"

"He did. Dammit, he did. The bastard just south of me is a supercilious Ropes and Gray prick. He has five grown children, all with nicknames like Cubby and Mish. Collegiate swimmers, each and every one of them—you know the type. The black sheep of the family is the one who settled for Dartmouth." He shook his head. "Five damn kids, can you believe that?"

"And the neighbor bitched about the track."

"That he did. He made me feel . . ."

Peter trailed off.

"This was before Rinn?"

"Oh yes. This Ropes and Gray prick managed to make it sound as if I'd put in a trailer park. While Gus was at camp that summer, I had two men bulldoze the whole mess and haul away the fill. I'm not sure Gus has ever forgiven me."

Pause.

"Ever *forgave* me," he said to his highball glass. "I've been speaking in the wrong tense, haven't I? Please accept my apologies. Also, please leave me."

Peter turned to the bartender, but she was already building his next drink.

She was a good bartender.

In sunlight again, I blinked. Looked up and down the block, saw no sign of Randall or Rinn. Which was a drag, because I had a lot to say to both of them.

Hell.

Checked my watch. I could hit the shop. That was the thing to do. See if Andrade was pulling his weight. Shuffle paperwork. Call a few slow-pays.

I climbed in my truck and aimed west.

Randall called as I clunked from traffic light to traffic light on Route 9.

"So what's the big deal with these iPods?" he said.

I hesitated, not knowing anymore how much I should—*could*—tell him.

"Are you, ah, alone?"

"Yes. You know, a little flirting with lovely Rinn doesn't have to mean I'm trying to get in her pants."

Kid reads me like a book. A comic book.

"It doesn't *have* to," I said. "But it usually does."

"Look, let's get past that. What's up with the iPods?"

I decided to trust him. Hell, he was Randall. I organized the story, then told it in thirty seconds.

When I finished, he was quiet for a long time.

"Well?" I finally said.

"A wrench has been well and truly thrown."

"Well?"

"Each iPod holds music, and not a lot," he said. "Ridiculously small playlists, actually, given the capacity."

"What kind of music?"

"Jazz. There's a set by Ron Charles on one iPod and a set by Brubeck on the other. Must have been one of his last shows."

"So?"

"The sets were recorded live at the Hi Hat. They're introduced by the owner and impresario. None other than."

I said nothing, feeling it sink in.

"These iPods," Randall said, "are love letters from Charlie Pundo to Rinn Biletnikov."

CHAPTER THIRTY-TWO

We switched roles.

Me: the cool one, running alternative scenarios up the flagpole, trying to give Rinn or Pundo or *somebody* the benefit of the doubt.

Randall: righteously pissed, ready to kick some ass, not overly concerned about whose.

We met at the cemetery near the Biletnikov place. Randall insisted on it—wanted to surprise Rinn, which meant we couldn't park in the driveway. We cut from the cemetery to the guesthouse, passing the clearing where Rinn had found Gus's body.

Black-red hole in a black sweatshirt. Bangs across the forehead like a boy . . . hell, say it . . . like Roy asleep after a long day in the sun.

I tightened my jaw. Kept moving.

Randall found the guesthouse key as easily as I had. Once we were inside, he asked where the other iPods were, pounded down the hall, came back with all of them.

Then we waited.

I tried to calm him, but the excuses I made for Rinn sounded weak even to me. It was hard not to assume that, at the very least,

Charlie Pundo had a thing for her. Did it run both ways? Whether it did or not, the fact that she'd hidden it from me and the cops forced us to take a fresh look at her.

"I should have known," he said at one point, arms folded, looking out the window. "Given the Crump story."

"What Crump story?"

"Their deal. He didn't tell you?"

"She was interning for Biletnikov when Donald came sniffing around for money, right?"

"Sure, but there's a bit more to it than that."

"So tell me."

"Crump oozed into Thunder Junction one day, hat in hand. He made quite the impression, as you might imagine."

"I can see it." I smiled, thinking about how old Donald's getup would go over in Cambridge, where uptight people pretended not to be uptight.

Then I thought of Donald collapsing onto me in a Hopkinton parking lot, the blown-out exit wound in his left temple. And stopped smiling.

Randall went on. Crump had worked Thunder Junction's offices like the pro he was, cycling through as many employees as he could in search of a weak link.

He thought he found it in Rinn Biletnikov, college girl. He worked her, charmed her, got her business card.

What Donald Crump didn't realize: that day, he was more mark than shark.

"Clever," I said. "Think that up yourself?"

Randall shrugged, smiled, continued.

An after-work drink at a local bar confirmed what Rinn had already figured out: Donald was looking for eyes and ears inside Thunder Junction.

"Rinn agreed to be those eyes and ears," Randall said. "For a price."

He looked a challenge at me. But given the timing, it wasn't much of a challenge.

I laid my thumb alongside my nose. "She needed more of this."

He mock-clapped for me. "Gus and Brad had worn out their welcome with Teddy Pundo. And Rinn had crossed that line, the one with which you're far more familiar than I, separating want from need. Where that particular substance was concerned."

I thought it through.

It worked.

The timing, the connection, the familiarity between Rinn and Donald.

But wait.

"Biletnikov wound up hosing Crump good and hard," I said.

"Right you are."

"Rinn must have been part of that hosing."

"An integral part."

"She used him to score, then double-crossed him?"

"Precisely." Long pause. "She is something, is she not?"

I shook my head. Damn right she was.

We waited some more. I played with the new info on Rinn and Donald. Did it change anything? Did it make me more or less likely to look at anybody as Gus's killer?

I was still thinking at three o'clock, when Randall said, "Here they are." We watched them pile out of the BMW: tipsy Peter, making for the main house without saying anything to anybody. Rinn, heading our way. Haley, who'd driven, lagging behind to pull Emma from her car seat.

I sat in the room's comfiest chair like a spectator. This was Randall's show, and I wanted to see how he played it.

Answer: harsh.

Rinn keyed her way in, closed the door, saw us, jumped half a foot.

"What the *hell*?" she said, her right hand over her heart. She looked at Randall, who was leaning on the bar that separated the living room from the tiny kitchen.

Then she looked at me.

Then back at Randall, whose face told her he was the boss right now.

She set hands on hips. "What the hell, Randall? Scare a girl half to death."

Instead of saying anything, Randall tossed a double handful of silver-wrapped boxes at her feet.

She looked at them, puzzled at first. Then her eyes sharpened and she put a hand over her mouth.

"Oh," Rinn Biletnikov said.

Then she said it again.

Then she sank toward the floor, dropping into a peasant crouch, ending up with rump against calves and both forearms covering her face. Like a kid hoping if she got small enough, she could disappear.

"Explain," Randall said.

Rinn didn't move.

"To us or to Lima. Your choice."

She stayed in her you-can't-see-me crouch until he pulled his phone and asked me Lima's number.

"No," Rinn said, dropping the arms. Her eyes were wet. "No."

Then she crawled around the floor picking up scattered iPods.

I sneaked a sideways look at Randall. I'd never seen him this way. He must've felt even more for Rinn than he'd let on.

Now he felt like a jackass. Embarrassment had turned his crush into fury.

I rose and found a box of Kleenex. Gentled the iPods and boxes from Rinn's arms, steered her to the couch, told her I'd put everything away.

She said, "They go—"

"I know."

Half-beat pause. "You? Not him?"

"I searched the main house. Figured I ought to search here, too."

"Tell me about you and Charlie," Randall said.

"Easy there, hotshot," she said as she sat.

I may have smiled as I walked down the hall to put away the iPods. You could knock Rinn Biletnikov off her game. But not for long.

By the time I got back, she'd wiped her eyes and crossed her legs and started. "When I told you about Peter's issues, I didn't tell you everything."

"That's putting it mildly," Randall said.

Her eyes flashed. "Do you blame me? I left off where things turned ugly."

I said, "They weren't already?"

Rinn ignored that. She was talking to Randall now. I don't know if she felt for him some of what he felt for her, but she *wanted* something from him. Approval? Understanding?

"When it became clear that Peter and I weren't going to accomplish any baby-making the old-fashioned way," she said, "I gritted my teeth and looked into alternatives. I was willing to take one for the team."

"In vitro, et cetera," he said.

She nodded. "Peter flew into a righteous Russian rage and told me to stop researching the matter immediately. He was almost clinically paranoid by then. He frothed that Boston's medical community is an incestuous one, and he'd be damned if he'd have everybody knowing his business. He, ah . . ."

We waited.

The sun had worked its way around. Outside, shadow now covered the cottage porch and half the backyard.

"He had an alternative proposition," Rinn said in a voice that wasn't hers, the voice of a shy eighth-grade girl.

Randall said, "And that proposition was?"

"He proposed to have Gus knock me up," she said. "He proposed to pay us a million-dollar flat fee apiece to make a baby and keep quiet about it."

You could barely hear her.

I sat with my mouth open. The word that jammed itself in my head: "freaks." Goddamn freaks, the lot of 'em. Give people all the money in the world and what do they do? Dream up new ways to be rotten.

"Dear God," Randall said, sliding to the couch, wrapping arms around Rinn. "Dear God."

She cried into his chest.

We let her.

Randall stroked her hair.

"It was *awful*," she said after a while, blubbering so I barely understood. "We were *buds*! We were *pals*! The Three Musketeers, Gus and Brad and Rinn."

"Peter's never admitted it to me," I said, "but he had to know Gus didn't like girls. I'm guessing part of what drove him was to . . . alter that. Fix it. Couldn't make his own privates work right, so he took a shot at his kid's."

"That's not the most gracious or politically correct way to put it," Rinn said, dabbing her eyes with a Kleenex. "But it's accurate enough." She blew her nose.

Randall said, "It appears the experiment was a success?"

"A dismal failure. In every way."

He looked a question at her.

Rinn shrugged. "Gus and I gave it the old college try. No luck. Our sessions became grotesque reenactments of my efforts with Peter. Can you see how miserable that would be for Gus?"

Randall said, "Not so hot for you, either."

"By then, you'd told Gus all about how his dad couldn't get it up," I said. "I'm betting it was one of the things you all made fun of Peter for."

"Gus always thought of himself as pansexual, an if-it-feels-good-do-it type," Rinn said. "Our epic bedroom failures forced him to reevaluate. They ruined our friendship, of course. They made Brad hate my guts. He was always much more into Gus than Gus was into him."

Freaks.

Rinn half-laughed. "About the time I was ready to break out the turkey baster, along came an opportunity that seemed to solve everything."

"Charlie Goddamn Pundo," Randall said.

I took an easy guess. "Somewhere along the line, during your big cocaine spree, Charlie fell for you."

"We met at the Hi Hat and fell for each *other*." Now she locked eyes with me. "I *told* you, this is not a one-way street for me and never has been. Charlie has been places. He's done things. He's got this . . . he's got something similar to what *you* have."

I said, "A truck payment he can't afford and a drinking problem?" Neither of them laughed.

"Did Pundo know you were pregnant? And that the baby was his?" Rinn nodded.

"How'd he react?"

"He was thrilled. He'd always wanted a girl, believe it or not."

"I can see where he would have struck you as impressive," Randall said. "Especially after you'd been palling around with Peters and Guses and Brads."

"Half-men and boys and potheads," I said. "And you've got that bad-girl side to you."

"Exactly." She shook her head to clear it. "Charlie and I became a furtive item. Meanwhile, I was procuring coke from Teddy on a regular basis, and Charlie knew nothing about that—he would have killed Teddy if he had. When I learned I was pregnant, I confided in Gus. It seemed so . . . *elegant* to have the baby."

"Peter would think she was Gus's, with that lovely Biletnikov DNA," Randall said. "The rest of the world would think Peter was a testosterone champ, makin' whoopee with his gorgeous young wife."

"And you and Gus would pocket a million apiece," I said. "But what did Pundo think of the plan?"

"It didn't bother him. He said he wanted a daughter, not *credit* for a daughter."

We said nothing for awhile. "There's one other thing I want you to know," Rinn said, "though I assume it's too late for you to ever respect me. The minute, no, the *instant* the pregnancy was confirmed, I quit the cocaine like that." Finger snap. "Everything else, too, including booze. I found I didn't want it anymore."

She sneaked a glance at me.

"You're a goddamn saint is what you are," I said.

CHAPTER THIRTY-THREE

The mind reels," Randall said as we walked the path to the cemetery.

"Freaks," I said.

"So what's our move?"

I thought about that as we stepped from woods onto manicured grass. His car and my truck were maybe fifty yards away.

"From the get-go, Donald acted like he had dirt on Peter Biletnikov," I said.

"And?"

"Not 'and.' 'But.' He was vague as hell. I put it down to con man's instinct, the urge to always hold back. Maybe it was something else, though. What if he suspected this freak show but hadn't confirmed anything when I first met him?"

Randall knew where I was headed. "He did confirm it eventually. And the confirmation got him killed."

"By whoever killed Gus, most likely. Anybody who looked ready to blow the secret got wiped out."

"And who wanted the secret kept in the worst way?"

"Peter Biletnikov," I said. "And Charlie Pundo."

He leaned on his car. "Peter I'll buy. The man's all about appearances, and the second wife with the bouncing baby means *way* more to him than it should. He's got inadequacy issues, paranoia issues. Maybe he goes a little crazy when the secret looks shaky."

"But you're not sold on Charlie Pundo?"

He shrugged. "A wiseguy bangs a young broad who digs outlaw types. This is not unprecedented." Randall's voice: bitter, brittle.

"I guess. But the iPods. That's Harry High School stuff. Mixtapes, remember those?"

"It was mix *CDs* when I came along, gramps. But okay. Point taken. It's out of character."

"Unless it's not."

He looked at me.

"Unless," I said, "there's more to that character than we know."

I climbed in my truck and headed for Charlene's place.

Charlene wasn't home. I found Sophie in her room, laying out her cheerleading uniform and gear.

"Almost forgot," I said, sitting on the edge of the bed. "Big competition tomorrow. Worcester?"

"Springfield." She didn't look at me. She grabbed a can of hairspray and a brush that had rolled toward my hip when I sat, moved them a few feet. Davey, who spent twenty-three hours a day on the bed, opened one eye. I knew my other cat, Dale, would be under the bed, ready to swat my ankle when I rose.

Sophie looked over her array, still not lifting her eyes.

"What's wrong?" I said.

"Jessie's gone again."

Hell. "Same guys?"

"No, she left with Kaydee. She borrowed a hundred dollars from me."

"Where's your mom?"

"Where do you think?"

Work.

"There's nothing we can do," Sophie said. "Is there?"

"I guess not."

I stood. Sure enough, Dale took a rip at my boot. It's how he asks for attention.

I carried him downstairs, told him he could help me put a frozen pizza in the oven. He lay in my arms like a baby, white belly up, and chirped. He does that.

While the pizza heated, Charlene texted. She'd be home in fifteen minutes. I texted back that dinner was under control. Then I looked at my cell, weighed it in my hand. What the hell. I dialed Lima.

"Where do you stand on the shotgun?" I said when he picked up.

"At the corner of Who's Asking and Go Fuck Yourself," he said. "You got a set of balls, Sax."

"I'm going to tell you something you don't know."

Pause. "Okay. Listening."

I hit Lima with the bomb about Charlie Pundo and Rinn Biletnikov. I hard-sold, starting with the iPods.

"You saw those iPods while you tossed the Biletnikov place," he said when I finished. "Just like you said you would."

I said nothing.

The line was quiet awhile.

"It's interesting shit, I'll give you that," Lima finally said. "But where does it *take* us? Where does it hook up to Almost Home or the Biletnikov kid?"

"Seems to me," I said, "a few more steps will get you there. Somebody's jealous. Somebody's being squeezed for dough."

He sighed. "My first homicide. Why couldn't I get a gangbanger blasting a gangbanger while a dozen wits and a security cam watched the whole thing?"

"Where are you with the shotgun?"

"The tat for your tit." He laughed.

I said nothing.

"Good news, bad news," Lima said. "The good's that ATF, DHS, and FBI jumped when they heard about the piece. Turns out there's this cat in the Czech Republic. A little man, they say, 'bout ninety years old. He starts with a single stainless-steel billet, crafts a shotgun in any configuration you like, ships 'em all over the world. All the customer needs is a suitcase full of money. Price per gun starts at a hundred grand. The Feds would love to cream this dude mostly because he makes fools of them—he's got a bunch of tricks for shipping the weapons one piece at a time."

"What's the bad news?"

"The Feds have about as much sway in the Czech Republic as they do on the moon. They know exactly who made the piece, but there's not a damn thing they can do about it."

"Shit."

"Yeah, shit."

"Let me nail something down," I said. "Just for the hell of it. Is the shotgun from Crump's SUV the one from Almost Home and Gus?"

He said nothing.

"I'm not asking for court-of-law proof," I said. "Come on, Lima. You know, or think you know. Same gun?"

"It has not been ruled out."

Now *I* said nothing.

"It's all I'm allowed to say." He sounded sorry about it.

I didn't give a rat's ass if he was sorry.

"My pizza's ready," I said. And clicked off.

It wasn't a good night, what with the cardboard pizza and Sophie mourning and me thinking about the case and Charlene trying to pretend everything was okay.

But we got through it.

At two in the morning, the home phone and my cell rang at the same time. The cell was a Framingham cop. The home line was a reporter from the *MetroWest Daily News*.

Both callers said my shop was on fire.

It was two thirty by the time I got there.

Ladder trucks, engines, pumpers, ambulances, cop cars. Half a dozen sirens screaming at each other. The fire crew had axed a hole in the roll-up door, busted out all the windows. They were hosing like crazy. It looked like the fire was under control, and this was mop-up time.

I stepped. I stared. I felt heat on my face.

My jaw: slack.

A cop asked who the hell did I think I was and tried to chase me off.

Another cop told him I was the owner.

I said nothing to either of them. I just stood and watched and thought.

There were at least two customer cars inside. They were junk. It looked like more customer cars in the parking lot were goners, too, between the hoses and the heat. I wondered if Floriano had backed up the computer. I wondered about my insurance. I wondered if we'd kept up with all the EPA and OSHA bullshit. The insurance companies love to find a regulation you missed, then screw you with it.

I wondered, in other words, the things you wonder while you watch your business burn.

With no warning, I felt like I'd been punched in the gut. I dropped to a knee. The nearest cop asked if I was okay. I nodded. He said wait here, then left. Came back in thirty seconds with what had to be the boss firefighter.

I stood. We shook hands.

He said he was sorry, then yelled in my ear. "How many waste-oil drums you got?"

I held up one finger.

"How full?"

I had to yell myself. "Been two weeks and change since they pumped it out. Must be pretty full by now."

He mouthed: *Fuck*.

On cue came a deep, dull thump as forty gallons of dirty oil caught fire.

A new round of flames jetted from the windows and the bashed-in door. Neighbors screamed. Firemen backed up, controlled but fast. Every cop in sight started herding civilians away.

I backed from the heat on my face. Matt Bogardis, the cop, came over. He walked me to a cruiser where we didn't have to yell.

"Your neighbor saw something," Matt said. "Or heard, actually."

"Which neighbor?"

"The guy owns the aquarium-supply store. He sleeps on a cot in his back room. I guess his family life ain't so hot."

"What'd he hear?"

"A window breaking. Just before she caught."

I looked at Matt.

"While the fire was under control," he said, "I took a quick look at the window. I wanted to see if maybe it popped once the heat built up."

"Did it?"

He shook his head. "There's no glass in the alley. It broke from the outside in. Your place was firebombed, Conway."

Then Matt patted my shoulder and asked what I needed and said things about nobody being hurt and thank God for insurance, huh?

I wasn't listening, and I wasn't thinking about insurance.

I was thinking about the Pundos.

I was thinking about how they were going to pay.

CHAPTER THIRTY-FOUR

This was the third shop I'd owned. It was the most successful by far, but I wasn't married to it the way I'd been to the previous two. Maybe because we'd been up and running less than a year. Maybe because we worked mostly on Japanese cars, rather than the BMWs and Mercedes I loved.

Maybe because Charlene had bankrolled this one.

By the time the cops and the firemen were done interviewing me, there was no sense trying to sleep.

Besides, I was enjoying my revenge plan. Savoring it. Felt like I *finally* had a clean target: the House of Pundo. Sure, I'd had my eye on Peter Biletnikov for Gus's murder. But this changed that. A firebombing was a gangster move all the way. I would've tipped to that even if I hadn't watched Charlie Pundo's guys torch his warehouse.

No way would I call Randall this time. He'd just talk me out of it.

I was going west hard and hot, and if the Pundos weren't nervous about it, they ought to be.

That was the plan, anyway. The 4:30 A.M., false-dawn, shivering-on-the-bumper-of-a-fire-truck plan.

But false dawn's a rough time.

All the gung ho had trickled from me, leaving me instead with the image of Gus dead in his backyard, a few feet from the motocross track he made as a kid.

I was fighting to get the gung ho back when my cell rang.

Charlene.

I'd filled her in at three. She shouldn't be awake at four thirty.

"Jessie was arrested last night," she said. Her voice: equal parts exhaustion, panic, competence. She was holding herself together. Barely.

"Tell me," I said.

"She was running with a pack of college kids. Some crazy off-campus loft party, as far as I can tell. I'm in Worcester. They'll release her to me soon, and then we go straight to family court."

"On Saturday?"

"They set it up special. They had to. There are a couple hundred kids here. It was a rave that turned into an orgy that turned into a riot."

"Hell."

"The police broke it up twice. The third time, some of the boys got mouthy and started bumping the cops. A car got turned over. The cops called in the riot squad. Conway?"

"I'm here."

"The policeman at the desk says Jessie was loaded." Sadder than I've ever heard her.

"Booze? Meth? Pills?"

"I don't know. Her pupils were dilated, she was abusive, she couldn't follow directions. Or wouldn't. They . . . Conway, they hogtied her with those puh . . . puh . . . plastic handcuffs to get her in a police car. The man at the desk said they had no choice . . ."

Charlene wept.

My heart hurt.

I said, "I can be there in twenty-five minutes."

"No! Hang on." She blew her nose and took a breath I could hear. "I can take care of this end. I need you to handle Sophie for me."

"Okay." Then I remembered the cheerleading comp.

In Springfield.

"The team meets at ten at the Civic Center," Charlene said. "She needs her uniform, and a high ponytail, and her bag, and a water—"

"She's got it under control. Had it all laid out last night. I saw it."

Charlene gave me numbers for her sister—I hate her and she hates me—and Sophie's coach. After the comp, the girls would go out for dinner as a team. I should make sure Sophie wound up in somebody's car. "Take good care of her. It's a buh . . . buh . . . big day for her. And it'll be wild at the Civic Center, all those girls running around. Buh . . . buy her flowers, okay?"

I said I would.

"And the shop," she said, really losing it. "Why *now*, why all this at once?"

"Don't worry about the shop," I said. "I got you covered."

"Yes," Charlene said. "You do. Thank you. I love you." Click.

A comp in Springfield.

Huh.

I sighed, rubbed my eyes, went to my truck.

"How old do you have to be," I said, "before you remember things?"

"*That* came out of nowhere," Sophie said.

Sophie: sweater and skirt in white, gold, blue. Across the top: CO-LONIALS. Ponytail tied high on her head with blue and gold ribbons. Glittery stuff in her hair. Sneakers white as a movie star's teeth.

We were on the Mass Turnpike, logging westbound miles. It'd been a quiet ride. I was thinking about the shop. Surprise feeling: freedom. No urgency about rebuilding, reopening. Instead: something that felt an awful lot like relief.

That would be an interesting conversation with Charlene. She's not big on letting the spirit move you. She believes in hard work and lots of it.

Floriano wouldn't suffer. He had standing offers from two indie shops that I knew of.

I did feel bad for Andrade. Like Floriano and me, he'd lost six or eight grand in tools. Mine and Floriano's were insured. I doubted Andrade's were. Mental note: ask if he needed help getting by until his elbow healed.

When I pictured Fat Teddy Pundo lobbing the Molotov cocktail in my back window, then hopping in his Mercedes with Boxer the wheelman, my temples pounded. Black, red, black.

I needed to send my head in a different direction.

That's why I asked Sophie about memory.

"How old?" I said.

She smoothed her skirt, flattening each pleat. "There's not as much consensus as you'd think. Most experts agree four is the age at which genuine, lifelong memory begins. Now many people report recollections from much earlier, but the hard research explains these as implanted memories—stories that were told around the dinner table for so long, and in such detail, the subject mistakenly believes he recalls the event itself."

"Anybody ever tell you you're pretty smart?"

She shook imaginary pom-poms, looked straight through the windshield. "Hold that line!"

I smiled.

"Why did you ask?" Sophie said after a mile or so.

"Something happened the other day."

She looked at me. I thought about baby Emma being placed in my arms. The jolt. How I'd been everybody at once: Emma, me now, baby me, my mother then, my mother now.

It had felt so real.

I tried to form up the words. Didn't have much luck.

"It's hard to explain," I said.

"The reason I ask," she said, "and the reason I've looked into it . . . I remember something myself. From when I was younger than two. Eighteen months, or thereabouts. It's very general. But I swear it's a memory, not a memory of being told something. I *know* it is. I think . . . I think we can remember broad concepts before we're three. Specifics? No. Concepts? Yes."

"What do you remember?"

She stared dead ahead, palms on skirt, so long that I asked again.

"Echoes," she finally said. Her voice was tiny.

"Echoes," I said.

"I've always hated them. All my life. A while back, I asked Jessie if she knew why. She teared up and kissed my head and finally told me."

I waited.

"When I was about one and a half, Mom . . . Charlene . . ." Her voice dropped so much I leaned sideways to catch what she said next. ". . . Charlene sold everything in our apartment. The furniture, the housewares. The rugs."

"To get high," I said.

"To get high." Sophie swallowed. "The only thing she *didn't* sell was my high chair. She set me in it and told Jessie to watch me. I cried all morning. In my high chair. With no furniture and no rugs . . ."

"The place echoed." My throat was tight as I said it.

We neared our exit. We'd be at the Civic Center in ten minutes.

Sophie said, "Do you know what Jessie did?"

"What?"

"When the carpet store down the block opened, she carried me there. She asked the man if we could just sit on rugs for a while." She swallowed. "Maybe the man knew Charlene, or knew of her, because he gave us two of those carpet samples the size of a doormat. We took them home and sat on them the rest of the day. Now *that* part I got from Jessie. But the echoes I remember."

"She carried you."

"There and back. And the two samples. She was eight."

I paid the toll.

"Your turn," Sophie said. "What's your early memory?"

I shook my head.

"Not fair. I told you mine. Is it specific, or is it more of a concept? A feeling?"

I thought it through, reached back for that moment Haley set Emma in my arms. The bolt. *I felt loved. I felt forgiven. I felt pure.*

"I remember being warm," I said.

"Sounds legit to me," Sophie said.

CHAPTER THIRTY-FIVE

The Civic Center was a nuthouse, all right. Five hundred or more girls, eight to thirteen. Pumped up, massing in every corner, every stairwell. Blue-white-golds, red-and-whites, blue-and-whites, crimsons, kelly greens, Carolina blues, purple-and-golds, black-and-silvers. Impromptu cheers, laughs, screeches. Volunteer moms counting noses, dazed dads lugging bouquets.

We found the other Shrewsbury Colonials. Sophie forgot all about me in half a second. Head coach: no-nonsense woman about my age, short brown hair, runner's build. I introduced myself so there wouldn't be a problem later when I picked Sophie up.

I grabbed a seat, one of three thousand spectators grouped in the western end of the arena. On the floor: mats, judges' tables, TV gear. Production people, judges, behind-the-scenes workers, all walking around trying not to look self-conscious.

Filling the eastern end: the cheerleaders, squads sitting together to wait their turn. Breaking into spontaneous line dances or cheers when a new song blasted over the PA. The only song I recognized: Queen's "We Are the Champions."

The girls knew them all.

In spite of everything, I caught myself smiling. Picked out Sophie, forty yards away. I waved, but she didn't see me.

When the PA went quiet for a few minutes, I called Floriano. Got voice mail. Left a message about the fire, said let's talk, asked him to check in with Andrade.

Our end of the arena filled. Buzz grew. An emcee with a wireless headset shushed everyone. National anthem, "America the Beautiful," convocation.

The competition began.

Some of the routines were impressive: choreographed to the hilt, girls flying everywhere. Truth be told, though, after twenty minutes they all looked the same to me. I just wanted to see the Colonials. I picked out Sophie again. This time she was looking for me. She smiled, waved.

I zoned out. Thought about the shop, the Biletnikovs, Jessie. I didn't know who her father was—doubted Charlene knew herself—but the smart money said he was a junkie or a drunk or both. Kid was born behind the eight ball.

New movement, a sense of something not right, snapped me back. I cleared my head. Across the way, in a mostly deserted section up high, I caught motion.

I looked.

It took a half beat to register.

Teddy Pundo. Up in the nosebleed seats, standing by himself, holding a half-assed sign, Sharpie on cardboard:

YEA SOPHIE B!!
U GO GRRL!!!!

He was staring across at me.
He was licking his lips.
He was thrusting his hips in time to the music.

While a squad of ten-year-olds from Lunenburg performed, I exploded from my seat.

Into the tunnel, take a hard right. I passed concessions, a table selling roses, a table selling cheer gear. Running as fast as I could, semi-controlled.

Semi-controlled.

It was the right term. It tied up more thoughts and events and people than I can explain. Roy. Charlene, Sophie, Jessie. Gus, his belly three shades of blood. Donald Crump, spilling from his Escalade, carrying me to the pavement.

Semi-controlled.

I used it all, used *them* all. Pumped everything into arms and legs, running just so, goddamn *flying* if you want the truth.

Semi-controlled. Black, red, black.

Rounded a corner, saw Teddy's cardboard sign on the floor near the ramp. No Teddy.

Ducked into the arena, picked out Sophie. Giggling, standing, her coach and a couple of moms keeping an eye on the girls. Sophie was safe.

I sprinted half the arena's circumference. No Teddy. He'd left the building.

Good.

It was time to get this done.

Fat Teddy Pundo forfeited everything the second I saw that sign.

I shot down to street level, semi-controlled. Crashed outside.

With the competition going full blast, it wasn't crowded out here.

I sprinted the three blocks to my on-street parking slot, working keys from my pocket as I ran.

As I swung around the front of my truck, I heard a tire chirp, a six-cylinder howl. Coming at me: a maroon Nissan Altima. Teddy.

He tailed you all the way from Charlene's place, and you didn't make him because he wasn't in his usual ride. You are one stupid fucker.

Thinking this as Teddy came hard, deep in the throttle. I tossed myself onto my hood, tucking my legs beneath me. Teddy creased the F-250's left flank. His right-side mirror brushed the sole of my left boot.

I jumped from the hood as Teddy grabbed a hard left at the end of the block, the Altima's overworked front tires squalling, smoking, trying to slow and steer at the same time.

The creasing had jammed up my driver's door. That cost me seconds: I sprinted to the curbside, climbed in the passenger door, fumbled and shrugged into the driver's seat, took off. Slid around the left-hand turn.

No Teddy.

I pounded the dash, cursing the world, just about weeping in frustration.

I pictured Fat Teddy following me from Charlene's house with Sophie at my side.

I thought of the police report Lima'd slipped me, the Guatemalan girl.

I thought of Teddy's sign. YEA SOPHIE B!!

He knew her name.

He forfeited everything when he let you see he knew her name.

The thought calmed me for a moment, made me feel semi-controlled.

But where'd he go?

I pounded the dash again.

Calm down. He's got to be headed for the Hi Hat.

Really? He doesn't exactly have the Charlie Pundo seal of approval.

He's not a rocket scientist. The Hi Hat is home. The Hi Hat is safe. Where else would he go?

I breathed myself calm, took a few seconds to think things through. I'd left Sophie alone at the comp. Was that smart?

It wasn't ideal, but it seemed like the right move. The coach had a good head on her shoulders, and the Civic Center was a public place packed with a couple thousand people. Better to have Sophie there while I tracked Fat Teddy than to lose him and spend the rest of the afternoon playing defense.

You sure?

Hell, I'm not sure about anything.

I drove.

Five minutes later, I parked across from the club in almost exactly the spot I'd used the first time Randall and I came here.

The maroon Altima was parked out front, just past the club's front door and the massive twin glass panes that fronted the joint.

Perfect.

Black, red, black.

I idled. I pictured Fat Teddy Pundo lobbing a Molotov cocktail. I pictured him doodling west on the pike, two cars back, invisible to dumb-ass me.

Black, red, black.

I revved my truck, dropped the shift lever in drive.

Half a plan . . .

I paused.

If you use your own truck, you might as well just take care of business, then sit on the curb in cuff-me-officer position.

But what else was I going to use? Hot-wiring a car, especially a modern one, is TV-detective bullshit. There are too many wires, too many computer fail-safes and lockouts. I've worked on cars all my life, and I couldn't hot-wire one if you gave me all day and a shop manual.

The Altima. This is Charlie Pundo's block. This is home. Nobody's ever stolen a car from a Pundo and lived to brag about it.

Huh. Would the keys be in it?

Worth a look.

Three minutes later, having driven around the block and parked in a spot that'd keep my truck off the Hi Hat security cams, I speed-walked past the Altima and cut a glance at its interior.

Keys. Right there in the ignition. Doors unlocked.

Knew it.

I didn't hesitate. I stepped around the car, not looking either way, and climbed in. Fired it up. Backed up a hundred yards. Popped it in drive, hit the throttle.

I picked up speed in a hurry.

The club came at me fast.

I put both hands on the steering wheel and braced myself.

I hit the curb at a harsh angle. The wheel bucked. I hung on.

When I hit one of the plateglass windows, I was doing forty-five.

I was semi-controlled.

CHAPTER THIRTY-SIX

Everything exploded. My nose broke on the air bag. I nearly passed out from the pain.

Things went quiet then.

I was inside the club.

I kicked my door open.

Sitting not three feet from the nose of the Altima was Fat Teddy Pundo.

His mouth was frozen in an O.

Half-wondering where Boxer was—guarding the boss in the office out back?—I looked around. There were no customers unless I'd run them over. Behind the bar stood today's barkeep: a redheaded woman in a white oxford-cloth shirt. I looked at her once, then turned back to Teddy. Don't know where she went, but I never saw her again.

Things turned slow. Things turned precise. I knew that feeling, remembered it from my racing days, loved it. It was my edge: Teddy Pundo, bully-boy freak with a gangster daddy, didn't know the feeling at all.

He was dead already and too stupid to realize it.

He rose, reaching behind his back with his right hand. I took two steps, boot-crushing plateglass and aluminum window trim. Without taking my eyes from Teddy, I reached for what was near: a chrome barstool with a black padded seat.

I grabbed the stool high on one leg. It was good and heavy, but to make use of its weight I needed to adjust my grip. I tossed it in the air like I was trying to wreck the ceiling fan above. Hell, I nearly did.

Nearly.

Instead: got both hands on one leg. Now I had a useful grip on the stool, a right-handed batting stance. I shifted my stride, sliding my left foot out front and setting up my backswing.

Teddy Pundo loved his black leather car coat—probably thought it made him look thinner—but he was having a hell of a time finding his gun in there.

What a shame.

His eyes went big as my backswing apexed and I stepped toward him again.

Finally, from behind his back came a matte-black semiautomatic.

When the world slows, the way it had for me, you see everything. Your brain operates at absolute maximum, vacuuming info.

I used to race against a guy who was blind as a bat. Couldn't read a stop sign until he'd run it, wore Mister Magoo glasses just to get his socks on. But you know what? He didn't need the glasses to race. Damnedest thing. He said once the green flag fell, he had the vision of a twenty-two-year-old fighter pilot—until he saw the checkers.

I believed him. He was a damn good driver.

I mention this because even as I began my swing, even as Fat Teddy Pundo squeezed the trigger, I saw the gun was a SIG Sauer P226. I was pretty sure it was the fancy Blackwater version.

Like I said: your brain takes in everything.

I also noticed the 9mm round hissing past my left ear as I swung the barstool.

Goddamn Teddy made the luckiest move of his life, cringing and backing away. The stool was supposed to flatten his temple, but instead it just knocked the SIG flying and smashed his nose.

And then I was vulnerable as hell: unable to stop the stool's follow through, I let it sail toward the club's stage and found myself way off-balance, all weight on my left foot, torso parallel to the floor.

Give Fat Teddy credit: he knew what to do.

He kicked me in the stomach as hard as he could with a pointy black shoe.

I won't lie: it hurt bad. Felt like the shoe clipped an organ or two on its way through my rib cage and into my spine.

I went to hands and knees.

I fought for breath.

I tried to uncross my eyes.

Teddy did what I would've done: he took a half second or so to steady himself and then kicked again.

If he'd connected, he might have knocked me cold.

But in spite of the pain and that instinctive panic when breath is gone, I was still seeing everything in slow motion.

I knew he was going to kick before he did. I even knew he'd use the same foot.

I got my right hand off the floor and my right forearm to my side a tenth of a second before the pointy shoe arrived.

New pain numbed the arm from the elbow down.

But I captured the foot.

Teddy Pundo said, "Hey." Like he'd caught me cheating at a board game.

I said nothing. Reached across my belly with the other hand. Breathed—boy, did that feel good.

And rose.

"Hey," Teddy Pundo said.

I don't know if it was my grip or the look on my face, but his eyes finally lit up, showing something other than stupidity as he came to realize how bad things were looking for him.

"Hey," he said.

I twisted his foot.

"My dad," he said.

Twist.

"Hey!"

Twist.

"My dad! Money! *Hey!*"

We began a dance. Teddy: hopping on his free foot, grabbing at me, fighting for balance. Me: twisting him, forcing him to hop. Most of my strength was gone—adrenaline seeped out while pain seeped in.

I was trying like hell to put him down, where I could fall on him and choke or blind him. But he had balance you wouldn't believe.

I hopped him across the floor to a potted plant on a stand.

I hopped him into a few wire chairs. He grabbed one and swung it at me, but had to let go and windmill for balance.

I heard sirens, far off. That made sense: even in Springfield, even on Charlie Pundo's private block, you couldn't drive a car through a window without lighting off a 911 call or two.

I needed to hurry.

So use his hopping against him.

I breathed, heaved. I hopped Teddy in a way that forced him to put his back to the club's intact window.

Then I leaned in and hopped him backward.

We picked up speed. The momentum helped me. The hops lengthened. Teddy's eyes went wide. I gave one last shove, noticing the sirens were a little louder, and fell forward.

He went through the window backward.

Quarter-inch plateglass exploded.

Teddy went down.

And stayed there.

I rose and stepped to him.

The base of Fat Teddy's spine was hung up on the windowsill, eighteen inches above floor level. He was bent way too far backward. The top third of the window quivered, still in its frame.

I stood over him. I looked down at him.

Then I looked up. At that top third of intact window.

Teddy's eyes followed mine.

He opened his mouth.

He tried to say something.

I wasn't interested in whatever he had to say.

I kicked the window frame and stepped back.

And watched glass guillotine his belly.

Then I looked away.

I breathed.

I worked angles.

Sirens sirens sirens, making it hard to think.

The state of Teddy Pundo's body didn't help.

I'd seen a lot.

But nothing like that.

I wanted out of this club, away from this place.

I began to shake.

You can shake later. For now, think.

I did.

The shakes stopped when I had a plan.

Forcing myself to ignore the sirens, I looked at the ceiling. I knew Charlie Pundo had sprinklers in his office to protect his records, but I didn't see a setup out there—which seemed impossible, but there it was. Maybe the club had been grandfathered in, or maybe the city of Springfield had looked the other way when Charlie launched the Hi Hat. Either way, I was grateful.

I stepped to the Altima, reached through the driver's window, turned the key to the on position. Cocked an ear, made sure the fuel pump was running.

Moved to the front of the car, wrenched up its buckled hood. Found where the fuel line connected to the intake manifold. No time to be pretty: I yanked the thin metal line as hard as I could.

Got what I wanted: a stream of gasoline on my fist.

Squinted around the bottom of the engine bay until I spotted the oil filter. Leaned, got a grip, hoped the filter wasn't overtightened.

It wasn't. I spun it off. Oil gouted to the car's belly pan, then to the club floor.

I grabbed a tablecloth, bunched it in the engine bay. Gas began to soak it.

Did the same with two more tablecloths.

Grabbed a basket of matchbooks from the bar, stuffed them in the tablecloth nest. Lit one book, touched it to the cloth.

The mess made a soft *fwump* as it caught.

Sirens: loud loud loud.

Then it was out the club door and a dead-nuts sprint for my truck.

I drove, forcing myself to keep it slow. Soon as I could, I grabbed a left and rolled toward the Interstate.

When I heard, and even felt, the *ka-fwump* of the Hi Hat catching fire, I damn near smiled.

Not for long.

My cell rang. A number I didn't recognize with the local 413 area code.

Huh. I picked up.

A man's voice, away from his microphone, said, "Shush, honey. Shush. Here he is."

Pause.

Sophie Bollinger said, "Conway?"

I stabbed the brakes, stopped dead in the middle of a block.

The man's voice came on again. "Gotcha, friend."

Frind.

Boxer.

CHAPTER THIRTY-SEVEN

Black, red, black.

First thing that came to mind: *You left Sophie alone. You thought it through, and that was your decision. You killed her.*

I said the second thing that came to mind. "I'm going to kill you."

"Many have tried, friend, many have tried."

"I killed Fat Teddy not five minutes ago."

It threw him. The pause told me so.

But it didn't throw him far. "Even better," Boxer said. "I was getting good and sick of carrying that one. Look, Sax, I've got something you want and you've got something I want."

I did?

I thought about playing it clever.

Then thought again. Clever doesn't work out so hot for me. I said, "What is it that I've got?"

"The shotgun."

"Cops have the shotgun. They found it in Donald's Escalade where you planted it."

He sighed. "Belay the silly games, friend. The *other* shotgun."

Well.

Well well well.

Something half-clicked, but Boxer spoke before I could lock it in place.

"Here's what you do to get this little honey back safe and sound, Sax . . ."

"What's Charlie think about your play?"

He said nothing.

"Charlie sign off on kidnapping a teenage girl as leverage?"

"Somebody's not thinking straight." Boxer said it to Sophie but stage-whispered for my benefit. "Somebody's not focusing on what he needs to do if he ever wants to see your cute ponytail again, darlin'."

It stabbed my heart, the way it was supposed to. But it didn't work, didn't mask what he wanted it to mask.

Boxer was off the reservation—his tag-team effort with Teddy at the Civic Center showed the pair of them had partnered up to end-run an old man they saw as soft. I'd wondered if that was the case. This call confirmed it. Charlie Pundo didn't know shit about their move. And would be pissed if he learned of it.

When he learned of it.

I'd make sure he did.

Once I pieced this together, still sitting in my truck on a shitty block in Springfield, I came to understand my leverage. Just like that.

It hurt my heart.

It hurt so bad.

I needed baby Emma, and I needed her fast.

"Gonna take me some time to get that gun out here," I said.

"You've got an hour."

"That's not enough."

"Has to be."

"Do my best." I checked my watch. "Where?"

Long pause. "You know the old Algonquin Mills building? In Chicopee?"

"Tell me."

He did.

Then I did the hardest thing I'd ever done in my life. I held my phone at arm's length and looked at the red END button.

And pressed it.

Pressing that button felt like slitting Sophie's throat.

I tamped down the doubt. Had things to do.

First move: call Randall.

He answered, thank God.

I said, "Are you with Rinn right now? In Sherborn?"

"Come on, haven't we . . ."

"Are you?"

He picked up on my tone. "Sure. Why?"

"Listen up and do *all* this to the letter. Leave Rinn there. Don't tell her anything about anything. Grab Haley and the baby *now,* and make tracks for this address." I said it.

He wrote it. "It'll take what, an hour and a half once I round up the gals?"

"Do it in an hour."

"What?"

"Or as near as you can. Randall . . ."

"Easy, amigo."

"They've got Sophie."

Half-beat pause. "Here I come."

Click.

I dug Charlie Pundo's card from my wallet. Called his cell. Left voice mail.

It was a hell of a voice mail.

Now I had to hope he checked it. Guys his age, you never know.

The beat-up mill sat on the eastern bank of the Connecticut River, with killer views of the Berkshires to the west. It had the grand shape, the red brick, the arched windows. Inside, it would have the high ceilings. In a better city, it would've been carved into half-million-dollar condos.

But this wasn't a better city. This was Chicopee. The arched windows were busted out, and the river stank.

I sat in my truck. Looked the place over, figured angles, tried to strip it back to a pure tactical problem of strengths and weaknesses and probabilities. The way Randall did when we watched shows on the Military Channel about famous battles.

A corner of my head knew I was tricking myself, forcing myself into cold-analysis mode to avoid thinking about what I'd done to Sophie.

Jesus Christ, what if I'd killed her?

Stop. If you need to trick yourself, trick yourself.

I breathed.

Didn't see any sign of Boxer, which was an edge. He thought I was hauling ass back to Sherborn for the shotgun he wanted so bad. He thought he had plenty of time.

Why's Boxer hot to trot over the shotgun?

Because he was the killer. Maybe Teddy was the idea man—though even that doesn't seem likely—but face it, Boxer was on the trigger.

It was one of the first ideas Randall and I had tossed around. Boxer, the pro shooter, had gone steaming into Almost Home to prove you couldn't mess with Teddy Pundo, who was now the king-shit dealer in Springfield. But Boxer had never seen Gus Biletnikov, and he'd blown away poor Weller, who just happened to be in the wrong room.

That had to be embarrassing. Boxer had covered by cutting down Gus with the same shotgun, after stealing a pair of Donald Crump's boots and somehow squeezing his feet into them. Then he'd killed Crump, already the top suspect, and had planted the shotgun to wrap the package in a way no cop would ever question.

Two things had gone wrong, though. First, a teenager had decided to videotape his first handjob.

And second . . . well, what? There was a screwup with the plant.

Which probably explained why Lima was hemming and hawing about the shotgun.

What was the screwup? I'd know soon enough.

It all worked. But it forced me to think about Teddy for the first time since . . . since the Hi Hat. The world wouldn't miss Fat Teddy Pundo, but part of the reason I'd . . . done what I'd done was because I pictured *him* cutting down Gus, pictured *him* blowing a hole in the kid who looked just like Roy.

I began to shake.

But not much, and not for long.

That's for later. For now: focus. Do what needs to be done. Get Sophie out of the jam you got her into.

I waited.

Text messages from Haley told me Randall was driving hard on the pike. She asked three times what the hell was going on and why I'd had them bring Emma.

Three times I ignored her. I didn't like thinking about Emma. About the way I was playing this. I shuffled approaches and scenarios, trying like hell to figure another move that could save Sophie.

I didn't find one.

News radio talked about a big fire in Springfield. They called the club the Hard Hat. They get everything wrong.

Checked my watch, decided to risk a little recon.

From Boxer's point of view, this was a good spot for a meet. The road was empty: frost-heaved and weed-cracked, it had serviced the mill and some related businesses, and had more or less died when they did. A miserable chain-link fence surrounded the mill and its parking lot, but the fence had long since been rendered useless by punks and thieves: I saw three gashes you could walk right through, and the main gate sagged open.

The big-ass parking lot—a couple acres easy, this place must have been something in its day—served as a moat for the mill itself. The joint had been built to last and built with pride, designed by men who couldn't picture anything ever topping hydropower. Squinting, I counted thirty-plus steps leading from the edge of the parking lot to the massive front entry. Place looked like the Supreme Damn Court, but with only four columns.

If I were Boxer, I'd get here soon. I'd walk those steps, sit Sophie down, and lean—half hidden in case anybody brought a long gun to the party—on one of those giant stone columns. I might bring a pair of field glasses, and I might bring help.

Boxer thought he would wait up there and watch me bring his incriminating shotgun, hat in hand.

Boxer thought he would kill me, then Sophie. Then he would whistle a little tune and drive away.

He thought.

I worked things through in my head, and I'll be damned if I could figure a trump card. I would have my leverage, the leverage I could barely stand to think about. Other than that, all I had was a voice mail to Charlie Pundo.

And how many guys Pundo's age had I known who never checked their voice mail, who didn't even know *how* to check it?

Hell.

I called him again.

Voice mail again.

I sighed. Time to stash my truck. I'd scoped out a good place half a mile away in another dead parking lot, back of a Wise potato chips delivery truck with four flats. Boxer might take a quick recon run up and down the road. I was better off if he didn't know I was here.

The sun's drop toward the Berkshires was building steam when I returned to a decent vantage point across the way, behind an eight-foot stack of pallets.

I was just in time. Teddy Pundo's black SUV nudged the mill's gate open, slow-rolled a loop around the parking lot, and ended up where I'd guessed: the base of the steps.

So Boxer had skipped the recon run. That was good news for me. It meant he was a little sloppy, a little overconfident.

I watched him step out, open the door behind him, tug Sophie's arm. She stumbled from the SUV, then let Boxer speed walk her to the top of the steps. She wore her cheerleading outfit, of course. To me she vibed okay physically. But I was a long way off.

As I'd guessed he would, Boxer hustled her behind a stone column.

A black BMW X5 rounded the corner and idled to the gate, Randall knowing where to find me because I'd texted him the info. I flagged down the BMW, checking my watch as I neared Randall in the driver's seat.

"You flew," I said. "Thanks."

"Is that him?" Randall gestured toward Boxer.

I nodded.

"Where's Sophie?"

"She's with him. Stashed behind the column to our right."

He nodded, looked, thought. "Tactically," he said after a few seconds, "this couldn't be much worse."

"I know."

"What's our plan?"

"*Your* plan is wait here," I said. "With Haley."

His eyes went hard.

Maybe mine went harder, because he said nothing.

As I walked to the BMW's right rear door, my phone rang. Boxer. I picked up.

He said, "What kind of game you running over there, friend? Why the spectators?"

I turned and looked at him, a hundred yards off. "Do you want to get this swap done, or don't you?"

Pause. "I'm not sure how well you can see from there, Sax, but my favorite little nine millimeter is half a meter from the glitter on sweet Sophie's cheek."

"I'll keep it in mind."

"Do." He clicked off.

I opened the door. I leaned over Emma's car seat.

She smiled up at me as I fumbled with straps.

Next to her, Haley sat. She'd been poleaxed by the sweep and pace of things, but she was coming out of it. "What are you doing?"

I said nothing.

"What exactly are you *doing*?"

I got the car-seat straps undone.

"Absolutely not!" Haley said, hurling herself across the bench seat, putting her torso between me and Emma.

Then she said it again.

And again, spittle-soaking my arms.

I was set to coldcock Haley to avoid losing time when Randall popped her door open, leaned in, got his hands beneath her armpits, and whipped her away like she was a rag doll.

"Shush," he said. "Shush. It's going to happen. It has to happen. Let it happen. Come to me."

She babbled and screamed and pounded his chest. I paid no attention: had by now lifted Emma up and out.

I didn't let myself feel, didn't let myself think about the way I planned to use the baby.

You know the part of the vision exam where you cover one eye with a plastic paddle and look at the chart? That strange feeling as the covered eye *wants* to help, *strains* to help?

The instant I'd settled on this plan, I'd forced my head into that mode. Couldn't let myself look at how awful, how unthinkable the plan was. At how rotten *I* was for putting it in play.

Emma was a lever. My only lever. She was my best chance—not a great chance, not even a good one, but the best chance available—to get Sophie back alive. Right now, she was nothing more.

I'd put a plastic paddle over the part of me that knew better. I *had* to.

Damn, but she was a good baby. Even with the craziness around her, she just cooed and looked at me and got a decent grip on my nose.

"You remind me of my cat Dale," I told Emma. "He's a good cat."

Before I was ten paces from the BMW, I heard Randall trot to me. He patted my shoulder. "You're a good man," he said.

I thought it was weird of him to pull a war-movie stunt like that. Until I felt something slip into the back pocket of my jeans, felt Randall tug my T-shirt to cover it. I realized my torso was blocking Boxer's view of Randall. "It's a ridiculous ladies' gun," he said. "A twenty-two with a pair of rounds. But it's all I could dig up at Casa Biletnikov."

I remembered the piece—had spotted it when I tossed the house.

Good old Randall. He'd found that thing, or demanded that Haley produce it, in a *hurry*.

I walked west toward Boxer and Sophie.

CHAPTER THIRTY-EIGHT

Jeez, this Emma was in a jolly mood. Must have napped most of the ride, then drained a bottle. Or done whatever makes babies happy.

As we crossed the parking lot, she smiled at me some more. I smiled back, dipped my nose for her to grab, kept my left arm high to block as much sun as I could.

When we were halfway across the lot, my phone rang.

I ignored it.

I looked left and right, head on a swivel. Had an icy feeling in my rib cage, wary that one of Boxer's boys was on sniper duty. And I was still hoping to spot Charlie Pundo.

That hope hadn't been much to start with, though, and it was fading fast.

When I reached the base of the steps, Sophie said, *"Ow."*

I looked up. Boxer had elbow-jerked her. He had her squeezed tight against his left side, had his 9mm shoved against her face in a way that forced her mouth open. A corner of my brain wondered why he wasn't toting the Desert Eagle he seemed so proud of.

But Boxer was paying Sophie no mind. He was staring at Emma, and his face looked like it was boiling.

"You clever motherfucker," he said. "You clever, stupid mother-fucker. You're now responsible for any bodies that drop today, friend. And drop they will."

"Not going to argue that," I said. Then to Sophie: "Sorry, hotshot. We'll just be a minute here."

The sweet little trouper nodded as best she could with a gun in her cheek. I wondered if she knew how my heart felt, wondered if she knew how hard it was for me to play it calm, one pro to another, with Boxer.

She was smart. She likely knew.

"I see you know who I'm holding," I said to Boxer. "So you know her history. You know what she means to your boss."

He chuffed a mean little laugh. "That fairy hasn't been my boss for five years. Hasn't been *a* boss in five years, not by any real measure."

It was a bluff. Boxer was scared of Charlie Pundo. I could hear it in his voice, see it in his body language.

"So you hooked up with Teddy to end-run him. To push him out."

"New York and Providence tolerated Charlie's silly dalliances. Why wouldn't they? Less for him meant more for them. Fat Teddy decided to grow a pair of balls, get back in the game, show the others who really owns Springfield."

"Teddy was dumb as a box of rocks. I'm guessing you helped him decide."

"Could be." Boxer made a crooked smile. "I owe you a debt of gratitude regarding Teddy's bad morning."

We were quiet maybe twenty seconds.

"I need you to know something," I said.

"What's that?"

Quick as I could, I shifted Emma to my left arm, reached behind me with my right, and brought the silly little pistol around.

I set its barrel against Emma's milk-white temple.

The baby cooed.

There was a wail behind me, far off. Haley.

"That one," I said, nodding at Sophie, "means as much to me as this one means to Pundo."

"Do you have the balls, Sax?"

"Do you?"

I watched him measure. I watched him think.

He was a gunman. A pro.

He knew his odds were rotten if he tried a shot from this distance with a handgun.

Still, I spread my feet. What I've found, guys firing downhill shoot low. A wide stance gave me a better chance that if Boxer did try, his round would zip between my legs.

He made his crooked smile again. "That a pistol? Or a toy for Emma?"

"It's not much of a pistol," I said. "But then, it doesn't have to be."

"You wouldn't."

"I'll say it again. That one means as much to me as this one does to Pundo."

"Well it's a Mexican standoff, then, isn't it?"

We stood that way. I caught Boxer cutting his eyes to his right, my left, and that icy feeling ran through my rib cage again. It's the feeling you get when you're exposed, a target. The feeling that makes you hunch over without knowing exactly why.

The look told me Boxer thought he had help. And that the help was probably positioned on loading docks a hundred yards to my left. It made sense: Boxer could've dropped a man there on his way in from the main road. It would explain why he hadn't driven past while I stashed my truck.

It hit me full: Boxer was stalling, hoping for long-gun help that for whatever reason hadn't come.

"The shotgun you're after," I said. "You used it at Almost Home.

Then you used it on Gus. Then you planted it on Crump. You thought you were packaging everything up in a way the cops couldn't resist. But something went wrong. What?"

Half-beat pause, then: "The fucking weapon that wound up in Crump's fucking truck hadn't been fired in five fucking years is what went wrong."

"How'd you manage to screw that up?"

"You tell me, friend."

Click.

It hit me hard.

I told him nothing. But I knew.

Spurnings and strikings.

Matching Western duds. Matching Harleys. Matching BMWs.

Matching shotguns. The best in the world, made by a little Czech the Feds couldn't stand but couldn't touch.

Peter and Rinn.

Well well well.

The surge of knowing lasted maybe ten seconds. Then Emma clucked and shifted, and I looked down at her.

And saw the joke pistol against her temple, where I'd laid it.

And the eye-exam paddle fell away.

And everything left me but shame.

I hot-potatoed the gun across the weedy lot, shifted to hold Emma in both arms, looked up at Boxer.

My knees began to shake.

"What are we *doing*?" I said.

"We're doing what we do."

I shook my head. "I'm not. Look, I didn't know about this shot-gun deal until you told me just now. Never heard about any second gun, don't have a damn clue where it might be. Can't help you. Do what you need to do. But Jesus, leave the girls out of it."

I half-turned, put finger and thumb in my mouth, cut loose with a whistle, made a come-here gesture.

Boxer said, "What gives, friend?"

I ignored him. Randall started across the lot, but I exaggerated a headshake. He stopped, pointed at Haley. I nodded. She started toward us at a dead sprint.

I turned back to Boxer. His gun still pressed Sophie's cheek. Her legs were shaking. Like mine.

"I'm going to pass the baby to the nanny," I said. Was surprised at the calmness of my voice. It was a hell of a time to feel serene, but I did.

"Then," I said, "I'm going to walk up those steps and take Sophie from you. Then we'll all walk away, and you can deal with your problems and I'll deal with mine."

Boxer cut his eyes to his right one more time. Maybe it hit him that the cavalry had chickened out, because his shoulders dropped an inch. When he spoke again, he seemed tired. " 'Fraid it can't happen that way. If you make the mistake of walking up these steps, I'm going to wait for a nice, easy shot. Then I'm going to drop you."

Sneakers slapped. Haley, panting, was at my left shoulder. I passed her the baby without turning, heard the sneakers retreat.

"God grant me the serenity to accept the things I cannot change," I said.

"Come again?"

"Never mind. Here's the thing: if it plays out your way and you drop me, you don't need Sophie. Can we agree on that?"

"You're jumping ahead, Sax. You're skipping around. What you need to do is think about getting me my shotgun."

I sighed.

And looked Boxer in the eye.

And stepped up.

Then again.

"That's far enough, friend."

Fucking *frind*. "Where are you from?" I said. "Australia?"

"Given present circumstances, I'll ignore the insult. I hail from South Africa." *Seth Efrica.*

I took two steps. "You're a pro. Once you take care of me, you don't need Sophie. And you *know* you don't need her."

"Don't force me," Boxer said, taking the 9 from Sophie's cheek and aiming at me.

"Conway, don't!" Sophie said.

"Shush," I said.

And took two steps.

My relationship with Boxer was shifting with each stair climbed. My altitude began to match his. His features came into focus. He was overtanned. He would get skin cancer someday.

I walked. I felt serene. I felt ready.

I felt pure.

I was a dozen steps from the top.

Then ten.

"*Con*way," Sophie said, sobbing.

Eight steps to go. Boxer's belt buckle was brass and shaped like Texas. Go figure.

Half a dozen steps to go.

"For Christ's ever-loving sake," Boxer said. "Have it your way."

He firmed up his stance.

He raised the 9.

He sighted down it.

His eyes were green. I hadn't noticed that before.

I spread my arms wide, giving him as much center-mass target as he could ask for, and took one more step. My gaze did not drop.

He began to squeeze the trigger.

The gunshot wasn't as loud as I'd expected.

Sophie screamed.

I froze.

I felt nothing. I didn't hurt.

I looked down at my chest.

Huh?

I grabbed the neck of my T-shirt. I ripped all the way down its front.

No blood.

Sophie screamed again.

I looked up.

Boxer's chest had exploded.

He toppled toward me.

He hit facedown.

He slid a few steps, stopping at my feet.

Now I saw the small entrance wound heart-high on his back.

I looked up a third time.

In the grand doorway of the shut-down mill, holding at his side a big-ass handgun with a suppressor as long as a paper-towel roll, stood Charlie Pundo.

Who apparently knew how to check voice mail after all.

CHAPTER THIRTY-NINE

Y ou took out the sniper?" I said to Pundo. I was breathing hard—
each of us had taken one of Boxer's legs, and we were dragging
him deep into the mill.

"Sure," he said. "I took one look and saw the punk had to be on
the loading docks. He never knew what hit him."

"Was it the one with the red beard?"

He nodded. "How'd you know?"

"I totaled the other one's hand."

"You did, didn't you? That seems like a long time ago."

We towed the body into a massive room with skylights and angled
toward a pair of four-by-eight-foot doors set in the floor. Pundo took
a ring at one end of one door, indicated I should do the same at the
other end.

Given its size and the fact it was sheet steel, the door opened with
ease that surprised me. Must have some sort of counterweight system. It also had a detent that let it stay open when we let go of our
rings.

I looked down. At nothing. No light, anyway. The pit below might
be twelve feet deep or a hundred and twenty.

Its smell just about knocked me over.

Pundo didn't let on that he noticed the stench. He came around to my side. He took an arm. I took a leg.

"On three," he said.

We tossed the body. Pundo closed the huge door on his own, then dry-wiped his hands like he'd just taken the kitchen trash to the garage. I took a quick inventory, realized I felt the same way. Didn't much like myself for it. But then, today's list of things I didn't like myself for was a long one.

"You've done this before," I said. "With all the other nightclub owners, I guess."

Pundo ignored the nightclub crack. "Sure, I've been here. How do you think *he* knew about the place?" He jerked a thumb over his shoulder. "I told him is how. FBI ever opens that door, twenty agents'll make their careers."

We hustled out the mill's smashed front door and took in the scene.

Randall had deputized himself. He'd made the two-shot pistol disappear and had done what he could—not much, but more than nothing—with Boxer's blood. Now he stood at the Biletnikov SUV, which he'd pulled to the base of the steps. Haley sat in its backseat, bottle-feeding Emma. Next to that vehicle sat a green Subaru Forester. It didn't strike me as much of a gangster ride, but it had to be Pundo's—Randall had found it while we'd done body disposal.

Sophie stood away from Randall, away from the cars, away from everybody. She stood by herself. Hugging her sides, even on a warm late afternoon, even in a cheer sweater. Her legs still shook.

She stared up at me.

Before today, Sophie'd seen a lot. More than any thirteen-year-old should see.

But she'd never seen a man she loved lay a pistol to the head of a baby.

Could I ever get her back?

Pundo was saying something, looking at me funny.

I said, "Huh?"

"You think she'll come back with me?"

"Who?"

"The nanny. Haley."

"Why do you want her to?"

"I'm not letting Emma out of my sight. Not after today, not for a good long time. I'll take her myself if I have to, but it's better for everybody if the nanny comes along."

"Emma and Rinn," I said. "They're what you wanted."

"They're *all* I wanted. Since the first time Rinn came in the club. She *does* something. She's *got* something. She's . . . she's worth the shame. You know?"

"But you're letting her stay with Peter. You're letting the world believe your kid is his."

"If that's what Rinn wants." He shrugged.

I said nothing.

We stood there, side by side.

With the sun low behind the mill, fun-house shadows stretched nearly across the parking lot.

"Your daughter," I said. "Emma. If I'd seen any other way."

"I should kill you for that."

"The way Emma is to you?" I said. "Sophie's that way to me."

"I get it. And you didn't make the first wrong move. *They* did, when they snatched her."

I nodded. "Teddy and Boxer."

"Who's Boxer?"

I'd forgotten that wasn't his name. It didn't matter much now.

"Never mind," I said.

Pundo said, "You know what I ought to be madder about? But can't get worked up about?"

I knew what he was going to say. His son. I'd guillotined him, then left him to burn.

"My club," Pundo said. "Specifically, my record collection. I was due to have a fire wall and better sprinklers installed next month."

Holy shit.

Charlie Pundo didn't know his son was dead.

That was fine.

Better than fine. It was likely the reason Boxer was dead and I wasn't. But you never know.

Losing a son like Fat Teddy Pundo wasn't like losing most sons.

Maybe Charlie didn't know because he didn't want to know.

He was staring at me. When he spoke, he sounded tired. "Don't deny you torched the place, Sax. Don't try for clever. You're half-clever, which is the worst. You're like a guy who's almost a good chess player. But only almost. You burned my club because you thought I burned your garage."

I said nothing. *Keep thinking that way, Charlie.*

He said, "You know who burned your fucking garage?"

I said nothing.

"The Andrade kid, the sad sack you crippled, then hired 'cause you felt guilty. I believe you AA types call it making amends."

Andrade.

Black, red, black.

"The sad sack's been coming around the Hi Hat damn near every night," Pundo said. "He got wind you and I were beefing, and I guess he was smart enough to hope the enemy of his enemy would be his friend."

Of course.

Pundo was right: I was half-clever. On a good day.

"Every night," he was saying. "Bending Teddy's ear, talking big about making you pay, about hitting you where you live. From me he wanted a pat on the head, or a cookie, or some damn thing. Teddy finally told him to beat it." Another half laugh. "How'd those amends work out for you?"

Down below, Randall clapped his hands twice and made a can-we-get-on-with-it gesture.

Pundo and I walked down the steps. "Haley will come with you," I said. "She'll do whatever's best for the baby. You can bet on it. You're in luck there."

I was right. Pundo and I tag-teamed Haley. At first, she didn't want to believe he was Emma's father. Once we convinced her—once Pundo convinced her how much he cared for the kid—she took diaper bag and baby seat and switched over to the Subaru without hesitation. She had tunnel-vision love for Emma.

I strapped the baby seat in Pundo's car, following Haley's instructions. When she declared it secure, she looked at me and said, without any change of expression, "You are an *awful* man."

"Yes," I said.

"You act like you're helpful. You act like Mister Troubleshooter. But you are *awful*."

"Yes," I said.

And stepped back and closed the door.

Randall wondered out loud what to do with Teddy's Mercedes. It was sure to grab the eyeballs of any cop who cruised this road. Pundo made a thirty-second phone call. When he clicked off, he said the SUV'd be gone in ten minutes and on a boat for Cape Town tomorrow.

Club owner. Jazz fan.

Then it was time to split up. The vibe was weird. It was as if summer camp was ending and we were all piling in with our folks to ride home—but something terrible had happened at camp, something nobody wanted to talk about.

"Well," Randall said.

"Well," Pundo said.

Nobody looked anybody in the eye.

When Randall dropped me at my F-250, both of us assumed Sophie would ride with me.

She didn't.

Wouldn't.

Instead, she took shotgun in the Biletnikov BMW, which Randall would drive back. Folded her arms, stared through the windshield.

Hell.

CHAPTER FORTY

Once we hit the pike eastbound, Randall buzzed me.

I said, "She okay?"

He knew who I meant. "She's out like a light. Before she crashed, I quizzed her on the snatch. The poor cheerleading coach was in over her head. She had fifteen dads, most of whom she'd met only once or twice, swooping in for their girls. Boxer glided up behind a bouquet of roses and elbow-walked Sophie right out of the Civic Center."

"Just like that."

"Just like that. At least the coach won't call in an Amber Alert." Pause. "Imagine the day Sophie had."

"Jesus."

Randall said, "What state secrets did you and Charlie Pundo pass back and forth up on those steps?"

"For starters, he doesn't know about Fat Teddy."

"What *about* Fat Teddy?"

Whoa.

I realized how little Randall knew of the day. Organized it all in my head, told him a two-minute version.

When I finished, he was quiet. We sat, each with a phone to our ear but saying nothing, all the way from exit 7 to exit 8.

"Wow," he finally said. "Are you okay?"

"Sure."

"Cut the shit, my friend. Are you *okay?*"

I thought it through. I took my time.

"I'm okay with Teddy," I said. "Or as okay as I deserve to be. As to the way I used Emma? I don't know. Can you . . . do you think . . . what would *you* have done?"

"Like virtually everybody else on the planet, I would have washed my hands of Gus Biletnikov and Company a long time ago. So I wouldn't have found myself in your situation or anything like it. And I don't mean that as a criticism."

"I picked up some dirt from Boxer, too," I said.

"The late and unlamented. What dirt?"

"You won't like it."

"Oh?"

"The shotgun the cops found in Crump's truck *isn't* the one used at Almost Home. Or on Gus. And that makes sense. Lima's been real closemouthed about that gun. Now I know why: it was one of those things the cops hold back to shake out the liars and the phony confessors."

"Meaning?"

"Boxer said there were *two* shotguns. Identical. He planted one on Crump so the cops'd think everything was wrapped up tight. But Boxer got screwed, accidentally or on purpose. He did Almost Home and Gus, so he had to know what the gun looked like. But when it came time to make the plant, he brought a dud."

Randall said nothing. I could feel the concentration as he worked through it.

"A matched set," I said.

"Holy shit," he said.

At the exact same time, we said, "Spurnings. Strikings."

"Peter," Randall said. "Brad."

"Brad my ass," I said. "He's a couch-bound pothead. It's Peter and Rinn we need to look at again."

Charlene packed a heavy slap. I got instant whiplash, and my busted nose began to bleed.

We were in her kitchen. Her sister leaned on the stove, smoking a generic white cigarette and just about purring at the fight. Like I said, I hate the sister and she hates me.

Jessie was on the great-room sofa, staring at her phone but soaking in everything. Family court must have released her. I wanted to hear about that. It didn't look like I'd get a chance, though. Not now.

Sophie had woken up when Randall exited the pike, had called home to say we'd be there in ten minutes.

And here we were.

"And you *didn't* call the cops? How *dare* you!" Charlene said to me. Then she turned on Randall. "And you! You're the smart one. How did you allow this to happen, Randall Swale?"

Charlene had been in a good mood when we entered, likely because Jessie was home. But as soon as Sophie saw her, the kid gave in to the tears she'd hidden from me—the tears reserved for Mom.

Even to me, the story of Sophie's last few hours sounded bad as I told it. And I left out a fair amount.

I shook my head, chasing away the whiplash. Jessie was looking at me from the corner of her eye. I spoke to her. "Glad you got sprung."

"Don't make nice with her!" Charlene said. "In fact, don't ever talk to my girls again. Just get out."

I stepped close so I could speak quietly, without feeling like the sister was taking notes. But Charlene flinched, stepped back, deadened her eyes, crossed her arms. "Get *out of my house!*"

"Please don't chase him away," Sophie said. "He was only—"

Charlene whirled. "*Shut up!*"

Sophie popped an inch straight up. Even the sister flinched. Charlene swept to Sophie, who'd started crying hard again.

Charlene: her back to me, arms wrapping her daughter. "He's not a good man, honey. Sometimes he tries, but he screws everything up. Shush now, honey. He's *not* a good man."

I backed from the room. I left through the front. I closed the door as quietly as I could.

Had the truck in reverse when Jessie followed me out and trotted down the concrete stairs to the driveway. Was she here to gloat? To pile on?

She stood at my window. I rolled it down.

She stared at the road. Gulped once or twice, clenched her jaw. Whatever she wanted to say, she was having a hard time with it.

I waited.

Finally, she said, "He doesn't."

"Doesn't what? *Who* doesn't?"

"Roy. He doesn't use. He never has. Wouldn't even drink a beer, wouldn't smoke a cig."

My chest went big.

"It was always a big point of honor with him," she said. "It was why . . . a big reason, anyway . . . we broke up. It was like living with the Hardy Boys. I couldn't take it."

"Well, hell," I said. "Thanks. For telling me."

"He always said he had two strikes against him in that department."

I thought that through. "Me, of course. What was the other one?"

"He said you were both strikes. That you counted double."

Then Jessie Bollinger made a tiny corkscrew smile and light-footed up the steps.

CHAPTER FORTY-ONE

I headed for Sherborn in full dark. It was a lucky break that Randall was still trying to calm Charlene—I wanted a crack at Rinn before he could swoop in to protect her.

Peter? Sure, I wanted a shot at him, too. But mostly at Rinn. She was the spurner, the striker. I had her pegged as the brains behind this second shotgun. I also had questions about how she fit in with the Pundos. Even with Boxer and Fat Teddy gone, I owed it to Gus to nail down every last detail, every last player.

She wasn't there, dammit. I read the guesthouse's nobody-home vibe at a glance, spare-keyed my way in anyway to confirm, then walked up the slope to the main house.

Peter answered the door. Took his time, but finally answered. Looked at me over his reading glasses, holding a thick magazine with a wristwatch on its cover.

You never know what's going to set you off.

The magazine did it.

Images bombarded me . . .

A pistol laid alongside Emma's pale skin.

Gut-shot Gus with bangs across his eyes.

Sophie's cheek deformed by Boxer's favorite handgun.

Teddy Pundo speed-hopping backward toward plateglass . . .

. . . And Peter Biletnikov was sitting at home reading a magazine about *wristwatches?*

"Where's your baby, Biletnikov?" I said, my jaw so tight I could barely speak.

He said nothing.

I slapped the magazine from his hand.

That didn't feel like enough, so I slapped his face. Hard, half-ashamed even as I did it, unable to stop myself. The slap spun his reading glasses to the floor. "Where's Emma? Doesn't look like you're beating the bushes to find her. Doesn't look like you've called the National Guard."

"The baby's with Haley," he said, looking truly puzzled.

"Yeah, but where? And why?" I stepped into the hall, forcing him backward.

"That is not your business," Peter said. "Is it?"

"It's as much mine as it is yours. I'm as much Emma's daddy as you are."

For the first time I'd seen, the Russian red drained from Biletnikov's cheeks. He backed three steps into his great room and plopped to a hassock, hitting it mostly by luck.

I let him stew.

He sat there a good long while. Elbows on thighs, face hidden in hands. "Rinn told you," he finally said. "A secret like that . . . I knew it would come out."

"It's worse than you think," I said. "Gus wasn't the father either."

That popped his face from his hands. "Of course he was."

I squatted to set my face level with his. "No. And deep down, I think you knew it. There's an ugly suspicion in an ugly corner of your ugly brain. So you tell me. Say the ugly suspicion."

He said nothing.

Was I savoring this?

Yeah.

Did I like myself for savoring it?

No.

Biletnikov was dripping silent tears now, refusing to meet my gaze like a dog that'd peed on the rug.

Still haunch-squatting, I reached for his chin with my left hand. I squeezed the chin, but only a little. I turned his face to mine. "Say it. Say it out loud."

"Puh-Puh-Pundo."

I nodded. May have smiled some, too. I let go his chin and rose, ignoring the pops from both knees.

"He was so . . ." Biletnikov said. "He exuded this . . . I *took* her there. To his club. I introduced them, dammit. Dear God, the look on her face when he joined us at the table, when he invited us to the after-party. The pair of them could have gone at it then and there."

Peter Biletnikov began to really cry then.

I let him.

What else was I supposed to do?

The wristwatch magazine had tripped something lousy in me. I'd decided to destroy him. To strip him naked.

And I had.

And it didn't feel good at all.

It felt awful.

I gave him maybe three minutes to blubber. Then I said, "Pull yourself together."

Blubber blubber.

"Tell me about the shotguns."

He used his shirt to wipe his face. "What about them?"

"A matched set, right? Made by some crazy little Czech?"

"How did you know this?"

I ignored that. "Why the crazy Czech? I know Rinn was jerking you around, making you buy everything in pairs. But why not just get a couple of nice Benellis or Purdeys?"

"The best of everything." He had the thousand-yard stare now, looking at nothing, speaking in a hollow voice. "That was our watch-word. *My* watchword. I heard about the Czech from hunting friends. The guns cost a hundred thousand apiece, and getting them here cost another quarter of that."

"Best of everything," I said.

"For Rinn," he said.

"Where do you keep them? I tossed the place."

"You did? Well, you wouldn't have. Found them, that is. I had a gun safe buried in a corner of the basement. Exquisitely disguised, really."

"So whoever took them knew where they were beforehand."

He nodded.

"Rinn knew," I said.

He said nothing.

"Where is she?"

He said nothing.

The doorbell rang.

"Better get it," I said.

"No," Peter Biletnikov said. "I believe it's for you. It's Detective Lima."

Hell.

"You called," I said. "It's why you took so long answering the door."

He said nothing.

I sighed, walked toward the front hall.

I stopped.

I turned. "Almost Home I get. When that happened, I doubt you even checked your gun safe. No reason to. But then *Gus* got shot. Your *son*. Nearby. You'd known for a while about weird shit going on with Rinn, Gus, Brad, the Pundos. Didn't you check on your guns then? Didn't you wonder what the hell was happening around you?"

He said nothing.

"Only reason I can see for doing nothing at that point," I said, "is that you knew. And you didn't want to know."

Nothing.

I turned, took a few more steps. Sighed. Opened the front door.

Lima said, "Whole bunch of people looking to talk with you."

"Cuffs?" I said.

"Anything you want to tell me?" he said.

"Nah."

"You going to shoot it out with me on the ride over?"

"Nah."

"No cuffs then."

Lima didn't have to let me ride up front, but he did. I appreciated that.

"When did you know the shotguns belonged to Biletnikov?" I said as soon as he made the hard right from the gravel drive.

"We went back with a search warrant after Crump got shot. By then, we'd put together enough customs data to convince a judge Biletnikov was doing business with the crazy Czech. When Biletnikov saw the warrant, he folded and showed us his safe."

"No shotgun?"

"Both gone. Biletnikov was surprised as hell."

"Find any cartridges?"

"Half a box. Bird shot, like what was used on the kid Gus."

I began to speak. He held up a hand. "We're not stupid. We asked Biletnikov if he ever used heavier shot. One-aught, specifically."

"And?"

"He said yeah, he probably had."

"Probably."

"Probably."

I let a few seconds pass. Then I said, "Are you guys looking for Rinn?"

"Why should we?"

I was stunned. "Don't you like her for it now? At least enough to scoop her up and talk to her? Hell, how many people knew about those shotguns? Or where to find them?"

"Crump could've known. He was friendly with Rinn."

"You can barely say that with a straight face. Come on, Crump had the frozen-up shotgun in his truck. An obvious bad plant."

"A plant? Maybe. Obvious? No. You've got tunnel vision for Rinn."

It was quiet as we rolled through downtown Framingham.

"What happened out there?" Lima said. "In Springfield?"

I said nothing.

"Reason I ask, I'm about to dump you in a room with a couple of assholes who're licking their chops."

I said nothing. Thought things through, or tried to.

Lima said, "I told you a few things about Teddy Pundo. I know you remember."

I waited.

"Every crime scene's a clusterfuck," he said after a long pause. "Add a fire, now you got clusterfuck squared."

Where was he headed with this?

"What I'm saying, a scene like that, it's hard as hell to know what happened to who when. Somebody might look at the scene and say, 'A guy got beat to death in a nightclub, then the nightclub got torched.' They might make it sound like cold hard facts. A done deal."

We swung into the barracks parking lot.

"But somebody *else*," Lima said, "might say, 'No, the guy crashed his car into the nightclub, climbed from the car, and stumbled around while he bled out.' The way lawyers and experts work, they could see it either way. Depending on how they wanted to see it."

"Depending on who was signing their paycheck."

He nodded and snapped his fingers so that he ended up pointing at me. "That's all I'm saying."

CHAPTER FORTY-TWO

Contrary to what I said before, sometimes the cops really *are* jerks once they've got their mitts on you.

Especially when they think you've been ripping around the state killing gangsters, torching buildings, and making them look like jackasses in the process.

First, I realized why Lima'd let me come here without cuffs and riding shotgun: he knew it would be the last decent treatment I'd get for a while. Two dicks who looked nearly like twins—six-three, steel-gray crew cuts, gray suits, greyhound builds—had dropped him to errand-boy status. His only job that night was to bring files and coffee to the hot-box room.

Lots of coffee, none of it for me. The greyhounds worked me over. They knew a fair amount about me, including the big-time resources Charlene could and would use to get me out of there, so they made sure I never saw a phone.

The greyhounds said they were the state police OCTF. Didn't say they were *with* the OCTF, said they *were* the OCTF. From their questions, I figured out it stood for Organized Crime Task Force.

I had well and truly stumbled into a jackpot.

I'd been in jackpots before.

I'd been in rooms with cops before.

I knew what to do.

I said nothing. And lots of it.

I said nothing for hours and hours.

I said so much nothing one greyhound wanted to hit me, and I'm pretty sure it wasn't part of any good-cop, bad-cop routine.

At one point, maybe four o'clock in the morning, Lima brought in a pair of steaming Styrofoam cups and, as usual, two packets of Splenda for one of the greyhounds. He set it all on the table next to an array of pics.

The pics: A pro headshot of Charlie Pundo. A long-lens shot of Teddy Pundo in his favorite jacket and shades. A similar shot of Boxer. (The greyhounds said his real name, but he'd always be Boxer to me.) A grainy security-cam shot of me running through the Springfield Civic Center.

Lima had called it just right. The greyhounds pummeled me with what they called facts. Facts about me, and Teddy, and witnesses, and car chases, and how Teddy had died.

They said they knew Boxer was the Almost Home trigger man. I noticed they didn't say how they knew that, but it didn't surprise me. They pummeled me with questions about Gus's murder, coming at me from a dozen angles the way cops do. The questions were engineered to get me to say Teddy was Gus's killer. *Might* have been. *Could* have been. *Had the opportunity*. Blah blah blah.

I said nothing. I'd figured out to my own satisfaction that Boxer killed Gus, too, erasing his Almost Home screwup. He'd stolen a pair of Donald Crump's little cowboy boots, managed to cram his feet into them, and thrown off the cops that way. When you'd seen Teddy in action the way I had, it was clear he didn't have the chops to cut down a man at point-blank range.

I said nothing. Let the greyhounds figure all this out if they could.

After a few hours, it hit me: the greyhounds wanted Fat Teddy as

Gus's killer as a way to go at Charlie Pundo. They'd probably spent years building one of these RICO deals. Those cases are usually ninety-percent bullshit: tax evasion and parking tickets. The greyhounds had to be licking their chops at the thought of a Pundo, *any* Pundo, shooting a man.

If they ever saw that trapdoor in the Chicopee utility building, the one where Charlie dumped bodies the way most people toss beer cans, they would goddamn faint.

They wouldn't get any help from me.

They had just run through their facts and questions for the twentieth time when Lima, deadpan, set down their coffees and picked up the old cups and pretended not to listen.

I spoke for the first time since they'd brought me in. Looked at Greyhound Number Two and said, "Splenda?"

Lima was good. He held his deadpan.

The greyhounds had bragged about how long they could bury me here—they claimed seventy-two hours was doable—so you should have seen the looks on their faces when my lawyers, meaning Charlene's lawyers, rolled in at 9:01 A.M.

How did the lawyers know I was there? Hell, how did *Charlene* know?

A quick text from Lima would have done the trick. But I never did find out for sure.

The greyhounds played it stubborn like a pair of six-year-olds, so it took a while, but that afternoon I walked out the front door into a stone-colored day. Randall idled in his Hyundai, reading something on his iPad.

"Take me to my truck," I said.

"You're welcome," he said, stowing the iPad. "Of *course* we were worried. Of *course* we got no sleep. But our world revolves around you, and besides, your gratitude makes it all worthwhile."

"It's at the Biletnikov place."

"I know. As is everything and everybody else."

"What's that mean?"

"While you were manufacturing license plates, Rinn and Haley fetched Emma and returned home."

"Rinn came back to Sherborn? To *Peter*?"

"That's home, all right. I came from there. Rinn invited me over to referee the big reunion."

"Yikes."

"And how."

"The way I figured it," I said, "Rinn would either run off with Charlie or say good-bye and good riddance to the kid. After everything that's happened."

"You weren't the only one who saw it that way."

"What changed her mind?"

He shrugged. "Motherhood is motherhood. Genes is genes."

"But she was a *terrible* mother. The worst. You saw her."

"Day to day, where the details are concerned, she was terrible. This I'll grant. Conceptually, though, she's a caring mother who loves Emma."

"So is Rinn going to change diapers conceptually? Feed the kid at two in the morning conceptually?"

"That is her stated goal. Again, genes is genes."

Money is money.

I kept the thought to myself—didn't want to rub Randall's nose in what a louse Rinn was.

But it made sense. Whatever bad-boy lust Rinn had felt for Charlie Pundo, it was likely out of her system. Peter was richer, tamer, and a lot closer to Boston. If you wanted to be cynical about it.

We were quiet awhile, easing along Sherborn's horse-farm roads.

"You had something with her," I said. "A connection."

"I won't argue that."

"Tough girl to have a connection with, and a tough time to have it. Between the empty-suit husband and the gangster and the new baby and a murder in her backyard."

He smiled some. "I won't argue that either."

I said, "What are you going to do?"

"I'd like to say I'll sleep for fourteen hours. But I don't think it's in the cards, due to this." He tapped the large Starbucks in the cup holder. "How about you?"

"Charlie Pundo wants to see me. He left three voice mails and a dozen texts while I was locked up."

"Do you want to see *him*? Is it wise?"

Pause. "I owe him that much," I finally said.

"Owe him you do. So does Sophie."

"Yeah."

"Has Charlie figured out you were behind his only son's demise?" Randall said.

"Yup. Had to happen eventually. I bet the cops told him, hoping to stir up some shit."

He nodded.

"But when I asked before," I said, "I wasn't talking about your plans for today. I meant"—I made a spreading circle with my hands, my arms—"what are you going to *do*?"

"We're here."

We were.

I waited for Randall to answer my question.

He didn't.

"Whose car is blocking my truck?" I finally said.

"That's Brad's. You can get around him on the grass."

"What's he doing here?"

Randall shrugged.

I looked at his face.

He looked straight ahead.

I started to say something.

But didn't. Climbed out instead.

Randall had been wrong: I couldn't get around Brad's car. I sighed, trotted to the guesthouse.

Nobody home.

Up the hill to the main house. Annoyed, hungry, headachy, wanting to hit the goddamn road for goddamn Springfield.

Heard voices, sharp but not yelling, as I approached.

The voices settled when I knuckle-rapped the door.

Rinn answered. Her cheeks looked hot, and she brushed hair from one eye.

"Here you are," I said.

"Can I help you?" she said.

"Brad's blocking me."

"Not to worry," he said, and came into view.

Holding Emma.

Who didn't seem to mind.

But I did.

I didn't like the picture. Didn't like it at all. It was off.

I said, "Everything okay?"

"Hunky," Brad said. "Dory, even. Let me clear the way."

He passed the baby to Rinn and walked down to his car.

"Everything okay?" I kept my voice low this time, eye-locking her.

"Everything's fine," she said.

I didn't want to leave her there. Everything was off, wrong, grainy.

"You sure?" I said, and nodded toward the car that Brad was pulling aside. "You cool with him?"

"Yes. You can leave. *Please* leave." Rinn stood her ground.

She was in charge of her baby for the first time, I told myself. Nervous as hell, probably got a lousy sleep.

And the sooner I got done with Charlie Pundo, the sooner I could wash my hands of the whole lot of them.

That's what I told myself.

I left.

I shouldn't have.

Ninety minutes later, I climbed from my truck and stood on the side-walk of Charlie Pundo's 1965 dreamworld.

Behind me was the little grocery, its fruit and vegetables fresh as ever. Above me: its green-and-white-striped awning. I took an apple, tucked a dollar in a little box, ate. Man was it good. Hadn't realized how hungry I was.

I looked up and down. Even the burned-out, blown-out Hi Hat didn't hurt Pundo's effect much. The debris had been policed up, the sidewalk in front of the club swept. You got the feeling they'd have the place rebuilt in six weeks, tops. Can-do, 1965 style.

Next to the club: Arturo's, the tailor. Then a parking lot.

For a church.

Charlie Pundo's church.

Catholic, of course.

It was where I would find him, of course.

I strolled. A beer and wine place ("We Sell No Hard Spirits"), a candy shop, an honest-to-God record shop.

This block ought to make me sad. It was pitiful.

It didn't make me sad.

I angled across the street, entered the red-brown brick church's side door.

Inside, between the heavy beams above and a gray day that couldn't fire up stained glass, the place was dark.

He was there. Of course.

The only one in the dark space. Last pew on the left, near the center aisle. Staring ahead at the altar, at the skinny Christ on a cross.

I approached Charlie. Didn't mean to walk soft, but I did. Church'll do that to you. Even when I stood eighteen inches from his side and just behind, he took no notice of me.

His suit, like so much around here, seemed straight out of 1965. Brown, nearly shimmery, with a white shirt and a skinny brown necktie.

"The sun hits it," I said, "that stained glass must be something."

CHAPTER FORTY-THREE

I t is," Charlie said. He did not turn. He showed no surprise. He slid three feet to his left.

I sat next to him. "You let her go easier than I would've thought," I said, looking straight ahead like Charlie.

He cocked his head. "Emma? Or Rinn?"

"Emma."

He lipped a *puh* sound. "They held the cards. Rinn and Peter."

"Not the DNA card."

"I play that card, I fuh"—he flinched like he expected the Jesus up front to shoot lightning from his eyes—"I screw up Emma's life for a good long time. Besides, you got any idea what the discovery phase of a custody trial would turn up?"

I thought about the abandoned mill, the stench from the body dump. I nodded. "A pretty good idea, yeah."

We were quiet awhile.

"My problem," he finally said, "I'm immersive, as a smart lady friend of mine once put it. When I jump in, I jump in with both feet. Back when I was in the thick of the life, I got out of bed every morning looking for reasons to beat on guys. To torch their offices, bust their fingers, humiliate 'em in front of their families."

"What happened?"

"Jazz happened. Nah, that's not it. Life happened. I changed. I got sick of it. Then one day I chucked it all, or as much as they let me, and hitched everything I had to the Hi Hat."

"Both feet," I said. "All in."

Charlie looked at me for the first time. "Got a feeling you know a little something about that. About jumping in now and asking questions later."

I said nothing.

"When I look back," he said after maybe thirty seconds, "all the signs were there that my own guys, led by my own *son*, were screwing me. I didn't see it because I didn't want to see it."

That made me think of Peter Biletnikov, playing dumb while his fancy shotguns were used to blow holes in people.

I said, "You know what happened to Teddy? How it ended with me and him?"

"Teddy the freak who was all set to slit my throat and take my action?"

"No. Teddy your son."

Charlie said nothing.

"Nobody should lose a son. But what he did, a kid . . . a *girl* I care about was at—"

He raised a hand. "I know as much as I need to know. Say no more. He was a true disappointment."

So that was that.

"Deep down," I said after a while, "you knew your own guys were gunning for you. But you hated getting pulled back in. You were tired of it. It wasn't your thing anymore."

"Yeah."

"I could tell in the skate park. That wasn't your idea at all, was it? You seemed . . . tired."

"That's the word. Like I said, you know a thing or two about all this. How tired it makes you. That's the part people, civilians, don't get."

"I get it." My voice was so low I don't know if he heard me.

Charlie checked his watch, sighed, grabbed the pew ahead as if to pull himself up.

"Wait," I said. "Almost Home. The halfway house. Did your man, the guy I call Boxer, don't even tell me his real name again 'cause I don't care, did he go in there looking for Gus?"

He nodded. "That's what I heard when I leaned on a few people, yeah. They decided since I'd turned into a jazz sissy who forgot how to be a criminal, they needed to turbocharge their rep, at least while they were getting started. You know, 'Don't even think about messing with us, look what we do to skimmers and slow-pays.'"

It made sense. "Teddy told Boxer what Gus looked like. He went in all jacked up, blew away the wrong kid. So he had to do it all over again out in Sherborn."

"Nah," Charlie said, standing, twisting at the waist the way people do when they've been sitting a while. "That one he didn't do."

I froze. "What?"

Pundo hadn't picked up that this was huge to me. He kept twisting, now with both hands at the small of his back. "He drove me to Smalls that night to catch a set by Eli Degibri. I dragged Teddy along, hoping against hope to civilize him."

"What's Smalls? Where is it?"

He looked at me like I'd asked who was buried in Grant's Tomb. "The Village. West Tenth, I think."

"New York?"

"Of course New York. I'm leaving."

I gave Charlie Pundo a ten-step head start while my head tried to arrange new facts.

Boxer hadn't killed Gus.

So who had?

Outside, I caught up to Charlie and peppered him with questions: double-checking, triple-checking. He was casual. He was dead certain. He wasn't hiding anything—why would he cover up for the jerk who'd tried to blindside him?

I sifted old info, new info. Shuffling along just behind Charlie, not paying much attention, I bumped into him when he pulled up.

We stood before the tailor shop. The little man inside was straight out of a Disney movie: the slight stoop, the smile that was sad but only a little, the chalk marks on his trousers where he wiped his hands. When he spotted us, he made a just-one-minute gesture and bent over a big padded table that dominated the shop.

"They can take a lot from me," Charlie Pundo said, "and indeed they have. My wife died at forty-two. The only girl I've loved since up and hauled my baby back to that dipshit Biletnikov and told me I'd damn well best stay mum about it. My consigliere and my only son humiliated and backstabbed me. *You* came along and torched my club and my sweet, sweet record collection."

He sighed long and deep. "But I've still got Arturo. I'll always have Arturo. Good-bye, Sax. Don't come around again. Not for a while, anyway."

I barely noticed.

I was watching Arturo. Watching him slice through gray wool with a curved-blade X-ACTO knife. He made it look so easy. Used a thin paper template, but you got the feeling he could do it freehand if he wanted.

I stared.

I stared because I knew who killed Gus Biletnikov.

And it wasn't Boxer.

And it wasn't Fat Teddy.

CHAPTER FORTY-FOUR

The moon was one night short of full.

It lit the Biletnikov place as nice as you could ask.

But both the main house and the cottage were blacked out.

Which wasn't right.

I'd flown. I'd learned my truck's front wheels shimmied when you hit a hundred and fifteen. It was usually a ninety-minute drive. I'd shaved that by twenty minutes.

I'd called Randall, Rinn's cell, the Biletnikov home line, Lima's cell. I'd even had Information hook me up with Brad Bloomquist's apartment line.

Voice mail everywhere.

The only one I'd left a message with was Randall. Told him to get the hell over to the Biletnikov house fast and do whatever he needed to protect them from Brad.

Brad Bloomquist.

Whose car was still here in the drive, just ahead of Randall's.

Brad Bloomquist: Mister Mellow, called himself The Dude after some guy in a stoner movie.

Brad Bloomquist: lover of Gus Biletnikov, who apparently didn't love him back anything like enough.

Brad Bloomquist: stoner-stalker who moved from Cape Cod, the perfect locale for the likes of him, to a nowheresville apartment in Framingham—to be near Gus.

Brad Bloomquist: crazy-jealous when Gus, who he called his first love, got it on with Rinn at the sick behest of Peter Biletnikov.

Brad Bloomquist: who was tight with Gus and Rinn during the spurnings-and-strikings days. Which meant he would have known about Peter's fancy shotguns.

Brad Bloomquist: whose apartment featured a table like Arturo the tailor's, and all the leatherworking tools you could ask for.

Brad Bloomquist: who must have stolen a pair of boots from Donald Crump, then sliced most of the leather away and worn them like thong sandals.

That's the part that had clicked as I looked at Arturo the tailor in Springfield. Brad's size 16 feet would have hung out of Donald's boots all over the place—but the prints would point straight at Donald.

So add another line to the résumé. Brad Bloomquist: a lot more sneaky-clever than he looked.

A few other things had clicked for me on the way here.

The Almost Home hit had been pro city, the shooter—Boxer—calmly blowing away a pair of witnesses just because they turned up in a stairwell.

But the killing of Gus had been a different deal. Amateur hour, a passion kill using bird shot from Peter Biletnikov's gun safe.

It all clicked. I'd had a long, hundred-and-fifteen-mile-an-hour drive to beat myself up for not seeing it earlier.

Why is Brad's car still here? Why is a compound that ought to be a beehive, baby and all, blacked out?

I grabbed my small flashlight, climbed from my truck, stepped lightly across gravel to the main house's front door. Felt my heart jumping. Breathed myself calm.

The door was not locked.

A shooter in the dark would aim chest-high. So I got low. Crawled across the front hall.

Soon as I hit the kitchen, I smelled it: copper and fizzled firecrackers.

Which meant, I knew, blood and gunfire.

Not fresh. Not old either.

Didn't need my flashlight. The moon was plenty. I crawled toward the hallway that led to a day nursery for Emma.

As I cleared the kitchen's island, I saw her.

Rinn.

On her back, soles of her shoes aimed at me. One rested sideways on the floor. The other pointed at the ceiling.

The blood pool beneath her was going crusty on top.

It was a big pool.

No pulse. Dead dead dead.

Her pretty hair covered most of her face and one eye.

I crawled through Rinn's blood. I crawled down the hall to the day nursery.

I rose.

Huh?

No crib.

I racked my brain, replayed the day I'd tossed the place. Yes. There'd been a crib, a little mobile with planets, the mobile high above, no risk of the kid grabbing anything.

So where was the crib?

A window smashed.

I ducked instinctively even as I figured out the noise had to've come from the guesthouse.

I straightened. I ran, feeling Rinn's blood on my hands and knees where I'd crawled through it.

Out the front door, take a right, down the hill.

Thunder. A shotgun blast. It lit up the cottage's big front window.

I pinwheeled in grass gone slick with dew. Moon at my back as I neared the guesthouse.

There was a light in its window now: Brad Bloomquist was all done caring who saw him do what. I saw him framed perfectly by the picture window, looking at something I couldn't see on the floor before him.

He'd broken open a single-barreled shotgun.

He was inserting a cartridge.

I lengthened my stride.

I looked ahead.

I timed it out.

I hurdled a little landscaping bed that fronted the cottage porch. The ball of my foot hit the porch railing nicely. The railing wobbled some—things you notice when your head's set on full-maximum intake—but held.

I pushed off.

I closed my eyes.

I went through the picture window headfirst.

CHAPTER FORTY-FIVE

At the Hi Hat, I'd been protected by a car.

This hurt worse.

I hit hardwood heavy and ugly. My shoulder made a ratcheting sound.

I ignored pain. I stood.

Bloomquist had spun my way, wearing a look of dumb surprise. The room's only sofa separated us.

I saw what he'd been staring at while I approached.

Haley. On the floor. Half-hidden from my view by the sofa.

But only half.

She was bleeding hard. Streams like something from a squirt gun jetted from the right side of her chest. From her neck and face. From her hairline.

She was pulsing blood, but she was *alive*. Staring up at me. Blinking, but not truly seeing.

Bloomquist said, "Huh."

And he smiled.

And he pulled the trigger.

I threw myself backward to the floor.

It felt so slow. It felt hopeless, useless. I saw, took in, sensed *every-thing*. It seemed I could draw a picture of every pellet that left the barrel.

During the instant I was laid out horizontal in midair, looking up, not yet on the floor, I watched pellets pass over my busted nose. I swear I did.

It seemed that way, anyhow.

Then my head hit hard, and both my feet stung like hell—shot had hit the soles of my boots.

I wasn't dead. I wasn't even hurt that bad.

I shook my head to clear it, shook it like a wet dog.

That's when I saw Randall. Off to my left, in the small kitchen area. I couldn't see much of him, but what I could see showed pin-prick blood.

Same as Haley.

All this registering in my head in some tiny part of a second.

While the main part of my brain screamed at me that a single-barreled shotgun takes time to load.

I crossed over the back of the sofa without touching it. I got my left hand on the shotgun's barrel before Bloomquist could move it. With my right hand, I went for his left eye.

I didn't get it—the eye squinched shut in time—but the move kept him on defense. Brad Bloomquist might be a three-time killer going on four, but he'd never had a serious man try to thumb out his eyeball.

Wish I could say the same.

We grunted. We wrestled. Standing there, toe-to-toe, while Randall and Haley bled out three feet away.

Bloomquist was a big fucker. Once he spread his legs and planted those feet, there was no moving him.

In a few seconds—all this felt slow but happened fast—he realized there wasn't a lot I could do with him. He started to feel confident.

Still clinging to the gun's butt and trigger guard with his right hand, he found my ear with his left.

And twisted.

I shrieked. Couldn't help it.

He twisted harder.

Cartilage popped. Then flesh tore.

I reached a tipping point. The ear, the shoulder, my head. They were adding up. I needed out *fast*.

Bloomquist was making sounds now like a man getting off, his grunts growing stronger and longer each time he tore at my ear.

Time to do a little playacting.

I made myself shriek again with the next twist. I set my right knee on the floor like a man who'd been beaten. I even loosened my grip on the gun's barrel a hair—just enough to goad Bloomquist into a final overconfident push.

It worked. He let go my ear so he could wrench away the shotgun with both hands. Then he could reload at his leisure and put me down.

On one knee, my head was now level with his belt buckle.

I drew back my free right hand.

Then I funneled every last bit of energy and hate into my right shoulder.

Then I punched Brad Bloomquist in the balls as hard as I could.

He doubled over so hard his teeth clicked my collarbone.

He made exactly the sound you'd expect.

He let go the gun.

Just like that.

The gun fell to me so fast it surprised me. Momentum spun me against the sofa.

At the same time, Bloomquist straightened.

With my back to him, I now had both hands on the shotgun's barrel in a baseball-bat grip. Just as I'd held the barstool in the Hi Hat.

I didn't hesitate.

It wasn't exactly a baseball swing. It was more of a Wednesday-night-league softball swing, a don't-give-a-damn, home-run-or-pop-up swing. Weight transferred from my right foot into the thigh and hip, up through the torso, out through the arm muscles.

It was a hell of a torquey swing.

The gun's maple butt connected with Brad Bloomquist's temple.

He was a big man. The impact jerked him off his feet anyway.

It caved in the temple.

He went down next to Haley. Her squirt-gun bleeding began to wet him.

Haley's mouth moved. She pointed at nothing.

I told her hush, told her she was going to be okay.

I didn't believe it.

The cottage landline was on the granite kitchen countertop. I fumbled at it, dialed 911.

"Do you know where I'm calling from?" I said when a lady picked up.

"Yes sir, what is the nature of your emergency?"

"Send everything," I said. "Send everyone."

I didn't bother to hang up.

Haley again. Pointing. Trying to prop herself on an elbow, slipping in her own blood. "Ma ma ma," she said.

"Emma?"

She nodded, fell back, lay still. Her pulse was strong. She was going to live.

I scuttled to Randall. He was out cold, oozing blood from his forehead, but now I saw his shotgun wounds were few and minor.

Well I'll be damned.

I rose.

It was hard.

I weighed a thousand pounds. My joints were filled with busted lightbulbs. Cool air where my ear ought to be attached felt odd. The rest of me just felt awful.

I thumped one slow step at a time down the hall, dreading every pace.

What had he done? What had Brad Bloomquist hauled off and done?

Tried the door to my left first, Rinn's bedroom. Hit the light.

Nothing. It was no different than when I'd tossed the place.

I heard something from the other room.

Cocked my head, heard it again, whipped open that door, flipped on the light.

And saw it. The crib that used to be up at the main house was now in here, crowded among the sacks and stacks from Rinn's shopping expeditions.

I heard nothing. Had I imagined it?

Forced myself to take a step toward the crib.

Then another.

And there she was.

Emma.

Pink pajamas with footies. Matching pink hat with a butterfly sewn on.

She was tangled in a yellow blanket. Didn't seem too happy about it.

Or about the sudden light.

She blinked. She squinched. She began to cry.

But not for long.

Because I picked her up.

I held her to my belly, to my chest.

I put my back to the ceiling light to make it less harsh on her.

I shook.

I heard something. Cocked my head to confirm. Sirens, all three types. Headed this way.

Emma was looking up at me. Her eyes were blue and pure. She looked like she wanted to ask me something.

I leaned to her.

I kissed her forehead.

I drew back.

I'd left lip prints: Haley's blood, Rinn's blood, Randall's blood, mine.

My tears.

The sirens were loud now, damn close. The noise threw Emma for a loop. I saw it in those pure blue eyes.

To settle her, I began to dip one knee, then the other.

Again.

Again.

Rocking her, feeling the rhythm of it.

Emma closed her eyes, sirens or no.

She smiled some.

Or maybe I imagined that.

Dip one knee. Dip the other.

I looked up, saw the first blue lights strobe into the Biletnikovs' drive.

I looked back down at Emma's sweet face.

"In the great green room," I said, "there was a telephone."

CHAPTER FORTY-SIX

Just a bench facing a four-pack of public tennis courts on a perfect mid-May day, a Windbreaker-in-the-morning, T-shirt-in-the-afternoon day.

Sophie and I had made it our regular spot. It was close enough so she could bike over. And it was shielded from Route 20 by trees, so if Charlene happened to drive past she wouldn't see us.

Wouldn't see *me*.

I was out of the house until further notice.

Randall was alive.

So was Haley.

So was Brad Bloomquist. More or less. They'd induced a coma to make it easier to pluck skull fragments from his brain. From what I heard, he wasn't coming out of the coma very well.

I had trouble getting bent out of shape over that.

The cops had found a diary in Bloomquist's apartment. A real Unabomber job, Lima'd called it: tiny, precise block printing all about Brad's unquenchable love for Gus. And what would befall anybody who came between the two of them.

Brad had smelled trouble when Gus finally agreed to spend a

month in rehab. He'd moved to Framingham from the Cape to set up stalker headquarters.

As Brad had feared, the Gus who came back from Hazelden wasn't sure where he was at in a hundred ways, including sexually—but he knew for sure he wasn't with Brad.

Brad went nuts. Betrayed by his one true love, he filled a dozen pages in the journal that night. Revenge plans, mostly.

Step 1 of his revenge: he knocked on Teddy Pundo's door and offered to lead him to the slow-pay who'd cheated him for a year and laughed about it.

Teddy, prodded by Boxer, was interested.

When Brad ponied up a fancy shotgun from Peter Biletnikov's well-hidden gun safe, which he'd learned about during his Three Musketeers days with Gus and Rinn, Boxer (and therefore Teddy) was even more interested. A major statement was needed if they were to show the world, especially the New York Mob, that weak old jazzman Charlie Pundo was no longer the boss of Springfield. The shotgun looked like a low-risk way to make the statement.

Boxer never asked if the ridiculously expensive shotgun had a twin. Hell, who would?

Per Brad's diary, it was Boxer who blasted away at Almost Home. It went pretty much the way I'd figured: Boxer had a decent description of Gus and he knew which room to look in, so poor old Brian Weller got it. Not to mention the others, who were just standing on the stairs at the wrong time.

The snafu rattled Boxer. Even a pro—hell, especially a pro—will think twice after taking the wrong three lives for no reward.

Brad Bloomquist's revenge plans: hit by a big-ass setback. He took it out on his diary and played for time.

The shotgun went back in the gun safe until the night Brad, already setting up Donald Crump for the frame job, swiped a pair of Donald's boots, trimmed nearly all the leather away, and wore them like flip-flops while he killed Gus.

Unlike Boxer, who had his own supply of heavy-gauge shot, Brad had to scrounge through Peter's ammo. That explained why lighter bird shot was used to blow Gus open.

Back went the shotgun into the safe—until Brad talked Boxer into completing the frame on Donald by killing the con man and hiding the shotgun in his spare-tire well.

Boxer the consummate pro, who was getting uneasy because of me, jumped at the chance.

But Brad slipped him the wrong shotgun, the *other* shotgun. Was it an intentional move by a guy who'd gotten hooked on lies and scams? Or was it a mix-up on Brad's part because he didn't know much about firearms?

His diary didn't say.

Boxer didn't know there *was* a second gun, and the two looked identical.

The frame-job shotgun, it turned out, was frozen from disuse and lack of cleaning.

Which was the only thing that prevented the frame from being perfect.

A bicycle bell is one of the last old-fashioned sounds.

I heard one and smiled, knowing it belonged to Sophie.

She covered my eyes with her hands and said, "Guess who?"

"Bad breath, dishpan hands, cheap ring. It could only be . . ."

It was an old gag by now—we visited every few days—but she laughed and came around the bench and sat next to me. "Who goes first today?" she said.

"You, of course."

"Davey's asleep, as usual. Dale spends every waking moment missing you, as usual."

"And your mom?"

"Your name does not pass her lips."

"As usual." We said it at the exact same time. And both tried to smile. And almost did.

"How's the new shrink?" I said.

"Better than the other one. Much better, actually. She's so young I forget she's a shrink. We just . . . talk."

"Does it help?"

"It helps more than counting down the minutes while listening to the first shrink suck cough drops. He was a dud."

I started to speak. My throat went tight. I forced my way past it. "The things you saw that day. Nobody should . . . if I could take it back . . ."

Sophie patted my arm.

"Question," I said. "Did you ever tell Charlene about the baby? About how I used Emma in Chicopee?"

"No." She stretched the word. "I can't decide whether that would make things better or worse."

"Same here. Best not tell her."

"Would you really have . . ."

"Don't ask it again, Sophie."

"Sor-*ry*." She folded her arms.

I said, "Anything on Jessie?"

She slumped against the bench. "Still nothing."

In the days of chaos, with Randall in the hospital, me scrambling to stay out of jail, media hyenas everywhere, and Charlene somehow coordinating everything without slacking at work, Jessie had gone on a paper-hanging spree in Worcester County, forging checks to the tune of nearly six grand and withdrawing the maximum on her mother's bank card each day.

Then she'd split for parts unknown.

I'd spaced. Sophie was saying something.

"What?" I said.

"I said your son seemed sad when I told him. He had no idea Jessie was gone. I'm sure of it. In case you thought they'd run off together."

"You spoke with Roy? Just like that?"

"He returned my call in fifteen minutes."

I closed my eyes. "How'd he sound?"

"He sounded like you," Sophie said. "Only lighter."

"I was a beanpole myself at his age."

"That's not what I meant."

We were quiet.

"I know," I finally said. "I'm glad he sounds that way."

We hushed up as two men and two women, none of them younger than seventy, set their gear on the next bench over and hit the court for mixed doubles, the four of them chattering away.

"Your turn," Sophie said.

"It looks like the insurance company will pay off on the shop. They're pissed about it, but they'll pay."

"You still haven't dimed out Andrade, have you?"

I said nothing.

"*Conway!*"

"Like I said, they're paying off. If I had to dime him to get the dough, I would."

"Bullshit you would."

I smiled.

Sophie said, "Job prospects?"

"I've got a standing offer in Springfield. Trouble is, I can't spell consigliere."

She gasped. "You *wouldn't!*"

"I wouldn't. But it was nice of Pundo to ask."

The foursome warmed up. They could really play. They all liked creeping up to the net. Sometimes the ball went back and forth a half-dozen times without touching the ground.

"Everything's going to be different," I said. "You know that."

"It doesn't have to be." But her voice told me she knew what I meant. How could she not?

"Got no shop," I said. "Got no Charlene. Not sure where I stand with the Barnburners. Different. Just warning you."

We were quiet awhile.

When Sophie finally spoke, I knew what was coming before she said it. "Are you sleeping?"

"Here and there. Not really."

"And you won't see someone about it, and you certainly won't take a pill."

"No and no."

Rinn had been Brad Bloomquist's final kill. And, judging by the diary, the one he'd most looked forward to.

He'd planned to kill her baby while Rinn watched.

See, by the time Peter and Rinn and Gus and Pundo did their sick little sleight of hand over who fathered Emma, Brad had been frozen out by the group—he'd let his true colors show here and there, and nobody trusted him.

So Brad was in the same club as Peter, thinking Gus was the proud pop.

And that, more than anything else, drove Brad around the bend. To be tossed aside by his one true love, who then switched over to *girls,* of all things, was good for a couple of spittle-flecked diary pages every night. The diary told the cops that Brad had high hopes for his meeting with Gus in the apartment—Brad had big plans to convince Gus to rekindle.

When things didn't play out that way, Brad killed him instead.

The day I'd interrupted Brad and Rinn in the guesthouse, just before I left to meet Charlie Pundo, Brad had been threatening the baby, telegraphing his plans to Rinn. He'd scared her enough that she didn't dare say anything to me.

I'd felt the bad vibe.

I'd ignored it.

And Rinn had died.

And that was for me to live with.

When I tried to sleep lately, when I got down to that place where you either doze off or don't, I always felt her blood on my elbows and knees. The blood I'd crawled through.

I didn't doze off much.

Roy, Jessie, Gus, Sophie.

Emma.

At night, in bed, I thought about them all. Pasts and futures. I tried pushing words and facts around to make things better for any of them. All of them. When sleep finally drew near, I could damn near convince myself I'd pulled it off, had done something differently that changed everything.

I always woke up sweaty and sheet-tangled.

A tennis ball took a wild hop and came over the fence. Sophie rose, underhanded it back to the oldsters, and sat again.

She'd been reading my thoughts. "Emma is the only winner," she said. "Relatively speaking."

"Relatively speaking."

Pundo had put the squeeze on Peter Biletnikov. Had strong-armed his way to a private paternity test, which proved what everybody already knew. Pundo gave Biletnikov a simple choice: give up the baby quietly and never hear about it again, or fight the process and find himself in court and on TV for a very long time.

It was a bluff, and a good one—Biletnikov didn't want a trial any more than Pundo did.

So Biletnikov was long gone, and Emma was with Pundo.

As was Haley. She wouldn't let the kid out of her sight. Charlie was fine with that.

Sophie said, "Do you still think Charlie will stay with Haley?"

"I'd bet a paycheck on it. When I visited, Pundo was shopping for a big house in Longmeadow, the ritzy suburb out there. And Haley's got a good heart. Emma will make out like a bandit."

"Good for her."

We were quiet awhile.

Finally, I said, "Remember we talked about little kids remembering things?"

"I know what you're thinking," Sophie said. "Emma's about seven months old. You're wondering if that's *too* early for memories. You're hoping it is."

"Is it?"

"I don't think so."

"You think Emma will have her echoes."

"Emma will have her echoes," Sophie said.